Will continued towards[...]g a home-made pushcart at a run caught up with him and passed him. Round the corner came a girl. The pushcart collided with her, and down she went with an involuntary yell.

'Oh, crikey,' gasped the boy, a lad about nine.

'Hard luck,' said Will to the girl, and stooped to help her up. Winded, she gazed up at him. She saw the tanned face of a soldier under a peaked cap, and concerned eyes. Will saw a young lady with bobbed jet-black hair clasped by a knitted blue hat with a bobble. Her grey eyes looked cross. 'Are you hurt?' he asked. She winced and looked at Will in an accusing way. 'Now look what's 'appened, I've hurt me knee.'

''Ere,' said the boy, 'Can't yer put 'er in me cart, mister, an' push 'er home? I'll come with yer so's I can take me pushcart off yer. There y'ar, mister, wheel 'er home in me cart.'

'Right, up you come, Daisy Bell,' said Will. He stooped, and the girl gasped and grabbed at the hem of her frock as he lifted her.

'Oh, I won't – you're not to – me in a pushcart at my age? I won't – oh, me legs, I don't believe it!'

'Off we go,' said Will. He turned with the cart and proceeded to retrace his steps. 'What's your name?' he asked the flushed and outraged young lady.

'Oh, you 'ooligan,' she breathed. 'I don't give me name to 'ooligans that've put me in a kid's cart. Well, it's Annie Ford, if you must know, and I hate yer.'

Also by Mary Jane Staples

SERGEANT JOE
RISING SUMMER
DOWN LAMBETH WAY
KING OF CAMBERWELL
THE LODGER
OUR EMILY
TWO FOR THREE FARTHINGS
THE PEARLY QUEEN

and published by Corgi Books

ON
MOTHER BROWN'S
DOORSTEP

Mary Jane Staples

CORGI BOOKS

ON MOTHER BROWN'S DOORSTEP
A CORGI BOOK 0 552 13975 0

First publication in Great Britain

PRINTING HISTORY
Corgi edition published 1993

Set in 10/12pt Linotype Plantin by
County Typesetters, Margate, Kent

Corgi Books are published by Transworld Publishers Ltd,
61–63 Uxbridge Road, Ealing, London W5 5SA, in Australia
by Transworld Publishers (Australia) Pty Ltd, 15–23 Helles
Avenue, Moorebank, NSW 2170, and in New Zealand by
Transworld Publishers (NZ) Ltd, 3 William Pickering Drive,
Albany, Auckland.

Printed and bound in Great Britain by
Cox & Wyman Ltd, Reading, Berks.

To Wendy and Jeffery

ON
MOTHER BROWN'S
DOORSTEP

THE INCIDENT

It was in December, 1924, when a ward sister in a London hospital noticed that the door of a drugs cupboard had been neatly forced open. A large bottle of chloroform, new and unused, with its glass stopper still sealed, was missing. She reported the matter immediately to the matron. The police were called in to investigate the theft. They talked to all members of the staff and to walking patients. They made enquiries among out-patients, and checked up on visitors known to have entered the hospital on the day in question. They wondered, of course, why the thief should want chloroform. It brought them eventually to the reasonable assumption that the person was an outsider, a clever crook who had done his homework and had lifted the chloroform with the intention of using it to put prospective victims to sleep.

That theory looked remarkably like fact when, a month later in January, 1925, a Lewisham jeweller entered a police station in what appeared to be a state of inebriation. He reported having been chloroformed by a heavily masked man who came into his shop just as he was about to close up. When he recovered consciousness some time later, his takings for the day were missing. The thief left no fingerprints and had not yet been traced.

Among other things occupying the attention of the police in 1925 was the usual list of missing persons. The list included three young girls. Ivy Connor of Bermondsey had disappeared in February, Mary Wallace of Rotherhithe in October, and Amy Charles of the Old Kent

9

Road in December. Their disappearances had been investigated without success and their case files were still open.

CHAPTER ONE

The March day was brilliant, the air crisp, the sun sharpening the sooty chimneys and rooftops of Walworth. Fog might arrive overnight and blanket London tomorrow, but today the weather made people feel cheerful and lively. It was 1926, the year of the Bright Young Things, with flappers showing their legs in short skirts, smoking cigarettes in long holders, and being jawed at by the law for the wildness of their ways. Some responded by flinging their arms around upbraiding bobbies and kissing them. The law and the Church and Mother Grundy were collectively shocked, of course.

In Walworth's East Street market, some women shoppers were wearing their best hats to celebrate the arrival of the sun. William Edward Brown, in the khaki uniform of the East Surreys, took in the old familiar scene with a sense of nostalgia. He could not count the number of times he had ducked and dived under stalls as a boy, looking for discarded fruit such as specked apples or slightly pulpy oranges. His family had been bitterly hard-up during the post-war years, but his mum had never lost her smile and his dad had never let go of hope.

William was known as Will. He had kicked against being called Willy and fought street kids who had tried to label him so. Entering the Army as a drummer boy at the age of fifteen in 1921, he sailed with his East Surrey battalion for service in India in 1922, and during the next four years he had come to know that India, with its teeming cities, its many religions, its cultural variations

11

and its extraordinary mixture of peoples, was something he'd need a lifetime to understand. But he hadn't done so badly; he'd got along with the Indian regiments of the British Army. Indian soldiers served with pride and distinction alongside the British, particularly in the flare-ups on the North-West Frontier.

Will reached the rank of full corporal when he was only nineteen, having distinguished himself in a bloody battle against the Pathans. Subsequently, however, something went wrong with his chest. He had moments when he found it difficult to breathe. His commanding officer ordered him to go sick, and he finished up in hospital in Poona. Conditions were better there, the air was finer and not laden with sultry heat. But as soon as he was discharged and rejoined the battalion in Delhi, his chest began to complain again. He was invalided home and given three months leave, during the course of which he was to attend a London chest hospital once a week. He'd been home just over two weeks, had visited the hospital twice and heard the worrying word asthma mentioned, although oddly enough smoky old Walworth seemed to be doing him good. He hadn't had one attack since arriving home.

He was enjoying his reunion with old Walworth and with his family, getting to know brother Freddy and sisters Sally and Susie all over again. Well, everyone was five years older. The whole family had gone barmy when he walked in on them with three months leave in the bag. His sisters fell on him, and Susie went all moist-eyed because he would be able to attend her wedding three weeks from now. The man in question was Sammy Adams, reputed to be Southwark's most well-known businessman. Will had felt immediate pride in Susie. At twenty-one she'd grown into a picture postcard beauty. Besides which, she was a typical flapper in her 1926 outfits. She took him as soon as she could to meet Sammy and all the Adams family, showing him off as her soldier brother, which went down well with Boots, Sammy's eldest brother. Boots had fought with the West Kents in France and Flanders during the Great War. He asked Will what the pay was like now. Lousy, said Will, but the grub's free. Same old tight-fisted Army Paymaster, said Boots, and what are the socks like? I think I've been wearing your leftovers, said Will. Boots asked if they'd got darned toes. Darned heels as well, said Will. Yes, they're mine, said Boots.

Susie was as happy as a lark about everything, and head over heels as well.

'Ain't I a lucky girl, Will?' she said in the old way.

'Not as lucky as Sammy,' said Will.

'But I wasn't anybody when I first met Sammy.'

'Well, you're somebody now,' said Will, 'and Sammy knows it. You hold on to that, Susie, you need to be on top with a bloke like him.'

'I am on top,' laughed Susie.

'Are you?'

'All the time,' said Susie. 'Mind, Sammy doesn't know it.'

Will didn't think his parents had changed much. His mum was still plump and placid, his dad still wiry and cheerful, and making light of the gammy leg he'd brought out of the trenches. He thought the Army had done a lot for Will, and said so. Done me brown, said Will. At which his mum said she'd never seen anyone more brown, then asked exactly what it was he'd got to go to the hospital for each week. Just to check up on the nurses, said Will. Well, I never heard the likes of that before, said his mum, coming all the way home from India to see if the hospital nurses are behaving themselves. That can't be right, she said. I expect Will's got a bit of India in his system, said

Mr Brown, and the hospital's got to get it out of him. There's funny things that can get into a soldier in India. Still, there must be nice things as well, said fourteen-year-old Sally, because they've made our Will all brown and handsome. I bet the girls will all go potty about him. I'd like some of that, said Will.

After his second visit to the hospital, Will let his family know that all he'd got was a little touch of asthma. Freddy asked what asthma was. Will said something like a cold on the chest.

'That's a blessin',' said Mrs Brown, 'I thought it might be one of them Chinese diseases like gangrene.'

'Mum, 'ow can you catch a Chinese disease in India?' asked Sally.

'What's gangrene?' asked Freddy.

'Nasty,' said Mr Brown.

'I think I'll buy you some thick woolly vests while you're 'ome, Will,' said Mrs Brown. 'They'll keep your chest warm.'

'Make it itch as well,' said Will.

'What's gangrene?' asked Freddy.

'It's what you get if your leg falls off and the doctors don't put the right kind of ointment on it,' said Susie.

'I ain't fallin' for that,' said Freddy. 'I mean what's the use of puttin' ointment on a leg that's fell off? I ain't daft, yer know, Susie.'

'Not much,' said Sally.

'And only now and again,' said Susie.

'There y'ar, Will,' said Freddy, 'you can see what I 'ave to put up with from me skin-and-blisters. They'll give me a complaint one day, and I'll 'ave to come to the hospital with you.'

'Good idea, Freddy,' said Will, 'you can help me check up on the nurses.'

14

'Cor, I fancy that,' said Freddy.

Will, his thoughts on his family, came out of the market and entered King and Queen Street. Kids just out of school were racing towards East Street. It was a thing with some Walworth kids to go to the market on their way home from school, and to do some scrumping for apples under the fruit stalls.

Walking to Browning Street, he saw a woman approaching, shopping bag in her hand and her best Sunday hat on.

''Ello, soldier, ain't another war on, is there?'

'Not here,' said Will.

'Thank gawd for that, I ain't got over the last one yet.'

'Never mind,' said Will, 'your titfer's in the pink.'

'Me 'at?' said the woman. 'What's wrong with it?'

'Looks like spring,' said Will. 'I like it.'

'Fancy me, do yer, soldier?' twinkled the woman.

'Yes, I'll pop round on Sunday,' said Will.

'Me old man'll chop yer legs orf.'

'So he should,' said Will, 'that's what husbands are for.'

The woman laughed and went on. Will continued towards Browning Street. A boy wheeling a home-made pushcart at a run caught him up and passed him. Round the corner came a girl. The pushcart collided with her, and down she went with an involuntary yell.

'Oh, crikey,' gasped the boy, a lad about nine.

'Hard luck,' said Will to the girl, and stooped to help her up. Winded, she turned on her back and gazed up at him. She saw the tanned face of a soldier under a peaked cap, and concerned eyes. Will saw a young lady with bobbed jet-black hair clasped by a knitted blue hat with a bobble. Her frock was rucked, her black lisle stockings showing to her knees. Her grey eyes looked cross. 'Are you hurt?' he asked.

'Did you knock me over?'

'Not me,' said Will.

'Me pushcart done it,' said the boy.

'You were lookin' at me,' said the girl to Will in an accusing way. She sat up. She winced and rubbed her right knee. She winced again. 'Now look what's 'appened, I've hurt me knee.'

'Sorry about that,' said Will. 'Let's try getting you up.'

'What, on one leg?' she said spiritedly. 'I'll look daft.'

'Oh, 'elp,' said the boy, 'you ain't broke yer leg, 'ave yer?'

'I'd better not have,' said the girl, touching her knee gingerly, 'or me dad'll push both your faces in.'

A woman came across from the other side of the street. She looked like one of Walworth's numerous motherly bodies.

''Ere, young man,' she said to Will, 'what's that gel doin' on the pavement?'

'She's bumped her knee,' said Will.

'Excuse me, if you don't mind,' said the girl, 'it was the other way about.'

'Is it 'urting?' asked the motherly body.

'Oh, no,' said the girl, 'it's just swellin' up, missus, that's all.' She was cross. She ought to be home by now, getting tea for her brother and sisters.

Looking at Will, the motherly body said, 'She can't just sit there on the pavement.'

'I know,' said Will, 'but she's against standing on one leg.'

The girl looked as if she didn't think that very funny. Another woman hurried up.

16

'What's 'appened?' she asked. Happenings were meat and drink to Walworth's motherly bodies.

'Me pushcart accidental 'it the girl's knee,' said the boy, who wanted to get home himself for a bit of tea.

'Oh, ain't that a shame? Oh, yer poor dear,' said the second motherly body to the girl, 'that's just what 'appened to me niece Ivy, she done 'er knee in two days before 'er weddin' and 'ad to walk up the aisle on crutches. Is it painful, ducky?'

'Oh, no,' said the fed-up girl, 'it's only cripplin' me.'

'That's what it done to me niece,' said the second motherly body. 'What's 'er soldier friend doin' about it?' she asked the first woman.

'Well, 'e'll 'ave to do something,' said the first woman.

'He's not my soldier friend,' said the girl.

'Couldn't you carry 'er to 'er home?' suggested the second woman to Will.

That was out as far as Will was concerned. He'd been advised to avoid that kind of exertion, and he certainly didn't fancy having an attack before he got the girl home. He'd be no help at all to her then. All the same, he couldn't walk away.

'Where'd you live?' he asked her.

'Blackwood Street,' she said. Blackwood Street was off the market.

'All right,' he said, making up his mind that he'd got to give it a go, 'up you come and I'll carry you.'

The girl, taking in his lean manly look, didn't fancy him carrying her at all, not at her age.

'I ain't bein' carried,' she said. 'I'll lose all me dignity, I'll get catcalled by the street kids. I'm seventeen, I am.'

'Better to be carried than to stay here gettin' trodden on,' said Will, who felt it would all have had its funny side if the girl's knee hadn't been so obviously painful.

17

'Excuse me,' said the girl, whose dignity was already suffering, 'but I'm not bein' carried. I'll 'ave to hop on one leg.'

'Yes, you got to get 'ome somehow, ducky,' said the second woman. 'Me sister fell over down Petticoat Lane one Sunday, an' got trod on till she was nearly ill, and it didn't do 'er back no good, either.'

''Ere,' said the boy, 'can't yer put 'er in me cart, mister, an' push 'er home? I'll come with yer so's I can take me pushcart off yer. I'll be late for me tea an' get a clip, but it won't 'urt. Me mum don't believe in knockin' me 'ead orf. There y'ar, mister, wheel 'er home in me cart.'

Bright idea that, thought Will, it solves everything.

'Right, up you come, Daisy Bell,' he said. He stooped again, and the girl gasped and grabbed at the hem of her frock as he lifted her.

'Oh, I won't – you're not to – me in a pushcart at my age? I won't – oh, me legs, I don't believe it!'

Resistance was all too late then. Will lowered her into the pushcart bottom first. It was a solid wooden crate on bicycle wheels. Her knees were up, her legs showing.

'There we are,' said Will.

'Yes, she fits in quite comfy,' said the first motherly body.

'You'll be all right now, love,' said the second, 'the soldier'll get you 'ome. 'E seems a decent chap.'

'Decent?' gasped the girl. 'Look what he's done to me, put me in this cart with me legs showin' – I'll die in a minute.'

'Off we go,' said Will. He turned with the cart and proceeded to retrace his steps, the cart running easily over the pavement, the boy following. 'What's your name?' he asked the flushed and outraged young lady.

18

'Oh, you 'ooligan,' she breathed, 'I don't give me name to 'ooligans that've put me in a kid's cart. Well, it's Annie Ford, if you must know, and I hate yer.'

'I'm Will Brown. Nice to meet you, Annie. Sorry about your knee, but with luck, it'll only be bruised.'

'Never mind me knee, what about me dignity?' said Annie, dreading street kids. Sure enough some appeared. They goggled at her. A fat one sang out.

'Where did yer get that gel, oh, yer lucky feller,
If I get tuppence from me mum, would yer like to sell 'er?'

'Oh, I'll kill him,' gasped Annie. 'Oh, look at people lookin', they'll think I'm only ten years old.'

'You look like a young lady from here,' said Will, pushing the cart on towards the Lane. The East Street market was known as the Lane.

'Oh, don't mind me,' said Annie bitterly, 'just keep lookin'. I like bein' in a pushcart with me knees up and me legs showin', don't I?'

'I'm not lookin',' said Will.

Annie, who was facing him, gritted her teeth. People were looking and gawping, of course. Oh, the shame of it, at her age. It was worse when they reached the market, where Will turned left. She was sure everyone in Walworth was there.

'Oi, Tommy Atkins,' said some grinning middle-aged man, 'did yer buy them goods off a stall?'

'Yes, five bob the lot,' said Will, and Annie fumed.

'Five bob?' said the interested party. 'You should've 'ad 'er wrapped up in fancy paper for that, an' tied with ribbon as well.'

Will grinned and pushed on, crossing the street.

'Did you hear that, did you hear what 'e said?' demanded Annie.

'I expect you'd look nice in ribbon,' said Will, trying to cheer her up.

'Oh, you saucy devil, you didn't ought to be a soldier, you ought to be locked up till you can treat a girl proper.'

'How's your knee?' asked Will, the boy still behind him.

'Oh, thanks for askin',' said Annie.

A passing woman said, 'Givin' yer sister a ride, are yer, soldier?'

'Not so's you'd notice,' said Will, 'she's just a new friend of mine, and we're getting to know each other.'

'I wouldn't be his sister or his friend, not if he gave me a sackful of diamonds,' fumed Annie. 'He's a demon, he is.'

'Cheer up,' said Will and pushed on.

'Look, I don't want you to think I'm not grateful,' said Annie, 'but how would you like to be wheeled 'ome in a pushcart?'

'Won't be long now,' said Will.

'Oh, blessed agony,' breathed Annie. He had turned into Blackwood Street. 'I know what's goin' to 'appen now, all the kids are goin' to look.'

Kids were there all right. They stopped their street games to stare. Recognizing Annie, they came running up.

'Crikey, look at you, Annie!'

'What's the soldier wheelin' yer in that cart for?'

'Is that yer knees showin'?'

A girl darted from an open door and came to a halt in front of the pushcart. She addressed Will indignantly.

''Ere, that's our sister you've got in there, mister.'

'She hurt her knee,' said Will, 'so I've given her a ride home.'

'Crikey, me an' Charlie wondered why she was late,' said fourteen-year-old Nellie Ford. ''Ave yer really 'urt yer knee, Annie?'

20

'Yes, and me pride as well,' said Annie.

'You kids, push off,' said Nellie, like Annie in her looks.

'Can't we see 'er knee?' asked a small girl. 'I never seen an 'urt knee except me own. I seen a bunion, me mum's got one—'

'Push off,' said Nellie. The kids backed off for about a yard.

'Right,' said Will, 'I'll carry Annie indoors. You lead the way,' he said to Nellie. 'Up you come again, Daisy Bell.'

'She ain't Daisy Bell, she's Annie,' said Nellie.

'Well, she'd look just like Daisy Bell if she had a boater and a bicycle,' said Will. He lifted Annie. She clutched the hem of her frock. 'Thanks for the loan of your pushcart, young tosh,' he said to the boy, who at once made off with it before foreign street kids could get their hands on it.

'This way, mister,' said Nellie, and Will followed, Annie up in his arms, legs dangling, frock rucked.

'Crikey, Annie,' called a precocious boy, 'I think yer knickers is showin'.'

Annie gave a tight little scream as Will carried her indoors.

CHAPTER TWO

The Ford family, renting their house in Blackwood Street for twelve bob a week, consisted of Mr Harold Ford, a forty-two-year-old ganger on the LSER, his three daughters Annie, Nellie and Cassie, and his son Charlie. His wife, unfortunately, had developed pneumonia during the last year of the war. It proved fatal, as pneumonia nearly always did. She lay in the South London cemetery now, under green turf and a headstone. The vicar of St John's Church had approved the wording.

'RUTH ANNIE FORD. Born 1888, died 1918. Wife of Harold Stanley Ford and mother of Annie, Nellie, Charlie and Cassie. OUR MUM.'

Annie was her dad's right hand now. She had any amount of spirit and as much bossiness as was necessary to get the better of twelve-year-old Charlie. She wasn't averse to chasing him with the brush and pan. The back of the brush was good for whacking his bottom, and the pan good for giving his head a thump. Charlie complained she'd knock it off one day. She told him he wouldn't miss it.

'Course I would,' said Charlie, 'I couldn't even walk about without me loaf of bread, nor see where I was goin', neither.'

'Dear oh lor',' said Annie, 'what a shame.'

Not that affection wasn't there. Annie had a characteristically warm cockney heart under her scolding exterior, and was very fond of her family, especially her dad. But someone had to keep them in order, her dad as well.

22

Sometimes on Sundays she'd make them all go to church with her.

'You too, Dad,' she'd say.

'Well, Annie, I was thinkin' about mendin' the chair that's—'

'No, you weren't. Go and put your Sunday suit on. And you, Charlie – here, where you off to, Cassie? Come back here. Sit on 'er, Nellie, till we're ready. Charlie, you goin' to put your suit on, or do I 'ave to belt you one?'

Charlie, strong-willed, was a holy terror who needed belting occasionally. Annie made do with thumping him and applying her own will, which was just as strong as Charlie's. So whenever she said they'd all got to go to church with her, Charlie went too. Annie could fashion hurtful beds of nails for defaulters.

Her dad gave her a hand with meals at weekends, but he was always home too late to be a help on weekdays. Still, he never failed to do full justice to what she set before him. Everyone had to wash their hands before they sat down to a meal. Annie was nearly ten when her mum died and could remember how particular she'd been about clean hands at meal times. She remembered lots of things about her lively pretty mum, nice things, and Annie meant never to let her down. She could never quite understand why the Lord had taken her when she was only thirty. Nellie asked a question on those lines once, and their dad said he supposed the Lord often took the ones He liked best while they were still young. Nellie said she didn't want the Lord not to like her, but she didn't want to be liked so much that she'd have to go to an early grave. Wouldn't it be better if the Lord took people like Mrs Potter? She's not young, said Charlie, she's ninety and she's got whiskers. Still, age before beauty, said Nellie. Not when it's got whiskers on, said Charlie. You Charlie, said

Annie, don't you talk like that about kind old ladies.

Annie could sort Charlie out fairly well most times. Ten-year-old Cassie was a different problem. She was a dreamy girl with a vivid imagination that took her into the realms of never-never land far too often. A neighbour would stop Annie and say something like what's all this I hear about your family being invited to tea at Windsor Castle next Sunday afternoon? Or, Annie love, I can't hardly believe your dad swam the Channel last week, there wasn't nothing about it in the papers. Or even, fancy your Charlie saving a girl from drowning in the Serpentine last week and being given a gold medal by the King.

It could all be traced back to Cassie, and Cassie would get a talking-to.

'Now, you Cassie, you've been tellin' stories again.'

'Me, Annie?'

'Yes, you. I saw Alice Miller down the Lane. What d'you mean by tellin' 'er Dad's goin' to get a job at Buckingham Palace?'

The Royal Family and much of what was associated with it featured prominently in Cassie's inventive mind.

'Annie, I only said Dad might. Well, 'e might one day. The King and Queen 'ave to 'ave men doin' jobs there, they couldn't do them themselves, they 'ave to sit on their throne mostly. I bet Dad could do a good job at Buckingham Palace.'

'Cassie, you little 'orror, the best job Dad could do would be to stop you tellin' all these fancy stories about us. You even told Mrs Woodley last week that Dad used to be a sea captain. If you keep on like this, you'll never go to 'eaven.'

'Well, I don't want to go yet, Annie, honest, not before Mrs Potter.'

If Charlie could be thumped for being a bit of a

tearaway, there wasn't much that could be done about Cassie and her imagination, except hope that she'd grow out of it. All their dad did about it was to cough a bit. Annie told him he could cough as much as he liked, but none of it would cure Cassie. No, but it's a help to me, said her dad. What sort of help? It stops me falling about, said her dad.

Cassie, Nellie and Charlie were all attending school. Annie had a job from ten until four with a grocer near the Elephant and Castle. The grocer, Mr Urcott, was a really kind bloke, he let her work those hours so that she could see to the family in the mornings and get home in time to make a pot of tea and do some bread and marge for herself and her brother and sisters. Supper came later.

Banging her knee against that pushcart meant she had failed them today. It also meant she'd arrived home in a mortifying way for a girl her age, even if she knew she couldn't have got there by herself on one leg. She'd never live that pushcart down. Neighbours would ask if she really had been wheeled home in it by a soldier.

Will sat her down on the edge of the kitchen table. With its solid legs and square deal top, it was the kind of table seen in most Walworth kitchens, and the kitchen itself, with its oven range and its window facing the back yard, was like a thousand others. The range fire was alight, burning very slowly, the coals covered by a pinky-white ash. China filled the dresser shelves and cups hung from hooks. Will thought the kitchen had a homely look similar to his mother's. He didn't think Annie and her family were too hard-up. Her sister's gymslip and white blouse had quite a new look, and the blue frock she herself was wearing was quite pretty.

'What yer doin' that for, sittin' Annie on the table?' asked Nellie, intrigued at having a soldier in the house.

'I'm taking care of her knee,' said Will, and stood back to regard Annie, who at once brushed at the skirt of her short frock and covered her knees. Crumbs, thought Nellie, what's our Annie gone all shy for?

Annie stared accusingly at Will.

'I don't know why you keep lookin' at me,' she said. 'I never met anyone who does more lookin' than you. I might not 'ave bumped into that pushcart if you hadn't been lookin' then.'

'We've had all that,' said Will, smiling. Crikey, thought Nellie, ain't he handsome? 'Where's your mum?' asked Will.

'She died when we was young,' said Nellie.

'Oh, sorry,' said Will, who couldn't imagine what it must be like for a family to have no mum. His own mum had always been there, placid, affectionate and un-critical.

'But we got a nice dad,' said Nellie.

'That's a consolation,' said Will. 'About the knee, Annie—'

'Never mind me knee,' said Annie, 'you're not gettin' a look at that too.'

'Pity,' said Will, 'I like knees. Well, girls' knees. Anyway, Annie, from what I've seen of yours, I'd say you've just bruised the right one. If it's a bit stiff, put some liniment on it.'

'Yes, all right,' said Annie, 'and thanks ever so much, I'll try and forget how you dumped me in that pushcart. Nellie, where's Cassie and Charlie?'

'Charlie's next door,' said Nellie. 'Pam Nicholls sauced him over the wall, so 'e jumped over it so's 'e could chase 'er into 'er kitchen and smack 'er up-an'-downer.'

'I'll kill the little 'ooligan,' fumed Annie.

'What's her up-and-downer?' asked Will.

''Er bottom,' said Nellie, giggling.

'Jamaica Rum?' said Will, grinning.

'Charlie calls it up-an'-downer, I don't know where 'e got it from,' said Nellie.

'Wait till I get my hands on him,' said Annie.

'Oh, it's all right, Annie,' said Nellie, 'Pam likes it. That's why she sauced him. Oh, an' Cassie's gone to look for Tabby. Tabby's our cat,' she said to Will. ''E's always goin' off an' gettin' lost. Annie says she'll drown 'im one day.'

'Nellie, have you all had a bit of tea?' asked Annie, her knee feeling stiff.

'Yes, I did some bread an' marge,' said Nellie. 'an' Charlie made a pot of tea. 'E only took 'alf an hour. Annie, could yer do with a cup yerself?'

'Yes, I could,' said Annie, 'but you're not to make it, you'll 'ave another accident with the kettle.'

'I upset the kettle once, when it was boilin',' said Nellie to Will. 'Not over meself, thank goodness, over the gas stove. Annie won't let me go near one now. Would you like a cup of tea yerself now, mister? I'll try an' get Charlie in.'

'I'll make it,' said Will, 'I've got plenty of time.' He was making a leisurely thing of his leave, as he'd been advised to. 'Annie ought to rest her knee on her bed, of course. Come on, Annie, I'll carry you up.' He could manage that, he thought.

'Oh, no you don't,' said Annie. 'I don't let soldiers I 'ardly know carry me up to me bed. Nellie can help me up the stairs when I've had that cup of tea. You really goin' to make it?'

'Where's the kettle?' asked Will. 'There it is.' It was on the hob, and he transferred it to the top of the gas oven in the scullery. He searched for a match.

In the kitchen, Nellie whispered, 'Oh, ain't he 'and-some, Annie? Fancy you findin' a nice soldier like 'im.'

Since Annie knew that her dignity had taken a hiding, she said loudly, 'Well, I won't say he wasn't helpful, nor that he 'asn't got a kind heart somewhere, but dumpin' me in that pushcart with 'undreds of people about, I wonder I didn't die of bein' looked at. I expect some soldiers – what's that I can hear?'

'It's 'im,' whispered Nellie, ''e's laughin'.'

'Well, he would, wouldn't he?' said Annie, even more loudly. 'He was laughin' all the time he was wheelin' me home. Some soldiers would have covered my legs up, but not 'im, oh, no. He let all the street kids have a look.'

'Yes, and Eddie Marsh said 'e saw yer knickers,' said Nellie.

'Oh, you Nellie, wasn't it bad enough havin' that little 'ooligan speak the word without you speakin' it as well?' fumed Annie.

'It's all right,' said Will from the kitchen, 'I didn't see them myself.'

'Oh,' breathed Annie, 'I'll spit in a minute.'

'Annie, you shouldn't spit,' said Nellie, 'Dad wouldn't like you to.'

'Got a teapot in there?' called Will. 'And some tea?'

Nellie took the teapot and caddy out to him.

'You goin' to stay and keep an eye on our Annie till our dad gets 'ome?' she asked, putting the question in the belief it was a sister's natural duty to help an older one enjoy a romance. Annie mostly turned her nose up at young men. She said she was too busy to go walking out with any of them, and that she liked her family best, anyway. Nellie knew she was wild with this soldier for putting her in a pushcart, but she wasn't actually turning her nose up at him. If she had been, she'd have spoken

28

very politely to him, thanked him for bringing her home, and asked her, Nellie, to show him out. Instead, she was giving him what for and not making any move to get off the table and hop to a chair. It was like she was waiting for him to carry her up to her room, even though she'd said he wasn't to. And Nellie thought her knee hadn't suffered a mortal injury, she was hardly taking any notice of it. 'I don't mind if you stay,' said Nellie, as Will stirred the pot, 'only me an' Charlie can't do much with her at times, specially if she's a bit upset, poor woman, an' needs someone to see she rests 'er knee.'

There was a muffled little yell from Annie.

'You Nellie, I'm listening to you!'

'Poor what, Nellie?' asked Will, grinning.

'Yes, poor woman,' said Nellie. 'Mind, she's ever so nice really, and our dad says she's pretty too. So does 'Arold Seymour down the street, 'e's potty about 'er, but 'e's got ginger 'air and Annie 'ates ginger 'air. D'you think she's pretty?'

'You Nellie!' yelled Annie. 'I'll smother you!'

'There, you can see she's upset,' said Nellie.

'Poor woman,' said Will, waiting for the tea to draw.

'I heard that!' cried Annie, who had never felt more put upon since she'd become a young lady. 'I'm not a poor woman!'

'We'll be with you in a moment,' called Will.

'What's yer name?' asked Nellie.

'Will Brown, from Caulfield Place.'

'That's a nice name. What's them stripes on yer sleeve for?'

'To show I'm a corporal and can order people about,' said Will.

'Crikey, can yer really? You goin' to order Annie about?'

'What'll happen if I do?'

'Oh, she'll think you're ever so manly,' said Nellie.

Annie could hardly believe what she was listening to. That Nellie, talking as if butter wouldn't melt in her mouth.

'Here we are,' said Will, bringing the teapot in. 'How about some cups and saucers, Nellie, and some milk and sugar?'

Nellie supplied the requirements.

'I'm still sittin' here like a lemon, you know,' said Annie.

'All right, let's try a chair,' said Will, and lifted her and sat her on one. Annie was a slender girl of five feet seven. She was proud of her legs and happy about her bosom, which was happy about itself. Well, it was firm and didn't joggle about like some other girls' bosoms did, especially if they didn't wear decent stays. Any bosom that didn't joggle felt happy about itself.

'I'm not goin' upstairs,' she said, 'there's the vegetables to do.'

'I'll help Nellie do them,' said Will, pouring the tea, 'I've got to do something to make up for puttin' you in the pushcart.'

'Well, it's kind of you,' said Annie, 'but I'm sure you've got to be on your way soon.'

'Time's my own until six,' said Will.

'We'd best let 'im help, Annie,' said Nellie. ''E's a corporal and can order people about, can't you, Will?'

'On top of that I'm bossy as well,' said Will.

'Don't I know it,' said Annie darkly.

Well, bless me, thought Nellie, two bossy people together, what a lark. And where's our Cassie got to, that's what I'd like to know. Wandering about in a dream, I shouldn't wonder, and looking for the cat.

30

CHAPTER THREE

'A sailor suit?' said eleven-year-old Freddy Brown in horror.

'A nice sailor suit would look lovely for Susie's weddin',' said Mrs Brown, his affable mother.

'Not on me it wouldn't,' said Freddy. 'I ain't goin' to wear no sailor suit, not for Susie's weddin' nor anyone else's. I'll fall down dead. You wouldn't like that, I bet, me fallin' down dead in the church.'

'But, Freddy love—'

'I'm eleven, I'll 'ave you know,' said Freddy, 'I ain't six.'

'Still, you'd look ever so sweet in a sailor suit,' said Sally, his fourteen-year-old sister. They were just home from school. They lived in Caulfield Place, off Browning Street, Walworth. Easter was approaching, so were the school holidays and so was their sister Susie's wedding. It was a time of excitement for the Brown family, and for the whole street. A cockney wedding wasn't the sort of event that concerned only the bride and her family. Everyone wanted to know everything about it, and Mr Brown kept saying to Mrs Brown that the way things were going the bridegroom would finish up finding himself married to every female in Caulfield Place. And Mrs Brown kept saying of course he wouldn't, he'd get charged with multiplied bigamy if he did.

'No sailor suit, if yer don't mind,' said Freddy resolutely.

'Perhaps Freddy wants to be a bridesmaid, Mum, and wear a pink frock,' said Sally.

'Here, leave off,' said Freddy, eating a slice of cake to keep the wolf from the door until supper.

'Well, all right, love,' said Mrs Brown, a natural peacemaker, 'perhaps a nice dark grey suit, then, that you could wear afterwards for Sundays.'

'With long trousers,' said Freddy.

'Long trousers at your age?' said Sally.

'I've made up me mind I ain't wearing shorts at Susie's weddin',' said Freddy, 'they ain't important enough.'

'Oh, I don't know about long trousers,' said Mrs Brown, cutting away surplus greenery from a firm cauliflower. 'You are only eleven, Freddy.'

'All right,' said Freddy, 'I won't wear no trousers at all, just me shirt, waistcoat an' jacket.'

'Oh, yer rotten 'orror,' said Sally, 'I'm not goin' in that church if you're not wearin' any trousers.'

'Can't 'elp it,' said Freddy, 'me mind's made up, I'm not wearin' no trousers unless they're long ones.'

'Well, listen to 'im,' said Sally, 'just wait till Dad comes in, I bet 'e'll make you sing a different tune.'

'I bet 'e won't,' said Freddy, 'I bet Dad wouldn't wear no trousers, either, if Mum tried to put 'im in shorts for Susie's weddin'.'

'Dad's a man, you soppy date,' said Sally, 'you're only a boy.'

'Can't 'elp that,' said Freddy, 'me mind's made up.'

'Now, Freddy love, stop actin' up,' said Mrs Brown.

'Crikey, what a life,' said Freddy. 'Me mate Daisy's moved and me mum won't let me wear long trousers. I 'ope this kind of bad luck ain't goin' to last me all year.'

'I'll speak sympathetic to your dad,' said Mrs Brown placatingly, 'but as for Daisy, she and her fam'ly couldn't help 'aving to move, love.'

Young Daisy Cook had been Freddy's best street pal. She and her family had moved because their house had a rather unhappy history. A grisly murder had taken place there twelve years ago, in 1914.

Freddy, eyeing his sister, took on a puzzled expression. 'What's 'appening to Sally?' he asked. His young sister, who had fair curly hair and hazel eyes, was getting pretty. And something else. Crikey, she'd stopped growing short, she was shooting up. He'd been taller than her, even though three years younger. Now she was suddenly above him. All in a few months. 'Here, what're you wearin', sis?'

'Me?' said Sally, her blue school gymslip short. 1926 was the year of exceptionally short hemlines. Legs were in. Or legs had come out, according to how one thought about the fashion. 'What d'you mean, what'm I wearin'?'

'Whose legs you wearin'?' asked Freddy.

'Not yours,' said Sally, 'or Susie's.'

'Look at 'er, Mum,' said Freddy, 'she's standin' on some kind of stilts.'

'Oh, I see what you mean,' said Mrs Brown, and smiled proudly at Sally. 'Yes, she's goin' to be as tall as our Susie.'

'Something's goin' on,' said Freddy. 'Come on, you Sally, let's 'ave a proper look at them legs of yours, I don't want me friends sayin' you're walkin' on someone else's.'

'Keep off,' said Sally. Freddy, as larky as any Walworth boy, sped around the kitchen table to get at her. Sally yelled and rushed.

'Mum, stop 'im!'

'Now, Freddy, leave Sally be, there's a good boy,' said Mrs Brown placidly. In all her forty-three years, nothing had ever seriously ruffled her, except the possibility, during the war, that her husband Jim might not survive his terrible life in the trenches.

'Mum!' shrieked Sally, as Freddy kept after her.

'Freddy, stop teasin' her,' said Mrs Brown.

'Someone's got to see whose legs she's wearin',' said Freddy, but gave up when Sally put herself behind their plump mother.

'Oh, yer daft ha'porth,' said Sally, 'how can anyone be wearin' someone else's legs?'

'Yes, it beats me,' said Freddy, 'unless you bought a pair of long wooden ones down the market. I dunno what I'm goin' to do if me mates find out one of me sisters is walkin' about on wooden legs.'

'Now you're talkin' silly, love,' said Mrs Brown, going into the scullery to peel potatoes at the sink, 'our Sally's got nice natural legs.'

'Yes, but 'ave yer seen what's been 'appening to them lately?' asked Freddy.

'Sally's growin' up,' said Mrs Brown.

'I remember Susie growin' up once,' said Freddy.

'Now how could anyone remember Susie only growin' up once?' asked Sally.

'Well, I was only little at the time,' said Freddy.

'You're potty,' said Sally. 'Mum, don't you think it's lovely our Will bein' 'ome for the weddin'? Susie nearly cried when she saw 'im.'

'It beats me, girls nearly cryin' when they're 'appy,' said Freddy. 'Mind you, Mum, I dunno that me brother's all that well.'

'He's just got a bit of a chest,' said Sally.

'He'll be all right now he's home and not 'aving to suffer all that terrible heat,' said Mrs Brown.

''Ope so,' said Freddy. 'Well, I think I'll go an' see if Ernie Flint'll lend me 'is bike on Sunday, so's I can cycle to Brockwell Park.'

'I'll come with you as far as Cotham Street,' said Sally,

'then I'll go an' see Mavis.' Mavis Richards was a close friend. They shared the giggly little secrets of schoolgirls.

'I don't know I want you ridin' bikes, Freddy,' said Mrs Brown, 'not with Susie's weddin' next month, you might fall off and hit your head on the road.'

'With an 'ead like's he's got, I bet Dad would get a bill for road repairs,' said Sally.

'Our Sally's nearly a comic sometimes,' said Freddy.

'Bless 'er,' said Mrs Brown.

'And 'er wooden legs,' said Freddy.

Out he went with his sister. Sally was bare-headed, Freddy wearing a blue cap. From the open door of a house shot the figure of a neighbour, Mr Higgins. He was a tram conductor whose duties sometimes brought him home early, sometimes late. After him came a rolling-pin. It struck him between his shoulder blades. Down he went. Following the rolling-pin came Mrs Higgins. Mr Higgins was thin and bony, Mrs Higgins was buxom. Freddy and Sally could tell she was riled. She had a wealth of dark brown hair, the pins were loose and it was all over her head and face.

'Get up,' she said to her fallen husband, and she retrieved the rolling-pin.

'What for?' asked Mr Higgins, feeling safer on the pavement.

'So's I can give yer another one,' said Mrs Higgins. 'I don't like 'itting you when yer on the ground.'

'I can't get up,' said Mr Higgins, 'I'm wounded, and me leg's broke as well.'

'I'll give you wounded,' said Mrs Higgins. 'Look at 'im,' she said to Sally and Freddy, 'would yer believe 'im capable of it?'

'Capable of what, Mrs Higgins?' asked Sally.

'Kissin' and cuddlin' 'is lady passengers, that's what.'

'Is he supposed to?' asked Freddy.

'Is 'e what?'

'Well, I only asked,' said Freddy.

''E's forbidden,' said Mrs Higgins, 'but 'e done it. Stay where you are,' she said to her husband, giving him a rap on his head with the rolling-pin. 'Mrs Blake saw it all this mornin', at the market tram stop. Me own 'usband, would yer believe, and in front of everyone in Walworth.'

'Now would I do that?' said Mr Higgins, his conductor's uniform dusty from the pavement. 'I'd lose me job.'

'That's what I've been tellin' yer,' said Mrs Higgins, 'and don't answer me back in front of Sally an' Freddy, they'll think I don't get no respect from you. Mrs Blake told me that when she saw it 'appen, she near dropped dead with shock.'

'Pity she bleedin' didn't,' muttered Mr Higgins.

'What's that? What's that you said?'

'I said I think me leg's bleedin'.'

'Shall I get 'im a bandage an' some ointment, Mrs Higgins?' asked Sally.

''E don't want a bandage, not yet 'e don't,' said Mrs Higgins. 'I'll give 'im what for when I get 'im back indoors. 'E'll need a doctor then, not a bandage. To think after all these years I'm burdened with the shame of what 'e's done today, and in public too.'

'Look, me pet,' said Mr Higgins, 'I just 'elped a lady off me tram with 'er foldin' pram and baby. Yus, and a shoppin' bag as well. She 'appened to be overcome with gratitude, I suppose—'

'She what?' said Mrs Higgins threateningly.

'She was overcome with gratitude, Mrs Higgins,' said Freddy. 'I mean, that's what Mr Higgins just said.'

'Well, what else would've made 'er give me a kiss?' said Mr Higgins. 'I asks yer, me love, what else? I didn't kiss 'er meself, nor cuddle 'er, it's against the regulations.'

'You're answerin' me back again,' said Mrs Higgins.

Along came Mr Ponsonby, a lodger in a house farther down the Place. An eccentric, he was fifty years old, his lean body clad in a black frock coat, black drainpipe trousers, and a grey waistcoat. He also wore a bowler hat, a red bow tie and elastic-sided boots. And he carried a rolled umbrella. At first glance he seemed a dapper man, but a closer inspection revealed crumbs on his waistcoat, wrinkles in his bow tie and a dent in his bowler. And his boots were dusty. On the other hand, his smooth unlined face had a very neat look, as if nature had taken pains to put each feature tidily in place. Sometimes his expression was querulous, and sometimes that of a kind and gentle man. He could often be heard talking to himself. 'Dear me, dear me, what a day, what a day.' That sort of thing.

Up he came in dainty pigeon-toed fashion and looked down at Mr Higgins.

'Mr Higgins? Dear me, what's this all about?' His voice had a piping lilt.

'I ain't sittin' 'ere of me own accord, yer know,' grumbled Mr Higgins.

'No, of course not, of course not,' said Mr Ponsonby.

''E fell over,' said Sally.

'Ah, who is this I see?' enquired Mr Ponsonby, and peered at Sally. He smiled. 'Ah, yes, a young lady.'

'She ain't a young lady, she's me sister,' said Freddy.

'Now now, Freddy,' said Mrs Higgins, 'course she's a young lady, anyone can see that. My, ain't yer growin' up nice, Sally? Yer goin' to rival Susie in a year or two. What're you doin'?' she demanded of her husband.

'I was thinkin' of gettin' up,' said Mr Higgins.

'I'll knock yer block off,' said Mrs Higgins, 'I ain't finished with you yet.'

37

'Come now, Mrs Higgins, have a peppermint drop,' said Mr Ponsonby, and produced a paper bag from his pocket. He always had peppermint drops somewhere on his person, and offered them generously to all and sundry. The street kids knew this, and sometimes ran after him, asking for one, and he always obliged. He sucked them regularly himself, and breathed peppermint fumes.

'Don't mind if I do, I need something,' said Mrs Higgins. As she helped herself from the bag, Mr Higgins came to his feet and disappeared indoors. It didn't fool Mrs Higgins.

'Gotcher!' she cried. 'I'll learn yer!' And she went bouncing in after him.

'Tck, tck,' said Mr Ponsonby and peered at Sally again. 'Ah, yes, Sally, our pretty young lady. Have a peppermint drop.'

'Oh, thanks,' said Sally, and took one. In return, she gave Mr Ponsonby a happy little smile. Life was doing her proud at the moment. Not only was she going to be a bridesmaid in three weeks time, she had also started to grow again after a gloomy year of thinking she was going to end up as a real tich of a girl. She was positive she could actually feel her legs getting longer every week. Not every day, of course. Every week. With fashions so short, and flappers showing their knees, no girl who had just had her fourteenth birthday wanted to have legs that hardly went anywhere. It was bliss that she'd shot up inches in just a few months. Mind, she still had to wear dreary old black lisle stockings for school, but Susie had recently bought her imitation silk ones for Sundays. They made her lengthening legs feel ever so posh. Susie, her sister, though, wore real silk nearly all the time. Well, she had ever such a good job, of course, as personal assistant to her fiancé, Sammy Adams, who was boss of Adams Fashions and other enterprises. Sally could hardly believe he was going to be her brother-in-law. When she left school at the end of the present term, perhaps she could get a job in one of his shops.

Mr Ponsonby blinked in the sunshine of her smile.

'Charming, charming,' he said. 'Well, good afternoon, good afternoon, I must get to my lodgings.' He put the bag of peppermints away, then turned and began to retrace his steps. Freddy and Sally went after him.

'Excuse me, Mr Ponsonby,' said Sally, 'you're goin' the wrong way.'

'No, no,' he said, stopping, 'I'm going to my lodgings, I have things to do.'

'Yes, but you're still pointin' the wrong way,' said Freddy.

Mr Ponsonby blinked again.

'Dear me, so I am, so I am,' he said.

'It's back there,' said Sally, 'in Mrs Mason's 'ouse.'

'Thank you, thank you, how kind. My, you are a pretty girl. Have you had a peppermint drop?'

'Yes, thanks,' said Sally.

'One can't be too careful.' Mr Ponsonby regarded brother and sister cautiously. 'One is never sure who has had one and who hasn't. Dear me, what a day, good afternoon.' And off he went to his lodgings, the point of his umbrella clicking on the pavement. He stopped to inspect a chalked hopscotch design. 'Bless my soul, what's that doing there? Never mind, never mind.' He hastened on.

'Ain't 'e funny?' said Freddy.

'You didn't get a peppermint drop,' said Sally, as they turned into Browning Street.

'Nor I didn't,' said Freddy. 'I'll take two next time 'e offers, 'e won't mind.'

39

'Bet he won't even notice,' said Sally. 'Don't he talk posh, though? Mum says 'e's prob'bly come down in the world.'

'Yes, 'e prob'bly 'ad a wife that took to drink an' drove 'im to ruin,' said Freddy. 'Still, 'e don't go around cryin' about it.'

'No, but he blows 'is nose sometimes,' said Sally.

'What's that got to do with it?'

'Well, lots of people blow their noses to 'ide they're cryin',' said Sally.

'Susie blew her nose a little bit when our William came 'ome,' said Freddy.

'There you are, then,' said Sally. She parted from him at Cotham Street, where her school friend lived. Freddy stopped for a moment to watch her. He grinned. She was walking as perky as anything in her short school gymslip. Showing off, just because her legs were getting longer. But he couldn't help grinning, he was fond of Sally, the cheeky one of the family.

He called after her in the fashion of a street urchin.

'Oi, darling, 'ow's yer farver's tadpoles?'

Sally turned, saw him grinning, put a thumb to her nose and then went on. A man coming the other way took notice of her. Tall and muscular, his eyes were dark and hollow beneath the peak of his flat cap, as if he didn't sleep very well, and his black serge overcoat was unbuttoned, his watch chain showing. Sally bridled because he was staring at her all the time during his approach. She didn't like his eyes one little bit, nor their fixed stare. And he was coming straight at her, as if he was going to knock her down and walk over her. Sally had to dodge aside, and as he passed her his body seemed to bruise the very air.

''Ere, d'you mind?' she said with spirit, but he just kept going, nor did he look back. Ugh, I don't like his kind, thought Sally, I like the ones that Susie likes. Sammy Adams, and his brothers, Boots and Tommy. Why wasn't there another brother, a younger one? One for her?

She laughed to herself then and went on to her friend's house.

Freddy, on his way to Ernie Flint's home in Rodney Place, approached a factory. Well, it had been a factory once, but had caught fire some years ago. It had all caved in except for a section at one end that used to house offices and store-rooms. A high wooden fence had been erected around the devastated property, but kids could squeeze in because the double wooden gates had been busted open one time, and the repair job had been makeshift. When kids did get in, they played around over piles of bricks and rubble. They couldn't, however, get into the section still standing. The door was padlocked and all windows heavily boarded up.

Passing the sagging gates, Freddy was brought to a stop by a girl's voice.

''Ere, you boy, come 'ere.'

He went back to the gates and saw a face visible through the gap.

'What's up?' he asked.

'I've lost Tabby,' she said.

'Who's Tabby?'

'It's our cat, of course. Can you come through 'ere and 'elp me find 'im?'

'Well, I'm on me way to—'

'You'd better come and 'elp or me dad'll wallop yer. I don't like lookin' by meself, not in 'ere.'

'All right, I suppose I'm not specially busy,' said Freddy, and squeezed his way through the gap. The girl, ten years old, looked him up and down as if she needed to be convinced he was capable of finding a lost cat. Well-brushed raven hair hung down her back. The black elastic of a straw boater was around her neck, the boater itself resting at the back of her head. Her face was a bit dusty, her gymslip likewise, but Freddy could see she had round brown eyes that were like Daisy Cook's. 'What's yer name?' he asked.

'Cassie Ford. What's yours?'

'Freddy Brown. Me fam'ly lives in Caulfield Place.'

'Oh, I know Caulfield Place,' she said, 'ragged kids live there.'

''Ere, mind yer tongue,' said Freddy, 'I ain't a ragged kid.'

'Well, all right,' said Cassie graciously, 'but what about me cat? Could yer start lookin' for it? Then me dad won't wallop yer. 'E's good at wallopin' boys. He give one to the boy next door last week, and it nearly done 'im in. When the boy's dad came round about it, Dad gave 'im one too.'

Crikey, what a crackpot, thought Freddy. Still, all girls were a bit potty. Not that he minded. He liked girls, and you had to accept they were off their chumps most times.

'All right,' he said, 'but you sure your cat's in 'ere?'

'Yes, a girl told me she'd seen 'im go in. Only I don't like bein' in 'ere alone.'

Freddy looked around. Mounds of bricks, mortar and rubble littered the place, the bright sunshine picking out all kinds of colours. Over on the right was the still standing section. It looked a bit desolate, even in the crisp daylight.

'All right, you stay 'ere, Cassie, and I'll go lookin'.'

'No, I'll come with yer,' said Cassie. 'I don't want to be alone when one of them skeletons comes up out of the ground.'

'Eh?' said Freddy.

42

'Yes, didn't you know that if you're alone in 'ere a skeleton comes up and rattles its bones at you?' said Cassie.

'Well, I'm blowed,' said Freddy solemnly, 'is that a fact?'

'Fancy you not knowin' that,' said Cassie.

'Well, like me dad says, you live an' learn. Come on, then, and if we do see a skeleton rattlin' its bones, I'll chuck all these bricks at it.' Freddy started walking and looking. 'What did yer say yer cat's name was?'

'Tabby,' she said, close on his heels. ''E's always gettin' lost.'

'You'd be better off with a canary,' said Freddy.

'I don't want a canary, I want our cat,' said Cassie, and she followed Freddy around the large area of collapsed walls and roofs, around the mounds capped with brick dust, and they both kept callng the cat's name. In and out of the gaps they went. 'Tabby, Tabby, come 'ere, will you!' called Cassie in exasperation.

'I'll chuck some stones about,' said Freddy. 'If 'c's around, that'll make 'im show 'imself.'

'Don't you throw stones at our cat, you might 'it 'im,' said Cassie indignantly.

'I dunno it wouldn't serve 'im right if 'e's always losin' himself,' said Freddy. 'And if you ask me, I don't think 'e's in 'ere.'

They reached the still intact section.

'Oh, lor,' breathed Cassie, ''e couldn't be in there, could 'e?'

'Don't see 'ow he could be,' said Freddy, 'it's all boarded up. Mind, we could go an' see if the door's open.'

'I ain't goin' in there meself,' said Cassie, 'it's 'aunted. Me dad's Aunt Tilda lived in an 'aunted house once, and it turned all 'er hair white, and me dad 'ad to go an' see what was 'aunting it, and it turned all 'is hair white too, and when 'e was only twenty.'

'Rotten 'ard luck, that was, Cassie.'

'Yes, our milkman said it made our dad old before 'is time.'

'Did 'e find a ghost?' asked Freddy.

''E never said, I expect it was too 'orrible to talk about.' Cassie eyed the boarded windows apprehensively. 'We'd best go,' she said.

'Wait a tick, let's 'ave a look,' said Freddy, and made a beeline for the padlocked door. He'd noticed something. It was the padlock, it was hanging loose. The thick steel staple hadn't been pushed in. He removed the padlock, released the metal bar and pushed the door. It swung open. ''Ere we are, Cassie,' he called, 'we can get in.'

'Oh, don't,' begged Cassie, 'you might get struck down or ate up.'

'But someone's been in,' said Freddy, 'and yer cat might've followed. I'll take a quick look, I won't give anyone time to eat me up.'

'You goin' in all by yerself?' Cassie was awe-struck. 'Can't you just put yer 'ead in and call Tabby? Oh, suppose 'e's trapped in there an' can't get out?'

'I expect all 'is hair's turnin' white, like yer dad's,' said Freddy. 'Still, I'll give 'im a shout.' He put his head in and bawled the cat's name. Nothing came of that, except the echoes of his voice, which ran hollowly about. 'Some cat,' he said, 'turned invisible, prob'ly. I'll 'ave a look, Cassie, might as well.'

'Oh, lor',' breathed Cassie. All the kids who lived close by said the place was haunted at night. Cassie thought it could be haunted by day as well, and the kids weren't too sure because none of them came and played around the brick hills any more.

'You stay there,' said Freddy, and went in, seeing how worried she was about her daft cat. He entered a wide passage with doors on either side. The dusty floor was marked, proving someone had been in. The light from the open front door showed up the marks. Perhaps a night watchman came on duty sometimes. Or perhaps the owner came and took a look at the place now and again. He opened each door in turn, but saw only empty dusty storerooms. They all said a silent hello to him in the gloom of boarded-up windows. No cat appeared. There were stairs at the end of the passage. They creaked as he climbed them. He stopped when he reached the landing, he had a sudden odd feeling of being sort of cut off from the humming life of Walworth. It was even gloomier up here, and very silent. But despite the gloom he glimpsed a large spider scuttling along the foot of a wall between doors. It made no sound. Well, spiders didn't, they were always silent. Bluebottles weren't, nor bees, nor birds. And monkeys, talk about chattering, they could beat the band at the Zoo. But spiders, they'd invented silence, they had.

He stood still for a little while. He wasn't a boy who suffered from nerves, but he had to admit it felt a bit creepy up here. Still, he'd better see if the cat had got trapped in any of the rooms. He moved along the landing, and the floorboards creaked under his feet, breaking the silence. He supposed everything was as dry as dust. He reached to open the first door, then held back as a plaintive little miaow came to his ears. That was the sound of a cat all right. He opened the door. Another empty room and no cat. I don't know that Cassie would like that, she'd say he'd just heard the ghostly miaow of a cat that had died up here.

'Come on, Tabby, is it you or not?' he called. That brought a second miaow, and it pointed him at the next door. He opened it. All gloom again, but the room wasn't bare and empty. He made out a table, a chair, and a truckle bed with rumpled blankets. On the table was a candle in a holder, and something else. He squinted. It was a sealed and labelled tin of corned beef. He heard a little movement then, and out from under the blankets leapt a cat. It darted past him and whisked through the door, a streaking bundle of tabby fur. Moments later he distinctly heard a glad yell from Cassie. His nose began to twitch, to pick up all kinds of smells. Cat smells, he supposed, mixed with others. The others probably had something to do with a watchman spending nights up here now and again. That was the reason for the bed, blankets and corned beef. And the reason why the padlock hadn't been pushed home was probably because the bloke had been all bleary and careless the last time he'd left the place.

Freddy closed the door and shut the smells in, but as he went down the stairs he thought some of them were following him. He heard Cassie calling.

'Freddy, come on out, I've got Tabby, and you ain't fell down a hole, 'ave yer?'

He walked through the passage and emerged into the late afternoon light. Talk about the joys of fresh air and sunshine, especially as there'd been a lot of fog about up to a week ago. It was nearly like summer now. Well, spring, anyway. He pulled the door to, slipped in the padlock and fastened it with a click. He turned. The cat was in the girl's arms, doing some daft purring.

'Good idea if you got that cat chained up,' he said.

'Oh, yer cruel thing,' said Cassie. 'But fancy Tabby gettin' in there.'

'Well, I did say 'e might've followed someone in, there's a room upstairs that looks like it's used by a night watchman, except I dunno what 'e's got to watch.'

'More like a ghost, I bet,' said Cassie. 'Wasn't you brave, goin' in by yerself? Me dad's brave too, 'e saved an 'orse once from drowning in the sea.'

'How'd it get in the sea?'

'It fell off a ship,' said Cassie, cuddling her cat.

'You sure?' said Freddy. 'I never 'eard of no 'orse fallin' off a ship before.'

'It slipped,' said Cassie. 'Or something,' she added after a moment's reflection. 'It was when me dad was a sea captain, and 'e 'ad to jump in and rescue the poor thing, it couldn't swim. They give me dad a medal.'

'Who did?' asked Freddy, walking back to the gates with her.

'I can't remember. Well, yes, it was the Horse Savin' Society, I think. Yes, that was it. Mind, that was before 'e took to drink.' Cassie sighed and her cat purred.

'That's funny,' said Freddy, 'I was only sayin' to me sister Sally earlier that a neighbour of ours prob'bly 'ad a wife that took to drink an' brought 'im to ruin. 'As yer dad brought yer mum to ruin?'

'No, me mum died when I was little,' said Cassie.

'Well, I'm sorry for yer about that, Cassie.'

'It's all right, I 'elp me dad as much as I can,' she said.

They rounded the final heaps of rubble and reached the gates, on the insides of which kids had chalked anti-social messages.

'*I hate Eddie Banks.*'

'*I hate his bruvver.*'

'*Loopy Lily Jarvis luvs Billy Palmer.*'

'*What, him? She's loopy all right.*'

'*Elsie Nunn's got a fat bum.*'

'*Cissy Dawes don't wear no drawers.*'

'*YES I DO!!!*'

'Don't read them, they're rude,' said Cassie.

'Come on,' said Freddy, and they squeezed their way out, the cat staying happily in Cassie's arms. 'Where d'you live?'

'Blackwood Street,' said Cassie.

'That's not far from us,' said Freddy. 'Well, I might see you around, Cassie, if I don't see yer cat first.'

'We used to live in a mansion in Dulwich,' said Cassie. 'That was when me dad worked at Buckingham Palace, servin' the King an' Queen. 'E used to take them their 'ot cocoa at night.'

'You sure?' said Freddy, hiding a grin.

'Course I'm sure,' said Cassie, 'they liked 'ot cocoa. Well, goodbye, Freddy, thanks for findin' Tabby.'

'So long,' said Freddy. She went one way cuddling her cat, and he went the other. Well, he thought, there's some girls a bit barmy, some a bit dozy, and some real crackpots. Still, as his dad always said, blokes had got to live with that.

He found Ernie Flint at home and asked about the loan of his bike. Ernie said not likely, his bike wasn't for lending, specially not on a Sunday. Get a bike of your own, he said. Me dad can't afford it, said Freddy. Bet your sister can, said Ernie, the one that's getting married. Girls about to get married can be a real soft touch, you could ask some of them for fifty bob easy and they wouldn't even remember giving it to you, they're at their soppiest when they're getting married.

'I dunno that Susie's soppy,' said Freddy.

'Bound to be,' said Ernie. 'You could ask 'er for a fiver, seein' what a good job she's got, and if she ain't soppy enough to give yer as much as that, tell 'er you'll just take 'alf that amount. You can buy a decent bike for fifty bob.'

'Crikey, I knew you'd got a bike, Ernie,' said Freddy, 'I didn't know you'd got brains as well.'

''Ow would yer like a punch in the eye?' said Ernie.

'I don't think I'll stay for that,' said Freddy, 'it might spoil me supper.'

He went back home, whistling with optimist cheerfulness as he thought about touching Susie for the price of a bike. Of course, he wasn't sure if her feelings about getting married really were soppy. She didn't act soppy, not Susie, but she did go about sometimes looking as if she'd lost a penny and found ten quid. But she never went off to work wearing odd stockings or forgetting to put her hat on or what day it was. That would have been a sign that she really was soppy about her engagement to Sammy. Still, she was up in the clouds sometimes. Promising, that was, thought Freddy.

CHAPTER FOUR

Will was ready to leave. It was after six, the best of the bright March day was over, the sun was deserting the Western sky, and sharp twilight was waiting in the wings. The chimneys and rooftops of Walworth were growing a sombre colour. Will had helped Nellie prepare the vegetables and to put them on, and a dissected plump rabbit was stewing. It had all been sending Annie mad, not being able to look after things herself on account of her stiff knee. She felt like a back number.

Will had met ten-year-old Cassie. Her hair was long, not bobbed, and she had dreamy eyes and an even dreamier smile. But she looked breathless when she heard about how Annie had come to meet this soldier. She obviously thought it the most romantic meeting ever, and Annie had a ghastly feeling she was going to say so. She prevented that by demanding to know where she'd been, and Cassie said she'd had to go and find Tabby and that a boy had helped her. What boy? Oh, said Cassie, he was the son of a lion tamer who'd just come back from darkest Africa to look after the Trafalgar Square lions for the King. They're not real lions, you silly, said Nellie, they're statue lions. Yes, he's got to keep them polished, said Cassie. I'm going to write about it in my diary, she said, and about Annie meeting a royal guardsman. He's not a royal guardsman, said Nellie. No, but he could be, said Cassie, and went up to confide her imaginings to her diary.

Will also met Charlie, a boy with a shock of untidy hair

and socks down to his ankles. Charlie thought Will had done a good job bringing Annie home after she'd hurt her knee. He brought her in a pushcart, said Nellie wickedly, and Annie gritted her teeth because Charlie, being what he was, made a lot of that.

'Cor, in a pushcart,' he said, 'our Annie and all. Bloomin' 'eroic, that was. I bet even Tarzan couldn't 'ave got 'er in a pushcart. I'm 'eartbroke I missed it. 'Ere, could yer put 'er in it again, Will? Yer don't mind me callin' yer Will, do yer? I ain't met no-one 'eroic before. Could yer put Annie in the pushcart again so's I could see it with me own mince pies?'

'Oh, you little 'ooligan,' said Annie, 'if I didn't have a stiff knee I'd boil you in the copper.'

'And besides, we don't 'ave a pushcart,' said Nellie.

'And besides, if I tried it,' said Will, 'she'd boil me as well. If she didn't have a stiff knee.'

'That's it, everyone laugh,' said Annie bitterly.

When Will was ready to go, he offered to carry her upstairs so that she could rest her knee and have her dad bring her supper up to her later.

'Well, all right,' said Annie, 'I suppose it's best – oh, mind me frock!' Will had lifted her. He carried her out of the kitchen, and she went on about her frock much as she had before. Charlie, following on with Nellie, couldn't think why Annie was having problems.

'What's she fussin' about, Nellie?' he asked. 'I can't see nothink wrong with 'er frock.'

'It's not 'er frock,' whispered Nellie, 'it's just that she ain't never met an 'andsome soldier before.' She darted, squeezing ahead of Will on the landing to open the door of the back bedroom, which was Annie's. 'In 'ere, Will,' she said, 'our Annie sleeps in this room.'

'Right, let's do the delivery job,' said Will. He carried

Annie in and placed her on her bed. She tugged at the hem of her frock. 'All right?' said Will.

Just the hint of a smile showed on her face.

'Thanks ever so much, honest,' she said.

'Don't mention it,' said Will, and it happened then. It came suddenly, the tightness in his chest, the sensation of constriction and the shortness of breath. He'd be coughing and wheezing in a few moments, an embarrassment to everyone. 'Got to go now. Good luck, Annie, you too, Nellie and Charlie.'

They all stared at him as he walked straight out.

'Crikey, 'e's gone,' said Nellie.

'Nellie, run down and make sure he knows I'm grateful really,' said Annie, 'tell 'im thank you again.'

Nellie dashed out, ran down the stairs and caught Will at the front door. He'd picked up his peaked cap from the kitchen.

'Annie said she's ever so grateful really, an' wants to thank you ever so much,' said Nellie.

'Pleasure,' said Will, wheezing now.

'Oh, 'ave yer got a cold?' asked Nellie.

'Sort of,' said Will huskily, and left, pulling the door to behind him. Nellie went back upstairs.

''E's got a sort of cold,' she said.

''E didn't look as if 'e had,' said Charlie. 'Blimey, what an 'eroic bloke, gettin' you in a pushcart, Annie.'

'If you mention that once more, Charlie, your life won't be worth livin', d'you hear?' said Annie.

'Yes, an' what did you do to Pam Nicholls?' asked Nellie.

'Well, I did 'ave a go at tryin' to push 'er foot into 'er mouth—'

'You what?' yelled Annie.

'But 'er mum come in then an' give me a thick ear,' said

Charlie, rubbing his left one. 'That Pam, she told 'er mum to give me another one. Just wait till I get 'er alone, I'll push both 'er feet into 'er mouth.'

'Nellie, get the chopper and hit your brother with it,' said Annie.

'Yes, in a minute, Annie,' said Nellie. 'I wonder if Will's comin' back sometime?'

'Of course not,' said Annie. 'What would 'e want to come back for?'

'Well, 'e might want to see if your knee's all right,' said Nellie.

'More like 'e'd want to give Annie another ride in a pushcart,' said Charlie.

'Oh, you wait, you 'eathen,' breathed Annie, 'as soon as me knee's better I'm goin' to hit you with the chopper meself, and don't think I won't. Didn't I tell you not to mention pushcarts again?'

'I only said what Will might do if 'e comes round again,' said Charlie.

'I don't know why you and Nellie call him Will,' said Annie.

'It's 'is name,' said Nellie.

'You shouldn't be familiar when you've only just met 'im,' said Annie. 'Look, both of you go down and make sure the supper's cookin' properly. Don't let anything burn, and mind how you handle the saucepans, Nellie.'

'All right,' said Nellie, and down she went with Charlie. Nellie descended quietly. Charlie's descent created a minor earthquake. Annie lay looking at the ceiling. She thought about being wheeled home in that pushcart. Her at her age, and him as good as laughing all over his face.

I might as well die and not have any supper.

No, I won't, I'll have some supper and die later.

*   *   *

53

Outside, Will leaned against the railings. He tried to let his body relax, he tried to keep still, but he wheezed like an old man with bronchitis, and a periodical cough racked his chest. He supposed he'd brought it on himself by carrying Annie upstairs. But just doing that had brought on the attack? He could see what was going to happen if his condition didn't improve. He'd be invalided out of the Army at the ripe old age of twenty.

The attack began to ease a little after ten minutes. He watched the street kids. He heard the faint sounds of Walworth traffic. Trams, omnibuses, horse-drawn vehicles. Not like Indian traffic. Bullocks provided horse-power out there. But not cows. Cows were sacred. If one sat down in a crowded city street, it could cause prolonged congestion. Well, if it wouldn't move, no-one tried to make it, so it stayed there.

As to the heat, it sapped a bloke's energy unless you ate lots of curry. He couldn't count the number of times he and other East Surrey men had longed for the April showers of home, and for things like the smell of eggs and bacon, the taste of fish and chips, the savoury flavour of hot faggots and pease pudding, and the creaminess of a rice pudding with a golden-brown skin just out of the oven.

Come to that, even street kids could be missed. Look at these, he thought, ruddy monkeys, the lot of them. Walworth kids never changed. This bunch were no different from those of his own generation. All generations scrapped, argued, broke windows, kicked tin cans and got their ears clipped by their dads. But they all grew up cheerfully and optimistically, with exceptions. That counted, cheerfulness and optimism.

It took over fifteen minutes before his breathing became normal, and a few more minutes before he decided to go on his way.

'What's that about our Annie?' asked Mr Harold Ford, a railway ganger of five feet ten and rugged all over. Just home from his work, his jacket was off. He always took it off the moment he entered the kitchen. His waistcoat was an old leather one, his shirt of thick striped flannel, and his trousers were of hard-wearing corduroy. There was a scarf around his neck and a belt around his trousers. He had a little round bald patch to his black hair that had inspired Cassie into asking him if he was going to be a monk later on. He said he liked the thought but didn't think he'd ever be holy enough.

'Yes, our Annie's upstairs, Dad,' said Nellie, and told him how her sister had bumped her knee and been brought home by a nice soldier. In a pushcart.

'What's that?' asked the Gaffer. Everyone called him that on account of his ruggedness. It made him look like a man who was in charge. 'Did you say a pushcart, Nellie?'

'Well, the soldier said it was the best way to bring 'er.'

'Oh, me old Adam, a pushcart?' said the Gaffer, trying to hide a grin. 'Where'd the soldier come from?'

''E didn't say,' said Nellie, 'except 'e did tell me 'is fam'ly live in Caulfield Place and 'e's 'ome on leave.'

'I think 'e comes from Windsor Castle,' said Cassie, 'I think 'e guards the King and Queen there.'

'Who said?' asked Charlie.

'Well, it's only what I think,' said Cassie, 'and only the way 'e looks.'

'Now 'ow can anyone look like Windsor Castle?' asked Charlie.

'You kids work it out,' said the Gaffer, whose ruggedness actually hid a heart made of marshmallow, 'while I go up an' see Annie.'

Up he went. He found Annie's knee was just a bit stiff

and bruised. Be all right in a day or so, he said. Annie wasn't too concerned with that, apart from thinking she might have to hop to work tomorrow. She still had indignity on her mind. So she regaled her dad with an account of the purgatory she'd suffered being wheeled home in a boy's pushcart with thousands of people all having a look at her.

'Thousands?' said the Gaffer.

'Yes, and all grinnin',' said Annie, 'and me with me knees nearly up to me chin.'

'Gawd save the starvin' poor,' said the Gaffer in a strangled voice, and suddenly wasn't there any more.

'Dad, where've you gone?' yelled Annie. She heard him out on the landing. He sounded as if he was choking to death. 'Oh, I don't believe it, you're out there laughin'! Call yourself me dad? You ought to be ashamed, laughin' like that, and don't think I can't 'ear you, because I can. What about the indignity I suffered, me a young lady near to eighteen.'

The Gaffer reappeared, his face red. He was coughing now. From her bed, Annie eyed him in outrage. He cleared his throat, rubbed his mouth, and made an attempt to come to terms with her feelings.

'Did yer say with yer knees up to yer chin, Annie?' he asked.

'You heard,' said Annie. 'Me, your eldest daughter.'

'Well, I ain't 'aving me best gel upset like that,' he said. 'I'll learn the bloke, Annie, soldier or not. I'll find out where 'e lives in Caulfield Place. It ain't far, I'll get 'im, and when I do I'll break 'is legs.'

'You'll what?' gasped Annie, sitting up.

'Break 'is legs, both of 'em.'

'Dad—'

'Don't you worry, Annie, I'll give 'im what 'e's asked

56

for, dumpin' you in a pushcart with yer knees up to yer chin, I'll make 'im wish 'e'd never been born.'

'Don't you dare,' gasped Annie, 'I'll never forgive you.'

'All right, Annie, just one leg.'

'Dad, you can't! It ain't Christian.'

'Ah,' said the Gaffer.

'Nor gentlemanly,' said Annie.

'Well, I'll grant yer that, Annie, breakin' legs ain't too gentlemanly.'

'Besides,' said Annie.

'Besides what?' asked her dad.

'Ain't it funny really, when you think about it?'

Charlie, Nellie and Cassie came running up the stairs to see what all the noise was about. Their dad was roaring with laughter, and Annie was giggling like a girl who'd forgotten she was a young lady of dignity.

CHAPTER FIVE

The evening had become cold and frosty, but Mrs Brown's kitchen was warm and cosy, the range fire glowing, and a supper of hot shepherd's pie was on the table, the potato crust patterned with crisp brown ridges. The house was old, going well back into the Victorian era, but its foundations and walls were solid and enduring. All members of the Brown family were present, and like the Adams family who had preceded them as tenants, they were never short of something to say. They were at it now, in response to what Will had said about a young lady who'd hurt her knee.

'Come again, Will?' said Mr Brown, a wiry old survivor of the trenches.

'Yes, say it again, Will,' said Susie.

'Yes, you'd best, love,' advised Mrs Brown, 'it sounded a bit funny.'

'It wasn't to her,' said Will. 'I decided I'd better not carry her, me in my condition, so I sat her in the pushcart and wheeled her home.'

'Crikey, you didn't, Will, did yer?' said Sally.

'How old was she?' asked Susie.

'She let me know several times she was seventeen and that I was mucking up her dignity,' said Will, 'but I had to get her home somehow.'

Susie laughed, and her engagement ring, a diamond solitaire, winked in the gaslight.

'Some palaver,' grinned Mr Brown.

'Wish I'd seen it,' said Freddy, 'only I went to Ernie

Flint's to see if I could 'ave a loan of 'is bike, not 'aving one of me own.'

Nobody took any notice of that. Will's way of getting a seventeen-year-old girl home was grabbing all the attention.

'I don't know I'd like bein' wheeled 'ome in a pushcart, and I'm only fourteen,' said Sally.

'Oh, but it must've been a nice ride for her with her knee hurtin',' said Mrs Brown proudly. She found it easy to be proud of almost anything her sons and daughters did, short of knocking a policeman's helmet off. She was against anything showing disrespect for the law.

'But the young lady didn't think it was nice, Will?' said Susie, twenty-one, and generally regarded as a corker, even by small boys still vague about why girls were different. And the vicar wouldn't tell them, except to say the ways of the Lord were wondrous.

'Yes, come on, what did she say?' asked Sally.

'Quite a lot,' said Will. Susie, sitting next to him, gave him a look. If Sally and Freddy were close, so were Susie and Will. She saw his little grin and how brown he was. The Army had done something for Will, made a man of him at twenty, and a good-looking one, with an air of self-confidence. An NCO's air of self-confidence. Susie could easily imagine a girl of seventeen dying of embarrassment at having him wheel her home in a boy's pushcart.

'What's a lot?' she asked.

'Well, most of it meant how much better off she'd have been if she'd never met me,' said Will.

'What a funny girl,' said Mrs Brown.

''Ere, listen, I met a funny one meself when I was on me way to Ernie Flint's,' said Freddy. 'Mind, I could've cycled there if I'd 'ad me own bike—'

'What's the young lady's name, Will?' asked Mr Brown.

'Talk to yerself,' muttered Freddy.

'Eat your supper up, love,' said Mrs Brown.

'Come on, Will, what's 'er name?' asked Sally.

'Annie Ford,' said Will.

''Ere, listen, I met a girl name of Ford,' said Freddy, 'it was the funny one, it was when I was on me way to—'

'Where's she live?' asked Sally.

'I dunno where she lives,' said Freddy, 'but I betcher she's got 'er own bike. If I 'ad me own—'

'I'm talkin' to Will, you blessed boy,' said Sally.

'Yes, where's the young lady live, Will?' asked Mrs Brown, beginning to think there might have been love at first sight if the young lady happened to have been pretty.

'Blackwood Street,' said Will. 'She's got a dad, two sisters and a hooligan brother.'

'So 'ave I,' said Sally, 'he's sittin' next to me. Is the young lady's brother purgat'ry to 'er?'

'Probably,' said Will. 'I was simply told about him by her sister Nellie. Anyway, they've all got each other but no mum. She died some years ago.'

'That's a shame,' said Mrs Brown.

'I don't know any Fords at our school,' said Sally.

'Sammy knows a Mr Ben Ford, a big fat man,' said Susie, and smiled reminiscently, knowing that Sammy's elder brother Boots had twice sorted out Fatty's troublesome bully boys.

Freddy, noting Susie's smile, thought this was a good time to try again.

''Ere, Susie, I like Sammy,' he said, 'I don't wonder you're romantic about 'im, seein' 'e's goin' to marry yer. 'As he got a bike? I ain't got one meself—'

'I wonder if Annie Ford and her fam'ly could be relations of Mr Ben Ford?' mused Susie. 'I hope not. Well, you'll have to take her some flowers, Will.'

'Eh?' said Will, and eyed Susie in suspicion. She smiled sweetly. Stone my brainbox, he thought, the way the female mind works. They were all the same, sisters, mothers, aunts, cousins and anyone else with a bosom. 'Watch what you're sayin', sis.'

Sally caught Susie's eye. Sally winked. Susie smiled again.

'But you should, Will,' she said, 'shouldn't he, Dad?'

'What?' Mr Brown exercised a cautious note on behalf of his eldest son. He knew about female minds himself. Well, you had to know a bit when you were married or you could wake up one morning and find your Sunday watch and chain had been pawned behind your back.

'Dad, just think,' said Susie, 'that poor young lady of seventeen bein' pushed home by Will in that home-made cart. Think of her feelings. I'd have died ten times over myself. Will's got to make it up to her.'

'Yes, course you 'ave, Will,' said Sally.

'Listen,' said Will, 'if I show up on her doorstep again, she'll chuck a brick at me. My face can't afford to stop a brick, it's the only one I've got.'

'Mrs Parks down in Charleston Street chucked a brick at Mr Parks once,' said Sally. 'It knocked all 'is teeth out, and 'e can only eat porridge now, and rice puddin'.'

'I don't suppose anyone 'ere could buy me a bike, could they?' suggested Freddy.

'I've been thinkin',' said Mrs Brown.

'Bless yer, mum,' said Freddy, 'I—'

'Not you, love,' said Mrs Brown, 'I was meanin' our Will. I think it might be nice if he did take the young lady some flowers now she's an invalid and don't have no mum. I expect she'd like some flowers.'

'Talk to yerself,' muttered Freddy again, 'that's it, talk to yerself.'

'What's up with Freddy?' asked Mrs Brown. ''E keeps talkin' to 'is supper.'

'Oh, don't mind me,' said Freddy, 'I ain't 'ardly 'ere.'

'Daffodils are nice,' said Susie, 'they're in the market now.'

'Yes, daffs 'ave just come out,' said Sally.

'I've got a special likin' for daffs,' said Mrs Brown, 'they were the first flowers your dad give me. Mind, he wasn't your dad then, of course, we'd only just met. Flowers always come first, Sally.'

'Then what?' said Sally.

'Us,' said Susie.

'Oh, a weddin' first, love,' said Mrs Brown placidly. 'Flowers, then an engagement, then a weddin', and then blessings.'

'What, us? We're blessings?' said Sally. 'Crikey, d'you mean Freddy as well? I don't call 'im a blessin'.'

'I ain't been blessed with no bike, I know that,' muttered Freddy.

'Daffodils, they'll do, Will,' said Susie.

'I'm not listening,' said Will, accepting seconds of shepherd's pie from his mum.

'I'll get them for yer, Will,' said Sally, 'on me way 'ome from school tomorrow. They're only sixpence a dozen down the market.'

'I've gone all deaf,' said Will.

'Sixpence and a penny for goin',' said Sally, 'I don't mind doin' a nice errand like that.'

'If I 'ad a penny for ev'ry errand I've done,' said Freddy, 'I bet I'd be able to buy me own bike.'

'Why am I bein' pushed?' asked Will.

'Because it's the nice thing to do, lovey,' said Susie, 'and you don't have to stay long enough for her to throw a brick at you. Is she pretty?'

'I'm barmy,' said Will, 'so's any bloke daft enough to mention a girl to a family full of females.'

'Excuse me, lovey, but we're half and half,' said Susie. 'Bet you two bob Annie Ford is pretty.'

'Will, would yer like to give me the sixpence now?' said Sally. 'And the penny for doin' the errand?'

Determinedly, Freddy tried yet again.

'If I 'ad a penny for—'

'Daffodils suit pretty girls,' said Mrs Brown, and Freddy's determination went to pot then.

'Biggest mistake I ever made, opening my mouth about Annie Ford,' said Will. 'In front of anyone in trousers, that wouldn't have mattered, but in front of anyone in bloomers—'

''Ere, d'you mind?' said Sally. 'I get enough of that from Freddy, 'e don't 'ave any respect for unmention ables.'

'I don't 'ave no bike, either,' said Freddy. 'Mind, it's a relief someone's noticed I'm alive, I can't tell yer what a blessin' that is. Now if I could just say—'

'Will, you still haven't told us if Annie is pretty,' said Susie.

'That's done it, that 'as,' said Freddy, 'I might as well go an' sort meself out a plot in the cemet'ry.'

'No, don't leave the table yet, love,' said Mrs Brown, 'there's syrup puddin' for afters.'

'Oh, all right,' said Freddy gloomily, 'I'll stay for that, a bloke can drown 'imself easier when 'e's got a full stomach.'

'Sit up, Freddy love,' said Mrs Brown, and brought the syrup pudding to the table.

'Susie, Will still 'asn't told us if Annie Ford's pretty,' said Sally.

'I didn't notice,' said Will.

'That's it, Sally, she's seventeen and pretty,' said Susie.

'Well, we hope so,' said Mrs Brown, serving the pudding.

'What're you up to, you hope so?' asked Will.

'I'm only sayin', Will love,' said Mrs Brown.

'Fancy our Will only just 'ome from India an' findin' someone seventeen an' pretty,' said Sally.

'Fancy findin' your syrup puddin' down your gymslip?' said Will.

'Funny thing, yer know,' said Mr Brown, 'I found yer mum when I was about Will's age.'

'Why, was she lost, then?' asked Freddy bitterly.

'Lost?' said his dad.

'I only asked,' said Freddy. 'Look, I dunno I can eat all this syrup puddin'. Still, I will. If it kills me, no-one'll notice, and it'll save me 'aving to drown meself.'

'Yes, eat it up, love,' said Mrs Brown fondly, 'syrup pudding's good for a growin' boy.'

'D'you want to tell us any more about Annie, Will?' asked Susie.

'Right, monkey, I'll come clean,' said Will, going on the attack, 'I only noticed her legs.'

'You shocker,' said Susie, putting aside any suggestion that she liked to see Sammy looking at her own legs.

'Not my fault,' said Will, 'they kept staring me in the face.'

'You listening to that, Mum?' asked Sally.

'Well, I must say you and Susie's both got ever such nice legs, lovey,' said Mrs Brown, equability undisturbed.

'Wooden ones, that's what Sally's got,' muttered Freddy.

'I didn't know that,' said Mr Brown.

'Well, 'ow could she get inches taller in a few months unless she's wearin' wooden ones bought off a market stall?' said Freddy.

'I don't think you can buy wooden ones off a stall, Freddy,' said Mrs Brown. 'You have to go somewhere special for wooden ones.'

'I bet she bought special ones from Mr Greenberg,' said Freddy, 'you can get anything from 'im. I bet if you looked, you'd see 'is sold label on Sally's.'

'Sounds a good bet, Freddy,' said Will. 'Let's all take a look after supper.'

'I'll scream for me mum,' said Sally, 'and I won't get the daffs for yer, not even if you give me tuppence for goin'.'

''Ere, listen,' said Freddy with reborn determination, 'if I'd 'ad tuppence for ev'ry errand I've done, I'd 'ave 'ad me own bike years ago. Mind, if Susie feels—'

'What's that blessed boy talkin' about?' asked Sally.

'I expect 'e'd like some more syrup puddin',' said Mrs Brown.

Bitterness uppermost again, Freddy decided to have his own back by dropping a bombshell. He addressed his mum. Loudly.

'I suppose Susie knows I ain't wearin' no trousers at 'er weddin'?'

'What?' said Susie.

'Nor I ain't,' said Freddy, 'I already informed Mum, an' she knows me mind's made up.'

'I'm dreamin',' said Susie.

'And I ain't wearin' no sailor suit, either, not at my age I ain't,' said Freddy. 'Just a scarf an' shirt. I just 'ope the day won't be windy. If it is, well, I'll just 'ave to grin an' bear it.'

Sally shrieked. Mr Brown hid his face in what was left of his helping of syrup pudding. Well, nearly. Will laughed his head off. Susie's face was a study.

Mrs Brown said, 'Bless us, Freddy, I don't know you

65

ought to 'ave said a thing like that. It don't sound a bit nice.'

'Can't 'elp that, Mum,' said Freddy firmly, 'I told yer, me mind's made up.'

'Well, take precautions if it's windy, Freddy,' said Will, 'wear a long shirt.'

'I've only got me short ones,' said Freddy.

Sally had hysterics and fell off her chair. Mr Brown choked on his pudding this time. Mrs Brown giggled like a girl. Susie held herself in check. She waited until the supper table had stopped rattling before she made herself heard.

'So your mind's made up, is it, Freddy Brown? Well, so's mine. You're goin' to wear a suit.'

'No, I ain't,' said Freddy, 'not unless it's got long trousers. I ain't wearing short ones, not at your weddin', Susie, and it ain't my fault if I ain't got long shirts.'

'Wear one of Dad's,' said Will.

Sally had more hysterics, on the floor.

'Listen, my lad,' said Susie, 'it's goin' to be a boy's suit or nothing.'

'I ain't wearin' nothing,' said Freddy, 'it ain't decent.'

'I mean you won't be there,' said Susie.

'Susie, I got to be there,' said Freddy, 'your weddin' is special to me.'

Susie smiled.

'Really special?' she said.

'Special special,' said Freddy.

'There's a good boy,' said Susie. 'Dad, buy him a suit with long trousers. You can get one at Gamages.'

'I'm ready to fork out, Susie,' said Mr Brown, who knew one thing for sure. Sammy Adams, important businessman and a decent bloke though he was, was getting a lovely, warm and generous girl on his wedding day, the kind a duke wouldn't say no to.

'There, that's settled,' said Mrs Brown happily.

'Mind, Susie, if I 'ad a bike as well, I could cycle to the church and do weddin' errands for yer,' said Freddy.

'Sally, get up off the floor, there's a love,' said Mrs Brown, 'you been down there long enough.'

'Talk to yerself,' muttered Freddy.

Later, Susie spoke to her dad.

'Dad, Sammy said he'd like to see you first thing in the morning.'

'What about?' asked Mr Brown, who was employed by Sammy as a full-time odd-job man.

'He didn't say.' Actually, Sammy had said he didn't think his future dad-in-law ought to be seen doing odd-jobbing around the offices and the Olney Road scrap metal yard. He'd have to talk to him, he'd said.

'Right you are, Susie, I'll go an' see 'im first thing in the morning.'

'Good old Dad,' said Susie, and then got Will on his own. Will at once said she'd got a look in her eye. 'Oh, I only want to ask if you've been all right today,' she said.

'Is this a crafty way of bringing up that girl again?'

'No, we were only pullin' your leg, love. I was wonderin' about your chest, that's all.' It was difficult for the family to believe Will had a serious complaint when he looked so healthy. If the doctors had talked about consumption, well, that really would have been serious. It was something Walworth people dreaded. 'You didn't get an attack through helpin' that girl, did you?'

Will thought about it and decided not to worry her.

'No, left me as fit as a fiddle, Susie.'

'That's good,' she said, 'only Boots mentioned that asthma can be a bit of an unsociable headache.'

'Well, I could do without it, and that's a fact,' said Will. His little grin showed. 'Specially at my age,' he added.

'That's right,' said Susie, 'so look after yourself. You don't know how pleased I am you're home for my weddin'.'

'I think you like the idea of marryin' Sammy,' said Will.

'Love it,' said Susie, 'even if we do have ups and downs.'

'Mum and Dad have had a few, I suppose.'

'Every married couple have some,' said Susie, 'but Mum's always been able to sort hers out with Dad.'

'Who's goin' to sort out those you have with Sammy?'

'Me,' said Susie, 'it'll never do to let Sammy be on top.'

'Never?' smiled Will.

'What? Oh, you,' laughed Susie, but turned just a little pink. Susie may have been twenty-one and adult, but she was still a virgin.

CHAPTER SIX

Mr Sammy Adams, managing director of Adams Enterprises, Adams Fashions and Adams Scrap Metal, had a handsome office above his established shop on the Denmark Hill side of Camberwell Green. Its old-style furniture was handsome, especially his large desk that sat on part of the square brown carpet.

Mr Brown knocked.

'Come in,' said Sammy, a tall young man in his twenty-fourth year and the energetic engine of the business.

Mr Brown entered.

'You wanted to see me, guv?' he said. It was a bit of an awkward relationship in a way, with his elder daughter Susie engaged to his young boss, and he'd settled for calling him guv. He'd tried Mister Sammy and Mister Adams, but come the engagement and he'd fixed on guv. Sammy didn't mind. Most of his employees called him Mister Sammy, distinguishing him from his eldest brother Boots, general manager of the business, whom they called Mister Adams. Sammy questioned whether this was right or not, seeing he'd founded the business. Boots said it was right all right, he was the eldest of the family and Sammy was still a lad. Ruddy rhubarb, said Sammy, did I hear you say that? It's a question of respect for my old age, said Boots. Sometimes, said Sammy, I ain't sure you're believable.

He looked up from his desk.

'Hello, Jim,' he said. That was how he'd always

addressed his hard-working and loyal odd-job man. 'Take a pew.'

'Nice of yer, guv,' said Mr Brown and sat down, not without thinking that it meant something serious was about to happen.

'How's the fam'ly?' asked Sammy, blue eyes showing, as always, something of his inner energy.

It's serious all right, thought Mr Brown.

'Fine,' he said. 'Well, except we can't 'ardly believe Will's got a touch of asthma.'

'Yes, perishin' hard luck,' said Sammy, 'and highly incredulous as well. But he'll beat it. Young man like him,' he added, speaking from the position of being as old as nearly twenty-four. 'I've been thinkin', Jim.'

'You do a lot of that,' said Mr Brown, frankly admiring.

'Well, if I don't,' said Sammy, 'me competitors'll start walkin' all over me, and gettin' walked over can hurt considerable. Jim, it's like this. You're Susie's dad, which for a start ought to earn you several medals. Now you can appreciate I don't want you as me dad-in-law mendin' our shop doors and keepin' our Olney Road scrap yard consistently tidied up.'

'You can give it to me straight, Sammy.' Mr Brown spoke as the future dad-in-law. 'You don't reckon it's right me workin' for yer.'

'You can chuck that notion out of the top window right now,' said Sammy. 'It's not good business, sackin' anyone who earns his wages as well as you do. But it won't look right, keepin' you doin' odd jobs here and at the scrap yard. Now, I'm about to acquire a new scrap yard in Bermondsey, Jim. You know all about scrap metal from bein' efficiently acquainted with the Olney Road yard. So I'm puttin' you in charge of the new yard in Bermondsey. You're startin' next Monday. You'll get a yard manager's

70

wage, of course. Is that proposition agreeable to you?'

Jim was gaping.

'Sammy—'

'Good,' said Sammy briskly, 'I like a man who makes up his mind quick.'

'I tell yer straight, you just flabbergasted my mind,' said Mr Brown, 'but that ain't goin' to stop me askin' if I can shake yer hand.' They shook hands across the desk.

'That's it, then, Jim,' said Sammy, 'I'm off out now.'

''Alf a tick,' said Mr Brown, 'you givin' me this job because you think I can do it, or because—'

'You're gettin' it because I've got trust in yer, Jim.'

'Well,' said Mr Brown, 'I'll say this much, young guv, if there's any bloke good enough for Susie, it's you.'

'As the manager of one of me scrap yards, you can call me Sammy in or out of business hours. Right, good on yer, Jim. Don't forget the weddin', you're givin' Susie away.'

'It'll be me special pleasure,' said Mr Brown.

Will Brown had been mentally toughened by his years of hard soldiering, but he still had a soft spot for his family, particularly his parents. His mother was just about the most easy-going woman alive. They'd known desperate poverty when the family lived in Peabody Buildings in Brandon Street, but his mum had never had a cross word for any of them, especially not for his dad, who had come out of the trenches with a gammy leg and no job until Sammy Adams had taken him on. Dad with his optimism and Mum with her ability to always make the best of things, had kept the family going even when hunger stalked and clothes were things of darns and patches.

So, being the son of his warm-hearted parents, Will arrived on the doorstep of Annie's home at half-past four

71

on the day after she'd suffered what she obviously felt was multiplied misfortune. Will knew he'd laughed, that he'd made her want to spit. So he was carrying a bunch of daffodils, wrapped all over. It would be asking for catcalls from street kids for a grown-up bloke, especially a soldier, to be seen carrying a bunch of flowers. He was still wearing his uniform. None of his old clothes fitted him, since he'd only been fifteen when he joined up as a drummer boy, and he hadn't yet bothered to shop for new stuff. But he had ordered a grey suit for Susie's wedding.

Nellie answered his knock. With Cassie and Charlie, she was home from their school in Trafalgar Street.

'Oh, 'ello,' she said, 'it's you.'

'I see it's you too, Nellie,' said Will, 'I thought I'd come and see how the patient is.'

'Our Annie? Oh, she went to work this mornin', at Urcott's the grocers, but Mr Urcott let 'er come 'ome at two o'clock. She was limpin' a bit. She's in the kitchen, she's just been chuckin' things at Charlie because 'e said she wasn't as bossy as when she was lyin' down. And she chucked the tea cosy at me because I said one of the street kids asked if she was goin' to 'ave another ride in a pushcart. Would yer please come in?'

'She's not goin' to chuck something at me, is she?' said Will, stepping in.

'Oh, it won't actu'lly 'urt,' said Nellie, closing the door. 'We're 'aving some bread an' marge an' cups of tea—'

'Nellie, who's that?' The voice of the young mistress of the house rang out loud and clear from the kitchen.

'It's yer soldier friend,' called Nellie.

'It's what?'

'It's 'im, Annie, 'e's come to see how you are.'

There was a short silence, then Annie called, 'Has he got that pushcart with him?'

'No, course 'e 'asn't, have yer, Will?' said Nellie.

'Well, is he laughin', then?' demanded Annie.

Nellie looked at Will. He tucked his grin away.

'No, 'e's not laughin', Annie.'

'He'd better not be. He can come in, then.'

Nellie led the way to the kitchen. Cassie and Charlie were sitting at the table, eating bread and marge and drinking tea. Annie was standing with her back to the range. On one leg. Her hand was on the back of a chair, supporting herself. She looked attractively slender in a jumper dress of dark green. The style was a bit out of fashion, particularly as it was waisted, but Annie had bought it half-price at a sale and it suited her. She'd shortened it to knee-length, and that was fashionable at least. Well, these days it was death to a girl not to look a bit fashionable.

'Good afternoon,' she said.

'Same to you,' said Will, inspecting her one standing leg.

'D'you mind tellin' me what you're lookin' at?' asked Annie, with Cassie and Charlie keeping the peace for the moment. She'd told them to.

'I'm lookin' for your other leg,' said Will.

'I'm restin' it,' said Annie.

'Yes, but where is it, upstairs on your bed?' asked Will.

'No, it's at the doctor's,' said Annie, and Cassie burped a giggle she'd tried to suppress. Charlie grinned.

'What's it doin' at the doctor's?' asked Will. 'Havin' an operation?'

Nellie spluttered.

'Annie, you've got it behind you,' she said.

Annie lowered it, and Will saw both legs then. Annie's eyes danced, and she laughed.

'Caught you there,' she said.

73

'Feelin' better, are we?' said Will.

'She was 'aving you on, Will,' said Charlie, 'she said she'd give me an' Cassie what for if we let on.'

'Well, it's my turn to laugh today,' said Annie.

Charlie said how's your father to Will, and then told Annie he'd got to go out and bash Georgie Simmonds. He owed him one on his conk. Annie told him to stay where he was or she'd tie him up. Cassie asked Will if he'd just come from guarding the Tower of London. Will said no, that was a job for the Beefeaters.

''Ere, 'ave yer fired yer rifle a lot?' asked Charlie.

'Now and again,' said Will.

'Christmas,' breathed Charlie, 'ow many blokes 'ave yer shot dead?'

'I hit an Indian elephant once,' said Will.

'Crikey,' said Cassie, 'did it fall down?'

'No, it hit me back,' said Will.

'Oh, did it squash yer flat?' asked Cassie in awe.

''Fraid so,' said Will, 'but I'm gradually fillin' out.'

Nellie let out a yell of laughter. Annie smiled.

'Would you like a cup of tea?' she asked.

'Thanks,' said Will.

Nellie brought a cup and saucer.

'What's in yer parcel?' asked Cassie of Will.

'Cassie, don't be nosy,' said Annie, pouring the tea.

'But it might be the Crown Jewels,' said Nellie, ''e might be mindin' them.'

'Cor, talk about bein' up the pole,' said Charlie.

'You can sit down,' said Annie to Will, 'if you'd be so kind.'

'Yes, Annie's honoured you've come and asked after 'er,' said Nellie.

'Let's see,' said Will, 'who's got a vase?'

'Oh, the Queen's got lots,' said Cassie.

'Well, can you ask her to lend us one?' said Will, unwrapping the daffodils and offering them to Annie. The golden blooms were a bright splash of colour against her dress. Annie stared.

'Oh,' she said.

'Just to make up for dumpin' you in the pushcart,' said Will.

'They're for me?' she gasped.

'They just need a vase and some water,' said Will, and Annie took the bunch and blinked at them. Will thought she looked very appealing in her surprise and uncertainty.

'Oh, ain't they lovely?' said Nellie, and dashed to the parlour. She came back with a tall vase and half-filled it with water from the scullery tap. She put the vase on the mantelpiece and took the long-stemmed daffodils from Annie, who for once looked as if she didn't quite know where she was. Nellie placed the blooms in the vase and spread them out. 'Look, Annie, ain't they a picture?'

'Yes, they're lovely,' said Annie, feeling all funny. Funny nice, of course.

Noting that Annie, vigorous in chastising him for some of his antics, didn't seem all there, Charlie said, 'I ain't keen on flowers meself, I think I'll go an' bash a hole in a wall with Georgie Simmonds' 'ead.' And he vanished before Annie knew he was even on his feet.

Will, drinking his tea, said, 'You girls managin'? Is there anything I can do? Old soldiers like me can be useful.'

'Old?' Annie came out of not being quite herself. 'Old?' she said. 'How can you be old?'

'The Army puts years on blokes.'

'Well, it's not put any on you,' said Annie.

'Don't you believe it,' said Will, 'I'm nearly a hundred in a way.'

'What way?' asked Annie.

'Mrs Potter's nearly an 'undred,' said Cassie.

'There you are, then,' said Will, 'some people do get to be that old.'

'You're not makin' sense,' said Annie.

'Anyway,' said Will, 'you're managin' to limp around and get on with things? No help needed?'

'Thanks ever so much, but no, I'm managin' fine,' said Annie, and took a little rest then by sitting down in the fireside chair. Her short dress let her knees show. Will looked. Annie pulled on her dress and covered her knees. 'Excuse me,' she said haughtily.

'Just havin' a look at your bruised knee,' said Will. 'Well, nice to know it's improvin'. I'll get movin' now. So long, girls.' Tabby the cat darted in then, made straight for Annie and leapt on to her lap. Annie gave a little yell and her knees showed again. Will grinned. 'I'm not lookin',' he said, 'I'm off.'

Nellie went after him to see him out.

'Thanks ever so much for comin' to see our Annie,' she said.

'Pleasure,' said Will. 'Tell her I'll send a pair of trousers round.'

'Trousers?' said Nellie. 'What for?'

'She'll know,' said Will, and went off laughing.

Nellie, returning to the kitchen, said, 'Will's funny, ain't 'e?'

'What d'you mean?' asked Annie.

''E said 'e'd send you a pair of trousers. 'E said you'd know why.'

'He said what?'

'A pair of trousers,' giggled Nellie, ''e said 'e'd send them round.'

Annie quivered all over.

'Are you laughin', Nellie?' she asked.

'Me?' said Nellie.

'I'm not,' said Cassie.

'I bet he is,' said Annie, 'I bet he went off laughin'. Did he?'

'Well, 'e wasn't actu'lly cryin',' said Nellie. 'Ain't 'e nice, though, Annie? It's a shame 'e didn't stay a bit.'

'I expect 'e's gone to Windsor Castle to make some lemonade for the Queen,' said Cassie. 'She likes lemonade. Annie, what's 'e goin' to send you trousers for?'

'Never you mind,' said Annie. 'Just wait till – Nellie, did he say he was comin' back again?'

'No, not direckly,' said Nellie, ''e only said about the trousers.'

'I bet he'll be laughin' all the way home,' said Annie. 'I – oh, blow, look at the daffs.' She was shocked at herself.

'Yes, 'e must like yer,' said Nellie, scenting romance, 'you ain't ever 'ad anyone bring you flowers before. Oh, if 'e don't come again, though, p'raps it's because 'e's finished 'is leave and is goin' back to the Army.'

Annie gritted her teeth. What must he think of her? She hadn't thanked him for them, not properly she hadn't. She'd been so astonished she'd hardly said anything. Oh, blow and bother.

'Where was it he said he lived?' she asked.

'Caulfield Place,' said Nellie, 'it's only down in Browning Street.'

'I'll 'ave to—' Annie stopped. No, she'd have to go in person, so that she could thank him properly, she couldn't just send a note. She'd be very nice about it, then she'd feel she could give him an earful about sending trousers round. She knew what he'd meant by that, even if her sisters didn't. And he'd better not laugh at her again. A young lady her age ought to be treated seriously.

CHAPTER SEVEN

'Sammy darling?' purred Miss Susie Brown, private secretary, personal assistant and exclusive fiancée to the managing director of Adams Enterprises Ltd.

Sammy, just back from a visit to his East End garments factory, looked up at her from his handsome old desk.

'Yes, what is it, Miss Brown?' he asked in strict businesslike fashion.

'Pardon?' said Susie.

'If you could hurry it up, Miss Brown?'

'I'll give you Miss Brown,' said Susie threateningly. Sammy had days when he tried to re-establish an authority she'd managed to knock sideways.

'Me principles relatin' to business hours—'

'Oh, yes, highly formal,' said Susie.

'Bless you, Miss Brown,' said Sammy, the youngest of his mother's three engaging sons. She'd brought them all up to count their blessings, and Susie happened to be top of his personal list. He thought the world of her and her status as his fiancée, even if he did sometimes wonder what had hit him. Her blue eyes mostly, which on a sunny day could sparkle like sapphires. In a stylish navy-blue costume that set off her fairness, not even a French count with arched eyebrows and a haughtifying family tree could have said she wasn't a stunner. She was all her own work too, allowing for the original contribution made by her mum and dad. She'd done it all on her own, she'd pulled herself up from being just another shabby and hungry-looking Walworth girl and turned herself into a May

Queen. Lovely figure too, and very high-class legs. Meritorious, it was, all the Adams female women owning high-class legs. Lizzy, his sister, to start with, Tommy's wife Vi and Boots's wife Emily, though Emily was getting a bit thin lately. In a few weeks, Susie's legs would join the high-class collection. Lovely girl, Susie. Sammy Adams, his mother had said, I never thought you'd have enough sense in your money-box head to ask Susie to marry you, I thought you had hardly any real sense at all. Actually, his feelings for Susie were such that he often didn't know whether he was upside-down or back to front. In a rash moment, he'd mentioned that to Boots. He should have known better, because Boots of course said well, Sammy, I'd say upside-down, since we all know Susie's been standing you on your loaf of bread for years.

Susie, viewing him lovingly, said, 'Sammy, you darling.'

'You want something,' said Sammy, feeling he was going to have to raid his wallet. He'd do it too. He was in the hopeless and helpless position of never being able to say no to her.

'You're a lovely bloke,' said Susie.

'This is goin' to cost me,' said Sammy.

'It's goin' to earn you a smacker,' said Susie. 'Sammy, you've given my dad a new job managin' our new scrap metal yard.'

'Think nothing of it,' said Sammy.

'I think everything of it,' said Susie, 'and you too.'

'Very good, Miss Brown, if that's all we'll now get on with our work.'

'It's not all,' said Susie, and came round the desk to bend over him.

'Miss Brown, not in the office—' Too late. Susie delivered a warm and loving smacker. Sammy yielded a principle or two and made an advance of his own. Inside the jacket of her costume, Susie quivered and straightened up.

'What's that doin' there?' she asked, and took his hand out.

'It's mindin' its own business, I'd say,' observed Sammy reasonably. 'Well, what's mine is yours, Susie, and what's yours is mine.'

'Not yet it isn't, and certainly not in the office,' said Susie. 'You're always breakin' your own rules, Mister Sammy Adams.'

'I don't recollect—'

'I do.'

'You sure, Susie?'

'Mmm, lovely,' said Susie, 'but kindly stop helpin' yourself to what's not yours till the weddin' certificate's signed. And even then, wait till we leave the church. I don't want you committin' unlawful sacrilege.'

'In front of the vicar? Perish the thought,' said Sammy, 'he's been my vicar man and boy, and I don't want to get struck by his lightning on me one and only weddin' day. It might be fatal. Fine thing that would be, gettin' married and goin' to me own funeral on the same day. All me old friends and neighbours would talk. Well, that's definitely all, Miss Brown, now let's get on with things.'

Susie laughed. There was no-one quite like Sammy, the driving force behind Adams Enterprises and its associate companies.

'Sammy love, you're sweet for what you did for my dad.'

'Well, I can't have me dad-in-law sweepin' floors, not when he's up to runnin' a scrap yard.'

'You're still a sweetie,' said Susie. 'Oh, there's something else.'

'If it's not business, I'm not listening,' said Sammy.

'Yes, you are. Sammy, we're goin' to have a horse and cart for our weddin'.'

'A whatter?' said Sammy, who had work to do, including reading every word of a contract relating to Adams Fashions.

'A pony and cart, actually.'

'I was under the official impression that me best man Boots is arrangin' to drive us from the church to the weddin' breakfast in our motorcar.' Sammy was the owner of a motorcar. He wore the approved peaked cap and goggles when driving it, which had made Susie tell him he looked as if he was about to enter a race at Brooklands. Sammy said he quite fancied that. Susie said she'd blow the car up if he got serious.

'Yes, I know about that arrangement, Sammy, but I've just been speakin' to Mr Greenberg. He's with Boots, they're talkin' about Mr Greenberg supplying our new upstairs offices with furniture. Sammy, you didn't tell me that both your brothers and your sister Lizzy all had Mr Greenberg's pony and cart for their weddings. I want that too, it's a fam'ly tradition now, and Mr Greenberg's goin' to be really upset if we don't ask him to do the honours.'

'Well, Susie—'

'I don't want any flannel.'

'I'm not in the habit—'

'Yes, you are, but like your mum says, you're a nice boy really.'

'That was fifteen years ago. I now happen to be—'

'Yes, you're lovely, Sammy. I'll ask Mr Greenberg to come and see you.'

'What's the use?' mused Sammy as Susie disappeared. 'I can't even answer her back now. I'm done for, I'm already gettin' careless about me overheads – here, hold on, what's this, a hundred per cent disclaimer clause in the event of delivery failing to be made on the due date? That's not friendly, Harriet, nor Christian.' Harriet de Vere was the chief buyer for Coates, a West End store with branches all over the South of England, and the contract was between Coates and Adams Fashions. 'That's not up for signin', Harriet me female alligator, that's up for discussion.'

Susie reappeared, in company with Mr Eli Greenberg, who had known Sammy as a boy and had long been his most obliging business friend. He was also a family friend. A family friend who doubled as an obliging business friend was priceless. Mr Greenberg advanced with his mittened hands lifted in a gesture of expansive pleasure. He wore an old round black hat and a dark grey overcoat with capacious inner and outer pockets. His grey-flecked black beard split in a happy smile and his white teeth moistly beamed.

'Sammy, my poy, vhat a pleasure, ain't it? You and Susie in a state of expectant marriage, vhat a joy to my heart, and vhat a fair princess, ain't she?'

'Hello, Eli, old cock.' Sammy stood up and shook Mr Greenberg's hand. 'Mind, I'm up to me ears.'

'Vhen veren't you up to your ears, Sammy? Up to your ears has cost me time and money, but who minds starvin' vhen it's in the name of friendship? The vedding, a blessing, ain't it?'

'I'm not denyin' it,' said Sammy, 'and I'm refrainin' from mentioning what it's going' to do to me wallet. I'm notin' your kind sentiments, Eli, and am takin' the opportunity to say Susie and self would be obliged if you'd do us the favour of transportin' us from the church to St John's Institute in your pony and cart.'

Mr Greenberg beamed again.

'Vhy, Sammy, vhat a pleasure, vhat a privilege. Already

I am invited to the veddin', now I am to cart you and Susie. Vell, don't I remember doin' the selfsame for Lizzy and Boots and Tommy? Vhat a privilege indeed, my young friend.' Mr Greenberg took out his large red handkerchief and blew his nose. 'You'll ask vhat vill I charge you. Not a penny, Sammy, not even a farthing. It vill all be for friendship and Susie's blue eyes.'

'You're a love, Mr Greenberg,' said Susie.

'Ah, vhat a fine turn Sammy has come to, Susie. Business is business, vun can't say it ain't, but vhere vould it lead a man to if he vas married to it and not to a young lady like you?'

'To my dad's chopper,' said Susie.

'Ah, such a joke, Susie.'

'It's no joke,' said Susie, and Mr Greenberg's deep chuckle rolled up from his broad chest and gurgled in his throat.

'Vell, I must be on my vay now,' he said, 'I have had the pleasure of obligin' Boots regardin' handsome furniture at a price that vill take the shirt off my back, and now I have to oblige a handsome lady.'

'If I had the time and wasn't church-goin', I'd oblige her meself,' said Sammy.

'Over my dead body,' said Susie, and Mr Greenberg departed still chuckling.

The moment the door closed behind him, Sammy said, 'This contract, Susie, is a pain in me posterior. There's a delivery clause in it which could make us walk the plank with nowhere to go but down. And the pirate captain is Harriet.'

'Miss de Vere of Coates?' said Susie.

'Selfsame,' said Sammy.

'Well, kindly let her know that you're mine, Sammy, not hers, and that you're not to be made to walk the plank so that she can rescue you from drowning, dry you out and get you into something comfy in her flat. Or I'll push her face in.'

'Don't like the sound of that, Harriet with her face pushed in,' said Sammy. 'It might be considerably detrimental to Adams Fashions. Further, Susie, my mother, bein' fond of you, wouldn't like to hear you talkin' in an unladylike manner. I'll deal with Harriet, I'll phone her and arrange to see her tomorrow afternoon.'

'Sammy darling, don't be silly,' said Susie. 'Tomorrow's Saturday.'

'Yes, I'll see her in the afternoon,' said Sammy.

'You won't,' said Susie.

'Did I hear you right, Miss Brown?'

'Yes, Mister Sammy Adams, you did. Tomorrow afternoon is when we're going out to buy the rest of our furniture.'

'Ah,' said Sammy. He had acquired a handsome house in Denmark Hill, and Susie, excited by all it meant, had been leading exultant charges into furniture emporia to help him spend his money. He'd had to tell her that each charge was causing him personal ruination. Susie, who knew him through and through by now, noted with affection that he accepted ruination manfully.

'You promised,' she said.

'Well, Susie, a promise is a promise,' he said. 'Is this one goin' to cause me serious injury?'

'Oh, it won't be fatal,' said Susie.

Boots came in then. Long-limbed, grey-eyed and twenty-nine, he was the man who held everything together. He had the gift of easy communication and a very whimsical side. Women always looked twice at him, and most of the office girls had crushes on him. His left eye, almost sightless, sometimes seemed a little lazy. He'd been blinded on the Somme. An operation had cured his right eye, but the left one was fairly useless.

'Still at it, Susie?' he smiled.

'I'm a slave to his nibs,' said Susie. 'This is his nibs.'

'His nibs would like to do some work,' said Sammy.

'Sammy, have you seen the contract I left on your desk?' asked Boots.

'I've seen enough to know we're not goin' to sign it,' said Sammy.

'The delivery clause?' said Boots.

'You spotted that too?' said Sammy.

'Can't let it stand, Sammy. Not as it is. Harriet de Vere is trying it on. What they'll do if delivery is late, of course, will be to accept the stuff at a reduced price. We'll lose our profit, they'll increase theirs.'

'You happen,' said Sammy, 'to be speakin' to the managin' director of Adams Enterprises, which is me, a highly sharp business bloke already arrangin' to smack Harriet de Vere's posterior.'

'She'll like that,' said Boots, 'lay it on like a man, Sammy, and she'll see a new clause is written in.'

'I'm hearin' things,' said Susie.

'Startling, perhaps,' said Boots, 'but glad you like that kind of action, Susie.'

'I'm glad too,' said Susie, 'glad you're jokin'.'

Boots winked, lazily, using his left eye, then asked how her brother Will was.

'Oh, he always looks fine,' she said, 'but if he's really asthmatic, he'll have to leave the Army, won't he?'

'Probably,' said Boots, 'and he'll have to fight for a disability pension. The Army's bound to say his condition wasn't brought about by soldiering. But they gave him a medical in the first place and must have passed him A1 for service or they wouldn't have taken him on. So he's got a case. If it comes to a fight with the Ministry of Bowler Hats, Susie, I'll pitch in with him.'

'Oh, that's so good of you, Boots,' said Susie. She knew he'd committed his help, that as a soldier of the trenches he'd stand with Will if necessary. She felt Will might need a pension if he had to leave the Army, because jobs were as scarce as ever and his asthma might limit him in what he could do.

'Work on Harriet, Sammy,' said Boots, and returned to his office.

'Sometimes,' said Sammy, 'I'm not sure if it's Boots who's teachin' me to suck lemons or if it's me heavenly Father.'

'Yes, he is heavenly, isn't he?' said Susie a little wickedly. 'Doreen says she can't sleep at night for thinkin' about him.'

Doreen was the general office maid-of-all-work, although she had an office boy to help her now.

'Well,' growled Sammy, 'you tell Doreen that if I catch her bringing her bed to the office to get some daytime kip, she'll get dropped on her head.'

'Oh, dear me,' said Susie, 'I'm not sure even that will cure her.'

'Well, oh dear me for nothing,' said Sammy, 'then I'll have to get your dad to chop her up, won't I? Now can we do some work, Miss Brown?'

'Yes, very good, Mister Sammy.'

A house damaged by fire in Rockingham Street, by the Elephant and Castle, was being demolished. The last of its walls collapsed under an iron pounding and amid spurting clouds of dust. Ten minutes later, the little gang of labourers packed up for the day. Henry Brannigan put on his long black serge overcoat, straightened his cap, and set off for his lodgings. He did not button the coat and it flapped as he walked. Tall and muscular, he might also have been handsome, but his face had lost flesh and his eyes were hollow. He lived with his sister and her husband in Stead Street, off Brandon Street. They'd given him a room after the death of his wife seven months ago.

A seemingly dour and introspective man, he did not mix well with people, but his sister, a lazy woman, did not mind having him as long as he paid his rent and didn't make work for her. He had no children, was set in his ways at forty-five and didn't intrude on either her or her husband.

He had a very obsessive habit when walking the pavements. He measured his strides to avoid treading on the lines that divided the paving stones. People who got in his way or stood in his way made his blood boil, for they could cause him to deviate and put him in danger of treading on a line. And if that happened, it ruined the whole day for him and it also meant bad luck.

He made a square turn into Larcom Street from the Walworth Road. Two approaching women blocked his path and intense irritation seized him. He did not check, however, he barged straight on, bruising his way between them. One woman staggered.

''Ere, you brute, what d'you think you're doin' of?' shouted the other woman.

'Time you learned to keep out of me bleedin' way.'

'Time you learned some manners!'

He went striding on. He crossed the street, walked past St John's Church and entered the paved path that led into Charleston Street. There he encountered a very lean man in a black frock coat. He carried a rolled brolly. One man or the other needed to step aside. Mr Ponsonby would have done so without argument, but Henry

Brannigan, rageful at this new obstacle, came straight on with the obvious intention of compelling him to shift himself. Offended, Mr Ponsonby came to a dramatic halt and Henry Brannigan was brought up short by the rigid point of the umbrella. It actually dug into his stomach.

'Sir?' said Mr Ponsonby querulously.

'Get out of my way.' Henry Brannigan struck the umbrella aside. That did him no good, for the point returned at speed and dug him in the chest.

'Manners, sir, manners,' said Mr Ponsonby.

'You bleedin' interferin' ponce,' said Henry Brannigan, and looked down at his feet. They were no more than half an inch from a line. He quivered, it was a hair's-breadth escape. If he'd trodden on it, it would have meant worrying about his immediate future and the advisability of changing or cancelling any plans he'd made. He didn't like doing that, but it didn't pay not to. Bad luck came along otherwise. As he'd told a coroner seven months ago, he'd trodden on a line coming home from work on a Saturday, and on the Sunday he'd taken his wife on a planned day trip to Brighton, not wanting to disappoint her by cancelling it. In the train, she'd got up to look out of the window, the door swung open and she fell out and killed herself. That was the worst bit of luck he'd ever brought on himself for treading on a line, and that only happened because some fool of a woman had been in his way. The coroner had the gall to make some very peculiar remarks about it, damn him.

He looked at the geezer with the umbrella.

'Well, sir, well?' said Mr Ponsonby impatiently.

'Lucky for you I ain't standin' on a line,' said Henry Brannigan. He did a measured sidestep and went on his way.

'Dear me, what an unpleasant fellow,' said Mr Ponsonby, and resumed his pigeon-toed walk.

Freddy Brown was on his way home. He'd been with Ernie Flint, his school mate, and Mrs Flint had given them both a cup of tea and a rockcake, just to keep them going until their suppers. Freddy thought his rockcake lived up to its name. Like eating a brick, it was, and tasted like one too. Must have been two weeks old. His mum's rockcakes weren't like that. Well, his mum knew and the whole family knew, that rockcakes were best eaten on the day they came out of the oven, and certainly not later than the day after.

Ernie had eaten his own rockcake as if he liked bricks. Freddy was going off Ernie a bit as a mate. He wouldn't lend his bike even for five minutes. If his old mate Daisy had had a bike, she'd have lent it every day.

Well, I'm blowed, he thought, there's that girl crack-pot. He was in Brandon Street and Cassie Ford was coming towards him. Grinning kids were catcalling her. And no wonder. She was leading her cat on a long piece of string that was tied to a ribbon around its neck. The cat was padding along on the lead as if it thought it was a dog.

'Watcher,' said Freddy, 'what's that you got with you on a piece of string?'

'Oh, it's you,' said Cassie from under her boater. 'What d'yer mean, what's that on a piece of string?'

'Ain't a pony, is it?' said Freddy.

'Course it ain't,' said Cassie scornfully, 'it's me cat.'

'You sure?' said Freddy.

'Course I am. Anyway, we don't keep ponies no more. We used to when we lived in the country, and we 'ad trained 'orses too.'

'Trained 'orses?' said Freddy.

'It was when our dad used to run a circus,' said Cassie. 'We 'ad elephants as well. Dad used to be an elephant tamer.'

'Was that before he used to be captain of a ship?' asked Freddy.

'No, after,' said Cassie. 'You've got crumbs down yer jersey.'

'Oh, just rockcake crumbs,' said Freddy. ''Ere, you got a sister called Annie?'

'Oh, she's the one that's a maid to the Prince of Wales,' said Cassie. 'She irons 'is best shirts.'

'Me bruvver Will met 'er last week,' said Freddy.

'Oh, is 'e yer brother? Ain't 'e good-lookin'?'

'Yes, so am I,' said Freddy, 'it's in the fam'ly, yer know.'

Henry Brannigan turned into Brandon Street then, and could hardly believe the cursed nature of the day. Two kids and a bleeding cat, and even a long piece of string, all in his way. First those two women in Larcom Street, then that ponce with the umbrella, and now these two kids and a cat on a string. He had to stop. At once the cat started to use his left leg as a rubbing post. He lifted his foot and kicked at the creature.

''Ere, don't you kick my cat,' cried Cassie. He glared at her. Freddy squared his shoulders. 'I'll tell my dad of you,' said Cassie. Kids, thought Henry Brannigan, bleeding kids. They all want doing away with.

'Get it out of my way or I'll squash it flat,' he said.

'Mister, you ain't nice,' said Freddy. 'You touch Cassie's cat and I'll whistle up all the kids in the street.'

'Get out of it before I knock yer brains out.' Henry Brannigan swept the boy and girl aside and strode away, drawing a hissing breath as he almost trod on a line. Cassie and Freddy stared after him.

'Well, I don't want to meet 'im again,' said Freddy.

'I expect 'e lives in an underground cave somewhere,' said Cassie, 'with witches and ev'rything.'

''Ere, d'you want to be my mate?' asked Freddy.

'I don't mind,' said Cassie.

'All right, come on, I'll walk yer 'ome,' said Freddy.

'Our first 'ome used to 'ave a drawbridge,' said Cassie, leading her cat.

'And a moat as well?'

'Annie fell in it once and nearly drowneded,' said Cassie. 'It was lucky the Prince of Wales come along an' saved 'er, because she 'ad to go to a ball in the evening.'

What a crackpot, thought Freddy.

CHAPTER EIGHT

On Sunday morning, Annie announced everyone was to go to church. Her late and adorable mum had liked her family to do a bit of church-going, about once a month. Annie always felt she had to follow the example.

Charlie, of course, shot out of the kitchen like an arrow from a bow, except that arrows never had socks down.

'You Charlie!' yelled Annie. 'Come back here!'

But the front door was already closing.

'I'll go after him,' said the Gaffer, and off he went too. 'Meet you in church, Annie, if I can catch 'im,' he called.

'Dad, come back here! Dad, d'you hear me?'

But the front door opened and closed again, and the Gaffer took off for the Sunday morning market at a smart pace. He might catch up with Charlie there and he might not. But he could rely on catching up with a half-pint when the pubs opened. He'd done his stint of helping prepare the Sunday vegetables.

'Well,' said Cassie, more sure than dreamy for once, 'Dad an' Charlie won't go to 'eaven if they keep dodgin' church.' She thought for a bit. 'P'raps they don't know there's free ice cream up in 'eaven.'

'Who said there was?' asked Nellie, putting a heap of potato peelings in a sheet of newspaper and wrapping them up for the yard dustbin.

'A lord did,' said Cassie.

'What lord?' asked Nellie.

'I dunno 'is name,' said Cassie, 'but 'e come out of 'is castle one day and said so. Everyone 'eard him.'

'I didn't,' said Nellie. ''Ere, take these out to the dustbin.'

'Yes, all right,' said Cassie, accepting the packet.

'Then take your aprons off,' said Annie, 'and we'll go to church.'

'What, now?' said Nellie. 'It's not 'alf-past ten yet.'

'Oh, so it isn't,' said Annie, looking surprised. 'Well, never mind, I'll let you two off, as Dad and Charlie 'ave dodged it. But I'll make sure we all go next Sunday, we don't want Mum turning in her grave. You keep an eye on the roast, Nellie, only don't try takin' it out of the oven, I don't want to find it's been on the scullery floor when I come back.' She took her apron off.

'Annie, you don't 'alf look nice in yer best frock,' said Cassie, holding the now soggy packet to her chest.

'It's Sunday,' said Annie.

'It's your bestest Sunday one,' said Cassie. Annie's bestest was a turquoise crepe de chine, paid for by her dad on the occasion of her seventeenth birthday. To her sisters it looked as expensively posh as real silk.

'Annie, you do look swell,' said Nellie.

'Is your soldier goin' to church with you?' said Cassie.

'Who?' said Annie.

'The soldier that's guardin' Windsor Castle,' said Cassie.

'Cassie, if you don't stop makin' things up,' said Annie, 'the cat'll get your tongue and you'll 'ave to do without it.'

'Oh, lor', will I?' said Cassie, not too happy about the prospect. But her irrepressible imagination chased the thought away, and she asked if the soldiers guarding Windsor Castle were given free ice cream in the summer.

'No, course not,' said Nellie, 'they've all got to wait till they get to 'eaven, the same as ev'rybody else. And if you cuddle them potato peelings much longer, they'll start comin' out of your ears.'

'I'll just go and put my mac on,' said Annie, 'then I'm off to church.'

'But it's still early,' said Nellie.

'Oh, I don't mind bein' early,' said Annie.

Susie was having an absorbing morning in partnership with her dad. They were working out table arrangements for the sit-down wedding breakfast at St John's Institute. Williamson's the caterers were looking after everything relating to food and drink. Mr Brown and Susie were taking care of protocol. Mr Brown had made a pencil sketch, and Susie had a list of everyone who would be there. They were sitting at the parlour table, keeping out of Mrs Brown's way in the kitchen. Susie said both families and their closest relatives had better be at the top line of tables. She counted and said that would amount to thirty grown-ups and children.

'Seems to me the Browns and Adams are a bit prolific,' said Mr Brown.

The front door knocker sounded.

'That can't be Sammy yet,' said Susie. Sammy was due to pick her up at noon and drive her to his mother's home for Sunday dinner there. The time now was twenty to eleven. Answering the door, she found herself looking at a dark-haired young lady with wide grey eyes framed by sooty lashes, and wearing a light mackintosh and a round rain hat. The day was showery.

'Hello,' said Susie.

'Oh, hello,' said Annie. Thinking that wasn't quite enough, she added, 'How'd you do?'

'I can't complain, and I'm not,' smiled Susie. Lord, thought Annie, who's she? She's stunning. 'Are you lookin' for someone?' asked Susie.

'Oh, I'm just callin',' said Annie, who had asked at

the first house where the Brown family lived.

'So I see,' said Susie, smiling again. Neighbours were passing by, going early to church. She took a more thoughtful look at the girl. Age? Yes, seventeen, she'd bet on it. Hurt knee? No, that wasn't obvious. All the same, she might be the girl. 'I suppose you're not askin' to see my brother Will, are you?'

Help, thought Annie, is this his sister? I think I've seen her about. She's really posh.

Susie looked a Sunday dream in a tailored spring costume made by Lilian Hyams, designer for Adams Fashions.

'Is your brother a soldier?' asked Annie.

'That's him,' said Susie. What had Will been up to, saying he hadn't noticed if the girl was pretty or not? She was all of that. And if anyone deserved her, Will did. He needs a helping hand. 'I think you're Annie Ford. Come in, we've heard all about you. Will's wandering around the Sunday market with Sally and Freddy, my sister and younger brother. Come on in, Annie.'

'Oh, I only called to thank him,' said Annie.

'Come in. Will won't be long.' Susie took the girl into the parlour. 'Meet my dad. Dad, look who's here.

Mr Brown looked. He liked what he saw.

'I don't think I've 'ad the pleasure,' he said.

'Well, you have now,' said Susie, 'this young lady is Annie Ford.'

'Pleased to meet yer, Annie,' said Mr Brown, rising and shaking her hand. 'But to me sorrow, I still can't say I know yer.'

'Of course you know her, Dad,' said Susie, 'Annie's the young lady who hurt her knee and—' She paused, she smiled. 'And was helped home by Will.'

'Well, I'm blowed, so you're her,' said Mr Brown with

95

a huge grin that gave Annie a sinking feeling.

'Oh, he didn't tell you how he helped me home, did 'e?' she asked.

'Well,' said Mr Brown, and let it go at that.

'Did he?' asked Annie of Susie.

'I'm Susie. Is your knee better, Annie?'

'Oh, he did tell you.' Annie gritted her teeth. 'It's not fair, I suppose everyone in Walworth knows now that he wheeled me home in a pushcart. Can you believe it? I'm seventeen, goin' on for eighteen, and I expect even when I'm ninety there'll be people talkin' about how I stopped the traffic.'

'Will never mentioned the traffic,' said Susie, trying to keep her face straight.

'No, but you know what I mean,' said Annie. 'Oh, wait till I see your brother. It's not that he doesn't 'ave some nice ways – well, I've come to thank him for the flowers he brought me, and it's upset me dignity again to find he told everyone about me in a pushcart.'

'Flowers?' said Mr Brown.

'Daffodils?' said Susie.

'Yes, they were lovely, a whole bunch,' said Annie, 'only I didn't thank 'im properly. I was a bit overcome.'

'I like bein' overcome by flowers myself,' said Susie.

'I'll overcome yer mum tomorrow, Susie,' said Mr Brown, 'I'll buy 'er some daffs on me way 'ome from work, seein' it'll be me first day in charge at the new yard. Now don't fret about that pushcart incident, Annie, I can tell yer Susie 'ad many a ride in one when she was young.'

'Excuse me, Mr Brown,' said Annie, 'it wasn't when she was seventeen, was it, and with 'er legs showin'?'

Mr Brown, who could put a cheerful face on most things bar an earthquake, said, 'Well, it's not all bad news,

Annie. I mean, there ain't too many girls that could stop the traffic in a pushcart.'

'Yes, cheer up,' said Susie, 'Will was only tryin' to get you home the best way he could.'

'Yes, but tellin' everybody,' said Annie. She glanced at Mr Brown. Mr Brown tried to look as if he thought a ride in a pushcart for a seventeen-year-old girl happened ten times a day in Walworth. Annie glanced at Susie. Susie looked reassuring. 'Oh, well,' said Annie, 'I'll just have to do my best to live it down. I don't suppose it'll take more than fifty years. I'd better go now or I'll be late for church. Will you tell your brother I called to thank him properly for the flowers?'

'We'll tell him,' said Susie.

'Mind you,' said Annie, 'it's only fair to say that if I do meet 'im again, I'll have to give him a talkin'-to for tellin' everyone about my indignity.'

'Oh, yes, do give him that kind of talkin'-to,' said Susie. 'We girls shouldn't suffer indignities in silence, or we'll never get the better of men, will we?'

Annie looked at her. Susie smiled. Annie saw a kindred spirit.

'Is he goin' back to the Army soon?'

'No, he's got a long leave, three months,' said Susie.

'Then I might 'ave a chance of givin' him a talkin'-to,' said Annie, and laughed. 'Well, it's been nice meetin' you both,' she said, and Susie saw her out. The church bell was ringing.

Mrs Brown appeared in the passage.

'Who was that, Susie?'

'Annie Ford.'

'What, the girl Will met? What did she want?'

'To thank Will for a bunch of daffs he bought her,' said Susie.

'Well, bless me,' said Mrs Brown, 'he did take her some, then. Wasn't that nice of him?'

'I think he bowled her over.'

'What was she like?' asked Mrs Brown.

'Just right for Will,' said Susie.

'Well, dearie me,' said Mrs Brown, 'd'you think Will might start askin' her out?'

'Well, Mum, while we don't want to keep on about the pushcart, the fact is Will owes her something for puttin' her in it,' said Susie, 'and he knows it. The daffs were only part-payment.'

Monday morning saw Mr Brown at the Bermondsey scrap metal yard. The double wooden gates were in good order, and so was the brick wall surrounding the yard. The rest was a mess. That included the large lock-up wooden shed. Sammy had said it'll be a tidying-up job for the first week, Jim. The shed's close to falling down, so there'll be a couple of men to help it on its way. They'll knock it down and prepare the site for a new shed that'll arrive in sections on Tuesday. You'll have a mountain of timber from the old shed to get rid of.

Granted, Sammy, Mr Brown had said. It could be burned in the yard, but that would be wasteful. Sammy said the natives of Bermondsey didn't like wastefulness, it would upset them. Right, said Mr Brown, I'll put a notice up on the gates, inviting them to come and help themselves to firewood. That'll get rid of it unwastefully. Sammy, who liked a bit of imaginative wordage, said you sound like one of my family already, Jim. Sort out what stock there is with Eddie Mason, your assistant, and let me have written details when they're ready. If any prospective customers look in, let them have a ten per cent discount on all standing stock to encourage them to clear us out. At present, the standing stock makes the place look like a junk yard. I'll pop in and see how you're doing from time to time.

Mr Brown knew Sammy was being typically himself. It didn't matter how much he was involved with all the big happenings, he still kept himself interested in everything else.

The large old shed was coming down. The men had the tarred roof off and had smashed it up. Now the boarded walls were being hammered, split and torn out. Huge heaps of timber were building up for the benefit of the poverty-stricken people of the immediate neighbourhood, who were always in need of fuel for their fires. Mr Brown had put the notice up on the outside of the gates, inviting people to come and collect free firewood at four in the afternoon. That would allow mums to send their kids as soon as they came home from school, and the kids would arrive with eager arms, large sacks, empty prams and home-made pushcarts. And it would keep everyone away until all the dismantling work had been done.

It was towards midday when the two men began to attack the floorboards, using long crowbars to lever the planks free from joists, which were set in a thick layer of gravel. At noon, Mr Brown sent his assistant, Eddie Mason, off to the pub for a beer and a sandwich. At about fifteen minutes past twelve, there was a sudden halt on the part of the workmen. Mr Brown, busy sorting out what there was in the way of brass, copper, lead and iron among the heaps of scrap, turned at the sudden silence. One workman, looking as if his face was drained of blood, said in a hoarse voice, 'Guv'nor, I think you'd better come an' take a look, an' then fetch the police.'

Mr Brown crossed the yard and looked at what the men had uncovered. An old soldier of the trenches, he'd seen death and he'd seen bodies that had lain unburied for days, but he too suffered a draining of blood at what he saw now.

Uniformed police and CID men had been and eventually gone, and the decomposing body of a girl had been taken away. Mr Brown felt sick. Some of the repercussions were going to land in Sammy's lap. The police had said nothing was to be touched for the time being, everything was to be left just as it was. Meanwhile, they had the job of trying to identify the dead girl.

Sammy being out for the day, Mr Brown went to the Camberwell offices to see Boots, the general manager. His wife Emily was with him. She was his shorthand-typist and worked from nine-thirty until three-thirty. She was just about to go. She was a lively and energetic woman of twenty-seven, but very thin. To Mr Brown she seemed a little thinner each time he saw her, as if her inner energy devoured all the goodness of her food before it had any chance to do something for her body. But she owned magnificent auburn hair and big green eyes, and it was in her eyes that all her energy seemed to show.

'Hello, Jim,' she said, 'thought you were at your new job in Bermondsey.'

'Well, I was,' said Mr Brown, feeling he didn't want to land Boots's wife with unpleasant news just when she was about to go home to spend time with her little son. It was the kind of news a man didn't like giving a woman. 'But I 'it a snag, which I ought to talk to Sammy about, only I just remembered 'e's up in London Town somewhere.'

'Kensington, among other places,' said Boots.

'Well, you can talk to Boots about it,' said Emily. 'Sammy's good at verbalisin', Boots is good at listening. I'm off to see young Tim.' Tim, her son, was four and a half years old. 'So long, lovey,' she said to Boots, and gave him a warm kiss. 'So long, Jim.' Off she went, her step quick, as it always was, much as if she was continually trying to beat the passage of time.

'Now, what's the trouble, Jim?' asked Boots.

'Nasty,' said Mr Brown.

'How nasty?' asked Boots.

Susie's dad recounted how the body of a girl had come to light. He had gone for the police, and they'd summoned a police doctor, who was of the opinion that the body had lain in the gravel under the shed floorboards for over a year. The doctor also said it would have been more decomposed than it was if it had been lying in earth.

'Hell,' said Boots, 'that's not a very good start, Jim.'

'Told yer it was nasty, Boots,' said Mr Brown. He got on well with Boots, who rarely turned a hair at setbacks. Sammy could be dramatic.

'Poor young girl,' said Boots. He supposed it was murder, and he disliked murder even more than most people. He'd been close to a grisly one in his teens, close enough for it to have been only a few doors away. He had memories of that which he would never forget. 'Think of her moments of terror, Jim.'

'Murder, that's what it was,' said Mr Brown, 'and 'anging's too good for the bugger who did it. The police 'ave made me shut down the yard for the time bein', and they've got the spare key for the gate padlock. The point is, what's it goin' to do to the business?'

'It needn't do anything,' said Boots. 'It's bloody unpleasant, but it's the previous owners who'll have to cope with the real worries. We've only just taken it over. Let's see, who were the previous owners?'

'Collier and Son,' said Mr Brown. 'I told the police.'

'D'you know when they stopped doing any real

101

business, Jim? Sammy said the place was pretty run-down.'

'I only know Sammy said on Friday that they hadn't done any business for gawd knows how long,' said Mr Brown. 'It seemed they was just 'anging on to the site. I suppose what you're on about, is that someone 'ad use of the place, and use of the shed, if you can call it use when you do a young girl in an' bury 'er there. An' he 'ad to 'ave that use without anyone gettin' suspicious the day after.'

'Such as noticing certain floorboards had been removed and replaced,' said Boots. 'Yes, you'd notice a thing like that, I'd say. Well, all right, Jim, it's not your worry, nor mine, nor Sammy's. The headache belongs to Collier and Son. We've just got a nasty taste in our mouths. Why don't you push off home and get Mrs Brown to make you a large pot of tea? You look whacked.'

'No, I'd rather do a bit,' said Mr Brown, 'I'll clean the shop windows.'

'I don't think Sammy would recommend that,' said Boots.

'I'd like to do something,' said Mr Brown. Boots's phone rang, and Susie's dad slipped out. He supposed Boots was right, that Sammy wouldn't want him to clean windows, not now he was a yard manager and only a few weeks away from being Sammy's dad-in-law. So he went to the firm's scrap yard in Olney Road, which was always busy, and where he could do some useful work for an hour or so before going home. Doing something would take that body off his mind.

Emily had decided to walk home, thinking it would be a lot more healthy for her than sitting in a bus when she'd been sitting at her typewriter most of the day. She walked briskly along Denmark Hill, liking the attractive look of its trees, houses and gardens. She'd never been able to do anything slowly, anyway. But she did get a bit tired more quickly these days. The doctor said she was anaemic, that she should eat more, especially lightly cooked liver. Actually, she didn't seem to want a lot of food, and a large plateful put her off. She thought it might be a good idea to go and see her old general practitioner, Dr McManus of Walworth, and get a second opinion.

She didn't want to get ill, that was certain. If she became a sort of invalid and couldn't be a proper wife to Boots, that woman Polly Simms, a teacher at Rosie's school, would be all over him, showing him how healthy she was herself. Emily knew Polly had had her eye on Boots for ages, and of course being upper class, she wouldn't think anything of trying to pinch someone else's husband. She wanted to pinch Boots all right, Emily was sure of that.

I'll fight that to me last drop of breath, she thought, I'll fight it even if I have to eat pounds of nearly raw liver every day. I'm not going to let any woman get her hands on Boots. I know we've got a good marriage, even if we have had one or two ups and downs. I just wish I'd given him more children, I know he'd have liked four, like Lizzy and Ned have. Oh, lor', could it have been me hidden anaemia that worked against me? It's only come out these last few months. I'll get to be a bag of bones soon instead of a wife.

Boots and Sammy had been so good, giving Susie's dad a job as a scrap yard manager. Sammy had mentioned the idea to Boots, and Boots of course had said well, as he's Susie's dad, yes, you could treat him as one of the family instead of a window cleaner. That was it really with Sammy and Boots and all the Adams. They made you one of the family if your connections were close enough. The family was what they lived for. It all came from their mum, Chinese Lady. The family was everything to her. Strangely, she could be much more critical of her sons than her daughters-in-law. But she was a cockney mum, and most cockney mums knew boys needed their ears boxing far more than girls did. Telling them off now that they were all grown up was a sort of substitute for boxing their ears.

Emily smiled as she let herself into the house. Tim, her lively four-year-old son, came running into the hall. Not feeling too tired after her walk, she hugged him, lifted him and kissed him smackingly.

'Is that you, Em'ly?' called Chinese Lady from somewhere.

'Yes, it's me, I'm home, Mum,' called Emily.

Home. That was the best word ever.

Annie had gone to her work in a thinking frame of mind. She kept asking herself if the present of that bunch of daffs had meant more than a nice gesture, if it meant Will Brown would come round and see her again. She'd had boys give her the eye when she was younger. Lately her dad had said it was time she had a young man. She wouldn't object if Will Brown asked to take her out, except she'd let him know she didn't want him laughing at her and treating her as if she was more of a joke than a young lady.

Her place of work, the grocer's shop in the New Kent Road, was large and always had a lovely grocery smell. The open sacks that lined the floor against the front of the counter gave off the aroma of currants, sultanas, raisins, rice, sugar, prunes and other items. Mr Urcott, in his spotless white apron, presided at the dairy counter, and had a miraculous way of shaping chunks of butter or margarine into neat oblongs and expertly wrapping them in grease-proof paper. He was a funny old bloke. Well, he was over fifty, had thinning hair and spectacles that always perched halfway down his nose. But he was really kind, he had a smile for all his customers and even for ragged kids who came to ask did he have a pound of broken biscuits for tuppence? If he said no, one of them was sure to say he'd break up a pound of whole ones, if Mr Urcott would like.

He kept his shop clean, and he kept two large cats, which padded around silently at night in search of any mice foolish enough to be drawn out by the smell of cheese.

The shop had been open for an hour when Annie arrived at her prescribed time of ten o'clock. Mr Urcott greeted her with a smile and a comment over the head of a little old lady customer.

'Well, here you are, Annie. Did you hop all the way?'

'No, I treated meself to a tram ride this mornin', Mr Urcott.'

'Best way too,' said the little old lady, who was wearing a granny bonnet. 'I 'opped all the way up our street once when I was a girl, and me drawers fell down. You don't want that to 'appen at your age, Annie, it'll upset yer dignity. So don't do no 'opping.'

'You can be sure I won't, Mrs Gurney,' said Annie.

'It's what comes of tapes wearin' out,' said the little old lady, not a bit concerned that Mr Urcott was listening. 'My granddaughter says elastic's best, but I don't trust elastic meself. Yes, now I'll 'ave two ounces of yer New Zealand butter, Mr Urcott, I can afford that this week. I don't know I can afford elastic, even if I trusted it.' She prattled away.

'Hello, Annie.' That greeting came from Mr Urcott's

other assistant, Miss Banks, a single lady in her thirties and a niece of the grocer. She was kind too, but more brisk than Mr Urcott. She looked after the opposite counter, and Annie helped her there. Annie also kept the shop looking tidy, and attended to all orders that required anything from the open sacks to be packeted up in twists of brown paper after being weighed. The shop was busy most days, its prices being competitive, its atmosphere laden with the appeal of a good grocery establishment that had well-stocked shelves, shining marble counters and cheerful staff. Striving, hard-up housewives knew they could get good value and a little gossip as well, if they wanted it.

Mr Urcott had three customers at his counter, and Miss Banks had four. Annie, donning her white apron, began to help. There was a lull after all the customers had been served, and Mr Urcott took the opportunity to ask Annie if her knee was quite better.

'Yes, thanks, Mr Urcott, it's only a bit twingey now,' she said.

'Twingey? Well,' said Mr Urcott, smiling benevolently at her over the top of his spectacles, 'if it gets hurtful twingey, Annie, you can sit down on one of the customers' chairs.' There were two chairs, one at each counter, mainly for the benefit of old ladies.

'Oh, I won't 'ave to do that,' said Annie.

The day passed pleasantly for her, she liked the work and her wages of ten bob a week were quite generous. Lots of factory girls only earned seven and six for doing a fifty-hour week. At a quarter to four, close to her finishing time, Annie was rearranging a shelf. Mr Urcott and Miss Banks each had a customer. Annie jumped as someone addressed her back.

'Afternoon, miss, and a pound of turnips, if yer please.'

She turned. Oh, help, it was him, and with a straight

face. But he wasn't in uniform, he was wearing standard Walworth casual clothes, trousers, jersey and jacket, and a brown cap. What was it he'd asked for? Turnips?

'That's daft,' she whispered, 'we don't sell turnips.'

'You sure?' said Will. Nellie had told him where her sister worked.

'Course I'm sure. We're not a greengrocer's.'

Will looked as if he might dispute that. Just for the fun of it. He'd returned an hour ago from his weekly visit to the hospital, where he'd been told his condition shouldn't be considered alarming, that he might merely be allergic to the Indian climate. So I might, he'd said, but what about the attack I had, exerting myself a little? Oh, that can be expected, but we still feel your condition is only temporary. Come and see us once a fortnight now, instead of once a week.

'All right, miss, no turnips, then,' he said, 'so I'll have four pounds of potatoes. Can you put them in a bag?'

'I'll hit you,' breathed Annie.

'What for?'

'You know what for. Comin' in here and playin' about.'

'No good askin' for some spring onions, I suppose, or a cauliflower?'

'How would you like a kick in the leg?' whispered Annie.

'Not much,' said Will. 'All right, how about a tin of Peak Frean's mixed biscuits for me mum?'

'Serious?' said Annie.

'Well, I don't think me mum fancies funny ones,' said Will.

'You'll come to a sad end, you will,' said Annie. With Miss Banks having served her customer, Annie became brisk. 'A tin of Peak Frean's mixed, you said, sir?'

'Thank you, miss, yes,' said Will 'and I'll have a bag of coal as well.'

'We don't sell coal, sir,' said Annie, 'you'll 'ave to go down a coal-mine for that.' She fetched the tin of biscuits. 'Anything else, sir?'

'Yes,' murmured Will, 'I'll wait for you outside, I heard you finish at four.'

'Pardon?' said Annie.

'Yes, not a bad afternoon outside,' said Will. 'Can I have one of your penny carrier bags for the biscuits?'

Annie put the tin into a carrier bag and Will paid, Annie eyeing him with the suspicion of a young lady who felt he might just have a pushcart waiting for her outside the shop.

'Good afternoon, sir, thank you for your custom,' she said.

'Pleasure,' said Will, 'pity about no turnips, though.' He departed, his face still straight, which made Annie sure he was laughing at her. And she was sure he wouldn't be outside the shop when she left.

But he was.

'You're here,' she said.

'Walk you home?' said Will, eyeing her in approval. She looked quite the young lady in a short skirt, red jumper and buttoned-up jacket.

'D'you mind tellin' me what you're lookin' at?' asked Annie.

'Just you,' smiled Will.

'Well, I just don't know,' said Annie, 'you're always lookin'. I never met any feller who did more lookin' than you. You could get both eyes blacked one day. And how did you know where I worked?'

'Nellie told me.'

'That's all very well,' said Annie, 'but what d'you

mean by comin' into the shop and 'aving me on?'

'I wanted a tin of biscuits,' said Will.

'You asked for turnips. And coal.'

'I forget myself sometimes,' said Will, and Annie laughed.

'You're daft,' she said.

'Now and again, I suppose,' said Will. 'D'you want to take a tram down to East Street?'

'What, under me arm or in a carrier bag?' asked Annie, having some of her own back.

'No sauce,' said Will.

'You can talk, you've got more sauce than all the street kids,' said Annie. 'And I'm walkin' home, thanks.'

'I was thinkin' of your knee,' said Will.

'How kind,' said Annie. She was still suspicious of him. 'You can walk with me, if you like, I always go home by the Walworth Road.' She liked the Walworth Road with its shops, its trams and buses, its people and its handsome town hall.

They walked to the Elephant and Castle.

'I was told you called at our house yesterday,' said Will.

'Yes, I wanted to thank you properly for the flowers,' said Annie. 'I'm sorry I didn't thank you properly at the time – oh, wait a minute, when you left you told Nellie you'd send a pair of trousers round for me, and you went off laughin' about it.'

'Did I?'

'I bet you did,' said Annie, as they turned into the Walworth Road. 'And what were the trousers for, might I ask?'

'To stop you worryin',' said Will.

'What about? Just tell me, go on. I didn't 'ave any worries at all until I bumped into that pushcart because you were lookin' at me.'

'Yes, it's all this lookin',' said Will, 'and I thought you could use a pair of trousers to cover your legs and knees up when I'm around.'

'Oh, I never heard anything so barmy,' said Annie. 'You're laughin' at me again. Anyway, how would you like to be a grown-up girl with her knees in the air in a pushcart?'

'You're not still worried about that, are you, Annie?' said Will.

'I'll never get over it,' said Annie, 'and I never thought you'd be rotten enough to tell your fam'ly about it, specially that nice sister and dad of yours. I bet it won't be long before everyone in London knows.'

'Only if it gets in the newspapers,' said Will.

'Newspapers?' Annie nearly fainted in public.

'They'll send reporters round to see you, and they'll take photographs.'

'Photographs of me?' gasped Annie in horror.

'In the pushcart,' said Will.

'D'you want me to die? I'm not bein' sat in any pushcart again, I can tell you, I'll—' Annie stopped and gave him a searching look. 'Oh, you rotten ha'porth, you're havin' me on again.'

'No, it could get serious,' said Will, 'they might drag me in and take photographs of me pushin' the cart with you in it and your knees up in the air. Strike a light, Annie, if the Army saw it, they'd throw me to the lions.'

'They wouldn't, would they?' Annie gave him another searching glance. Will tried to look worried but brave. It didn't work. 'Oh, you lunatic,' said Annie, 'you're doin' it again, laughin' at me. And you a soldier too, a corporal. Where's your uniform?'

'In my wardrobe,' said Will. 'I bought some civvies this mornin'.'

'Your sister said you were on three months leave, I've never 'eard of any soldier havin' that amount of leave before.'

'It's for good behaviour,' said Will, 'for bein' respectful to officers, nice to old ladies and kind to girls.'

'I'm not simple, I'll 'ave you know,' said Annie. 'Did you get three months leave as a reward for doin' something brave?'

'No, just for doin' three years duty in India.'

'India? Oh, no wonder you look so brown. What's it like there?'

'Hot, mostly,' said Will, and talked to her about that teeming continent. When they reached Caulfield Place down Browning Street, they stopped.

'Here's where you live,' she said. 'I'd best get a move on now and give Charlie and Nellie and Cassie a bit of tea.'

'How many young men come knockin' at your door?' asked Will.

'Hundreds,' said Annie.

'As many as that? Well, I suppose there's no point askin' if I can take you out when you've got—'

'Of course I 'aven't,' said Annie.

'All right,' said Will, 'how about a row on the Serpentine next Sunday afternoon, if the weather's fine?'

'You askin' serious?'

'Yes, d'you mind?' said Will.

'No, I like bein' asked out,' said Annie.

'Good,' said Will, 'I'll call for you at half-past two next Sunday.' He thought he could manage a gentle row on the Serpentine. There was no real exertion in that. He wouldn't be entering a boat race. 'That suit you?'

'A row round the Serpentine sounds nice,' said Annie.

'Don't fall out of the boat,' said Will.

'You'd better make sure I don't, or I'll pull you in with me.'

'I'm hopin' for a fine afternoon, not a wet one,' said Will.

Annie laughed, and they parted, Will strolling down Caulfield Place and Annie hurrying along to King and Queen Street, a little smile on her face.

CHAPTER NINE

Monday having been washday, the Brown family expected the usual supper of cold meat with mounds of piping hot bubble-and-squeak. But because it was Mr Brown's first day as manager of the new scrap yard, Mrs Brown put herself out to do grilled pork chops. However tasty bubble-and-squeak was, the cold meat just wasn't good enough for celebrating a proud day like this. Mrs Brown's scullery had been full of steam from the copper for hours, and the yard line was still laden with laundry. The scullery was still full of the smell of washing, but the door from the kitchen was shut tight to keep the smell from interfering with the aroma of the supper. Mr Brown had decided to say nothing about the grisly find at the yard. He didn't think he needed to upset his family, especially with Susie's wedding in the offing. In any case, it was nothing to do with Sammy's ownership of the yard. Any headaches belonged to the previous owners, Collier and Son. With luck, when it got into the papers, Adams Enterprises wouldn't even be mentioned. Boots was a godsend in cases like this, he'd know how to talk to the police and to any newspaper reporters if they asked questions.

Enjoying his supper, he came up with the opinion that his trouble-and-strife was worth her weight in roast beef. Susie said you mean pork chops, Dad. Sally said no, he meant gold. Same thing, said Mr Brown, seeing I'm talking about the roast beef of old England.

'Now, Jim,' said Mrs Brown, 'I don't want to be stood up pound for pound against roast beef.'

''Ow much roast beef would it be, then?' asked Sally.

'With any luck, a few 'undredweight,' said Mr Brown.

'Me a few 'undredweight?' said Mrs Brown, whose motherliness was constant and unvarying. 'Dad, you're askin' for a clip, makin' out I'm like the Fat Woman of Peckham.'

'I think it's the Fat Boy of Peckham,' said Will.

'Well, I'm not him, either,' said Mrs Brown.

'You're a nice comfy lady, Mum', said Susie, 'and worth all the pork chops in the Tower of London.'

''Ow many they got there, then?' asked Freddy.

'Millions,' said Susie.

''Ow'd they get millions?'

'Well, they order ninety every week for the Beefeaters,' said Will, 'but the Beefeaters won't eat them, they only like beef chops.'

'I never 'eard of beef chops,' said Sally.

'Well, you wouldn't, would you?' said Will. 'The Beefeaters grab them all.'

'Mum, if I 'ave to listen to any more jokes like that, I'll leave 'ome,' said Sally.

'Oh, don't do that, lovey,' said Mrs Brown, 'just finish your pork chop.'

'I 'eard a joke once,' said Freddy, holding his chop and biting at what was left of the pork. 'There was this absent-minded bloke, yer see, an' when 'e got to 'is work one day someone told 'im 'e was wearin' odd socks. "No, they ain't odd," he said, "I got another pair at 'ome just like these."'

Sally giggled. Mrs Brown smiled fondly. Susie smiled. Will grinned.

Mr Brown said, 'An' then what, Freddy?'

'Joke over,' said Freddy. 'Wake up, Dad. 'Ere, do all the fam'ly get presents at the weddin'? I wouldn't mind a bike meself.'

114

'Blessed boy,' said Sally, 'what's 'e talkin' about?'

'It's only the 'appy couple that get presents, Freddy,' said Mr Brown.

'I dunno what Susie's gettin' any for,' said Freddy, 'not when she's goin' to get all Sammy's worldly goods. Crikey, she'll get 'is motorcar as well, and I ain't even got a bike.'

'I'll buy you a bike, Freddy,' said Susie.

Freddy nearly swallowed his chop bone.

'Now, son, you can't eat that bone,' said Mr Brown.

'Did our Susie say something?' asked Freddy, slightly hoarse.

'She said she'll buy you a bike,' smiled Will.

'Crikey,' said Freddy, 'ain't our Susie lovely, Will? I bet there ain't many bruvvers that 'ave got a sister like her. I bet Ernie Flint's sister could eat broken glass. Susie, did yer really say you'd buy me a bike?'

'I have bought it, lovey,' said Susie. At Sammy's request, she had placed an order with Mr Greenberg and Mr Greenberg had said what a pleasure to see you, Susie, and what a pleasure to buy up certain textiles at certain warehouses for Sammy at ten per cent commission. Two and a half, said Susie. Susie, Susie, said Mr Greenberg, and sat down under the stress of a sudden heart attack. Seven and a half, he said faintly. Susie smiled, and Mr Greenberg recovered slightly. Four, said Susie. Mr Greenberg had a relapse. Susie fanned him. Six, he said hoarsely. Five, said Susie. Susie, Susie, you'll be my death, he said. But five is twice as much as two and a half, and you don't want to ruin us, do you, Mr Greenberg? Mr Greenberg settled for five and forgave Susie because of her blue eyes. Susie saw some bicycles among a mountain of stuff in his yard. She examined them. She found two very good ones and offered to take them both off Mr Greenberg's hands. On my life,

Susie, said Mr Greenberg, ain't it a pleasure at twelve and six each? Bless you, Mr Greenberg, said Susie. Eh? said Mr Greenberg. Thanks, said Susie. Mr Greenberg said did I hear a quid for the pair? No, I'm happy with twenty-five bob, said Susie. Done at a guinea, Susie, said Mr Greenberg. Susie laughed. She was happy to pay up. Earning twelve pounds a month, which few young women of her age did, her savings made her relatively affluent, and she had insisted on helping her dad with the wedding expenses.

'Susie, you really bought me a bike?' asked Freddy, blissfully agape.

'Mr Greenberg's deliverin' it tomorrow,' said Susie, 'with one for Sally as well. A lady's bike, and both nearly as good as new, with bells.'

'Oh, Susie,' breathed Sally in rapture.

'Bless you, Susie love,' said Mrs Brown.

'Seconded,' said Will, and Mr Brown looked affectionately proud of his one and only elder daughter. Sally jumped up and gave Susie a hug and a kiss. Freddy said he'd do all Susie's wedding errands for her, and what's more, he said, I won't come to the church in me shirt tails, I'll wear me new suit.

'What a blessin',' said Sally, 'we're all honoured, ain't we, Dad?'

''Ighly,' said Mr Brown.

'I'll wear me bicycle clips as well,' said Freddy.

'Not in the church, lovey,' said Mrs Brown.

'Well, all right,' said Freddy generously. 'Susie, we goin' to 'ave "Knees Up, Mother Brown" in the Institute?'

'Sammy says you can't have a Walworth weddin' without a knees-up,' smiled Susie.

'That you can't,' said Mr Brown.

'It occurs to me,' said Freddy, 'was—'

'Crikey, listen to 'im,' said Sally, 'fancy anything occurrin' to 'im.'

'Yes, was "Knees Up, Mother Brown" wrote for our mum, Dad?' asked Freddy.

'Funny you should ask that, Freddy,' said Mr Brown. 'It was the Sunday our Susie was christened, and we 'ad a bit of a do afterwards. Me and yer mum did a lively dance, and a bloke in a posh suit and a bow tie come up as yer mum was showin' 'er knees. 'E complimented 'er and asked me would I mind if 'e wrote a song in 'er honour, and what was 'er name. Seein' she'd become a mother, I said you can call 'er Mother Brown. 'E said 'e was much obliged, then went an' sat in a corner and wrote the song there an' then. Then 'e played it on the joanner. "Knees Up, Mother Brown", that's what it was, and everyone did a dance to it, and ever since everyone in Walworth's danced to it.'

'Dad, you scream,' said Susie, 'you just made all that up.'

'You ask yer mum,' said Mr Brown.

'Well, I do remember some saucy bloke comin' up and sayin' he liked me knees,' said Mrs Brown, 'but I don't remember him writin' a song about them. Well, I boxed 'is ears.'

Susie laughed. She listened as her dad talked about how he felt he'd had one over the eight when he first met their mum. She was that pretty he was sorry none of them had been there at the time. Freddy tried to puzzle that out while his dad went on to say that for the first time in his life he'd felt inebriated without a single drop of what you fancy having passed his lips. Susie listened to Sally pulling his leg, and to her mum announcing that Will had treated her to a lovely tin of biscuits after getting back from the hospital. It was a relief, she said, that the doctors had told him his asthma might only be temporary, and that they'd given him some special tablets to take, specially if it got temporarily chronic.

'Aspro, I reckon,' said Mr Brown, 'they give yer that for everything.'

'Yes, Henry the Eighth's wives were given a couple each after he had their heads chopped off,' said Will. 'but it didn't cure their headache.'

Susie laughed again. Will could be really funny, and he was letting his sense of humour make light of his condition. The evening sunshine was going, but its light was still lingering on the grimy rooftops of Walworth and touching the kitchen. It was a lovely old kitchen to Susie. She could rarely sit at the table in the evenings without thinking of the previous tenants, the Adams family. Sammy and his sister and brothers had all grown up here. She often felt that she and her family were an extension of the Adams. Sammy said life was all about families, that loyalties began with the family, and that if you didn't have loyalties you didn't have anything worthwhile to hang on to when you started slipping. She and Sammy would have a family. Two boys and two girls. That is, Sammy had said would she mind doing him the honour four times and come up with two of each. Susie said would he mind giving her a little help, since she didn't think she could manage everything by herself. Sammy asked if she'd write down exactly what he had to do, as he was dead ignorant about that sort of thing. So am I, said Susie, but we can practise together. What, now, in your parlour? said Sammy. No, when we're married, said Susie, so leave my legs alone. Now? said Sammy. Well, not exactly now, said Susie, not immediately.

It was definitely cold meat and bubble-and-squeak for

Gaffer Ford and his family. Annie had had to see to the washing, which Nellie and Charlie had collected from a bagwash on their way home from school. It had all needed to be sorted out and hung on the yard lines. Still, the bubble-and-squeak, crisply browned, was a treat any Monday.

Gaffer Ford thought of something.

'Seen any more of the soldier bloke that wheeled your knees 'ome in a pushcart, Annie?' he asked.

'You done it now, Dad,' said Nellie.

'Done what?' said the Gaffer.

'You're not to say that word,' said Nellie.

'No-one ain't,' said Charlie, 'and I got orders to bash any of the street kids that talk about it.'

'No, you ain't,' said Nellie. 'Annie didn't give you no orders to do any bashin'. You just said you would, it's yer 'ooliganism that makes yer want to go around bashin' people.'

'Charlie,' said the Gaffer, 'I 'ope I ain't goin' to have to take me belt to yer one day, which I've been recommended to by certain neighbours. Anyway, what word ain't I to say?'

'Pushcart,' piped up Cassie.

'Cor, she's said it,' groaned Charlie.

'Cassie, you know Annie's forbid it,' said Nellie.

'Yes, I don't want it ever mentioned again,' said Annie, 'not by any of you – Dad, is that you laughin'?'

'Bless yer, Annie, not me,' said the Gaffer.

'It's bad enough him always laughin' – no, never mind that,' said Annie, 'just get on with your suppers.'

'Who's 'im?' asked the Gaffer.

'Pardon?' said Annie.

'The one that's always laughin',' said the Gaffer, who knew the answer.

'Betcher it's 'er soldier,' said Charlie.

'If you must know,' said Annie, 'he came into the shop to buy a tin of biscuits for 'is mum, and I just happened to serve him.'

'Then what?' asked the Gaffer.

'What d'you mean, then what?' asked Annie.

'Did 'e come on 'orseback?' asked Cassie.

''Ow could 'e come on 'orseback for a tin of biscuits?' asked Charlie. ''Orses ain't allowed in grocers' shops.'

'Small 'orses are,' said Cassie.

'Cassie,' said Annie, 'stop givin' your meat to that cat.'

'It's only the bits of fat,' said Cassie.

'Did yer soldier 'ave a chat with yer, Annie?' asked the Gaffer.

'Well, he did walk down the Walworth Road with me on me way home,' said Annie, 'when I spoke to him about makin' a joke of what I suffered.'

'Cor, I bet 'is ears 'urt,' said Charlie.

'The Queen went down the Walworth Road once,' said Cassie dreamily.

'What for?' asked Nellie.

'Well, she 'ad some shoppin' to do,' said Cassie.

'What shoppin'?' asked Charlie.

'Oh, jellied eels an' pie an' mash, I think,' said Cassie. 'Yes, it was that, I remember now, they don't 'ave any in Windsor Castle, only liver an' bacon an' fairy cakes with pink icing. And plums an' custard,' she added, after a brief but thoughtful pause.

'Cassie,' said Annie, hiding a smile, 'I just don't know what we can do with you and all your fancies.'

'We could turn 'er upside-down an' shake 'em out of 'er,' said Charlie.

'No, we couldn't,' said the Gaffer, 'not our Cassie, she's one of me sweet'earts.'

120

'We could turn Charlie upside-down and make an 'ole in the floor with 'is big 'ead,' said Nellie.

'Yes, time we 'ad some 'oles knocked in the floor,' said the Gaffer. 'Anyway, so yer soldier walked you 'ome, Annie, did 'e?'

'Yes, and he asked me to go for a row on the Serpentine with 'im next Sunday, if it's fine,' said Annie.

'Annie, did yer say yes?' asked Nellie.

'I 'ad to be gracious and forgivin',' said Annie. 'You can't be church-goin' and not forgivin'.'

'You'll look nice in yer best Sunday frock, Annie, while you're standin' on yer dignity in a rowin'-boat,' said the Gaffer. 'I couldn't be more pleased for yer.'

'Ain't it nice, Annie's soldier bein' romantic about 'er?' said Nellie.

'Romantic's daft,' said Charlie.

'Annie, I'll come as well, if yer like,' said Cassie, 'there might be a circus with lion tamers in the park.'

'Cassie, you can't go, you silly,' said Nellie.

'I could take Tabby,' said Cassie, ''e's really a circus cat.'

'First I've 'eard of it,' said Charlie.

'Well, 'e can do circus tricks,' said Cassie, 'like puttin' 'is tail up in the air an' standin' on one leg.'

'I never seen 'im standin' on one leg,' said Nellie.

''E did it once, I saw 'im,' said Cassie.

'Then what 'appened?' asked the Gaffer.

'Well, 'e fell over,' said Cassie dolefully.

The family yelled with laughter. Cassie couldn't think why.

'You're a real scream, you are, Cassie,' said Nellie.

'She's our little coughdrop,' said the Gaffer.

'Who wants some marmalade tart?' asked Annie. They all wanted a slice of one she had made on Saturday evening.

'Can I 'ave mine 'ot?' asked Charlie. Annie said yes, put it in the fire for a minute. The family yelled with laughter again, and the Gaffer was certain of one thing then.

And that was that a man's kids were the best thing in his life when he'd lost his wife.

Mr Brown was at the Bermondsey yard again on Tuesday morning. Not that there was anything he could do. The police had said don't touch. He sent his assistant off to the Olney Road yard, which was busy and could use a bit of help. The police had appeared early. They were going to take away the boards that had lain above the corpse and give them a minute examination. Mr Brown asked why, and was astonished to hear them talk about fingerprints. Fingerprints on floorboards that had been walked on ever since that poor girl had been buried there? On the underside, said the police. It's smooth planking.

Mr Brown asked if the girl had been identified. The police said they were working on it, using a list of missing persons. Did they know how old the girl had been? Not yet. The pathologist would come up with that information pretty soon. Had they got any helpful information from Collier and Son? The reply made Mr Brown infer that Collier and Son had let their business go to the dogs on account of too much time spent in pubs. The father and his son had had no employees at this yard, they worked the business themselves. On and off. And mostly off during the last eighteen months. Mr Brown drew another inference, that the CID were investigating father and son. He asked if he could get rid of the stacks of timber. He'd taken down the notice on the gates after the body had been uncovered yesterday. The police said they'd be obliged if he left everything just as it was. Finally, he asked if they wanted to speak to Mr Sammy Adams, managing director of the firm that had bought the yard and the business just a week or so ago. The police said they had no plans to at the moment.

That was something, thought Mr Brown.

One of the closed double gates was pushed open and Boots entered the yard, raincoat over his arm. The day was showery.

'Morning, Jim,' he said, and introduced himself to the police. He spoke to them and received from them the same kind of information they'd given to Mr Brown, no more and no less. Mr Brown couldn't help noting how easily he conducted himself. He never seemed to let people bother him, whoever they were and however awkward they could get. Mr Brown knew him for a man to whom the fact of being alive in God's world was far more important than the attitudes of people. People seemed to amuse him, and he nearly always looked as if a hint of amusement was lurking in his eyes, even his almost blind one. He might not be amused at the moment. He wasn't. You could see that, you could see a steely light, and Mr Brown knew he was thinking of the man who had murdered that poor young girl and buried her body under a scrap yard shed.

Mr Brown knew his background, that he was the eldest of his redoubtable mother's four children, that he'd been born and bred in cockney Walworth, won a place in a grammar school, made himself temporarily famous as the most important defence witness at an Old Bailey murder trial and soldiered in the trenches of France and Flanders before being blinded on the Somme. He'd married the girl next door while he was still blind, and now he was the general manager of his brother Sammy's business. Mr Brown thought that for all its complications, Boots did the job standing on his head. Unlike Sammy, however, he did not seem ambitious. He seemed a contented man, although

123

his wife, Emily, once said there was a lot more to him than met the eye. His adopted daughter Rosie adored him. And, according to what Mr Brown had heard from Sammy in an unguarded moment, so did Miss Polly Simms, daughter of General Sir Henry Simms. Miss Simms had been an ambulance driver during the war, and although she had never met Boots while in France, Sammy said she complained bitterly that Emily had pinched Boots while her back was turned. But keep it dark, Jim, said Sammy, or there'll be ructions and my dear old Ma will start boxing ears all round. Not that Boots can't handle the situation. He's a family man.

The police, ready to depart, requested that Mr Brown and Mr Adams leave with them. They locked the gates and went on their way, the relevant floorboards wrapped in an old sheet. Boots took a stroll with Mr Brown.

'Good of yer to come,' said Mr Brown.

'Just wanted you to know it's not your problem or your worry,' said Boots, 'and that the scrap yard in Kennington is short of a manager. He's off sick. Would you care to take over, Jim?'

'That'll suit me, Boots.'

'I need to get back to the office,' said Boots.

'I'll push off to Kennington,' said Mr Brown. 'By the way, I've kept all this to meself.'

'So have I,' said Boots.

'I didn't want me fam'ly to know, specially Susie.'

'Everybody'll know soon, of course,' said Boots, 'but the papers might not mention it's now an Adams yard.'

'Well, with the weddin' comin' up, yer know, Boots.'

'We're all looking forward to it, Jim.'

'Special special it's goin' to be for Susie.'

'And a revelation to Sammy, I'd say,' said Boots, and the lurking hint of amusement turned into a smile.

The midday editions of the evening papers came up with the news of the discovery of a girl's body in a scrap yard in Bermondsey. The possibility that she'd been murdered was hinted at. Mr Brown felt certain the police had no doubts. The pathologist's report was expected today, and the papers informed their readers that the police were trying to establish the girl's identity by checking their lists of missing persons.

'Ah, good afternoon, Mrs Brown,' smiled Mr Greenberg as the good lady opened the door to him. 'And vhat a pleasant day, ain't it?'

'Oh, I suppose a nice drop of rain is doin' someone some good,' said Mrs Brown in her agreeable way. No disillusioned male could ever have said Mrs Brown was a contrary female. ''Ave you brought the bikes, Mr Greenberg?'

Mr Greenberg's small pony and cart stood outside the house. The well-known rag-and-bone man also had a horse and cart.

'Vell, how could I let Susie down? Vhat a happy young lady she is, ain't it? Might I bring the bikes in, Mrs Brown?'

'I'd be ever so obliged,' said Mrs Brown proudly. Some neighbours were on their doorsteps, watching through the light shower of rain. It could make any woman proud to have neighbours witnessing two bikes going into her house. 'And I'm that glad you're deliverin' now, as Sally and Freddy will be home from school in half an hour.'

'I vill bring them in at vunce, von't I?' beamed Mr Greenberg.

'And stay for a cup of tea,' said Mrs Brown.

'Vell, time ain't alvays money,' said Mr Greenberg, his

beard curling happily, 'and ain't this a house and a home of fond memories for me? Vhy, ain't it the only house that's known the Adams and Browns, all of vhich are my friends? I vill bring in the bikes and drink tea vith you vith great pleasure.'

'Leave them in the passage,' said Mrs Brown, and bustled back to her kitchen to put the kettle on.

Mr Greenberg unloaded the bikes one at a time and placed them in the passage. He returned to his cart to put the nosebag on his pony. He looked around for a moment. The shower of rain ceased its patter, the clouds broke and the sun came out, creating a rainbow over Walworth. Ah, such a country with its rain, its rainbows and its good people, thought Mr Greenberg. His love for his adopted country surfaced, and he took out his large red handkerchief and blew his nose. He thought of the trodden muddy streets of Russian villages, and the perils of being Jewish whenever a patrol of Russian police or Cossacks rode in. The tsars and their knout-wielding Cossacks had gone, and the Bolsheviks and their commissars had Russia now. They were no better than the tsars. Who would want to go back and live under them? Who would ever exchange a life with the people of London for a life under the Bolsheviks? There were a few people, ah, yes, who would never smile on a Jew, but did he not have a thousand friends who would laugh with him and crack jokes with him?

How busy he had been almost from the day he and his parents and his sisters had stepped ashore and taken their first steps over the soil of England. He had been fifteen then and was now just fifty. In all that time he had been too busy to find a wife. And now, when grey was peppering his hair and his beard, a woman had entered his house in the Old Kent Road. A woman of thirty-six, a widow, Hannah Borovich, who had three children, all boys.

126

'Mr Greenberg, shame on you,' she had said.

'Vhat? Vhat? You enter my house and address me in Russian, not even in Yiddish?'

'We are Russian,' she said.

'I spit on Russia.'

'Tck, tck,' said the handsome widow. 'It is time you were married, time you became a father.'

'To whom should I be married?'

'To myself. You are a good man, Eli Greenberg, and a kind one. I will take you for my husband and give my sons what they need, a father. Go to Rabbi Goldstein and tell him so.'

What could a man do with such a woman who had three sons all with dark liquid eyes and crisp curly black hair? Should he take a wife at his age and her three sons too? She was poor and was concerned for them.

What could a man do except think about it?

Mr Greenberg smiled, raised his round black hat to Mrs Brown's neighbours who were still on their doorsteps, then entered the house to drink tea with Susie's affable mother.

CHAPTER TEN

One could have said that Sally and Freddy came out of school in leaps and bounds, such was their rushing eagerness to get home and see if their bikes had come. School friends laughed and shouted at them.

'Go it, Freddy, old Nick's behind yer!'

'Leg it, Sally!'

That Sally and her growing legs, thought Freddy, it just ain't right. His sister was yards ahead of him and running fit to lick him to their door. Exuberant Sally ran on. Appalled at being beaten by a girl, and his sister at that, Freddy charged after her. Up through Walcorde Avenue they flew, Freddy gaining. Sally turned into Browning Street.

''Ere, you Sally!'

'Slowcoach!' called Sally.

Freddy belted after her and they were almost together as they turned into Caulfield Place. And there they almost sent Mr Ponsonby flying.

'Oh, 'elp,' panted Freddy.

'Oh, sorry, Mr Ponsonby,' said Sally. They stopped.

Mr Ponsonby, regaining his balance, straightened his bowler hat and peered at them.

'Dear me, what a day,' he said, 'what high spirits. Who are you?'

'I'm Sally, 'e's Freddy.'

'Ah, yes, Sally Brown. Charming, charming, such a sweet girl. And Freddy, yes, such a firework, my word, yes. Dear me, where are you going?'

' 'Ome,' said Freddy, 'to see if our bikes 'ave come.'

'Bikes?' said Mr Ponsonby, looking puzzled. 'Ah, bicycles, of course. Have a peppermint.' He produced the bag, opened it and proffered it. Sally and Freddy each took a peppermint while their feet fidgeted.

'Thanks ever so, Mr Ponsonby,' said Sally.

'Not at all, Sally, not at all. My, you're a pretty girl.'

'She's got special wooden legs,' said Freddy.

'He's barmy,' said Sally, and Mr Ponsonby peered at her legs.

'Dear me, dear me, well, I never,' he said, 'how very charming.'

'She just 'ad ordin'ry short legs before,' said Freddy. 'Well, we got to go now, Mr Ponsonby – crikey, look, Sally, that's Mr Greenberg's cart outside our front door – come on.'

Off they ran. Mr Ponsonby turned to watch them, a kind smile putting a crease in his tidy-looking face.

'Dear me, what a very nice photograph I could take,' he said, and helped himself to a peppermint. 'But one is so busy, so busy. I must get on. Now, where am I going? Ah, yes.' He turned about and twinkled off, rolled umbrella lightly tapping the pavement.

Having paid their joyous respects to the beaming Mr Greenberg, and gobbled up cake with their cups of tea, Sally and Freddy took up rapturous ownership of their bikes. Off went Sally to ride round and see her friend Mavis. Boys whistled at her legs.

'Soppy 'a'porths,' said Sally and cycled on.

Freddy just went careering around the back streets, having promised his mum and Mr Greenberg too not to tussle with trams and buses in the Walworth Road. Trams always come off best, said his mum. And Mr Greenberg said bikes were valuable as business goods, but boys were valuable to their families.

Pedalling from Rodney Road into Orb Street, Freddy spotted Cassie. She was meandering along and singing to herself. With a tyre-hissing swerve, Freddy crossed to her side of the street and stopped.

'Watcher, Cassie.'

'Oh, 'ello,' said Cassie.

'Like me bike, do yer?' said Freddy.

'Crikey, is it yourn?' breathed Cassie in awe.

'Not 'alf,' said Freddy, 'it's a present from me eldest sister. She's wealthy, yer know. Well, she is a bit.'

'Oh, does she wear furs?' asked Cassie. 'I 'ad an aunt once who wore furs. An' jewels. An' she 'ad 'er own carriage with four white 'orses. Only she fell on 'ard times and 'ad to go an' do the laundry for a wicked uncle.'

'Rotten 'ard luck,' said Freddy. 'Did it turn 'er hair white?'

'Oh, no, she 'ad lovely gold 'air,' said Cassie, 'and 'er wicked uncle tried to cut it off. 'E chased 'er all round the laundry room. Only 'e couldn't see where she was in all the steam, and 'e fell in the great big laundry tub.'

'Did 'e? You sure 'e did, Cassie?'

'Oh, yes, and it boiled 'im all over,' said Cassie.

'Did it drown 'im as well?' asked Freddy.

'Oh, no, 'is servants got 'im out,' said Cassie.

'And hung 'im on the line?'

'I think they 'ad to,' said Cassie, 'he was all soppin' wet. Still, me aunt did say he was sort of different after that. Is it really yer own bike?'

'Yes, like a ride?' said Freddy. 'You can sit on the carrier be'ind me.'

'Oh, could I?' Cassie was aglow with pleasure.

'Yes, come on,' said Freddy, and held the bike steady. Cassie perched herself astride the wire carrier.

'Oh,' she said.

'What's up?'

'It's all wiry,' she said, ''ave yer got a little cushion I could put in me knickers?'

'I dunno, you girls don't 'alf 'ave soft bums,' said Freddy. 'I suppose us blokes ought to carry cushions around, only we don't. Never mind, Cassie, use this.' He took his soft cap off and handed it to her. Cassie unperched herself and with no more than two or three facile movements she lodged the cap in the seat of her knickers. Then she frowned.

'It's all lumpy,' she said.

'Look, Cassie, as me mate you ain't supposed to complain,' said Freddy. 'Me old mate Daisy never complained not once.'

'I ain't complainin',' said Cassie, 'I'm just sayin', that's all. I'm just sayin' it's a bit lumpy.'

'Well, try it,' said Freddy, and Cassie perched herself astride the carrier again. ''Ow's that?' he asked.

'Oh, it don't feel 'alf so lumpy now,' said Cassie.

A boy came up.

'What's she doin' on yer bike?' he asked.

'Sittin',' said Freddy.

'You ain't supposed to give girls bike rides. Get 'er orf, and I'll ride.'

'She's me mate, Alfie Gibbons, and you ain't,' said Freddy.

'Bleedin' cissy,' said young Alfie Gibbons.

''Ere, Cassie, 'old me bike while I roll me sleeves up,' said Freddy.

'Oh, you goin' to 'ave a duel?' asked Cassie in excitement.

131

'No, I ain't, I'm just goin' to flatten 'is 'ooter,' said Freddy, who had a lot of his mum's equability but couldn't stand being called a cissy.

'Ain't you got a sword?' asked Cassie, off her perch and holding the bike. 'Me dad 'ad lots of swords once and 'ad lots of duels. 'E 'ad one once with a French duke. On 'Ampstead 'Eath. Dad cut 'is 'ead off.'

'Cor blimey,' said Alfie Gibbons, 'she's yer mate? She's as daft as old Ma Simmonds, who ain't got no teef, eiver.'

'Right, put yer dooks up,' said Freddy, sleeves rolled up and muscles flexed. Cassie's eyes grew big. It was the first time a boy had threatened to fight a duel on her behalf. Street kids were approaching, sensing an up-and-downer.

'I just remembered, I got to do some errands for me mum,' said Alfie Gibbons, and made tracks for his home in Stead Street.

Freddy rolled his sleeves down and Cassie said, 'Oh, 'e didn't give you a chance to bash 'im.'

'Still, it saved 'im goin' 'ome with a flat 'ooter,' said Freddy. 'Come on, let's 'ave our ride.'

Once again Cassie perched herself astride the carrier, Freddy's soft cap cushioning her bottom, and away they went. It was Cassie's very first bike ride and she pictured herself being carried away on a white horse by King Arthur, the horse galloping and six wicked uncles chasing after them.

Around the back streets Freddy cycled, but could hardly believe his ears when Cassie, coming out of her dreams, suddenly said, 'I'm 'ungry'. They had just passed the shop in Rodney Road that sold boiled sheep's heads for sixpence, or half a one for fourpence.

'Well, if yer don't mind, Cassie, I ain't stoppin' to buy yer any sheep's 'ead.'

'Ugh, I don't want no sheep's 'ead,' said Cassie, 'I was just sayin' I'm 'ungry, that's all.'

'Could yer wait till next time I see yer?' said Freddy, turning into Charleston Street. 'Then if I got a bit of pocket money on me I'll buy yer a toffee-apple.'

'Oh, I like toffee-apples,' said Cassie, legs swinging, hands holding on to Freddy. At the end of Charleston Street, he let the bike bump gently up on to the pavement and rode along the path separating St John's Church from the vicarage. This time he could hardly believe his eyes. It was that big bloke again, the one with a flapping overcoat and hollow staring eyes. He was striding straight towards them.

Henry Brannigan hissed with rage. A bloody bicycle and two bloody kids riding on it. Those kids, the ones who'd been in his way before. Look at that girl, she had her legs stuck out, curse her. She was bad luck, if any kid was. But he refused to stop, he came barging on, keeping to the measured stride that ensured he trod on no lines.

Freddy wavered and veered. The man, glaring, brushed the bike as he bruised his way by. The machine fell over, and Cassie and Freddy toppled and sprawled.

'Oh, yer rotten great elephant!' yelled Freddy.

'Bloody bikes, bloody kids, ridin' on pavements, I'll 'ave the rozzers on the pair of yer,' said Henry Brannigan in a growling roar, and strode on.

'I bet me bruvver Will 'ud kick 'is teeth all the way down 'is throat,' said Freddy. 'You 'urt, Cassie?' He helped her up.

'I don't like 'im,' said Cassie, brushing herself down, 'I bet 'e's someone's wicked uncle, I bet 'e tramples people to death under 'is 'orses, I bet 'e rides six 'orses at once.'

'Yes, but are you all right?' asked Freddy.

'Yes, course I am, I just fell over, that's all. Me sister Annie fell over last week and 'urt 'er knee.'

'That was when me bruvver Will met 'er,' said Freddy, examining his bike for dents.

'Yes, 'e looked at 'er, an' that was what made 'er fall over, she said.'

'Don't be daft, Cassie, 'ow could anyone fall over just by bein' looked at?'

'Well, she could see 'e was a lion tamer,' said Cassie, 'that was what done it.'

''E ain't a lion tamer, 'e's a soldier,' said Freddy.

'Yes, ain't 'e 'andsome?' said Cassie. 'I expect 'e'll get a job one day servin' the King an' Queen with their Sunday teas. They always 'ave strawberry jam with their Sunday teas, did yer know that, Freddy?'

'I suppose I know it now,' grinned Freddy.

'Can we do more ridin'?' asked Cassie.

'D'you like me bike, then?'

'Not 'alf,' said Cassie, 'an' yer cap's ever such an 'elp.'

'All right, we'll do more ridin' till our suppers,' said Freddy. 'Lucky there ain't no dents in me bike.'

'Your cap's got all creased, lovey,' said Mrs Brown when Freddy returned home alive and unscratched.

Freddy, taking his cap off, gave it a critical look, then banged it about on his knee.

'Yes, well, it's been in Cassie's bloomers,' he said.

'It's what?' said Will.

'It's what?' yelled Susie.

'Oh, dear,' said Mrs Brown.

'That blessed boy, you can't believe 'im, can yer?' said Sally.

'Bein' 'is dad, I want to believe 'im, but I ain't sure I 'eard 'im right,' said Mr Brown.

'I dunno what yer all fallin' about for,' said Freddy.

134

'Cassie rode on me carrier an' used me cap for a cushion, and it ain't my fault girls 'ave got soft bums.'

Sally had a fit, Susie shrieked with laughter, Will grinned all over, Mr Brown rolled his eyes and Mrs Brown said, 'It's best to say bottoms, Freddy love, specially in company. Now let's all sit down and 'ave supper.'

'Wait a tick,' said Will, 'I'd like to know who stuffed your cap down Cassie's whatsits, Freddy. Was it you, or did Cassie manage it herself?'

'Oh, don't,' gasped Sally, 'I'll fall ill.'

''Ere, can you see me doin' a thing like that?' protested Freddy.

'Not without usin' my imagination,' said Susie.

'Cassie did it 'erself,' said Freddy.

'Well, I suppose some part of the fam'ly honour's been saved,' said Will.

'I'm still goin' to be ill,' said Sally.

'It's a corkin' bike, Susie,' said Freddy, 'I really like yer for it.'

'Me too for mine,' said Sally.

'Well, if we could all sit down now?' said Mrs Brown, and they all took their places at the table for rabbit stew, highly succulent and flavoursome.

Mr Brown had brought an evening paper in and was sitting on it. It contained the news that the dead girl had been strangled, that the scrap yard in which her body had been found used to be owned by Collier and Son of Bermondsey and was now the property of Adams Enterprises of Camberwell. The pathologist had given her age as twelve at the time of death. This had enabled the police to narrow the field in respect of missing persons, and the police were interviewing a Bermondsey family whose daughter had disappeared thirteen months ago. They were also making enquiries in other directions.

They were, in fact, giving beery Mr Collier and his equally beery son a hard time.

Susie asked her dad how he was getting on in Bermondsey.

'Well, we're 'eld up a bit on account of 'aving to sort a lot of things out before we can start doin' any business,' he said.

'You'll do it, Dad,' said Susie, 'you're a good old sorter-out. Sally, don't forget that on Saturday afternoon you're comin' with me to our Brixton shop for a fittin'. We're meetin' Sammy's nieces Rosie and Annabelle there.'

The fittings were for Susie's bridal gown and the bridesmaids' dresses.

'Oh, I wouldn't forget that, Susie,' said Sally. 'I could cycle there on me new bike, if yer like.'

'No, you couldn't, lovey,' said Mrs Brown, 'we can't have you cyclin' in all that traffic.'

'I don't mind takin' 'er, Mum,' said Freddy, 'she can ride on me carrier, like Cassie did.'

'With a decent cushion down her whatsits,' said Will.

Hysterics ran around the table, but stopped when they reached Mrs Brown, who said, 'No, Freddy love, you're not ridin' any bike to Brixton, either.'

'There's a murder been done down Bermondsey way,' said Mrs Queenie Watts, who lived with her husband in Brandon Street and had her brother, Henry Brannigan, as a lodger. She was reading her husband's evening paper.

'There'll be a nasty one done 'ere in a minute,' said Stan Watts from the scullery. He was regarding the sink. It was full of washing-up. 'There's two days' dirty dishes out 'ere.'

'Oh, I ain't been feelin' up to things recent,' said Mrs Watts, hairpins loose and a button looking as if it was about to desert her blouse. 'I think I'm gettin' an 'eart condition. 'Ave yer read about this pore young girl that's got done in?'

'I've read it all right,' said Mr Watts, 'and I'll be readin' tomorrer about you bein' done in yerself.'

'That ain't a very nice joke,' said Mrs Watts.

'It ain't a joke.'

'Nor's me 'eart condition, I can feel it gettin' chronic. Now come in 'ere, Stan, an' pour yerself a glass of beer. I'll 'ave one too, it'll cheer me up a bit. I don't like readin' about murders.'

'One thing,' said Mr Watts, 'you won't get the miseries readin' about your own, you won't be doin' no more readin'.'

'Strangled she was, pore girl,' said Mrs Watts.

'So will you be, Queenie, if I keep comin' 'ome to this kind of mess,' said Mr Watts.

'Only twelve she was, did yer read that?' said Mrs Watts.

'Well, you're nearly fifty, but that won't save yer,' said Mr Watts. Resignedly, he filled the kettle and put it on a gas ring, knowing he'd got to do the washing-up himself. If his wife was lazy, she was still good-natured and always managed to give him a decent supper. Hearing footsteps on the stairs, he said, ''Enry's on 'is way out, Queenie. 'E's always goin' out, that brother of yourn.' The front door opened and closed.

'Well, 'e don't do no 'arm,' said Mrs Watts, 'and I expect 'e can enjoy a bit of company in a pub.'

'Not 'im,' said Mr Watts, ''e don't need company.'

'Course 'e does, Stan, 'e's still a grievin' widower and 'e knows 'e can get cheered up in a pub.'

'Always found 'im a funny bloke meself,' said Mr Watts, 'and it didn't do 'im much good losin' 'is wife

Matilda like that. Ruddy 'orrible that was, fallin' out of a train. Poor old Matty.'

'Don't talk about it,' said Mrs Watts, and let a shudder squirm its way through her stout and indolent body.

Lines at night didn't count if they couldn't be seen. It was only when they showed up under the light of shop windows or street lamps that they offered their challenge. It was then that Henry Brannigan had to step carefully. He sometimes had horrible dreams, dreams in which he trod on a pavement line and then had bad luck rushing at him in the shape of howling red-eyed wolves. In the night-marish dreams he ran like a madman, the animals at his back, and every dream always finished with him running until he fell off the edge of the world into a black void. His plummeting fall jerked him awake and brought him out of his nightmare.

He went out frequently at night to escape the solitude of his room. He liked walking, he liked to use his long vigorous stride to eat up the pavements, knowing the lines that couldn't be seen didn't matter.

It was damned dark tonight, with no moon and the starry sky blanketed by heavy clouds. The patches of light at intervals caused him to watch for the visible lines. Approaching a pub that cast faint light, he knew a few lines would show up. A man appeared, coming towards him. Henry Brannigan judged they would meet in the faint light. Damnation. It was always a challenge to him not to falter or check, so he kept going, eyes searching for the lines he knew would be visible, even if only faintly. The approaching man had a stride as determined as his own. Curse him. Calamity loomed. Then the pub door opened and a woman in a large hat and a long coat came out. It caused the approaching man to change step and to leave the pavement. It got him out of Henry Brannigan's way at a moment when lines appeared and he needed to lengthen his stride. He was able to do so freely, and a sigh of relief escaped him.

''Ere, 'alf a mo', dearie.' The woman was at his back, and his feet were in darkness again. He stopped. He owed her a favour, although she didn't know it. He turned. The faint light reached out to make her face visible. She was handsome after a fashion, but she was tarted up with paint and powder.

'What d'you want?' he asked.

'Make me an offer, lovey.'

He realized what she was, but he still owed her a favour. It wasn't often that someone's action was helpful. Usually it was the other way about. He parted his unbuttoned coat, thrust a hand into his pocket and drew out a silver coin, half a crown.

'Here,' he said, and gave it to her. Her hand closed over it, and its weight and its feel told her its value. She had had a blank evening, and no-one had even bought her a drink. She liked a drink, just one. She knew that a lot of drink didn't help a woman's looks, and she needed her looks. At thirty-eight she had to take care of them.

'Kind of yer, lovey,' she said, smiling up into his dark face, 'but can yer make it five bob? I've got a nice flat and you can stay till midnight, if yer like.'

'I don't go with women,' said Henry Brannigan, who would already have gone on his way if he hadn't felt that fate required him to be friendly as well as grateful. 'Out of respect for me late wife.'

'Oh, yer poor man, but what did yer give me this 'alf-crown for, then?' asked Madge Simpson, who'd been on the game for five years and knew how to keep an eye open for the coppers.

Henry Brannigan wasn't going to explain. People were bleeding idiots. None of them understood. That coroner hadn't understood. What a man had to do, he had to do.

'You 'ard-up?' he said to the woman.

'Who ain't?' said Madge Simpson.

'Well, keep the 'alf-crown.'

'You don't want nothing for it, lovey?'

'Nothing.'

'Yer a gent,' said Madge. 'Mind, I ain't fond of takin' something for nothing, I ain't come down to plain beggin' yet. 'Ere, come 'ome with me, anyway, an' keep me company for a bit. I'll make us a pot of tea and a sandwich, it's one of them evenings when customers don't seem in the mood.'

'I'm pleased to 'ave met yer, lady,' said Henry Brannigan, 'but I don't go in for keepin' company. Good night to yer.' And he went on his way. He entered the Walworth Road, which was full of lighted shop windows and street lamps. The pavements were bathed in light. His feet knew the Walworth Road paving stones well, he adjusted his stride to them.

''Ere, be matey.'

The woman had caught him up and was walking beside him, taking quick steps to keep up with him.

''Oppit, lady,' said Henry Brannigan, the familiar scowl appearing on his face.

'Don't be like that, lovey,' she said, and did a little one-two with her feet.

'What made you do that?' he asked, keeping relentlessly to his measured stride.

'I don't like treadin' on the lines,' she said, 'it's bad luck.'

'What?' Henry Brannigan could hardly believe his ears.

'Last time I trod a bit careless on a line, a customer did

140

it on me. Pulled 'is trousers on quick an' went off without payin', the swine,' said Madge. 'Not all me customers are gents, I can tell yer. 'Ere, I live in Amelia Street, it's just across the road. You can come an' spend 'alf an hour with me, can't yer? I can do with a bit of company – 'elp, I nearly 'it that crack. Cracks count as lines to me. Don't think I'm barmy, I ain't, I'm just superstitious. I don't walk under ladders, neither.' She stopped. 'Come on, share a pot of tea with me, I like yer, and I won't pester yer or ask to see yer wallet.'

'I'll do that, lady, I'll share a pot of tea with yer,' said Henry Brannigan, hiding the excitement of discovery. This woman felt the same way as he did about lines? 'Yes, I'll come with yer.'

'That's more like it,' said Madge, a good-natured woman, even if she was a fallen one. A fancy large-brimmed hat crowned her head, and her waisted coat owned a glossy collar of fox fur. She'd bought both items for a song down Petticoat Lane, and they gave her quite a posh look. But she didn't charge posh prices, her going rate was five bob. 'Come on, then, but don't tread on the tramlines.' She laughed.

'Tramlines count,' he said as they stepped off the kerb.

'What?' she asked.

'I'm careful meself about treadin' on lines.'

'Well, I never, are yer really?' said Madge. They crossed the road and she laughed again as they both took care not to tread on the tramlines. They reached the pavement. The road was darker on this side.

'We can walk easy now,' he said. 'Lines don't count, of course, if you can't see 'em.'

'That's right,' said Madge, entering Amelia Street with him. 'My, fancy you bein' superstitious as well, lovey. Ain't it a funny old world? Me lodgings ain't far down 'ere, except they're on the other side. Come on.' She took him across the street and to the house in which she lodged. She fished her key out of her handbag, slipped it into the lock and opened the door. A glowing gas mantle illuminated the passage. Lace curtains framed the approach to the stairs. 'This way,' she said, 'me dear old landlady don't mind me bringing gents 'ome. She 'ad gentlemen friends 'erself when she was a chorus girl up West.' Henry Brannigan closed the door and followed her up the stairs to the back room, where a slow-burning coal fire offered a warm cosiness. She took a box of matches from the mantelpiece, struck a match and applied the flame to a gas mantle. The onset of light drove away black shadows, and the room took on an inviting look. A rug of brown wool covered the linoleum in front of the hearth fender. Two leather-upholstered armchairs seemed slightly at odds with a kitchen dresser, but only in a friendly way. 'This is me livin' room,' said Madge. 'Me bedroom's on the landing, but we won't be usin' that, will we?'

'I ain't felt the need since me wife died,' said Henry Brannigan.

'All right, lovey, I ain't goin' to push yer. Take yer coat off, and yer titfer, and I'll put the kettle on.'

He took his hat and coat off and hung them on the door peg. She looked at him. His features were gaunt, his eyes dark and hollow, but he had the kind of strong-boned face that would have been handsome if there'd been more flesh to it. His black hair was well-brushed, his working clothes coarse and hard-wearing.

'Givin' me the once-over, are yer?' he said.

'Well, I like to see what I bring into me livin' room, ducky,' said Madge, and filled a tin kettle with water from a pitcher. She put the kettle on a gas ring. 'In me bedroom, well, I just shut me eyes. A gel can't be too choosy when it's what you might call a matter of business. Come on, sit down.'

But Henry Brannigan remained on his feet, placing himself with his back to the fire and eyeing her in undisguised curiosity. Madge removed her hat and coat, and his dark eyes flickered, for she wore a white high-necked lace blouse with a lace front and a red flared skirt saucily short. It was knee-length, and the frilled hem of a white petticoat peeped and flirted above legs in lace-up boots and black stockings. Her hair was auburn, her mouth generously touched with lipstick and her face heavily powdered. She was a good five feet eight and still handsome. She'd been kept by a man for ten years, from the age of twenty-three. She'd have preferred marriage, but he had a wife. When she was thirty-three, he stopped visiting her. He had always visited twice a week, on Tuesday and Friday afternoons. When he failed to appear, she waited for an explanatory letter. It never came, and she had no idea where he lived. He had always kept that from her. She thought he must be either ill or dead, but was unable to find out. She felt bitter about it. With his disappearance, her allowance stopped. She thought about getting a job, but it was 1921, and any job was hard to come by. She took herself up West one evening and met a young RAF pilot. She was willing, he was eager. He took her to a small hotel in Kensington and she slept with him. When she woke up in the morning, he'd gone, leaving her three pounds on the bedside table. Truthfully, she hadn't thought about money. She simply owned a very healthy body and it was a bit starved. She put the three pounds in her purse and left the hotel, the manager giving her a funny look on her way out. Blow you, she thought.

She started looking for a job, a decent one. She didn't fancy factory work, not a bit, and not after ten years of being kept in comfortable style. She tried her luck in some West End clubs, thinking a job as a dining-room waitress might suit her. That proved unsuccessful. She had no family. She was the only child of a Bermondsey docker and his better half, and they were dead. But she met a very nice gent by one of the clubs, and he gave her a whole five quid for spending the night with him. It enabled her to set herself up in cheap lodgings. And that was the start of her real fall from grace. She'd come down in the world since then, a long way down, and had finished up here while plying for trade in Walworth pubs. She had to keep her eye open for the rozzers. She hadn't ever been run in. A girl got her name in the papers when that happened.

'You're on the game, of course,' said Henry Brannigan.

'Well, how'd yer guess, lovey?' she smiled. She quite liked him. She felt he was a bit withdrawn, but he looked a girl in the eye and spoke frankly. Well, everyone on the game was always a girl. 'Like me workin' outfit, do yer?'

'Suits yer,' he said, 'you've got fine legs. Bit too much powder, though.'

'Eh?' said Madge.

'Tone it down, you don't want to look as if you fell in a flour bag. A bit less powder and not so much paint, an' yer'll look more like a lady than a pro. Men fancy ladies.'

'Saucy devil,' said Madge, but laughed. 'Like a sandwich, would yer?'

'A biscuit would do for me.'

'Sure?'

'Biscuit and a cup of tea, I don't need more.'

'Suits me too,' said Madge, and he watched her as she brought out a tin of biscuits from the dresser cupboard and prepared to make the tea. She chatted while she waited for the kettle to boil. He made responsive

144

comments. He was absorbed, even fascinated. What a find, a woman who shared his feeling that to tread on lines was bad luck. Kids played at it on their way home from school, giving yells if they failed, and pushing at each other to try to bring about failure. But it was a serious business when you were an adult, and sod kids who got in your way. He couldn't remember the last time he'd consorted with a woman apart from his wife. And his wife had gone now.

Madge made the tea, let it stand for a minute or so, then filled two cups with the steaming golden liquid. God's gift a cup of hot tea was, and nor was it unpleasing to have a man keeping her company, a man who wasn't here to go to bed with her. She got him to sit down in front of the fire, and she sat down herself, in the other armchair, each of them with a cup of tea and a biscuit. He was a strong-looking figure even seated. She was a woman who had an affinity with men, and so she sat, of course, with her legs and knees unveiled and the lacy hem of her white petticoat showing.

''Ow long you been watchin' lines?' he asked.

'Five years,' she said, 'ever since a bloke either died on me or walked out on me. Something got to me, something about bad luck an' good luck, and I'm superstitious up to the top of me corsets now.'

'Lines, I reckon, are put in yer way to test yer will power,' said Henry Brannigan, crunching biscuit with strong teeth. 'I ain't sayin' it applies to everyone, just to some of us. You're kind of kindred, lady.'

'Kind of tarty, yer mean,' said Madge.

'Not to me,' he said, 'except for yer paint an' powder, but that can easy be washed off. It ain't tarty to ask me up 'ere to share a pot of tea with yer, and to sit me in front of yer fire. That's human kindness.'

145

'What's yer name?' asked Madge.

He wasn't keen on offering his name to all and sundry, not since the inquest, when the newspapers had shouted it out.

''Ave I asked you for your name, lady?'

'No, but I'd like to know yours, seein' you just said something very nice to me,' said Madge.

'I'm Henry.'

'Just Henry?' Madge smiled. 'All right, good enough, Henry. And I'm Madge. I'll be thinkin' of you when I'm next walkin' the pavement an' dodgin' the lines.'

'That's it, you watch them lines.'

'Mind, I only do it sometimes. You can't be doin' it all the time, only when the mood takes yer.'

'You should do it all the time. Once you start, you're on the wheel of fortune, take it from me.'

'Oh, it don't count if you ain't botherin',' said Madge, and Henry Brannigan shook his head dubiously. 'More tea? Let's give you a refill.' She took his cup and saucer, got up and took the cosy off the teapot. She refilled his cup and her own. He thanked her in a sober way, looking at her in her white blouse and short saucy skirt. She sat down again, and he eyed her legs quite openly. She didn't mind. She liked a man to be frankly appreciative.

'What got you on the game?' he asked.

'Me legs?' she said jokingly.

'I shouldn't think so,' he said.

'Well, I'll tell yer, Henry, seein' yer keepin' me friendly company,' she said, and told him how she had been a comfortably kept woman for ten years before her lover just disappeared from her life. She recounted what happened after that. 'Well, I didn't fancy slavin' in a fact'ry. It spoils yer for fact'ry work, bein' kept by a gen'rous bloke who's fond of yer as well. Mind, I sometimes wish it 'adn't

146

spoiled me that much, I might 'ave got used to a job and ended up a respectable workin' woman, or even got married.'

Henry Brannigan thought for a moment, then said, 'I'll keep you.'

'What?' said Madge.

'A woman like you, and kind of kindred,' he said, 'you shouldn't be on the game. I'll make you an allowance. I've got savings, and the insurance money paid to me on the death of me wife, and I've also got me wages of two pound ten a week.'

'What?' said Madge again, staring at him. 'Listen, Henry, you've only just met me, and I ain't takin' that proposition as serious.'

'I'm offerin' serious,' he said. 'It'll keep you out of pubs, it'll keep you off the game, which'll turn you into an old 'aybag sooner than yer think if you don't give it up. You look an 'andsome woman to me. That day you picked up a West End gent and 'e paid yer for services rendered, I'd say that was a day when you trod on a line after startin' the fateful business of avoidin' them. That time with the clubman put you on the game, an' that was bad luck, I tell yer. It's bad luck for any woman the day she goes on the game. Now you get yerself a flat, say at twelve bob a week.'

'Twelve bob would get any woman an 'andsome flat,' said Madge, wondering if he really was serious.

'Well, like I said, Madge, you're 'andsome yerself,' said Henry Brannigan. 'I'll take care of the rent an' the cost of keepin' yerself in decent comfort.'

'As yer mistress?' said Madge.

'I ain't askin' for that, but I'll come to keep yer company frequent.'

'But you'll want yer pleasure, won't yer?'

'Just yer company,' he said, 'I'm short of company that suits me.'

''Old on, ducky,' said Madge, 'there's a ruddy catch somewhere. You'll keep me and only ask for me company now and again? Don't yer fancy me, then?'

'I ain't partial to usin' a woman like that,' he said, 'I'm more partial to sharin' 'er fireside, or doin' a bit of walkin' with 'er when the summer evenings come. We can beat the lines together.'

'Sounds nice,' said Madge, 'but not much of a bargain for you.'

'You look for a flat tomorrer,' he said, 'and I'll meet yer outside the town 'all at eight in the evenin'. Are yer willin'?'

'Henry, you're cheatin' yerself,' she said.

'Are yer willin'?'

'More like dreamin',' said Madge. 'No, of course I'm willin', but it's goin' to cost yer, Henry, for just me company. Rent an' keep cost more than a bag of 'ot chestnuts.'

'Just one thing,' he said. 'No more customers. You got that, lady?'

'That was included when I said I was willin'. I don't go in for cheatin' a man.'

'It don't pay a woman, cheatin',' said Henry Brannigan, and the ghost of a smile came and went.

CHAPTER ELEVEN

Sammy, who had left for Manchester on Monday evening without returning to the office, was back on Wednesday afternoon. In Manchester he'd been talking to mill owners. His new contract with Coates meant he couldn't take the slightest risk in respect of fabric deliveries.

Susie, hearing him enter his office, immediately went to see him.

'Ah, good afternoon, Miss Brown,' he said, hanging up his hat and coat.

'Ah to you too,' said Susie, and walked up to him, lifted her face and pursed her lips.

'Not in office time, Miss Brown,' said Sammy.

A kick arrived on his left shin.

'Take that,' said Susie. There had been other times in her prolonged and electric relationship with Sammy when she'd had to deliver kicks.

'You did that with your eyes shut,' said Sammy, and kissed her.

'That's better,' said Susie.

'Not bad at all,' said Sammy, 'but I think we'll have to stop meetin' like this in office hours.' But another kiss arrived, a lovely one to Susie. He had a man's fine firm lips, and didn't believe in pecking a girl.

'Now you're takin' advantage,' she said.

'Well, Susie, while I'm not purportin'—'

'While you're not what?'

'While I'm not purportin' to imply the Manchester girls don't have fashionable legs and female bosoms, the fact is

149

what you've got, Susie, is high-class and adorable all over. Mind, I haven't been all over yet—'

'Sammy!'

'So I'm speakin' blindly, you might say, but not without bein' confident and optimistic. Accordingly, when we keep meetin' like this I can't help takin' advantage – hold on, is me declaration of confidence amusin' you, Miss Brown?'

Susie, laughing, said, 'Sammy, I love it. More, please.'

'Later, Miss Brown, later. Did you see Eli?'

'I did, and he's goin' to put his nose into every suitable warehouse. Sammy, exactly why do you want him to buy up our kind of materials?'

'Well,' said Sammy, 'Harriet—'

'Miss de Vere.'

'The selfsame, Susie. Our summer fashions are sellin' like hot faggots in her branches—'

'Cakes. Hot cakes.'

'Same thing, Susie, except hot faggots are tastier and more nourishing,' said Sammy. 'Now, on account of that, Miss de Vere, who is actually a widow name of Mrs Bird, persuaded her directors to give us a huge contract for autumn and winter designs.'

'I know that,' said Susie.

'Well, I'm glad you do, Susie, it does me heart good to know your brainbox is tickin', because we've got to make sure we don't fall flat on our faces when it comes to delivery. I acquired promises in Manchester regardin' delivery of fabrics, and before I went there I had a specialized talk with Harriet—'

'Miss de Vere,' said Susie. Before becoming engaged to Sammy, she'd felt somewhat threatened by his attachment to his old girlfriend, Rachel Goodman. So she'd discouraged the development of anything but a strictly business relationship between Sammy and Harriet de Vere. Harriet

150

had found Sammy mesmerizing. However, she had subsequently met Boots and found him fascinating. Even so,
Susie was taking no chances. The horrendous casualties of
the Great War had resulted in a shortage of eligible men
and a worrying surplus of women.

'The obligin' lady—'

'I don't like that word,' said Susie.

'Let's say she was reasonable, then,' said Sammy.
'She'll have the delivery date altered to give us two extra
weeks. All the same, promises from the mills don't always
work out, which is why we want Eli Greenberg to nose out
our kind of materials in certain London warehouses and to
buy them for us.'

'But if the Lancashire mills come up with deliveries in
good time,' said Susie, 'we'll be stuck with all the fabrics
Mr Greenberg buys on our behalf.'

'Ah well,' said Sammy.

'Mister Sammy Adams, kindly explain what ah well
means,' demanded Susie.

'Yes, you've got it, Susie.'

'I haven't got it,' said Susie.

'Well, it could mean some of our competitors will be
dyin' of wantin' what we happen to have,' said Sammy.

'Sammy, that's not fair.'

'Eh?' said Sammy.

'You'll have cornered the market,' said Susie. 'It's not
nice.'

'Pardon?' said Sammy.

'It's not decent,' said Susie.

'Am I hearin' you correct, Miss Brown, or is there
something wrong with me listenin' equipment?'

'If I thought I'd helped you starve our competitors, I
just couldn't look the vicar in the eye on our weddin' day,'
said Susie.

'I'm glad you've got principles, Susie,' said Sammy, 'I've got some meself. Would I let our Shoreditch competitors starve for want of fabrics?'

'I hope you've still got some Christian goodness,' said Susie. 'And I've just thought, they'd be getting all they wanted from the mills. Except, of course, some firms do order from the London wholesalers.'

'Well, if our competitors couldn't get what they wanted from the mills, I'd sell them what they wanted from our stocks,' said Sammy.

'There's a good boy,' said Susie.

'At a fair price, of course.'

'Sammy?'

'One of me strictest business principles, Susie, is never to let me charitable inclinations interfere with the profits.'

'You're wicked,' said Susie.

'Well, we've got to live, Susie.'

'Yes, ruination's very upsetting,' said Susie. 'By the way Boots wants to see you.'

'If he's been enquirin' after me, you can let him know I'm here,' said Sammy.

'I don't think it was an enquiry,' said Susie.

'Watch what you're goin' to say next.'

'Oh, he just said tell Junior to come and see me as soon as he gets back from Manchester – Sammy, don't you dare!'

Sammy was after her. Susie fled back to her office. Sammy, grinning, went to see Boots. On the way he looked in on Emily, busy typing in her own little office. Its privacy related to the fact that she was the wife of a director.

'Hello, Em. Everything all right with you?' Sammy thought she was getting much too thin.

Emily's smile was overbright, so were her big green eyes.

'Hello, Sammy love. I'm fine. I think me lord and master's been askin' after you.'

'It's my serious opinion that Boots has been the fam'ly's lord and master since he first put on long trousers,' said Sammy.

'It's his posh education,' said Emily.

'I'm now goin' to sort him out,' said Sammy, and departed for his brother's office, where he informed Boots he was against being given messages by his personal assistant that made him sound like the office boy.

'Is that a fact?' said Boots.

'I hear someone's been referrin' to me as Junior,' said Sammy.

'First I've heard of it,' said Boots, and Sammy cottoned on.

'That Susie,' he said, grinning again. 'Wait till she's Mrs Sammy Adams.'

'We're all waiting for that,' said Boots. 'How did you get on in Manchester?'

'Manchester was what you call promisin',' said Sammy, 'but I'm buyin' in from London wholesalers in case the promisin' bit gets rheumatism. Before I took me train to Manchester, I had to talk serious to Harriet about that delivery clause.'

'You mean you floored her,' said Boots.

'Well, she fell about a bit,' said Sammy, 'but the delivery date's goin' to be put back two weeks. Now can I ask what you wanted to see me about?'

'The Bermondsey scrap yard's been temporarily shut down, Sammy.'

'It's what?'

'That's just between you, me and Susie's dad at the

moment,' said Boots, and went on to recount how a young girl's body had been found in the gravel under the shed floor. He'd been keeping in touch with the police, and an hour ago they'd informed him over the phone that the girl's identity had been established. She was the daughter of a Bermondsey couple, officially listed as missing from home thirteen months ago. Her name was Ivy Connor and she'd been twelve years old at the time. The pathologist had diagnosed strangulation.

'Jesus,' breathed Sammy, 'a twelve-year-old girl? The sod who did that to her ought to be put in an empty room with her father for an hour before they hang him.'

'I feel the same,' said Boots. 'Her name and the pathologist's report will be in today's evening papers. So far, Susie doesn't know the body was discovered in our scrap yard, and Jim's said nothing to her or any of his family. Further, he's kept the relevant page of their daily paper to himself. He doesn't want Susie upset with the wedding not far away, and she won't necessarily find out it concerns our Bermondsey yard unless the papers mention the firm's name again. On the other hand, there'll be an inquest, of course, and I don't doubt Jim will be called on to confirm he was present when the body was discovered. He and his assistant are working at the Kennington yard at the moment. How much d'you know about the previous owners of the Bermondsey yard, Collier and Son?'

'Couple of boozers,' said Sammy.

'I think the police are investigating them.'

'Waste of time,' said Sammy. 'Old man Collier and his son Walter as boozers are harmless except to their business. Listen, I think Susie'll have to be told.'

'I thought you might think that,' said Boots, 'but left it to you to decide.'

'The staff don't know?' said Sammy.

154

'Some do, those who read the newspaper accounts,' said Boots, 'but they're keeping quiet.'

'I'll tell Susie,' said Sammy, and did so at once. It was a shock to her, but she was her dad's daughter, she had his brand of resilience and was concerned more for him than for any shadow it cast over the wedding. She was concerned because the yard had been shut down just when he'd been appointed manager and because he'd had to see the body.

'I feel sick, Sammy. That poor young girl.'

'I share your feeling, Susie, and don't think I don't.'

Susie spoke to her dad that evening. She'd bought an evening paper on her way home. The details were all there, all relating to the grisly conclusion that the girl had been murdered and her body hidden in gravel under a shed in a scrap metal yard in Bermondsey. Reported missing from her home thirteen months ago, her murder was now commanding a full investigation by the police. There was no mention of Adams Enterprises as the present owners of the yard, but the report did state that the owners at the time of the murder were Collier and Son. It also stated that two men were helping the police with their enquiries.

Susie agreed with her dad not to discuss the matter with the rest of the family.

'You've come, then,' said Henry Brannigan in the evening twilight. The woman had got to the town hall before him.

'You didn't think I'd play you up, did yer, Henry?' asked Madge.

He looked at her. Her face was only lightly powdered, her lips not quite so richly carmine. She was wearing a smaller hat and a less fancy coat. She looked very respectable, in fact. She had a little smile on her face.

'Did yer tread on any lines gettin' 'ere?' he asked.

'Not one,' said Madge, 'I wasn't goin' to risk a bit of bad luck poppin' up and knockin' me off me feet. It can injure a girl. I must say you're lookin' a gent this evenin', Henry.'

He wore no coat. He was dressed in a serviceable blue suit that fitted him well, with a collar and tie and a trilby hat. His eyes looked deepset in his gaunt face. He was middle-aged, but his body was straight and without a paunch. She was willing to bet he was as strong as a horse, and that he was good in bed.

'You're lookin' presentable yerself,' he said, 'but don't think I didn't like what you wore last night, except for yer paint an' powder.'

'Oh, yer fancied me saucy skirt, lovey?' said Madge, smiling. 'You should've said, I'd 'ave worn it again tonight.'

'Good company you were,' said Henry Brannigan. ''Ave yer found a flat?'

'I found a really nice one in the New Kent Road, above that little paper shop,' said Madge. 'It's got its own door an' stairs at the side of the shop, and it's two nice rooms and a kitchen, it's all self-contained at ten an' six a week. You'll be able to visit when yer like, with yer own door key. I'll cook supper for yer sometimes, if you fancy that. D'yer want to come an' see it? Only I said I'd take it, it's fully-furnished and I gave the newsagent five bob as a deposit on the first week's rent. I couldn't afford to give 'im the lot in case you – well, you know.'

'In case I didn't turn up.'

'Well, a girl can't trust every man she meets, even if she does like 'im,' said Madge.

'We'll go an' see it,' said Henry Brannigan. 'I know that shop, we'll cut through Wansey Street. Watch the lines, it ain't dark yet, an' seein' we're after settin' you up in the flat, let's keep bad luck away from its door or we'll risk it catchin' fire the day you move in.'

'Yer a thoughtful man about me superstitiousness, Henry,' she said, and they began their walk, partners in their belief that it was unlucky to tread on lines, although Madge only practised this belief when the mood took her. They went down Wansey Street and made for Balfour Street, which would bring them into the New Kent Road. Dusk fell and the lines between paving stones began to be lost to the eye. Treading on them didn't count then. They passed the sagging gates of the destroyed factory. Madge made a comment. 'They ought to build a new one,' she said, 'an' give the people round 'ere a bit of work. I did 'ear a new one might be goin' up.'

'You 'eard that, did yer?' Henry Brannigan gave it some thought. 'Well, you ladies usually manage to 'ear more than men do.'

'Henry, you got a nice way of makin' a lady of me.'

'A woman like you, you've got the makings of bein' a lady, that's me honest opinion. I 'eard meself that this place is a kids' playground, which keeps 'em off the streets an' gettin' in people's way. Watch that lighted bit of pavement comin' up, the lines'll be showin'.'

Madge did a little one-two step at the right moment, and Henry Brannigan couldn't help being highly approving of her.

He liked the flat. It was very nicely furnished, the bedroom neat, the living room cosy and the kitchen just right. It had new wallpaper and an almost new gas oven.

'Yer really like it?' said Madge.

'Be a pleasure for me to keep yer comfortably resident 'ere, Madge. I'll give yer thirty bob a week to pay for yer rent and yer livin' expenses.'

'Thirty bob?'

'It'll keep yer respectable, an' now and again I might treat yer to some new togs. That fair, is it?'

'It's all that to me,' said Madge, 'but I still can't see what you get out of it.'

'I like yer, I like yer company, and I like bein' able to talk to yer,' he said. 'I'll pay you the allowance monthly. Here.' He took out his wallet and extracted six pound notes. Madge reckoned he had twenty of them in the wallet. It didn't give her ideas. If she'd become a tart, she'd never been a sly or calculating one. Henry represented the turn of the tide, a turn that was highly welcome to her at her age. 'That's yer first month's,' he said, and handed her the banknotes. 'I'll come an' see yer Tuesday an' Thursday evenings, and I'll take you out Saturday evenings an' Sunday afternoons. I know yer'll play fair with me.'

'You sure you know?' said Madge.

'I'm bettin' on yer.'

'I'm short of flour and bakin' powder,' said Mrs Brown the next morning. Her husband and Susie had gone to work, and Sally and Freddy to school, but Will was still around and thinking of going to the public library to borrow a couple of books. 'And I need some bakin' eggs as well.'

'What's bakin' eggs?' asked Will.

'Cracked ones that come half price. I'll have to go out, I can't start me bakin' till I do.'

'Well, I'm goin' to the library, Mum,' said Will, 'I'll get the stuff you want.'

'Oh, would you?' Mrs Brown spoke fondly. 'I'm a bit busy, love, I'd be grateful. I'd like two pounds of self-raisin' flour, a tin of bakin' powder, four cracked eggs that's not too cracked, and two pounds of caster sugar.'

'Right,' said Will, a little grin on his face as he decided which shop he'd patronize. 'Special reference to four cracked eggs not too cracked, eh, Ma?'

'If you would, love,' said Mrs Brown. 'You can take me shoppin' bag.'

'D'you mind if I don't?' said Will. 'I'm a bloke, not a mum.'

'Oh, you don't want to take no notice of what people might say,' said the affable Mrs Brown, 'and you'll have to carry the shoppin' in something.'

'I'll work it out,' said Will, who was keeping active but without putting himself under stress. He'd had a couple of mild evening attacks, that was all.

There were customers in the shop, and Mr Urcott, Miss Banks and Annie were all busy. Will, entering, hid himself behind a large lady whose voluminous apparel doubled her size. Her hat was a further help. Not until Annie finished serving her did Will become visible. It was like a Houdini trick to Annie. One moment there was only a large lady at the counter, the next moment Will materialized. With a grin on his face, of course. Still, he had a nice face, a sort of country face because it looked brown and healthy. A girl could put up with a grin on that kind of face. But he's going to sauce me, she thought, and prepared herself for verbal battle.

'Can I help you, sir?' she asked.

'Any cauliflowers, miss?' enquired Will.

'No, nor any coal, either, nor any soldiers' sauce, except yours.'

'What a funny shop,' said Will. 'Never mind, I'll try for two pounds of self-raisin' flour, two pounds of caster sugar, a tin of bakin' powder and four cracked eggs not too cracked.'

'I hope you're serious,' said Annie, bobbed hair smooth, neat and shining, grey eyes daring him to be joking.

'Mrs Brown is,' said Will.

'Mrs Brown?'

'My mother. She wants to do some bakin'. Go to a good grocer's, she said, where they serve you with a smile and don't give you any lip.'

'Any lip? You can talk,' said Annie. 'Are you really shoppin' for your mum?'

'It's me pleasure,' said Will.

'Nice you've got some good points, like bringing a girl flowers and doin' your mum's shoppin',' said Annie, and served him. The flour, sugar and baking powder were placed on the counter, and then she found four very acceptable cracked eggs for him. Brightly she asked, 'Have you brought your shoppin' bag, sir?'

A female customer spoke up. Like most cockney women, she wasn't given to reticence.

'Oh, is yer wife laid up, young man? If I was laid up, I don't know that my old man would let 'imself be seen with a shoppin' bag. I admire yer for not mindin'.'

'You don't seem to have it with you, sir,' said Annie, tongue in cheek.

'No, I left it on a tram with me handbag,' said Will. Customers laughed. 'Use this, miss.' He brought a folded brown paper carrier bag out of his pocket, the one he had bought previously from Annie. 'I'll give you shoppin' bag,' he murmured.

Annie placed his purchases in the carrier. The eggs, which she'd put into a brown paper bag, she rested carefully on top.

'There you are, sir, thank you for your custom – oh, and

you can get a nice strong straw shoppin' bag for sixpence down the market.'

'You can get carpet beaters too,' said Will.

'What for?' smiled Annie.

'Smackin' saucy bottoms,' murmured Will, and departed, leaving Annie not quite sure who'd won the battle. Still, it had been nice seeing him. She hoped he hadn't forgotten about Sunday, only he hadn't mentioned it.

'Mum, 'ave yer got a cushion I could borrer?' asked Freddy a few minutes after he arrived home from school.

'What d'you want a cushion for, lovey?'

'For Cassie.'

'Cassie?'

'Yes, that girl who's me new mate,' said Freddy. 'I'm takin' 'er for a ride on me bike again. She's outside.'

'Well, bring 'er in,' said Mrs Brown, 'you don't have to keep your friends on the doorstep.'

'Yes, go on, bring 'er in,' said Sally, 'me and mum would like to see where you put the cushion.'

'Bless us,' said Mrs Brown, 'don't you go puttin' no cushion where you shouldn't, Freddy, not like you did with your cap.'

'I didn't do it, Cassie did,' said Freddy, and went to the kitchen door. 'Cassie, come in,' he called, and Cassie entered the passage and came through to the kitchen.

'Oh, 'ello,' she said.

'You've got a sister called Annie,' said Sally.

'Yes, our Will's friendly with her,' smiled Mrs Brown.

'Are you Freddy's mum?' asked Cassie.

'Yes, I have that pleasure,' said Mrs Brown.

'We don't 'ave a mum,' said Cassie, 'she died. But we've got a nice dad that builds railway engines. 'E saved a lady from being eaten by lions once.'

'My, did he do that?' said Mrs Brown.

'Yes, it was when 'e was in darkest Africa,' said Cassie. ''E was a famous explorer, 'e was explorin' a jungle and 'e saw this lady. She was all tattered an' torn. Well, 'er clothes were. 'Er ball gown was nearly ruined by the lions' claws. They were runnin' after 'er.'

'Why was she wearin' a ball gown in a jungle?' asked Sally.

'She was goin' to a ball with an African prince,' said Cassie, 'only the lions ate 'im.'

Sally rolled her eyes. Mrs Brown smiled.

'My goodness, Cassie,' she said, 'why did they want to eat the lady as well?'

'Dad didn't say.' Cassie did a bit of thinking. 'Oh, yes, I remember now, it was for afters. Lions like afters.'

''Ere, Cassie,' said Freddy, who'd heard a lot like this before, 'd'yer want a slice of cake?'

'Yes, please, I'm not 'aving none at 'ome,' said Cassie, 'I told Annie I was 'aving a ride on your bike.'

'Here we are, love,' said Mrs Brown and cut slices for all three of them.

'Cassie, you 'aven't told us how your dad actu'lly saved the lady,' said Sally.

'Don't worry,' said Freddy, 'she won't forget to tell yer.'

'Yes, me dad got down from the elephant 'e was ridin',' said Cassie, eating cake, 'and 'e swept the lady up into 'is arms. Her hat fell off, but she didn't mind.'

'Fancy wearin' an 'at with a ball gown,' said Sally.

'Well, it was rainin' a bit,' said Cassie, rarely at a loss. 'Me dad said you should 'ave 'eard the lions, they didn't 'alf roar, 'e said.' Cassie ate more cake. ''E climbed up on his elephant with the lady an' they galloped off.'

'Crikey, you sure, Cassie?' queried Sally. 'I mean,

gallopin' elephants, I never 'eard of elephants gallopin' before.'

Cassie did some more thinking. She plucked at her fertile imagination.

'Well, it was galumpin' actu'lly,' she said. 'Elephants do a lot of galumpin' in darkest Africa. After me dad 'ad saved the lady, she wanted to marry 'im, but 'e was too busy at the time, so she gave 'im a lock of 'er golden 'air instead. And I think she sent 'im a Christmas card once, with robins on it.' She smiled at Freddy's mum. 'That was ever such nice cake, Mrs Brown. 'Ave yer got a cushion I could use for the bike ride, please?'

'Get one from the sofa, Freddy,' said Mrs Brown. 'Cassie, you mind you put it on the carrier, not anywhere else.'

'Yes, I can't put it in me things,' said Cassie, 'a cushion's too big. Our Aunt Eileen 'ad to kneel on a church cushion once, but it did 'er back in an' she 'ad to be lifted out of the pew by a fire engine. She was ever so blushin'. Well the 'Ouse of Lords was there, it was in St Paul's Cathedral.'

Sally had one of her hysterical fits. Mrs Brown just smiled placidly.

'Come on, Cassie,' said Freddy, wearing a huge grin, 'let's get the cushion.'

He and Cassie were outside a minute later with the bike. Sally brought hers out too. Cassie was placing the cushion on Freddy's carrier when Mr Ponsonby appeared.

'Well, dear me, dear me,' he said, 'what's all this on the pavement?'

'It's our feet, Mr Ponsonby,' said Sally.

'And our bikes,' said Freddy.

Mr Ponsonby peered and murmured.

'Good gracious, and a cushion too,' he said.

163

'Yes, it's for Cassie to ride on,' said Freddy. 'This is Cassie, she's me new mate.'

'Good afternoon,' said Mr Ponsonby, and raised his bowler hat.

''Ello,' said Cassie, 'you give me a peppermint once.'

'So I did, so I did. Did I?' Mr Ponsonby puzzled over it. 'What a charming girl. Ah, yes, and Sally too. You must all have a peppermint now. Dear me, what am I thinking of not to have offered them?' He produced the bag, and Sally, Cassie and Freddy took one each. 'Where is my camera? Bless me, two such pretty girls and I've forgotten my camera. Stay there and I shall bring it. Good afternoon, good afternoon.' Off he went, his pigeon-toed walk making him look as if he was twinkling over the pavement.

'Come on, 'e won't come back,' said Freddy. 'On yer get, Cassie, and I'll ride yer round the 'ouses. You can come, if yer like, Sally, I see you got yer wooden legs on.'

'Oh, she ain't got wooden ones really, 'as she?' said Cassie, sitting astride the cushion.

'Well, she used to 'ave ord'nary short ones,' said Freddy, 'so she went an' bought wooden ones down the market.'

'Golly, they look real,' said Cassie.

'You're both daft,' said Sally, and away she went on her bike. Freddy went whooping after her with his delighted passenger.

Henry Brannigan, on arrival home from work, put his head round the kitchen door. His sister was preparing supper for herself and her husband. Her crumpled blouse could have done with some ironing, and her hair could have done with some hairpins.

''Ere y'ar, Queenie.'

'What's this?' asked Queenie Watts.

'Box of choc'lates,' said her brother. 'I appreciate you fixin' me up with lodgings.'

Mrs Watts, taking the box out of its bag, gazed at it in bliss.

'Well, ain't you a love?' she said. 'And you ain't no trouble, 'Enry; I'm pleased to 'ave yer after all yer troubles. 'Ere, is that a new coat yer wearin'? It looks really nice on yer.'

'I reckoned it was time I 'ad a new one.'

'Listen, what d'yer go out a lot for of an evenin'?' asked Mrs Watts. 'You found yerself someone you like? Only you never come an' talk about yerself.'

'I 'appen to 'ave got over me troubles, Queenie.'

'That's good, 'Enry. Yer still a fine strong man, except yer don't always look as if yer put enough food into yerself, and yer don't go in for talkin' much. You could be welcome company for someone like a widder woman if yer talked a bit more.'

'It's been me troubles and me bad luck,' said Henry Brannigan, 'and all them street kids gettin' in a man's way.'

'Gettin' in yer way?'

'Specially some. Still, can't be 'elped.'

'Well, there's got to be kids, 'Enry.' Mrs Watts helped herself to a cream chocolate. 'It wouldn't be no life for anyone if there wasn't no kids. Mine are off me 'ands, of course, but I'm 'oping for some grandkids some day.'

'You could do with some 'airpins first, Queenie, if yer don't mind me sayin' so.'

'I don't know where all me 'airpins get to,' said Mrs Watts, and ate another chocolate.

'You could look a bit 'andsome if you took more time with yerself.'

'It's me back, yer know, 'Enry, it catches me something chronic, but the choc'lates'll cheer me up. Yer a good sort, an' don't you let street kids worry yer.'

'Young devils some of them arc,' said Henry Brannigan, and went up to his room.

CHAPTER TWELVE

The following afternoon, Sammy's mother entered his office. She was known to her family as Chinese Lady on account of her almond eyes and the fact that she had once taken in washing. She was in her fiftieth year, a slim woman of upright carriage and firm bosom. As she had once said to Boots, she didn't believe in letting anything become unfirm. Not that she'd been referring to her bosom. Never would she have mentioned it to any of her sons. She regarded bosoms as unmentionable, in fact. No, she'd been talking about women who let themselves go. Go where? asked Boots. Chinese Lady simply gave him a look. She'd been giving her eldest son those kind of looks ever since his schooldays, when he'd learned to use his tongue in a way she found highly suspicious.

She appeared in Sammy's office wearing a brown velvet toque hat and a beige-coloured raincoat. She looked sprightly. Boots was there as well as Sammy.

'Hello, who's this lady?' asked Sammy. 'Hold on, is that you, Ma?'

'I don't know how many times I've told you not to call me Ma,' said Chinese Lady. 'I don't mind any of us bein' poor, but I didn't bring any of you up to be common.'

'Who's poor?' asked Boots.

'You know what I mean,' said Chinese Lady, who always stuck to her guns however much her sons tried to confuse her. 'I don't want people tellin' me that Sammy's grown up common, specially now he's in business. Mind, it's not the sort of business I'd of expected of any of you, ladies' clothes and things I won't mention. I can't bring meself to even look in that shop window of yours downstairs. When I think of you, Boots, lettin' my youngest put things like that in the windows of all 'is shops, I wonder you sometimes don't feel uncomf'table.'

'I suppose I'm blasé about it,' said Boots.

'Don't you use them French words of yours to me,' said Chinese Lady, 'you know I don't hold with them, nor with them fast French females you learned them from durin' the war. Still, you come out of the war without gettin' your head blown off, so I won't go on at you about lettin' Sammy get a bit unrespectable in his business. I just hope he won't end up leadin' his whole fam'ly astray. Lizzy was only sayin' the other day that it's embarrassin' havin' all her brothers workin' in ladies' unmentionables.'

'I work in a suit myself,' said Boots.

'I do too,' said Sammy, 'you got my word for it, me old love.'

'Don't be familiar,' said Chinese Lady, 'you know what I mean. It's just not decent, designing things for female persons.' She was on her favourite hobby-horse, and Boots and Sammy knew it. 'I don't mind frocks and skirts and suchlike, but things, well, I can't hardly bear thinking about it.'

'I suppose I'm blasé about it myself,' repeated Boots. 'Well, I was taken into ladies' underwear by Emily at an early age. In Gamages.'

'I don't know how you can talk so disreputable,' said Chinese Lady, 'and usin' vulgar French words again as well.'

'You're a good old girl,' said Boots.

'And might I point out we don't design ladies' unmentionables ourselves?' said Sammy. 'We acquire them from manufacturers.'

'Kindly don't argue,' said Chinese Lady firmly, 'I don't like any of my children to be argufyin'.'

'Children? Who said that?' asked Sammy of the pile of work on his desk. He knew it was no good telling Chinese Lady he was up to his ears. 'Anyway, Ma, to what do we owe the pleasure of your visit and your omelette?'

'Omelette?' said Chinese Lady. 'What omelette?'

'I think he means homily,' said Boots.

'And what's that, might I ask? Another French word? If you must know why I'm here, I just happened to be passing.'

'Passing, yes, I see,' said Boots.

'Yes, I thought I'd better pop in and see what you're gettin' up to,' said Chinese Lady, who made a habit of that. She was, of course, proud of her sons' accomplishments, but was never going to encourage them to get above themselves. She was always saying to her daughter Lizzy that they were good boys really, except that Sammy didn't go to church as often as he ought to. Lizzy was of the opinion that Sammy was a live wire who'd only go to church regularly if he could sell the vicar a new organ, that Boots was a danger to well-behaved housewives and Tommy as honest as the day was long.

'Well, we won't keep you, Ma,' said Sammy, who'd been talking to Boots about the murder investigation. It seemed from today's papers that old man Collier and his son had been cleared.

'Also,' said Chinese Lady, 'I happen to be meetin' Rosie here from her school. I'm buyin' her a special little something for always helpin' me to wind me knittin' wool. Where's Susie?'

'I think she's workin',' said Sammy, 'it's what she's here for.'

That went over Chinese Lady's head.

'Perhaps I'll have a cup of tea with her in her office while I'm waitin',' she said.

'What's she sayin' now, Boots?' asked Sammy helplessly.

'She wants you to put the office kettle on,' said Boots, as Chinese Lady advanced on Susie's office door. At the door she turned, frowning.

'I've just remembered,' she said, 'I've been readin' about a murder done in a Bermondsey scrap metal yard. Boots, I hope it wasn't an Adams yard.'

'Well, old lady,' said Boots at his most reassuring, 'you can take it from me that we didn't own any yard in Bermondsey until a couple of weeks ago.'

'I don't know I hold with you and Sammy bein' in the scrap metal business at all,' she said soberly. 'There's a lot of shifty people in that sort of trade. It's no wonder there's been a murder.'

'Now don't give our yards a bad name, Ma,' said Sammy, 'we don't go in for anything shifty.'

'I should hope not,' said Chinese Lady. 'That poor girl,' she said, shaking her head. 'Still, I won't keep on at you about your business, I don't believe in bein' interferin', and I'm sure you both do your best. There's some mothers that have got worse sons, a lot worse. You're good boys most of the time. Well, I'll see Susie now.' She knocked.

'Come in,' called Susie, and Chinese Lady entered. Boots and Sammy heard Susie exclaim. 'Oh, what a nice surprise, Mrs Finch.' Finch was the name of Chinese Lady's second husband, presently abroad on Government business.

Sammy grinned. Boots smiled. Chinese Lady would get her cup of tea. Susie thought the world of her future mother-in-law.

'What a character,' said Sammy.

'Yes, not too many like her,' said Boots, 'she keeps putting us in ladies' unmentionables.'

Twenty minutes later an open sports car pulled up outside the shop. In it were Rosie, Boots's adopted daughter, and Rosie's favourite teacher, Miss Polly Simms. Rosie, nearly eleven, was fair-haired, blue-eyed and enchantingly vivacious. Polly, an ex-ambulance driver of the Great War, was twenty-nine, her rich chestnut hair styled in a Colleen Moore bob, her vivid good looks accentuated by her large and expressive grey eyes. Her sense of humour was irrepressible, although there was often a brittle note to it, a legacy of her years among the men of France and Flanders. She regarded all surviving Tommies as old comrades. Her special regard for Boots, a survivor himself, was of an incurable kind, and it caused her a great deal of heart-burning.

'I expect Daddy's got his nose to the grindstone,' said Rosie. She never thought about Boots as her adoptive father, simply as her one and only daddy. No-one, except perhaps Polly, quite knew just how much Rosie loved him.

'Frightful, if he finishes up with no nose,' said Polly.

'Oh, he'd just say that that would save him having to blow it when he got a cold,' said Rosie, and a little giggle arrived.

'Yes, he would say that, wouldn't he?' smiled Polly, a cloche hat cuddling her head.

'Nana says he's airy-fairy.'

'Is airy-fairy good or bad?' asked Polly.

'Well,' said Rosie, 'Nana's always saying it wouldn't have happened if she'd boxed his ears more often when he was younger.'

'Yes, I've heard her talking to him,' said Polly. She

spent most Tuesday and Thursday evenings at the house which Boots and his family shared with his mother and stepfather. She was coaching and cramming Rosie for a scholarship exam next January.

'I'd better go up and meet Nana now,' said Rosie. 'I'll say hello to Daddy first.'

'Yes, do him a favour, lift his nose off the grindstone for a few minutes,' said Polly.

'Whose nose?' asked Boots, and they looked up. There he was standing beside the car, a smile lurking.

'Oh, hello, Daddy, where did you spring from?' asked Rosie.

'I saw the pair of you from my window,' said Boots.

'You actually left your grindstone to come down and say hello?' asked Polly.

'What a blessing,' said Rosie. 'We don't want you to wear your nose away, Daddy.'

'Well, if I do I'll have a wooden one fixed,' said Boots, 'and the grindstone can have a go at that.'

Rosie laughed.

'We thought you'd say something like that, didn't we, Miss Simms?' said Rosie. 'Is Nana up there, Daddy?'

'Yes, she's waiting for you in Susie's office,' said Boots, and Rosie scrambled out of the car, said goodbye to Polly and ran into the shop. 'Thanks for giving her a lift, Polly.'

'My pleasure,' said Polly, 'the girl's adorable. So am I.' She looked up at him from the car. She couldn't help herself, she loved everything about him, his looks, his masculinity, his whimsical self and his lazy, almost blind left eye, which she always wanted to kiss. 'Well, say something.'

'Yes, all right, you're adorable, Polly. Can't stop, though, must get back to my desk.'

'Stinker. Look, couldn't we dash off to Paris together for a little while? Say for a year?'

'Sounds exciting,' said Boots, 'and French.'

'Do you mean I excite you?' asked Polly.

'Frequently,' said Boots.

'Well, then?'

'Well what?'

'You can manage a little adultery, can't you?' said Polly. A tram clanged by. People went by. The driver of a horse and cart whistled at Polly. She was oblivious of all the hustle and bustle of Camberwell Green, and didn't even hear the whistle.

'Polly, do you want to wreck my marriage?' asked Boots.

'Yes.'

'You don't mean that,' said Boots, who had had this kind of conversation with her before.

'Oh, come on, old love,' said Polly, 'meet me somewhere at midnight. Is it fair, is it even decent, for Emily to have all of you all the time?'

'I'll have to pass on that one,' said Boots.

'I hope you've heard that hell hath no fury,' said Polly. 'I've lived like a virgin ever since I met you, and I'm getting fed-up waiting for you to take me to bed. I'm going to sleep with the next man I meet, even if he's hairy all over.'

'Don't do that, Polly.'

'Bloody hell,' breathed Polly, 'why shouldn't I?'

'I'll break your leg if you do,' said Boots.

'You'll what?' Polly stared at him. He actually looked as if he meant it.

'Sorry, my mistake,' said Boots, 'it's none of my business. See you at the house this evening.' He went back to his office through the shop, leaving Polly almost giddy.

Suffering pangs of love, she thought, he cares, he actually cares.

Chinese Lady's special little gift to Rosie was a silver locket. She had already paid the Camberwell jeweller a deposit on it. She paid the balance and it became Rosie's. She could place heart-shaped cut-outs from family snap-shots inside it, one of Emily and one of Boots. Rosie was rapturous. She did the cut-outs as soon as she got home, and fitted them into the locket. One was a head and shoulders of Boots, the other of Emily and herself, their heads close together. Then, when she closed the locket, she and Emily were both kissing her daddy. Rosie felt blissful about that.

Henry Brannigan spent the evening with Madge in her new flat. He arrived with a bunch of flowers for her, which touched her considerably. But she still felt con-fused and uncertain, she still felt there must be a catch in the arrangement. She knew men well, of course. There weren't many who would give on a generous scale to a woman and ask for nothing in return. Henry had said company was enough for him. He didn't seem to quite realize exactly what he was doing for her. First and foremost he was relieving her of the wretched necessity of going out at night to pick up men in pubs. For three nights now she hadn't had to do that. The pleasure of keeping her body to herself surprised her.

She asked him where he lived. He told her.

'You've just got one room in yer sister's place?' she said. She had the fire alight and they were sitting in front of it. She wore the short skirt and teasing petticoat he had said he liked. 'Henry, that's daft, you livin' in one room

174

when you could easy afford a flat. Does yer sister cook for you of an evenin'?'

'No, I always eat a good meal midday,' he said.

'But you 'ave to 'ave something of an evenin',' said Madge.

'Well, I frequently pick up fried fish when I'm out walkin'.'

'You shouldn't 'ave to do that,' said Madge. 'I'll do a light supper for both of us every evenin'.'

'I wouldn't want to ask that of yer,' said Henry Brannigan.

'You 'aven't asked,' said Madge, 'I've offered. You come 'ere at seven every evenin' and we'll eat supper together. You like company, you said—'

'I like your company.'

'Well, I like company meself.'

'You're a good woman,' he said.

'I was once, I ain't able to call meself that now.'

'Perhaps you ain't been all that respectable, but that don't mean you're not a good woman.'

'Well, it's downright kind of you to say so, Henry.' Madge eyed his gaunt look. ''Ave you been sufferin' on account of losin' yer wife?'

'It's been on me mind,' he said.

'Still, you're lookin' a bit better since I first met yer,' said Madge. His eyes weren't so dark and brooding. He looked more satisfied with life. 'Didn't you 'ave any children?'

'No, no children,' he said. 'Nor you, of course.'

'No, nor me,' she said. 'Missed out on that, didn't I?'

'Now don't let it worry you,' he said. 'What you didn't 'ave an' what me an' Matilda didn't 'ave won't be missed. There's too many perishin' kids, anyway. They get under yer feet ten at a time in some places.'

'Henry, you can't blame kids for bein' born;' said Madge, 'and it would please me to 'ear you talk less uncharitable about them.'

'What's this? Givin' me orders, are yer, lady?'

'As if I would,' said Madge.

'Only jokin',' he said. 'Now, 'ow about a walk and pickin' up some fish an' chips?'

'You don't 'ave to break me arm, not over fish an' chips,' she said. 'I'll be pleasured to walk to the shop with yer, Henry.'

'We'll watch the lines, eh?'

'Henry, we don't 'ave to do that all the time, only when we're in the mood. I'll 'ave to take yer mind off doin' it all the time, or you'll get too serious about it.'

'We'll see,' he said.

'I'll put me 'at an' coat on,' said Madge.

They enjoyed a nice companionable walk down to the shop, and she went along with his wish for them not to tread on visible lines.

The inquest on the young Bermondsey girl was held on Friday. Boots attended, with Mr Brown. It was merely a question of the parents confirming what day it was when their daughter went out for a walk and never returned, and of Mr Brown confirming how the body was found. That, together with the post-mortem report, proved enough to bring in a verdict of murder by a person or persons unknown.

The Saturday newspapers published details of the inquest. Mr Brown, whose name was mentioned, collared the family's newspaper when it plopped on to the mat and took it to work with him. He did not bring it home with him. Saturday, anyway, wasn't a day when too many people sat down with their dailies.

Mrs Mason did mention the matter to her lodger, Mr Ponsonby, on his way out of the house, however.

'What, what?' he said.

'The pore gel, Mr Ponsonby, down Bermondsey way. Murdered, she was. It says so in the paper.'

'Dear goodness, what are we coming to, Mrs Mason?'

'Found in a scrap yard, 'er body was, by some workmen an' the yard manager. 'Orrible. I 'ope they catch the brute that done it.'

'What a day, what a day,' sighed Mr Ponsonby. 'What can be done to such people?'

'Hang 'em,' said Mrs Mason.

'Yes, indeed. Ah, now I've forgotten where I'm going.'

'Down the market,' said Mrs Mason.

'Ah, so I am, so I am.' Mr Ponsonby beamed at his landlady. 'Thank you.'

'Don't forget to come back,' said Mrs Mason.

It was mid-afternoon, and Mr Ponsonby, having found his way to the East Street market, was about to inspect the rosy apples on a fruit stall when he came face to face with the unpleasant person whose path he'd crossed some days ago. Certainly, he was dressed more acceptably, in a trilby hat and suit that looked new, but Mr Ponsonby recognized him immediately with his dark eyes and dark features. And, as before, they were in each other's way. Mr Ponsonby at once brought up his rolled umbrella to hold the fellow off.

Henry Brannigan stared at him.

'What's up with you?' he asked.

'Mind your manners, sir, I shall not give way,' said Mr Ponsonby.

'Eh?' Henry Brannigan gave the silly old sod a surprised look before realizing there was something familiar about him. His memory placed him among the many people with whom he'd had pavement confrontations. And that led him to recognition. 'Oh, it's you, you barmy old bugger,' he said.

'Stand off,' said Mr Ponsonby.

''Ello, 'ello, 'ello,' said the stallholder, 'you gents set for a ding-dong, are yer? Well, don't get in the way of me customers or me bananas.'

Henry Brannigan, his life much less bedevilled by fantasies since finding a woman who was a kindred spirit, pushed the brolly aside quite good-temperedly.

'No 'ard feelings, mate,' he said. 'It's only on pavements that I don't like people gettin' in me way.' He made a little detour, brushing Mr Ponsonby's shoulder unaggressively as he went by him.

'What an ugly fellow,' murmured Mr Ponsonby to his umbrella. 'Ought to be hanged, ought to be hanged. I must tell Mrs Mason. Now, what was I doing?'

CHAPTER THIRTEEN

'Well, just look at our Annie,' said Charlie.

Sunday dinner was over and everything tidied up. The Gaffer was ready to relax with *The People*, and Charlie, Nellie and Cassie were thinking of going to Ruskin Park, Cassie in the hope that the Prince of Wales would be there, when she could ask him if he'd mind giving her father a job guarding Buckingham Palace on a horse. As for Annie, she'd just come down from her bedroom in a pure white cotton dress with a scalloped hem that lightly danced around her knees. With it she wore a long string of beads and a round straw hat that sat on the back of her head like a crisp yellow halo. The dress, the beads and imitation silk stockings turned her into a fashionable flapper.

'That's our Annie?' said the Gaffer.

'Ain't she something, Dad?' said Nellie. 'Crikey, look at yer frock, Annie, I never saw that one before.'

'Oh, I've had it ages,' said Annie. She'd bought it yesterday, in fact, at Hurlocks by the Elephant and Castle during her short midday break. Twenty-four hours could be called ages by any girl not wanting to be accused of dolling herself up on account of a certain young man. 'Mind, it's the first time I've worn it. D'you like it, Dad?'

'Looks a treat, Annie,' said the Gaffer. 'Must've cost a packet, though.'

'Oh, a bit out of me savings,' said Annie.

'Well,' said the Gaffer solemnly, 'if you'd 'ad a bit more savings you could 'ave 'ad a bit more frock. I recollect there was an uncomfortable occasion when you were 'ighly embarrassed by the shortness of one of yer other frocks.'

'Dad, I told you never to mention that again,' said Annie. 'Didn't I tell you?'

'So yer did, Annie.'

'Well, I don't want to 'ave to tell you again, Dad, nor anyone else in this fam'ly. D'you all hear me?'

'Yes, Annie,' said Nellie.

'You Charlie,' said Annie, 'what're you grinnin' at?'

'Me?' said Charlie.

'Yes, you.'

A knock on the front door made Nellie dart.

'I'll answer it,' she said.

'I bet it's 'im,' said Charlie.

Nellie, finding Will on the doorstep, brought him through to the kitchen. The day being surprisingly balmy, he wore an open-necked cricket shirt, blue jacket, flannel trousers and no hat or cap. He said hello to everyone and took the opportunity to meet Annie's father and to shake hands with him.

'So you're the bloke,' said the Gaffer, taking a naturally long look at the young man who had wheeled Annie home in a pushcart.

'The bloke who what?' smiled Will.

'Who—'

'Dad, Annie said you're not to say,' warned Nellie.

'Oh, about the pushcart?' said Will.

'Oh, 'e's been an' said it,' breathed Cassie.

'Askin' for a wallop from Annie, that is,' said Charlie.

'Where is she?' asked Will.

'Mister, she's just there,' said Cassie.

'Strike me pink,' said Will, casting an eye over Annie in her pristine white, 'that's Annie? I thought it was someone's bridesmaid.'

'No, that's our Annie,' said the Gaffer.

'Don't take no notice of 'im, Dad,' said Annie, 'he's always talkin' daft. I don't know what 'is mum 'as done to deserve a son like him. Nor do I know what I'm doin' to be goin' out with him.'

'Might I have the pleasure of takin' her to Hyde Park, Mr Ford?' asked Will.

'You're welcome, Will,' said the Gaffer, smiling.

'I'll see he gets 'ome all right, Dad,' said Annie. 'I don't want 'is mum to worry about 'im. I expect she worries a lot about him bein' barmy. I'll 'old his hand for 'im when 'e gets off the bus.'

Will grinned. So did the Gaffer.

'Like the Army, do yer, Will?' he asked.

'On and off,' said Will.

'Well, we won't keep yer,' said the Gaffer, 'off yer go with Sergeant-Major Annie.'

'Oh, you just wait till I get back, Dad,' said Annie.

'Crumbs,' breathed Cassie, 'is Annie goin' to wallop our dad, Nellie?'

'Not till she gets back,' said Nellie, giggling. She and Cassie went to the front door to see the couple depart. They watched them walking up the street, Annie's light dress fluttering, her legs shining.

'Don't they look nice?' said Cassie. 'I expect they might meet Lord Percy in the park.'

'Who's Lord Percy?' asked Nellie.

'I don't know, I just read 'is name somewhere,' said Cassie dreamily.

The rowing-boat moved in a slow jerking fashion over the sunlit waters of the Serpentine. Will was exerting himself economically on the oars. Other boats skimmed or floundered according to skill or lack of it. Annie was in charge of the rudder. It was her first time in a rowing-boat, and there was water, water everywhere, plus the challenge of steering. She liked a challenge, however. Will had explained how to use the ropes, and she took up her fearsome responsibility with resolution. So far, they'd only collided with one boat after narrowly missing another, which she thought their fault, anyway, not hers.

Will was enjoying the outing, the March day was really warm, the Serpentine a pond-like playground. Laughter, yells and recriminations were constant on all sides.

'You Cissie, you'll drown us in a minute.'

''Erbert, stop splashin' me, d'you 'ear?'

'Blimey O'Reilly, some mothers do 'ave 'em, Alice, but fancy yours 'aving one like you.'

'Fancy yours not chuckin' you back under the gooseberry bush, Danny.'

Will liked Annie as a spectacle of early spring. Her self-confidence tickled him. She was sure other boats were at fault when a bump looked likely. She sat upright, hands holding the rudder ropes, her eyes alight. Will, pulling gently on the oars, smiled at her.

'Excuse me,' said Annie, 'but would you mind lookin' where we're goin'?'

'Annie, you're the one who has to look where we're goin',' he said. 'I can only look at where we're comin' from.'

'You sure that's where you're lookin'?' asked Annie, all too aware her legs were right in front of his eyes. 'I suppose you haven't got lookingitis, have you?'

'Is it my fault you're only wearin' half a dress?' grinned Will.

'Listen,' said Annie, 'this dress is highly fashionable.'

'Highly? Shortish, I'd say.'

'Still, I'm pleasured you like it – here, watch yourselves,

you two!' Annie raised an indignant voice to a boat bearing down on them. Will turned his head.

'Pull with your right hand, Annie,' he said.

Annie pulled. The boats collided. Her legs went up in the air.

''Ere, mate,' said a young gent in a Hackney accent, 'would yer mind tellin' yer lidy driver to watch what she's a-doin' of?'

'How's your own driver?' asked Will, keeping the boat steady with his oars.

'Glad you asked, mate,' said the young gent, pulling with one oar and pushing with the other. 'She's keen, I tell yer that. Yer keen, ain't yer, Clara?' he said to his girlfriend, who was pretty, plump and fairly sporty.

'Well, a girl can only get drowned once,' she said, and the young gent eyed Annie, who was right way up again, but considerably put out.

'Like to swop drivers, mate?' he asked Will.

'What's he mean, swop drivers?' demanded Annie.

'He means he fancies you,' said Will. 'How about you?' he asked the plump and sporty girl. 'D'you feel like swoppin'?'

'Well, you look all right,' she said, 'but can I trust yer? I can't trust Nobby; 'e squeezes me in all the places I didn't know I 'ad.'

'I don't know if Annie would go for that,' said Will, with the boats paddling around each other.

Annie, hardly able to believe what she was hearing, said, 'I certainly wouldn't. What d'you think I am?'

'You look a bit of all right from where I'm sittin',' said the young Hackney gent.

'You'll be sittin' in the Serpentine in a minute,' said Annie. 'You're common, and clumsy as well. You shouldn't be allowed in a boat. Will Brown, kindly start rowin'.'

183

'So long,' said Will to the matey couple, and rowed away.

'What d'you mean talkin' about that fat girl and me swoppin'?' asked Annie.

'Just passin' the time of day with them,' said Will.

'Did you bump into them on purpose just to get my legs up in the air?'

'I'll be frank,' said Will, rowing without pushing himself. 'I like a bit of a treat. You don't get to see too many legs in India. Cows' legs, yes, but they're not much of a treat, except to bulls, I suppose. By the way, the bump happened because you pulled on the left rope, not the right. Where're you takin' us now?' He turned his head again, then pulled hard on his left oar to avoid another collision. Annie tugged on a rope. By the grace of God it was the correct one, and they floated by the oncoming boat. But Will's sudden muscular pull brought on a familiar warning. He gritted his teeth. Of all things he didn't want an attack to turn him into a wheezing old man in front of a healthy young girl. Sod it, he thought, I'm going to be a sorry case for the rest of my life if I can't even row a slow boat round the Serpentine. He eased on the oars, paddling with them, waiting for an attack to follow the warning. Much to his relief, his breathing remained normal. He paddled on, towards the boat park.

Annie asked if they were going in. Will said they might as well, their time was nearly up and he fancied a little walk to the refreshment rooms. Would she like some tea? Annie's response was happily in the affirmative.

The tea rooms, always well patronized on fine Sundays, were crowded, but they found a table, and Will ordered a pot of tea, buttered fruit buns and slices of fruit cake. Annie enjoyed the occasion tremendously, and told Will he was being really nice to her. Will said so why had she poured him only a half-cup of tea? Annie said it wasn't good manners to have full cups in places like this.

'Blow good manners,' said Will.

'You've got to have good manners in public,' said Annie, who always remembered that although her lively mum enjoyed a laugh and a joke, she wouldn't stand for any misbehaviour, especially in public.

'You think a couple of mouthfuls of tea add up to good manners, you dotty girl?' said Will.

Annie made a decision there and then. She decided, definitely, that her dad was right, that it was time she had a young man, and that the only one she'd like to have was Will. Accordingly, she had to stop letting him confuse her, and take him in hand, just as if he was her young man.

'I hope you're not goin' to make a scene at your age, Will Brown,' she said amid the chatter and clatter of the tea rooms. 'I'm sure your mum wouldn't like you makin' a scene when you're takin' a young lady out. You can have more tea when you've finished that – oh, and would you like me to butter your bun for you?'

'Would you repeat that?' asked Will.

'Yes, I'll do it for you,' said Annie. It was, to her, a quite natural way of taking him in hand, of letting him see that as his young lady she didn't mind doing things for him. Will watched in amusement as she took his bun, sliced it in half, buttered both halves and gave it back to him. 'There, you can eat it now,' she said. 'Imagine, real butter and all. Will, don't you think you ought to take your elbow off the table in a place like this?'

'Here, half a mo',' said Will, 'are you tryin' to be a mother to me?'

'Course not, you silly,' said Annie, 'how could I be your mother at my age?'

'I've still got a funny feelin' you're tryin' it on,' said Will.

'Eat your bun,' said Annie. 'Isn't it nice in 'ere, Will?'

'Yes, Mother, very nice,' said Will.

Annie smiled. She enjoyed every moment of the tea, and was kind and gracious to her young man, letting him see she didn't act like a common person in public. Will, of course, had a terrible time trying not to laugh. He had a feeling, in any case, that a full-blooded laugh wouldn't do his chest any good. Little danger signals kept hovering.

Annie lingered over the tea because of her enjoyment. She made Will tell her about his family, all of them, and in return she told him any amount of things about her sisters, her brother and her dad, including what an imagination Cassie had and what a kind and homely man her dad was.

The waitress arrived with the bill.

'Everything all right, sir?' she asked.

'Yes, thanks, we'll come again, me and Mother,' said Will.

'Who?' asked the waitress, glancing at Annie.

'Don't take any notice,' said Annie, 'my young man's a bit funny at times.'

'So's my young lady,' said Will, and Annie experienced little tingles of pleasure. She watched him as he paid the bill, giving the waitress a tip, and she thought oh, he's really nice, I don't mind now how much he looks at me in my highly fashionable frocks. When they left she was very gracious in her thanks.

'It was a lovely tea,' she said, 'and you behaved really nice.'

'I had to,' said Will. 'Mother was watching me.'

Annie laughed, then said he'd still got room for improvement.

Will, strolling through the park with her on their way to

186

the bus stop, said he'd do his best. Annie said she hoped he would, as she didn't want to walk out with any young man who had as much sauce as he did. Mind you, she said, I expect there's some young men a lot worse. That sounds as if there's hope for me, said Will. Oh, I think you've got the makings, said Annie graciously.

They enjoyed a very companionable bus ride home, with Annie's shining knees showing, and both knees didn't mind him looking. When they reached her door-step, she was surprised and disappointed that he wouldn't come in. He'd trot off to his own home, he said. Annie wondered if he'd kiss her, but he didn't, nor did he say a word about seeing her again, and that left her very miffed. Will, however, had symptoms to fight, and they reached their inevitable peak the moment he opened his front door. He took himself straight up to his bedroom, and there his attack took its coughing, crippling hold of him. His mum came up.

'Will, we can hear you coughin' all over the house,' she said in concern.

'Give us – a minute – be all right – in a minute.'

'Can't I do something, lovey?'

Will couldn't reply, he was trying to suck in air. He'd taken one of the prescribed tablets and could only wait for it to work. He made a gesture, and Mrs Brown did the sensible thing. She left him to his privacy. As she went downstairs she thought, I hope it's not consumption, I just hope it's not, I'll have something to say to the Army if they've helped to give him consumption. No wonder he's gone up to his room instead of coming to tell us about his girl Annie.

Will was thinking, I'm a hopeless case, and that's a fact. I'm going to be as useful to myself or anyone else as a saucepan with a ruddy great hole in it.

Freddy had had a mixed-up afternoon himself. Calling on his new mate, Cassie, he found she was just about to go to Ruskin Park with Charlie and Nellie. He offered to take her on his bike. His mum had said he could do that as long as he didn't use the main road, where young boys on bikes could make tram drivers have fifty fits and give bus drivers nightmares. So he'd promised to get to the park through the back streets, which was easy.

'Oh, yes, I'll come with you, Freddy,' said Cassie.

''Elp yerself to 'er company, Freddy,' said the Gaffer, looking forward to putting his feet up with his Sunday paper.

''Ere,' said Charlie to Freddy, 'you don't go out with girls, do yer?'

'No, just me mates,' said Freddy.

'What yer goin' out with me sister for, then?' asked Charlie, puzzled but not aggressive.

'She's me new mate,' said Freddy.

'But she's a girl,' said Charlie.

'Well, that ain't 'er fault,' said Freddy, 'she was born like it. Me mum was born a girl. Course, she's a woman now.'

'Blimey,' said Charlie, 'you sure you ain't feelin' unwell?'

'You Charlie,' said Nellie, 'leave Freddy be. 'E can 'ave Cassie for 'is mate if 'e wants.'

'Well, I ain't complainin' about it, am I?' said Charlie. 'I'm just askin' 'im if 'e's all there.'

'Freddy looks all there to me,' said the Gaffer.

'Well, I ain't been taken' away yet, Mr Ford,' said Freddy. 'You ready, Cassie?'

'I'll just get me cat,' said Cassie.

'Not likely,' said Freddy, 'we ain't takin' that barmy cat

up the park with us. I don't mind yer takin' a cushion, but not yer cat.'

'All right, I'll just get me 'at,' said Cassie, and left the kitchen.

'I wish yer luck, Freddy, yer'll need it,' said Charlie, and went off to the park with Nellie, Nellie hoping to get off and Charlie hoping to find a few boys who needed bashing.

Freddy went out to mind his bike. Cassie appeared at the open front door and chucked a cushion at him to put on the carrier. Vanishing again, she reappeared with Tabby in her arms.

'Now look 'ere, Cassie—'

''E wants to come,' said Cassie. 'I asked 'im.'

''E's a talkin' cat now, is 'e?' said Freddy. 'Listen, as me mate you're supposed to do what I tell yer.'

'Me dad never said so. Freddy, Tabby wants to come, and I've got 'is string.'

'Oh, all right,' said Freddy, who had some of his mum's good nature, 'but I ain't 'aving 'im sit on me 'andlebars, you'll 'ave to 'old him.'

'Yes, I'll 'old him to me bosom,' said Cassie, whose imagination embraced a multitude of fancies. Getting astride the cushioned carrier with Tabby clasped to her, she added, 'Did yer know they could only tell the Sleepin' Beauty was actu'ally still alive because 'er bosom was 'eaving?'

'Oh, gawd,' said Freddy, but away he went, round to Portland Street and on to Wells Way. He cut through Church Road and other back streets to reach Champion Park, almost opposite the entrance to Ruskin Park. Cassie hummed a song all the way, and Tabby purred at her bosom. Or rather, her bosom-to-be.

At the park-keepers' hut just inside the entrance, Freddy asked if they'd mind his bike.

'Come again, me young lord?' said a park-keeper, smart in his brown uniform and brown bowler.

'Yes, could yer mind me bike, please, if I leave it 'ere? Only I can't take it round the park, it says so on the notice.'

'Well, me lord, what it also says on that there notice is that it ain't incumbent on me to mind bikes.'

'I ain't never seen that on the notice,' said Freddy.

'You sure you ain't?' said the park-keeper.

'Honest,' said Freddy.

'Well, blow me braces,' said the park-keeper, 'then I suppose I'll 'ave to think about mindin' it – here, wait a bit, what's that girl doin'?'

'Oh, she's just putting 'er cat on a piece of string so's she can walk 'im round the park,' said Freddy.

'Gawd love us,' said the park-keeper, 'mindin' bikes, cats on pieces of string, I'm hearin' things. I'll be hearin' an elephant on a yard of elastic next. Might I refer yer young lordship to the notice again?'

'Mister, I dunno it says anything about elephants,' said Freddy.

'No cats or dogs, that's what it says – here, where's she goin'?'

Cassie was away, walking, the cat following on its string lead.

'I'll go after 'er, mister, an' tell 'er,' said Freddy.

'You do that, me lord, and quick,' said the park-keeper, 'because if she runs into me superintendent, he'll drown the cat and 'er as well. And he'll sell yer bike in aid of the starvin' poor, of which I'm one.'

Freddy grinned. The park-keeper winked. Freddy ran in chase of Cassie. He caught her up. People were staring at the girl with a cat in tow. Boys were cackling and offering comments.

'What yer got there, a walkin' canary?'

''Ere, Lulu, yer bein' follered.'

'Does yer muvver know yer out?'

'Listen, Cassie, no cats nor dogs,' said Freddy. 'Nor elephants. We'll 'ave to take Tabby back and ask the park-keeper to mind it. 'E's mindin' me bike, so I expect 'e'll mind yer cat as well.'

'Tabby don't like bein' minded by park-keepers,' said Cassie.

'Well, if yer don't take 'im back—'

'Freddy, d'you think we might meet a lord or something? I just saw a lady lookin' like a Spanish senrika that was once captured by an 'andsome pirate that was really the Prince of Wales.'

'What's a Spanish senrika?' asked Freddy.

'Oh, an 'igh-born lady,' said Cassie. 'She was ever so upset at bein' captured because she was supposed to be meetin' an 'igh-born duke that was in love with 'er.'

'Well, I'm sorry about 'er 'ard luck,' said Freddy, 'but we've got to take yer cat back, and besides, everyone's lookin'. Cassie, I've got to tell yer, Tabby looks barmy on a piece of string.'

'No, 'e don't,' said Cassie, taking absolutely no notice of looks, stares, comments and giggles. 'Of course, the Spanish senrika didn't mind when she found it was the Prince of Wales who'd captured 'er. If we see 'im in the park, I'm goin' to ask 'im if me dad can guard Buckingham Palace on an 'orse for him.'

''Adn't you better ask 'im first 'ow he got on with the Spanish senrika?' said Freddy, trying a bit of sarcasm. 'Now look 'ere, Cassie, I never 'ad any trouble with me other mate, Daisy Cook—'

'Mummy, mummy,' cried a little girl, 'look, she's got a cat.'

'Well, she shouldn't 'ave,' said the maternal parent, 'it's not allowed, so come 'ere, I don't want you 'aving anything to do with what's not allowed.'

'There, yer see, Cassie?' said Freddy. 'There'll be a bloomin' riot in a minute.'

'Course there won't,' said Cassie, 'it's Sunday. The King don't allow riots on Sundays. Me dad told me so.'

Tabby's head suddenly slipped the string. The animal whisked in front of Cassie and ran into the path of a handsome lady in a flowery dress and a hat shaped like a pudding basin. Without hesitating, it sprang upwards into her arms, much to her startled astonishment. It purred blissfully.

Cassie stopped. Freddy stopped. Beside the handsome lady was a man who looked strong enough to squash Tabby with one blow. He also looked as if he was prepared to do just that.

'Ruddy blind 'ow'djerdo's,' he said 'now it's kids with climbin' cats in the park, would yer believe.'

Cassie and Freddy stared and blinked. It was actually him again, the man who'd knocked them off the bike some days ago. It's like bloomin' doom, thought Freddy.

'Oh, 'elp,' he breathed.

'It's all right, Henry,' said Madge. Henry was taking her for an enjoyable saunter round the park, and she was going to give him Sunday tea at the flat later.

Henry Brannigan inspected the boy and girl, laying his dark eyes first on Freddy, then on Cassie. Little glints appeared, glints of recognition.

'What's the idea?' he said. 'In me way again, are yer? Lucky for you this ain't a pavement.' The park paths were surfaced with tarmac.

'Henry, what're you goin' on at them for?' asked Madge, handing the cat back to Cassie.

They're haunting me, these two kids, that's what they're doing, thought Henry Brannigan.

'Cats ain't allowed in parks, nor dogs,' he said.

'Nor's elephants,' said Freddy, 'the park-keeper down by the gate just told me so.'

The handsome lady laughed at that, and even the man looked as if he had a bit of a grin on his face.

'We're sorry our cat jumped on yer, missus,' said Cassie nervously.

'That's all right, I like cats,' said Madge.

'Yes, all right, but just watch it, yer young perishers,' said Henry Brannigan, and resumed his saunter with Madge.

'Freddy, that was 'im,' whispered Cassie, cuddling Tabby.

'Don't I know it,' said Freddy, 'except 'e 'ad a Sunday suit on. Listen, what d'yer mean by sayin' it's our cat? It's yours. I wouldn't want a barmy cat like that, I'd sooner 'ave an 'eadache. I – oh, crikey, Cassie, there's a park-keeper comin'. Come on, bunk down 'ere.'

They did a quick bunk down a path that took them past the public conveniences. They met Nellie, who'd found a school friend, and together they'd found four boys who fancied having a lark with them. Nellie and her friend Pam didn't go in for larks, so the boys were settling for saucy chat and the girls were settling for giggles. Nellie wanted nothing to do with Cassie, not while she had her daft cat with her, so that left Freddy still in charge of her. He perforce had to keep her out of trouble. It almost wore him out. His old mate Daisy Cook hadn't ever been a trial to him. Nor had she ever talked about her dad being an executioner at the Tower of London. Cassie was insistent that that was what *her* dad had been.

'Yes, 'e 'ad to execute people that run off with the

193

Crown Jewels,' she said. 'The King put 'im in charge of them.'

'I bet that was a worry to 'im', said Freddy, 'I bet it didn't do 'is white 'air any good. Still, it must've got better, I noticed it's not white any more.'

'Yes, it made a recov'ry,' said Cassie.

Freddy took her home then, while he still had the strength to ride his bike. The park-keeper who had minded it for him turned a blind eye on Cassie's cat as she sneaked through the gate with it.

CHAPTER FOURTEEN

'It ain't what I'd like, guv,' said Bert Roper, the man who looked after the maintenance and the security of the factory Sammy was renting in Islington until his new one was built in Shoreditch. Bert and his wife Gertie, supervisor of the sixty machinists, were in the factory office with Sammy and his brother Tommy, the manager. All three sons of Chinese Lady had something to offer the kind of world she believed in. They had manliness and a liking for hard work. Chinese Lady was proud of what they'd achieved, but never said so. They'd only get above themselves, and that was another thing she believed in, a man not getting above himself. She'd often had to tell Boots he knew too much for his own good. Still, he had very distinguished looks. And Sammy with his blue eyes that always looked as if he had an electric motor behind them, was sort of arresting. As for Tommy, well, he was as handsome as his late father, Daniel Adams, and that was saying something.

At this moment, Tommy and Sammy were up against the prospects of a strike in the manufacturing side of the rag trade. All the trade union workers were threatening to come out, whether they could afford to or not, and few could. But bosses were trying to make a case for cutting wages, which were already sinfully low. Even non-union workers in some of the sweatshops were thinking of supporting the strike. Trade union agents were haranguing them. They'd been at the seamstresses in Sammy's factory.

'It's 'ard on Bert, yer see, Mister Sammy,' said Gertie, ''im 'aving been a docker an' still 'aving dockers for 'is mates. And it ain't too easy for me an' the girls.'

'I'm takin' your point, Gertie,' said Sammy. 'What you and Bert are sayin' is that he's goin' to come out.'

'I ain't said that yet, guv,' said Bert. He and Gertie were as loyal to Sammy as any two workers could have been, and even a bit more. Bert had given up his docker's card to look after the factory, and he knew it was as steady and well-paid a job as any East End man could have wished. 'We all know this fact'ry ain't a union shop, so I don't 'ave any legal standin' if I come out on strike, which would mean you'd 'ave the right to sack me. But I'm a union man at 'eart, and you're the only bloke I'd work for without a union card. In me 'eart, guv, I'm wantin' to support the strikers.'

'And not wantin' yer mates to turn their backs on yer,' said Gertie.

'I can 'andle me own discussions, Gertie,' said Bert.

'Not without me you can't, said Gertie. 'I'm yer wife, for better or worse. If you've got problems, they're my problems too. Mister Sammy, Bert's an upset man about all this.'

'So am I,' said Sammy, thinking of the new contract. 'I don't know anything more upsettin' than ruination.'

'Bert's got to make a gesture,' said Tommy, 'against low wages being cut to starvation level. And the girls are bein' got at. The local union officials want them to sign on and come out.'

'I've told them officials,' said Gertie, 'I've told 'em a dozen times that if they can look after us better than you do, Mister Sammy, then we might sign on. A good boss is better than a union card, I told 'em. You've got a lot of appreciative girls, an' they ain't goin' to change you for a union that'll be orderin' them to walk out on you every time some seamstresses somewhere else 'ave a complaint about their bleedin' boss – if yer'll excuse me French, Mister Sammy.'

'Well, Gertie old girl,' said Sammy, 'I'm not partial, as you know, to havin' you and your hands bein' called out on strike on account of trouble in some other workshop. Nor am I in favour of everyone in Adams Fashions bein' in an upset state, as Bert is.'

'We're goin' to be more upset when the strikers stop delivery vans gettin' through,' said Tommy. 'Wait a tick, though, we've got loads of materials comin' in from all over.'

'Which I duly advised you would,' said Sammy.

'You clever old cock,' said Tommy, 'did you get advance warnin' that a strike was on the cards?'

'I don't recollect I did,' said Sammy, who had had other reasons for getting Susie to go to work on Mr Greenberg while he'd been in Manchester. 'However, Eli's comin' up with the goods, is he?'

'We're up to the ceiling with stocks,' said Tommy. 'Quality varied, but all in our ranges. Bert's goin' to arrange the hire of a small warehouse in Canonbury Road to take the overflow. He knows the geezer who owns the place, so he'll give 'im a friendly goin'-over regardin' the rent.'

'My compliments,' said Sammy. 'Right, then, with considerable feeling I've got to admit Bert has his back to the wall, and Gertie and the girls likewise. So what I propose is that when the time comes, if it does, we'll run a banner outside the fact'ry. What'll be on it, you'll ask.'

'Yes, I'll ask,' said Tommy.

Sammy quoted what he had in mind.

'ADAMS FASHIONS SUPPORT THE STARVING

FAMILIES OF THE STRIKING WORKERS WITH DONATIONS FROM STAFF AND EMPLOYERS – DROP YOUR OWN DONATIONS IN THE BUCKET.'

'Bloody 'ell,' said Bert.

'Watch yer language,' said Gertie.

'Yer a bleedin' genius, guv,' said Bert.

'Hold on,' said Tommy, 'I'm not approvin' donations my girls can't afford, Sammy.' Tommy, in daily touch with his staff of seamstresses, knew just how hard-up most of them were, and how much they relied on the weekly bonuses they were paid on the understanding such payments weren't made known outside the factory. Sammy knew the girls generally, Tommy knew them individually, and Tommy had the softest heart of Chinese Lady's three sons.

'If I might continue?' said Sammy.

'Keep it simple,' said Tommy.

'My proposition,' said Sammy, who wasn't partial to words of one syllable, 'is that everyone donates half their wages while the strike's on, and that this sacrifice is gen'rally made known. It can also be communicated to the local paper. I'll donate the same amount, which'll be the sum total of all the staff donations.'

'Strike a light,' breathed Bert.

'Good of your pocket, Sammy,' said Tommy, 'but nothing doin' as far as the girls are concerned. They can't afford anything like 'alf of their wages.'

'I've got to say it's a bit more than I thought you 'ad in mind, guv,' said Bert.

'Fortunately,' said Sammy, 'I can inform you the firm's in the financial position of bein' able to reimburse everyone, so long as it's kept under yer titfers, which if it isn't might blow a ruddy great hole in the look of things.

You've got to be seen makin' the sacrifice. Kindly inform the machinists of same, Gertie.'

'Bless yer kind 'eart, Mister Sammy, yer the best boss goin', and yer smart as well,' said Gertie. 'We don't come out, we stay at work to 'elp support the strikers' fam'lies? We got yer. And 'oo's goin' to be able to say that that ain't better than a non-union shop goin' on strike, specially as you're donatin' too, out of yer pocket. Bert's right, Mister Sammy, yer a bleedin' genius, and 'im an' me couldn't 'ave put it nicer if we tried. Excusin' me French again.'

'Clever, I grant yer,' smiled Tommy.

'Bert still bein' in an embarrassin' position, however,' said Sammy, 'he'll stand outside the fact'ry to take charge of the collectin' bucket, or it'll get half-inched. Might I suggest, Bert, that to anyone who drops a coin in you say, "The starvin' fam'lies of the strikers cordially thank you, mate." Or missus, as the case may be. Now, you'll look as if you've come out, but if we need you to do a piece of work, I'd like to ask you to do it and to send Gertie out to keep an eye on the bucket. And if you could arrange for security to be kept goin', I'd appreciate it.'

'You'll need a bit of security, guv,' said Bert, 'because there'll be some geezers that'll think about firin' the fact'ry on account of it not bein' on strike.'

'Can I take it you've got no more worries?' asked Sammy.

'I'll settle for your wheeze, guv,' said Bert. 'Like you pointed out, it'll look as if I'm on strike, anyway, which I will be most of the time, an' besides, I'm thinkin' donations'll be more of an 'elp than closin' the fact'ry down.'

'Right,' said Sammy, 'and would you like to make it your business to see that all the donations land up where they're intended to?'

'With the strikers' fam'lies,' said Tommy.

'Be a pleasure,' said Bert.

'I know you're our boss, Mister Sammy,' said Gertie, 'but yer one of us and always will be. So's Mister Tommy.'

'We happen, Gertie, to have been born one of you,' said Sammy.

'Two of you,' said Tommy.

'Back to work, Gertie,' said Bert.

'Back to me girls,' said Gertie, 'and if what I tell 'em don't make 'em sing, me name ain't Mrs Gertrude Amy Roper.'

Left alone with his brother, Tommy said, 'Business wearin' you out, Sammy?'

'Business, sunshine, is what perks a bloke up,' said Sammy.

'Business,' said Tommy, 'is what 'ands you the perks.'

'Unfortunately,' said Sammy, 'you can't always dodge the contrary hand of fate.'

'You've got verbal tonsilitis, d'you know that, sonny?' said Tommy.

'Caught it from Boots and his educative infection,' said Sammy. 'I was sayin', I think, that fate's got provokin' ways of pokin' a finger in your eye.'

'You get problems, you mean,' said Tommy. 'So do the rest of us.'

'In my case,' said Sammy, 'I'm havin' to hope St John's Church stays upright next Saturday week. I don't want it fallin' down just as Susie's promisin' to love, honour and obey. Come to that, can I rely on her to obey yours truly?'

'I hope I can rely on her to poke a provokin' finger in your eye occasionally,' said Tommy, studying a batch of delivery notes from Mr Greenberg's warehouse contacts. It looked to him as if Sammy was cornering the stocks held by London wholesalers.

'I ain't appreciative of that kind of comment,' said Sammy. 'I'll remind you that as managin' director of Adams Enterprises, I've got problems other blokes never hear of.'

'Well, keep 'em close to yer chest,' said Tommy, 'because if your best friends get to hear they'll want some of them. I'd say what you'd say yourself, that most of the problems you've got are 'ighly desirable.'

'I can't hang about here any longer,' said Sammy, lodging some invoices in his business attaché case for Boots's attention back in Camberwell. 'All I've got time for is to inform you that you and Boots both come up with jokes that don't make me laugh. Give me love to Vi. I'm partial to Vi. Her jokes are funnier than yours. So long, Tommy.'

'Wait a bit – all this material Mr Greenberg's buyin' on our behalf – it's more than we need as a reserve—'

'Precautionary, Tommy, precautionary,' said Sammy. It wasn't a rag trade strike he really had in mind but rumours of a General Strike.

On his return journey to Camberwell, he made a detour that took him to the Bermondsey scrap yard. He brought his car to a stop outside the gates. They were barred and locked, the yard deserted, by order of the police. It could be they were going to keep it that way until they'd solved the murder. The place, of course, was now an object of morbid curiosity among the locals. Open, it would have attracted swarms of them. Sammy thought about the unfortunate young girl. It made him grit his teeth. Hanging was too good for any man who could strangle an innocent. It was hard luck on Susie's dad, the discovery of the body and the closing down of the yard, but that was nothing compared to the brutal ending of a young life. He could imagine the murderer having the run of the yard.

Old Collier and his son had often neglected it for days on end. But at least the investigation had moved away from the place and away from Adams Enterprises.

Why had he come here when he couldn't really spare the time? In the hope, of course, that he'd find the police there with the news that they'd laid their hands on the bloke responsible. A young girl. It could have been Rosie, Boots's adopted daughter, or Annabelle, Lizzy and Ned's girl, given different circumstances. Or Susie's lively young sister, Sally.

Sammy drove away, wishing the police luck in their investigations.

Scotland Yard had taken them over, and were conducting enquiries not only in respect of the murder but also in respect of two other missing girls. There was the possibility that the initial disappearance of all three girls was linked to a common factor. They were examining the missing persons file on thirteen-year-old Mary Wallace of Rotherhithe, who had disappeared in October, 1925, and twelve-year-old Amy Charles of the Old Kent Road, lost to her family in December. The parents of both girls were still making regular calls at their local police stations to ask if searches were continuing. Scotland Yard began to interview the parents, the neighbours and friends of the missing girls, as well as combing Bermondsey for any kind of information that might help to connect the dead girl, Ivy Connor, to a suspect.

'Annie me pet,' said the Gaffer over supper that evening, 'did we 'ear from you as to when soldier Will is doin' 'imself the honour of walkin' you out again in a rowin'-boat?'

'Doin' what?' asked Annie.

'Dad, yer silly,' said Nellie, ''ow can anyone walk Annie out in a rowin'-boat?'

'Well, yer know what I mean,' said the Gaffer. 'Is 'e callin' for yer again on Sunday, Annie?' He asked the question naturally, for he was quite sure Will appreciated his nice-looking daughter and had made some arrangements to see her again.

'I'm sure I don't know,' said Annie, feeling very put out that Will had made no arrangements at all. If he turned out to be a chronically casual type, she'd show him the door quick when he did happen to call, or if he did. Except that she hoped he wasn't like that, she really did.

'Well, I'm blowed,' said the Gaffer, and wished he hadn't asked.

'Oh, I bet 'e'll be on the doorstep soon,' said Nellie.

''E might be at Buckingham Palace,' said Cassie.

'She's orf,' said Charlie, rolling his eyes.

'Well, 'e might,' insisted Cassie. 'The King might be makin' 'im a lord.'

'A dustman, more like,' said Charlie.

'Course not,' said Cassie scornfully, ''e don't 'ave a dustman's smell. 'E's a soldier. And 'andsome,' she added, after one of her brief thoughtful moments. 'I expect the Queen fancies 'im a bit.'

'Well, I 'ope she don't, Cassie,' said the Gaffer, 'because if she does, the King might chop 'is 'ead off.'

'Cor, I'd like to be there,' said Charlie, 'I ain't never seen a bloke 'aving 'is loaf chopped orf.'

'Ain't you an 'orrible boy?' said Nellie.

'Funny you should say that,' said Charlie, chewing on a chop, 'one of me teachers calls me 'Orrible 'Arry. I told 'er me name's Charlie, but she went an' said I was still an 'Orrible 'Arry.'

'Well, Charlie, if you don't mend yer ways,' said the Gaffer, homely face stiff and stern for once, 'I'll mend 'em

203

for yer. You won't like it, me lad, you can be sure you won't, but it'll 'appen.'

Charlie went a bit red. Nellie, who didn't like uncomfortable family moments, said brightly, 'Annie, you never told us if Will liked yer new white Sunday frock.'

'What there was of it,' said the Gaffer, returning to his normal good-humoured self.

'I heard that, Dad,' said Annie.

'There, see what comes of talkin' out loud, Cassie?' said the Gaffer.

'Mrs Bell's parrot talks out loud,' said Cassie.

'Yes,' said Charlie, never subdued for long, 'it says things like 'ello, cock, and 'ow's yer farver?'

'It spoke to me once,' said Nellie.

'What did it say?' asked Cassie.

'"Who's a naughty girl, then?"' Nellie giggled.

'Cheeky old bird,' said the Gaffer.

'They got 'undreds of talkin' parrots in Windsor Castle,' said Cassie, 'an' goldfish as well.'

'Cassie, you're goin' cuckoo,' said Nellie.

'Yes, they got them as well,' said Cassie, 'the Queen likes cuckoos.'

'She'd like you, then,' said Nellie.

'Yes, I might be 'er maid one day,' said Cassie.

'Bless yer, Cassie,' said the Gaffer.

'Yes, bless her,' said Annie, fond of her dreamy, imaginative young sister.

'I went out with Freddy on Sunday,' said Cassie.

'We know yer did, an' with yer barmy cat,' said Charlie.

'Well, I'm Freddy's mate,' said Cassie, ''e told me so.'

'Wait till 'e finds out what's 'it 'im,' said Charlie.

The talk among the Brown family was mostly about the forthcoming wedding. Susie was having three bridesmaids, her sister Sally and two of Sammy's nieces, Rosie and Annabelle. The conversation was a trial to Freddy. He did his best to make it more interesting.

'That Cassie Ford,' he said, 'I dunno I ever 'ad a mate as scatty as her. Did I tell yer—'

'Susie, I do think cerise pink for the bridesmaids' dresses is lovely for a weddin',' said Mrs Brown.

'Wouldn't do for a funeral, though,' said Mr Brown, 'so it's lucky you only 'ave bridesmaids at weddings.'

'Funny ha-ha,' said Susie.

'I ain't wearin' pink meself,' said Freddy, 'just me new suit.' He'd been fitted out with a ready-made grey suit at Gamages. 'Did I tell anyone that when I took Cassie up the park on Sunday, she brought 'er cat and I 'ad to—'

'I do hope it'll be a fine day,' said Mrs Brown, 'I wouldn't want to go to Susie's weddin' under an umbrella; it wouldn't seem right.'

'Better than bein' rained on, Ma,' said Will, victim of two asthma attacks during the day.

'You could get Freddy to 'old the umbrella,' said Sally, 'then you could walk into the church all dry an' dignified.'

'Good idea,' said Mr Brown, 'we'll make Freddy official umbrella-'older.'

'I dunno I ought to 'ave a mate that takes 'er cat to a park,' said Freddy. 'Daisy Cook never—'

'Eat your supper up, love,' said Mrs Brown.

'Dad, you made up your mind yet about what kind of 'at you're goin' to wear?' asked Sally.

'Well, I've been offered the loan of a top 'at by an undertaker friend,' said Mr Brown.

'Bless us, Jim,' said Mrs Brown, 'I don't know it'll be right to wear any undertaker's hat.'

'Dad, it's out,' said Susie.

205

'I think I'll go for a bike ride up to Scotland,' said Freddy.

'Yes, all right, love, when you've 'ad your afters,' said his fond mum.

'What's the use?' muttered Freddy.

'Keep tryin', pal,' said Will, 'it got you your bike.'

Freddy's problem came knocking on his door after school the following day.

'Can I come on yer bike, Freddy? I've been 'ome and 'ad some tea an' cake, and Annie said you can ride me round a bit but not ma' .e me late for me supper.'

Freddy said how kind of her, then asked Cassie if she'd brought the cat. Cassie, long hair slightly awry and boater sitting on the back of her neck as usual, said no. Tabby, she said, had gone out with another cat.

'He's what?' said Freddy.

'Yes, 'e likes goin' out with another cat,' said Cassie. 'She's a lady cat. Well, I think she is.'

'I suppose 'e takes 'er to the pictures,' said Freddy.

'Yes, she likes the pictures,' said Cassie, 'specially Mary Pickford. Can we go on yer bike?'

'All right, you're still me mate, I suppose,' said Freddy. 'I was goin' round to see Ernie Flint, but I'll give yer another go.'

'Oh, does Ernie Flint go up in balloons?' asked Cassie.

'No, 'e just blows them up at Christmastimes,' said Freddy, and brought his bike out.

'Me dad went up in a balloon once,' said Cassie.

'I bet 'e's been down in a submarine as well.'

'Yes, 'e was a submarine captain once, I think it was in the war,' said Cassie. 'Freddy, you 'aven't brought a cushion.'

'Well, 'ard luck on yer bum,' said Freddy.

'I got to 'ave a cushion,' said Cassie,

'Oh, all right,' said Freddy, and went back to get one. Mr Ponsonby, who had been watching from the gate of his lodgings, came twinkling up to Cassie. He smiled down at her.

'My word, how pretty,' he said. 'Dear me, what a charming girl. Do I know you?'

'Yes, I'm Cassie. You give me a peppermint sometimes.'

'Well, everyone must have a peppermint,' said Mr Ponsonby. Out came Freddy with a cushion. 'Ah, Freddy, is this your pretty friend? Has she had her photograph taken?'

'No, but me sister Annie 'as,' said Cassie, 'it was when she was with the Prince of Wales in Hyde Park.'

'Dear gracious me, how delightful,' said Mr Ponsonby. 'Did you hear that, Freddy? This pretty girl's sister photographed in Hyde Park with the Prince of Wales.'

'Yes, can't 'ardly believe it, can yer?' said Freddy. 'I expect she 'ad tea with 'im as well.'

'Yes, they 'ad a whole pint of winkles with bread an' butter an' strawb'ry jam,' said Cassie. 'Well, I think they did.'

'Dear me, dear me,' said Mr Ponsonby, smiling gently, 'photographs are so nice to have. Come and see me about it. Goodbye now.'

Back he went to his lodgings murmuring to himself.

''E forgot to offer us any peppermints,' said Freddy.

'I've 'ad lots from 'im,' said Cassie.

''Undreds, I suppose,' said Freddy.

'Yes, I think so,' said Cassie.

'Come on, I'll 'ave to put up with you bein' scatty,' said Freddy, and away they went for a ride round the houses.

*　　*　　*

Mrs Mason, going up to her lodger's room, found him sitting in the window chair at a little table. He was beaming at a photograph on the table.

'Excuse me, Mr Ponsonby—'

'Come in, come in, Mrs Mason,' he said.

Mrs Mason, already with her head round the door, brought all of herself in. She had to admit he was an ideal lodger, he kept his room very tidy, made no fuss and grumbled about nothing. Whatever possessions he had, he kept them tidily locked away in his cupboard.

'I don't like 'aving to ask,' she said, 'but it's this week's rent, yer see. You don't 'appen to 'ave paid me yet.'

'Heavens, how remiss of me. Do forgive me.' Mr Ponsonby brought his wallet out from his inside jacket pocket. 'Let me see, how much is it?'

'Just five bob, Mr Ponsonby.'

Mr Ponsonby took a ten-shilling note from his wallet and handed it to her with a smile.

'There, that's for two weeks, then,' he said. 'Dear me, what a day, I must apologize for my forgetfulness.'

'That's all right,' said his good landlady, 'you don't forget very often. Who's the photo of, if I might ask?'

'Pardon?' Mr Ponsonby peered at her. 'Ah, yes,' he smiled, 'a niece of mine, young Clementine.'

'Oh, like the one in the song,' said Mrs Mason, and looked at it as he showed it to her in a proudly beaming way. He was a bit eccentric, so she said, 'Yes, what a nice girl.'

'Charming, charming,' said Mr Ponsonby.

What a funny old codger, thought Mrs Mason as she made her way downstairs to her kitchen. The girl in the photo had had her eyes shut.

'How's your young lady, Will?' asked Susie. She was in

the parlour with him. She was doing some embroidery and he was playing records on the gramophone bought from Sammy's East Street stall five years ago.

'Very healthy,' said Will.

'Why'd you say that?'

'Why not? It's true.'

'I think what you're really talkin' about is your health, not hers,' said Susie.

'Well, mine's a problem, hers isn't.'

'You old silly, you shouldn't talk like that,' said Susie. 'I thought she was very sweet. When are you goin' to take her to a cinema?'

'Suppose I had an attack watchin' Pearl White bein' tied to a railway line?' said Will wryly.

'Change the record, love,' said Susie. 'Put on "Happy Days Are Here Again".'

CHAPTER FIFTEEN

Annie, hurrying home after her day's work, turned into Browning Street from the Walworth Road and almost bumped into Will, who was on his way to see Dr McManus.

Startled, she still managed to say, 'Watch out, mind my knee.'

'Hello, Annie.'

'Hello yourself,' said Annie. ''Ave you been laid up?' It was a whole three days since Sunday and the Serpentine. And the weather was cold. She thought Will looked manly in a new overcoat, and as brown as ever. The sun of India had burned the brown into his face. But she thought he was a little bit drawn. Will had had three attacks during the day.

'Laid up?' he said.

'Well, I 'aven't seen you for ages, have I?' said Annie, then wished she hadn't said that because he really did look a bit drawn. 'No, I mean, 'aven't you been well?'

'A bit of a cold on me chest,' said Will. 'Let's see, d'you fancy the pictures tomorrow evening? There's a Tom Mix film on.'

'Honest?' said Annie.

'That's what my sister Sally told me.'

'No, I mean, you're invitin' me honest?'

'Lovaduck, Annie Ford, is there another way of invitin' you, then?' said Will, showing his amiable grin.

'I'll have you know me dad told me some young men have got crafty ways of invitin' young ladies,' said Annie,

210

'but I'll let him know my young man invited me honest.'

'I'll call for you at half-seven,' said Will, 'and you'll find out how honest I am in the back row of the Golden Domes.'

'I'll scream for the manager,' said Annie happily.

'That won't help you,' said Will, 'he's my uncle. See you tomorrow, then, Annie?'

'Yes, I'll risk it,' she said, 'but I think I'll bring a 'atpin.'

Will laughed. Annie couldn't help herself. She fell in love.

Susie mentioned to Boots the next day that her mum and dad had had a letter from Polly Simms. Polly was one of the many wedding guests. But she wasn't coming, after all, said Susie, she'd written to apologize for crying off, but she was having to go abroad as soon as the schools broke up for the Easter holidays at the end of this week.

'That's news to me,' said Boots without changing expression.

'Yes, she gives Rosie extra lessons at your house two evenings a week, doesn't she?' said Susie. 'I can't think why she didn't tell you. It's a pity she won't be with us, she's such good fun. I wonder what she's goin' abroad for?'

'Fun, I suppose,' said Boots.

He took time off from the office in the afternoon, and was at the school at twenty to four. Classes finished at four. Polly, called from her class by the headmaster, went to the teachers' room where Boots was waiting for her. Dressed in professional fashion, in a pale grey blouse and a dark grey skirt, she nevertheless managed to look as vivaciously appealing as always, her Colleen Moore bob curving to points that lightly kissed her cheeks.

211

'Hello, old thing,' she said, and her brittle smile arrived. Boots, standing with his back to the fireplace, his hat off and his overcoat unbuttoned, regarded her frowningly. 'Oh, dear,' she said, 'am I in the doghouse?'

'Why are you having to go abroad?' he asked.

'Who told you I was?'

'Susie. You wrote to her parents.'

'Well, one must do the right thing sometimes,' said Polly.

'Why are you having to go abroad?' asked Boots again.

'To get away from you,' said Polly. 'Darling, I love you dearly, but you give me nothing. You care for me, but you give me nothing. I'm expected to live with that kind of frustration? It's killing me. At home, I get on stepmama's nerves, I get on my father's nerves, and I get on my own nerves. If you care for me but won't love me, what's the point of my life here? There's my teaching, but that's not enough. I have to get away, and far enough to know you're not just around the corner. So I'm going to Kenya to stay with family friends out there, and to find a less frustrating life for myself. I'm leaving by boat this Saturday. The school breaks up on Friday.'

'Why haven't you told me anything of this?' asked Boots.

'I'm telling you now, aren't I, old thing? I was intending to let you know tonight, when giving Rosie her last cramming lesson. Look, old dear, I admit I've had my passage booked for some time, but gave myself the option of cancelling it in the hope you'd still become my lover. But you're too much of a family man, so I'm chucking you to give myself the chance of a new life by getting you out of my system. I'll never be able to do that while I stay here, using Rosie to find out what you're doing and even what

212

you're saying. I must give Rosie up. I shan't bother either of you any more.' There was just a touch of bitterness to that remark. She had tried, God knows she had, but she accepted now that he was never going to be unfaithful to Emily.

'Bother us?' Boots looked disappointed in her. 'That's not up to your usual standard, Polly. You can't really believe you've ever bothered Rosie, and certainly not me. Your friendship and affection have always been special to me.'

'Affection?' Polly drew a deep breath of exasperation. 'Is that what you think it is, affection? God, if it was only that, I'd be laughing, not running away.'

'Must you run?'

'Yes, I must.'

Boots let out a little sigh. He was a more sophisticated man than either of his brothers, but he was as much his mother's son as Tommy or Sammy. He believed marriage really was for better or worse, unless a wife or husband was totally impossible to live with. Emily was far from that. To make Polly his mistress would be to destroy all three of them in the long run.

'I'm going to miss you badly, Polly,' he said.

Polly regarded him in melancholy. She had known thousands of Tommies in France and Flanders during her years as an ambulance driver. Of them all, Boots was the finest, a man without airs and graces, a man with a whimsical tolerance of clowns and idiots, a man born in the heart of cockney Walworth who had come out of it simply as a man.

'Let me ask you for the last time,' she said, 'will you be my lover?'

'Polly—'

'No, you won't, will you?' The bitterness surfaced then.

'Well, damn you, ducky, for giving me nothing. I wish I'd never met you.'

She turned on her heel, a swift and willowy figure. She left. It was a gesture of finality. Boots stood there. Was it for the best? What a cliché. It did nothing for his emotions. He turned his hat in his hands and listened to the sounds of the school, a place of the young, the active and irrepressible young.

The door opened.

'Daddy?'

He looked at her, his Rosie, nearly eleven and already heart-breakingly pretty, her fair hair black-ribboned, her blue eyes a little sad.

'Hello, kitten.'

'Miss Simms said you were here. I've just finished classes. Daddy, Miss Simms – she's leaving us.'

'Yes, I know.'

'She said goodbye to me, and asked if you'd mind if she didn't come this evening.'

'Well, it's a blow, Rosie, but for a long time now she's been convinced you'll walk that scholarship exam next January.'

'But I'm sad, Daddy, aren't you?'

'People come and go, Rosie, friends come and go, it's all part of life.'

But he was sad, Rosie knew he was. Every gesture of his, every mood and, at times, every word, registered with her. He was the man who had given her a home and the warmth and security of family life. He loved her. More than anything else, that counted with her.

'I shan't ever come and go, Daddy.'

'You will, you know, later on.'

'No, I'm never going to leave you, never.'

And Rosie meant it.

*   *   *

Will, setting off to pick up Annie, was in a cheerful frame of mind. Dr McManus had been more open than the Army doctors, and was quite willing to offer a second opinion, while pointing out he was a general practitioner, not a specialist. He could say, however, that the cause of an attack was the swelling of the lining membrane of the minor bronchial tubes, but how this came about couldn't be generally determined. It might be because a patient was allergic to something like a feather pillow, but on others it might have no effect whatever. Certain foods such as eggs or strawberries could bring about the spasm that caused the swelling that caused the attack. Some sufferers were affected by living in a city or town, others by living in the country. How long had Will been home from India? About four weeks. And how many attacks had he had in that time? About eight or nine. That's two a week. That's not bad at all, said Dr McManus.

'Except that I've had most of them during the last ten days,' said Will.

'Which makes you think it's catching up on you?'

'It makes me think I've got asthma,' said Will, and Dr McManus smiled.

'Well, you have, Will,' he said. He'd conducted an examination and asked questions. 'Let's see, you were fairly free from attacks up to the last ten days. Have you been eating food generally different from what you had during your first two weeks home?'

'Not really,' said Will. 'Plain, but well-cooked and pretty nourishin'.'

'Let's look at your activities, then. What's been different about your activities over the last ten days?'

'Nothing,' said Will, 'I've been taking things easily gen'rally.'

215

'Was your condition worse in Indian towns and cities, than in open country?'

'No, definitely not,' said Will.

'Are you sure that over the last ten days your life hasn't seen a little difference?'

'Are you talkin' about excitement?' asked Will.

'Good question,' said Dr McManus.

'D'you mean I could be affected by the excitement of winnin' a bet on a horse race or landin' a job at five quid a week?'

'Stimulation of an asthmatic condition can be caused by a variety of agencies, Will, external or internal. It can be caused by the air you breathe, if the air contains an irritating factor, or an infection of the nose or throat. Or simply by the infectious nature of simple excitement. Have you had a winning bet lately?'

'No, nothing like that,' said Will. His little grin appeared. 'But I met a girl about a fortnight ago.'

'What kind of a girl?'

'Lively,' said Will. 'Stands up for herself and answers me back. Name of Annie Ford. Would you know her?'

'Yes,' said Dr McManus, 'if she lives in Blackwood Street with her family.'

'That's her,' said Will.

'And you've been seeing her?'

'Frequently,' said Will.

'Well, that's a change in your pattern of life, isn't it?' said the doctor.

'Hell's bells, I meet a girl and that affects my asthma?'

'Would you say, as a young man, that you find her exciting?'

'She's a saucebox,' said Will.

'Yes, an engaging girl.'

'I had an idea,' said Will, 'that physical exertion, such

216

as rowing a boat on the Serpentine, caused attacks.'

'That and a difference in your routine might have done it. Look, next time you have an attack, make a note afterwards of exactly what you were doing at the time, what your last meal consisted of, if you'd been sneezing or not, and whether you were in or out of doors. Then come and see me again.'

'I'll do that, doctor, and thanks.'

Annie found him in top form on the way to the cinema, and was sure he might be a candidate for a thick ear if he secured seats in the back row. But she was spared having to set about him, for he bought sixpenny seats halfway up the stalls.

'Lucky for you you changed your mind,' she whispered.

'Lucky for you, you mean,' he whispered back.

'Young men ought to be respectful to their young ladies.'

'And young ladies ought to say sir to their young men.'

'Yes, sir, three bags full, sir.' Annie was happy. She liked being with him and sitting close to him in the cinema, their shoulders touching. She really felt like his young lady. They enjoyed the programme. A Mack Sennett comedy featuring the Keystone Cops preceded the Tom Mix film. It made the audience roar. In the big film, Tom Mix was his usual breezy self. His cowboy and Indian films often had an amusing side, and he could sometimes give the impression he was taking the mickey out of the Wild West. Will bought ice creams before the film started, and Annie said he was getting to be quite a nice feller.

They went home on a tram, Will relieved he'd had no attack all day. He thought about what Dr McManus had said. Did it excite him to have met Annie and to take her out? Well, he had to admit she wasn't exactly unexciting, and her legs were a treat to his eye.

'You're a bit quiet,' she said.

'I'm thinking would it help to be a cowboy?'

'What sort of 'elp do you need, then?'

'All those wide open spaces must be good for most people. And I might leave the Army.'

'Honest?' said Annie. 'Oh, that's good.'

'What's good about it?'

Well, I'd like it, thought Annie, I'd like to have him just a few stree s away from me all the time.

'What's makin' you think about leavin'?' she asked.

'Cowboys and Indians, I suppose,' said Will. The tram was running smoothly, the traffic light at this time of night, and he liked the feel of Annie close beside him, thigh, hip and shoulder. Steady, mate, he thought, don't get excited, you might be allergic to excitement; your doctor said so. 'Is that good?'

'Is what good?' asked Annie.

'Leavin' the Army for the wide open spaces, joinin' the cowboys and Indians,' said Will. 'Didn't you say it was?'

'Oh, you daft thing,' said Annie, 'there's wide open spaces down near Brighton in Sussex. Dad took us there once, on the train. Besides, cowboys and Indians ride 'orses. You can't ride 'orses, can you?'

'Not without fallin' off,' said Will, 'but I can ride a bike.'

Annie laughed. Other passengers glanced at her. They saw a girl in happiness. Will saw a girl bright and alive, her hip and thigh communicating feminine warmth to his. His body, vigorous and healthy despite his asthmatic condition, stirred reactively. Steady, he told himself again.

They alighted at East Street.

Feeling peckish, Will said, 'Fancy some fish and chips, Annie?'

'Oh, who wouldn't?' said Annie, liking the offer

because it was just the kind of treat a girl could expect from a young man when she was his young lady.

So they walked along the Walworth Road to the fish and chip shop near Manor Place, where Will bought two helpings of rock salmon and chips. They put salt and vinegar on, and spent a happy time eating them out of the newspaper wrapping on their way back to East Street. Annie deposited the newspaper in the wire basket fixed to the lamp-post on the corner of the street, and then Will walked her home.

In the doorway of the Ford house, the cold night darkly enclosed them. Annie looked up at him. Her face seemed misty.

'Will, thanks ever so much for a lovely evenin',' she said a little throatily.

Will kissed her. He couldn't help himself. Blissfully, Annie received the kiss, her first romantic one. Oh, help, swoony. Her mouth clung to his, and she pressed close. Ruddy fire and hell, thought Will, as warning signals arrived. Kissing a girl was doing it to his tubes? He released her.

'Bless you, Annie,' he said.

'Oh, bless you too,' she said, breathless and rapturous. 'You'll come in, won't you, and see Dad and 'ave a cup of tea?'

Will's chest was tightening, but he felt it would be like giving her a slap in the face if he said no.

'A cup of tea sounds just what the doctor ordered,' he said. Annie opened the door and they entered, she in a quick way, he moving carefully, nursing his condition.

The Gaffer was up, the rest of his children in bed. He greeted Will with cockney heartiness, and Annie put the kettle on. Then she set about making some corned beef sandwiches with pickle for her dad.

'Good film, Will?' enquired the Gaffer, sitting at the table with him.

'Tom Mix? You bet,' said Will.

'Will was sayin' on the tram that he might leave the Army and go and be a cowboy,' said Annie, bobbed hair dancing a little as she sliced bread.

'Ruddy good idea,' said the Gaffer. 'Let's all push off an' get away from bosses in top 'ats an' gold watch-chains. Let's all be cowboys.'

'Me as well?' said Annie, a little glow on her face.

'I like the picture,' said Will.

'What picture?' asked Annie, spreading margarine on the slices.

'I reckon 'e means you on a cowboy's 'orse in yer 'ighly fashionable frock, Annie,' grinned the Gaffer.

'Dad, you're gettin' as bad as Will, and if you don't leave off I'll make you stand in a corner.'

'Gawd 'elp us,' said the Gaffer.

'Sounds fierce,' said Will. The tightness was easing.

'Yes, I'm the boss in this kitchen,' said Annie, and made the tea and the sandwiches. Then she sat down with Will and her dad. Her dad tucked into the sandwiches and they drank the hot tea. Will mentioned that Susie was getting married at St John's Church next Saturday week. Annie, at once intrigued, wanted to know who the bridegroom was. Will said Sammy Adams, and that he'd once run a glass and china stall down the market, where he'd first met Susie.

'Oh, I know 'im,' said Annie. 'I mean, I saw him lots there. He's a real lively feller, and good-lookin' too. I bet he's never put a girl in a—' She stopped. The Gaffer coughed.

'In a pushcart?' said Will.

'Blimey, yer done it now, Will,' said the Gaffer, 'that's a word that's forbidden in this 'ouse.'

'What do I do now, then, duck under the table?' said Will.

'What's he doin', where's he gone?' asked Annie, as his head and shoulders disappeared. She shrieked, knowing that under the table she was all legs. Will's head re-emerged.

'Dropped me teaspoon,' he said.

'I bet,' said Annie. 'I don't know how you can just sit there grinnin', Dad.'

'Well, a bloke can't 'elp droppin' 'is teaspoon,' said the Gaffer, frankly tickled by what was developing between his lovable daughter and her likeable soldier. He knew Annie far too well not to realize she was in high spirits and uncommonly happy. She'd had a tough time since the death of her mum, and she'd taken on all kinds of responsibilities while doing a job as well. It hadn't got her down, even though she'd never had much time to spare for herself or for boys. Now, when she was in her eighteenth year, it looked as if she'd got a young man. It was making her come alive. Well, Will was a bit of all right, and he'd got a nice sense of humour.

Will, remembering that a wedding guest had cried off, someone called Polly Simms, said, 'Like to come, Annie?'

'Come where?' she asked.

'To Susie's weddin'.'

'Me?' said Annie, eyes opening wide.

'There's room for you. There'll be dancin' at the Institute in the evenin'.'

'But your parents must've done all the arrangement,' said Annie, 'they couldn't take an extra guest now, could they?'

'Not extra big and fat ones, no,' said Will, 'but you're not big and fat. We could fit you in nicely.'

Annie went warm with pleasure, then made a face.

'Oh, I couldn't, Saturdays are Mr Urcott's busiest days, I couldn't ask 'im for the afternoon off.'

'Well, come to the Institute when you've finished work,' said Will.

'Oh, I'd love to,' said Annie.

'Good,' said Will, 'and now I think I'd better push off. Good night, Mr Ford.'

'Best of luck, Will,' said the Gaffer.

Annie saw Will to the front door.

'Thanks for the tea,' he said.

'It's been a lovely evenin',' said Annie, wondering if he was going to kiss her again. 'Oh, and thanks ever so much for the weddin' invite.'

'Wear your high fashion knockout,' said Will. 'Like to go to Ruskin Park on Sunday afternoon?'

'You're gettin' quite nicer all the time,' she said.

'Hope I can keep it up,' said Will, and went off with a smile, but without kissing her.

I'll have to go and see Dr McManus again, he thought, and ask him if kissing a girl is fatal to me asthma.

CHAPTER SIXTEEN

At the sound of the front door closing the following evening, Mrs Queenie Watts said to her husband, '''Enry's out ev'ry evenin' now reg'lar as clockwork.'

'Doin' 'im good,' said Stan Watts, 'makin' 'im more human. 'Ere, what's this out 'ere on top of the copper?'

'Oh, just some of 'is shirts,' said Queenie, 'I offered to put 'em in me Monday wash, if I'm up to doin' it.'

'But 'e uses the laundry, don't 'e?' called Stan from the scullery.

'Yes, but I offered. I 'ad a weak moment, I forgot about me chronic back.'

'What's 'e use three shirts in a week for?' asked Stan. 'They're bleedin' best shirts, look at 'em.'

'I can't see from 'ere,' said Queenie, lumpily lazing in a fireside chair, 'but I take yer word for it.'

'''Ere, yer know what three best shirts in a week mean, don't yer?' said Stan. '''E's got a fancy woman, that's what's takin' 'im out reg'lar ev'ry evenin' about the same time. 'Ere, wait a bit, there's a bloodstain on the cuff of one shirt, Queenie. I 'ope that don't mean 'e's cut 'is fancy woman's throat.'

'Oh, yer daft lummox, Stan. You don't suppose, do yer, that 'e cut 'er throat last night and 'as gone back tonight to bury 'er somewhere? 'E just 'appened to nick 'is wrist when 'e got back 'ere last night, 'e told me so, and 'e showed it to me. It's only a small nick.'

'Well, 'e's got some woman all right,' said Stan, 'dressin' smart like 'e does an' goin' out so reg'lar in 'is

223

new overcoat. And 'e don't look these days as if the rozzers are 'unting 'im down.'

''E couldn't help lookin' like that,' said Queenie. 'It was Matty fallin' out of that train that did it to 'im. 'E's gettin' over it at last.'

'And 'e's got a fancy piece that's 'elping 'im,' said Stan.

'Time 'e 'ad a little bit of what 'e fancies,' said Queenie indulgently.

After a nice homely supper of fresh haddock and poached eggs with Madge, Henry Brannigan took her for a walk along the Walworth Road. He, as usual, measured his strides whenever they reached a patch of light. Madge, as usual, fitted in with him, even though she was cheerfully disposed this evening to ignore the superstitions. Henry, however, was very set in the way he observed all the rules, and she didn't like to go against him.

'That one near caught the both of us,' he said, as they came out of the light cast by a shop window. Some shop windows always showed light, but most had their shutters up.

'Still, we both beat it,' said Madge.

'Well, good for both of us, eh? Like a drink? Say a port an' lemon?'

'That's nice of you, Henry. I don't know I ever met a man more gen'rous than you, nor more kind.'

'I ain't ever sure meself that dibs do a bloke much good by bein' kept in 'is pocket,' said Henry Brannigan. 'Dibs, yer might say, is there to be spent when there's something worthwhile to spend 'em on. A good woman's worthwhile, Madge, and it ain't nothing to do with bein' gen'rous. And I don't know I'd call meself kind, I'm more rough and ready, like.'

'A rough diamond, then, that's you,' said Madge, full-bodied and hearty, and surprising herself in her liking for taking walks with this strange and earthy man. The night was fine, the inky sky studded with a million tiny stars, the day clouds of early April swept from the heavens by a wind that had come and gone.

They crossed the road when they reached East Street, darkly empty of stalls. The tramlines, straight and true, faintly glimmered. They stepped over them, Madge doing so with a little laugh as they made for the pub on the corner of Penrose Street. The lamp above its door illuminated the paving stones. Madge, just a little bit careless then, trod on a line. Henry Brannigan emitted a sharp hissing breath.

'Shouldn't 'ave done that, Madge,' he said.

'Oh, it don't really count, Henry,' she said. 'I'm not in a superstitious mood tonight, I'm 'appy bein' out with yer.'

'All the same, I don't like it,' he said. 'Just take care tomorrer in case bad luck comes runnin' after yer.'

'I'll do that, Henry, I'll take care,' she said, sorry that she'd upset him.

'Good,' he said, and took her into the pub. It gave them a warm if fuggy welcome, the clay pipes of elderly cockneys issuing smoke. The place was fairly full, lively customers enjoying old ale at fourpence a pint from the barrel. A table, unoccupied, offered itself. 'You sit there, Madge, and I'll order up yer port an' lemon.'

He was a real gent, she thought, in the way he treated her, especially as a lot of people would just see her as an old pro. Still, she was off the game now. She sat down while he took himself to the crowded bar. Her handsomely mature looks drew the eyes of some men. She knew this pub, of course, she knew all the pubs and their noisy

225

cockney atmosphere and their sawdust floors. Walworth men and women liked their pubs.

A man, catching sight of her, gave her a second look, then elbowed his way out of a group of men and women. He shifted his cap a little until its soft peak was at a perky angle and walked across to Madge.

'Watcher, Daisy gel, ain't seen yer around lately,' he said, and winked at her.

Oh, blow it, thought Madge, he's been a customer of mine, I suppose. Daisy was the name she'd always used. She could rarely remember any of their faces, not generally she couldn't, and she'd hoped none of them would remember hers now that she wasn't tarted up.

'Beg yer pardon?' she said.

'Are yer booked, love?' The man wasn't at all bad-looking. He was about thirty, with a fine pair of shoulders and a scarf around his brawny neck. A faint sexual surge disturbed her healthy body. That was often the trouble. She *was* healthy. She liked men, except the pathetic kind who'd never been able to look her in the eye. Henry looked her in the eye like a real man should. She frankly fancied Henry. He was middle-aged but as strong as a horse, she could tell that.

'You after something, mister?' she said distantly.

'You offerin', Daisy? 'Ow about a bit of what I've 'ad before, eh? Bleedin' fine woman, you are, and 'ere's me 'ard-earned silver in advance.' His hand dipped into his pocket and came out with two half-crowns, which he placed on the table in front of her. Madge felt sick, then angry. 'Meet yer outside in twenty minutes, say?' The man gave her another wink.

A glass of port and lemon appeared. A hand set it down beside the heavy silver coins. That was followed by a pint glass of old ale, and Henry Brannigan, having rid himself of both glasses, addressed himself to the intruding third party.

'The lady's with me,' he said.

'Well, don't be greedy, tosh,' said the third party, 'I'm paid-up an' booked.'

Henry Brannigan drew a long breath. It seemed to expand him and to lengthen him. He picked up the half-crowns and dropped them into the third party's jacket pocket.

'Do yerself a favour, mate, an' bugger off,' he said.

'Watch yer north-and-south, cully, I ain't yer private doormat.'

'Would you be invitin' me outside?' asked Henry Brannigan.

'You want it, you'll get it.'

'Right.' Henry Brannigan glanced at Madge. 'Won't be a tick,' he said.

'Henry—'

'Look after me pint,' he said, and went outside with the man. No-one took any notice. Amid all the boisterous noise, the brief dialogue had gone unheard except by Madge. She sat stiffly, biting her lip. But she didn't have long to wait. Henry was back within a couple of minutes. He didn't look ruffled, and he didn't look heated. He sat down and picked up his glass of ale.

'Oh, me gawd, what've yer done to 'im?' breathed Madge.

'Hit 'im,' said Henry Brannigan. ''E won't be comin' back. I 'ope that'll show yer, Madge, that it don't do to challenge them fates.'

'What d'yer mean?' she asked.

'Trod on a line outside, didn't yer?' he said. 'An' bad luck didn't take any time to catch up with yer, did it? You're off the game now, so I'd say you count it as bad

227

luck to get an offer from a bloke when you're livin' respectable, don't yer?'

'So 'elp me, I don't want to go back on the game,' breathed Madge, 'nor 'ave anyone makin' an offer.'

'There y'ar, then, lady, don't risk it. Don't ask for bad luck to come runnin' after yer. It chased after yer when you trod on that line, and caught up quick with yer. I ain't partial to 'aving you accosted, not now you're keepin' yer bed to yerself. Well, the fates 'ave taught you yer lesson. Now 'ere's good 'ealth an' good luck to yer, Madge.'

Madge, a shaky little smile on her face, said, 'Bless yer, Henry, and 'ere's good luck to you too.'

They drank to each other, with Madge thinking he's right, you can't shut superstitions up in a cupboard whenever you feel like it, you've got to keep them out in the open all the time and pay respect to them.

Susie entered Sammy's office on Saturday morning the moment she heard him come in.

'Mister Sammy,' she said, consulting her watch, 'you're late.'

'Did I hear you say something, Miss Brown?'

'You did. It's nearly eleven, and I wasn't aware you had any appointments this mornin'. Lilian Hyams phoned and said to tell you all the autumn and winter designs are now finished in respect of suggested alterations by Miss de Vere. And Tommy phoned to say the hire of another warehouse has been arranged. And there's a letter from Shuttleworth Mills about their new cotton fabrics that wants answerin'. Eleven o'clock in the mornin' won't do, Mister Sammy, unless you've got a good excuse.'

'I'll come after you in a minute,' said Sammy.

'Yes, please – no, I mean no – not in office time. Just kindly explain why you're late, and if it's because you've been up to see Miss de Vere, I won't invite you to my weddin'.'

'Sometimes,' said Sammy, 'I get a painful feelin' I'd be better off deaf, you saucebox. I'd give you the sack if it wasn't for the fact that I'd miss your legs walkin' in and out of me office. What's kept me, you want to know? Well, I'm able to inform you, Miss Brown, that I've been to the Bermondsey Borough Council and offered them the scrap yard as a buildin' site, at the price we paid for the business, so that they could put up a block of municipal flats.'

'You want to sell that yard?' asked Susie.

'Well, I know your dad could get back to it in time, Susie, but there's always goin' to be some geezers nosin' about to get a look at where that girl's body was found. It's what's called morbid curiosity. You remember, don't you, a woman called Mrs Chivers, who was murdered a few doors away from where you're livin' now?'

'Yes, everyone in Walworth knew about that,' said Susie. 'Your fam'ly told me the full story. Boots was a witness at the trial of Elsie Chivers, the daughter, and so was your mum.'

'Boots got her off,' said Sammy. 'Our respected Ma said he gave his evidence like the Lord of creation, and juries take notice of the Lord of creation.'

'I can imagine,' said Susie. 'It must've been awful, a woman accused of murderin' her own mother. Em'ly said she wouldn't have hurt a fly. Yes, I can imagine Boots bein' impressive. He's got such an air, don't you think so?' Susie smiled teasingly. 'We all adore him, of course. Doreen says he makes her bosom rise and fall.'

'Might I remind you that I've told you before I won't have any adorin' on these premises, it interferes with business. Nor don't I want to see any bosoms risin' and fallin'. Tell Doreen a decent corset will solve her breathin' problems. Let's see, where was I? Yes, the point is, Susie, after the trial geezers from newspapers haunted the street for weeks. When they'd given up, along came the Nosey Parkers to look at the house and to ask questions. They kept comin'. Morbid curiosity, don't yer see, a bit of wordage Boots acquainted me with. It's goin' to be like that at Bermondsey, partic'larly if the police find the murderer and hang him. I don't want your dad to have to put up with staring eyeballs and queer questions. So I made the Council an offer of the yard, which they're considerin', and after that I made an offer for Rodgers and Company's scrap yard off the Old Kent Road. Which old man Rodgers accepted on the spot. That's the yard for your dad, Susie.'

'Sammy, oh, you lovely feller,' said Susie.

'Sound as a bell, your dad is,' said Sammy.

'Sammy, I'm goin' to be your best and only wife ever.'

'I'll try not to mind the expense,' said Sammy.

'I'll try not to as well,' said Susie. 'Tommy said he thinks you're usin' Mr Greenberg to corner all the textiles held by London wholesalers. I told him I was grievously afraid you are.'

'Well, we might get lucky,' said Sammy.

'It's just not fair,' said Susie.

'So you said before, Susie, but it's rattlin' good business. Now, kindly inform Ronnie to mount his bike and ride off to our Brixton shop with this box. They're expectin' it.'

The cardboard box, white, was on Sammy's desk.

'What's in it?' asked Susie.

'Silver-white bridal stockings,' said Sammy.

'Silver-white? Oh, let me see,' said Susie.

'You've already got your weddin' stockings, haven't you?'

'Yes, white, but not silver-white.' Susie picked up the box and sped into her office with it, closing the door behind her. Sammy grinned. Susie's legs in silver-white. Even a high-class reputable businessman could hardly wait.

When Ronnie, the office boy for two months, rode off to Brixton with the box, one pair of stockings was missing, a note from Susie in its place.

Sammy, having heard from Susie that Polly Simms wouldn't be at the wedding, after all, because she had to go abroad, felt a bit sorrowful about it. He liked Polly, the whole family did. She might be upper class, but could mix with all kinds. They'd miss her, the family, but it was just as well she was going abroad. She was a lot too fond of Boots, and Chinese Lady would raise the roof if Boots let it get out of hand.

Yes, just as well she was leaving.

A business acquaintance, a Covent Garden wholesale florist, popped in to see Sammy at twenty minutes past eleven. Susie had left at eleven – she had a hundred things to do, all in respect of the wedding. Josh Walker, who had gravitated from a flower stall in the East Street market to Covent Garden, owed Sammy a small favour. It was one of Sammy's profitable principles, to contrive for business friends or acquaintances to owe him favours.

'Well, 'ow's yerself, Sammy? In the pink, I see. Bloomin', as yer might say.'

'I might, if I didn't have headaches, Josh,' said Sammy.

'Oh, we all got those, Sammy. I'm just on me way to Peckham, so I thought I'd just look in on yer and 'and yer something for your fiancée, seein' yer doin' the honours with 'er next Saturday.' Josh Walker placed a long cardboard box on Sammy's desk. Sammy lifted the lid and

231

saw at least a dozen bunches of magnificent King Alfred daffodils.

'Josh, I'm overcome,' he said.

'Pleasure. Good luck, mate. I can tell yer, marriage don't actu'lly kill yer.'

'Is that a fact?' said Sammy. 'Well, it suits me, one of me main business ambitions is to stay alive.'

'I admire an ambition like that,' said Josh Walker, and shook hands and departed, a large grin on his face.

Sammy, left with a plethora of superb blooms, decided this was ladies' day. He called Doreen in, gave her three dozen and told her to share them out among the girls.

'Mister Sammy, oh, ain't you an angel?' said Doreen.

'Glad you mentioned that,' said Sammy, 'in me modesty I sometimes forget it.' He took another four dozen blooms through Susie's office to Emily's little sanctum. She was at her typewriter. She worked from ten to twelve on Saturdays, the rest of the staff from nine to twelve-thirty.

'Sammy?' she said, gazing huge-eyed at the King Alfreds. Sammy winced a little at her thinness. His affection for Emily, who'd been a godsend to the family when they lived in Walworth, was deep-rooted. 'Sammy, what're all those daffodils doin' against your waistcoat?'

'Nothing useful,' said Sammy. 'Josh Walker's just handed me a box of them. Here's some for you. There you are, Em. Look a lot better against your bodice than my waistcoat.'

'Sammy, all these?' Emily, always demonstrative, positively sparkled. 'I'll stand them in a vase in the hall, where everyone can enjoy them. And you can give us a kiss for bein' a lovely bloke.'

'Cost you tuppence,' said Sammy.

'Oh, still chargin', are you?' smiled Emily, cuddling the blooms. 'All right, let's go mad, give us fourpennyworth.'

232

Sammy gave her two smackers, one on her cheek and one on her good-looking mouth. 'Here, that's not a brother-in-law's kiss.'

'Just a tuppenny one,' said Sammy. 'All right, Em, are you?' He hadn't the heart to refer directly to her thin look.

'Me?' said Emily, who hated what was happening to her, and only talked about it with Boots and Chinese Lady. Chinese Lady was doing her best to stuff her with lightly cooked liver and almost raw red meat. 'Me?'

'I like to ask after the health of me close relatives,' said Sammy.

'Well, this one's fine, Sammy love.'

'Tower of strength, you are, Em, as our shorthand-typist and a close relative.'

'Well, bless yer cotton socks for sayin' so, Sammy, and you're not so bad yourself. We're all lookin' forward to the weddin', and me and Boots are prayin' marriage won't ruin you.'

'Kind of you, Em. You had a wartime weddin', so did Lizzy. If mine's as good as yours was, I'll face up to the consequent ruination.'

'Same old Sammy,' said Emily.

'Good on yer, love,' said Sammy. On his way back to his office, he said, 'By the way, you owe me fourpence. Pay me later.' Emily laughed.

Sammy then called Ronnie in, the office boy having just got back from Brixton. Sammy had finally given in to demands from the general office staff for a runabout lad, and sixteen-year-old Ronnie Jarvis of Camberwell, looking for a job and eager for anything, had been taken on two months ago. Sammy already had his eye on the lad. He was willing, adaptable and good-natured. He stuck stamps on letters as readily as he helped Mitch, the firm's van driver, to load and unload. And he assisted in the shop below whenever he was asked to. Sammy liked anyone who liked work.

'Right, Ronnie, got your bike at the ready still, have you?'

'At your service, Mister Sammy, sir,' said Ronnie, slim, lanky and pleasant-looking. Sammy approved the fact that he didn't sport a quiff or put brilliantine on his hair.

'Good. Saddle up, then, me lad, and kindly deliver this box to Miss Brown. I've scribbled her address on the lid. Mind you hand it in with my compliments, and don't damage the contents or you and your bike will be hanged upside-down, which will hurt considerable.'

'Mister Sammy, I can frankly tell yer I don't like bein' hurt considerable.'

'Highly sensible,' said Sammy. 'Kindly get movin', and when you've made the delivery you can go home, which you'll be entitled to if it takes you up twelve-thirty. Here's a tanner for doin' this special delivery.'

'Well, thanks, sir,' said Ronnie, 'and I'd like to say I'm pleasured to be included with the staff at your weddin', seein' I've only been workin' here for two months.'

'Can't leave any of you out,' said Sammy, 'or there'd be ructions. Off you go.'

Ronnie had contributed to the staff collection for a wedding present, and the money had been used to buy Susie and Sammy a chiming clock.

Off went the whistling office boy to Caulfield Place, Walworth, the box strapped securely to the carrier. A knock on the door of the Browns' house was answered by Sally. She blinked at the caller.

'Hello,' he said, the cardboard box balanced on his hands.

'Hello yerself,' said Sally, looking pretty nice in a Saturday frock.

Ronnie, who hadn't worked in the offices for two months without taking educational note of the verbal attributes of Boots and Sammy, said, 'Am I addressin' a lady member of the Brown fam'ly?'

'You 'ave that honour,' said Sally, deciding he was putting it on.

'Might I 'ave the further honour of speakin' with Miss Susie Brown?' asked Ronnie, deciding he wasn't in any hurry.

'Alas,' said Sally, who'd never yet played second fiddle to a boy's chat.

'What?' said Ronnie.

'Alas.'

'Alas what?'

'Miss Susie Brown, my sister, don't 'appen to be in,' said Sally, 'she's gone shoppin' from 'er work.'

'Oh, well,' said Ronnie, 'p'raps I might have another further honour.'

'You're comin' it a bit with all these honours, ain't you?' said Sally.

'Could I enquire your name?'

'What for?'

'I think I like you,' said Ronnie.

'That's nothing,' said Sally, 'ev'ryone likes me, even me brother Freddy. What's that box you're 'olding?'

'Special deliv'ry to Miss Susie Brown, with the compliments of Mister Sammy Adams. I'm 'is assistant.'

'No, you're not,' said Sally, 'that's Susie.'

'Yes, I'm his junior assistant,' said Ronnie. 'Shall I come in and wait? I don't mind havin' a chat with you in your parlour.'

'I'm thrilled,' said Sally, 'but alas.'

'Alas what?' asked Ronnie, grinning.

'Alas, I'm just goin' to have poached eggs on Welsh

235

Rabbit with me fam'ly,' said Sally. 'You honestly on the firm's staff?'

'I have that honour,' said Ronnie.

'You're not comin' to the weddin', are you, with all the staff?'

'I have that further honour,' said Ronnie.

'You're a sad case, you are,' said Sally, 'you talk like someone's butler.'

'Funny thing, I was once—'

'Well, never mind, you're a junior assistant now,' said Sally. 'You can give the box to me.'

'Pleasure. I'm Ronnie Jarvis, by the way. Who did you say you were?'

'I didn't. Well, all right, I'm Sally Brown.'

'Pleased to meet yer, Sally. D'you go out with fellers?'

'No, course I don't, I'm still only fourteen.'

'I used to be fourteen,' said Ronnie. 'You soon grow out of it. Here.' He placed the box in her arms. 'I might come and sit in your parlour with you sometimes, and bring my mouth organ.'

''Elp, I can 'ardly wait,' said Sally.

'Me neither,' said Ronnie, and rode off whistling. Sally giggled and took the box to her mum, who lifted the lid and saw it was full of daffodils. She was so overcome by Sammy's flowery gift to Susie that she hardly heard anything of what Sally said about the boy who'd brought them. So Sally had to say most of it twice.

Coming to, Mrs Brown said, 'Oh, was he a nice boy, then?'

'Well, 'e was honoured at just standin' on our doorstep,' said Sally.

'Why, is our doorstep special, then?' asked Freddy.

'No, but he probably thinks Sally is,' said Will.

236

'Our Sally's only fourteen, she's only just left school,' said Mrs Brown.

'Oh, you soon grow out of only bein' fourteen,' said Sally.

CHAPTER SEVENTEEN

On Sunday afternoon, Annie and Will took to the winding paths of Ruskin Park along with other people, of whom there were plenty. The weather had warmed up. A fine Sunday always brought the cockneys of Camberwell and Walworth to the park, as well as better-off people from the neighbourhood of Denmark Hill. Annie had been able to put on her second best Sunday dress and to wear it without a coat. Will said it was nearly as highly fashionable as her white one. Annie said she was keeping that for his sister's wedding, that she'd be able to get to St John's Institute by a quarter to five. Was there really going to be dancing in the evening? Yes, to a three-piece band, said Will, and 'Knees Up, Mother Brown' would be performed.

'Crikey,' said Annie, 'will the vicar be there?'

'Yes, just for the knees-up,' said Will, sauntering beside her.

'I bet,' said Annie. 'Anyway, I'm not goin' to do any knees-up in me highly fashionable dress, not with you lookin'.'

'And the vicar,' said Will.

Annie bubbled with laughter. The exciting little under-currents of being in love exhilarated her, but she kept her head, she didn't make the mistake of falling all over him in a manner of speaking. Of course, if he fell all over her – in a manner of speaking – she wouldn't mind that. She asked if he'd thought any more about leaving the Army. Will, who felt the Army's medical experts would make the decision for him, one way or another, said yes, he'd thought more about it, and that he'd make up his mind before his leave was up. Annie said she supposed it was sensible for him to take his time. It didn't occur to her to ask him how long he'd signed up for simply because she didn't know enough about the conditions imposed on a man when he entered the Army. Will said as soon as he'd made the decision she'd be the first to know outside his family.

'Me?' said Annie.

'Well, you're—' Will checked. Better not to say because she was his young lady. If he was going to suffer asthma all his life, he didn't think he could ask a girl to suffer it with him. Suppose, for instance, it took hold of him every time he made love to her? That wouldn't make any wife rapturous, she'd think she'd married a wheezing old man. Mind, he'd only had one attack these last few days, and that was when he woke up on the morning after taking her to see Tom Mix. So he'd attended Dr McManus's morning surgery. Dr McManus wanted to know exactly what had preceded the attack. Will said eight hours good kip. Dr McManus asked if he had feather pillows. Will said the Army doctors in London had mentioned feather pillows, but there'd been none in India, and in any case, this was the first time he'd had an attack while still in bed. Dr McManus wanted to know what was the last food he'd eaten the night before. Will said fried fish and chips. Might have been the frying fat, said the doctor, you might be allergic to its acidity. Will asked if he might also be allergic to being close to a girl, and he mentioned his evening out with Annie, their closeness in the tram and their extreme closeness when he kissed her.

'Are we talking about physical excitement, Will?' asked Dr McManus.

'You did mention that,' said Will, and the doctor said he

supposed the Army medical specialists had mentioned a hundred and one possible elements. Will said they'd mentioned over-exertion as something to avoid, but hadn't said a word about physical excitement. Ruddy hell, doctor, he said, if he couldn't even kiss a girl without his bronchial tubes taking a hiding, what was the point of marrying one? Dr McManus said thousands of asthmatic men and women were married. Yes, said Will, but perhaps they can all do what comes naturally without wheezing and coughing over it.

'Well, do those two things again,' said Dr McManus.

'What two things?'

'Kissing your young lady and eating fried fish and chips. But not on the same day. Let's see if one or the other affects you. If not, then do what you did before, enjoy them near to each other.'

'Sounds barmy,' said Will.

'It might well be,' smiled Dr McManus. 'Do you carry your tablets about with you?'

'I do now,' said Will.

'You should.'

So there it was, then. It wouldn't do at this stage to give Annie any impression that he was courting her. It wouldn't be fair to her. Annie deserved a bloke who was a hundred per cent fit.

'Come on,' she said, 'what's on your mind?'

'Oh, just the Army,' he said, 'and if I'm goin' to be in or out of it.'

Annie wondered if his relationship with her had been anything to do with his idea about giving up the Army. She hoped he would.

They stopped by the tennis courts, all of which were being used.

'Let's sit and watch for a bit,' she said. There was a

bench vacant and they seated themselves. On another bench were a strong-looking man and a handsome woman. They were watching a tall man in a white cricket shirt and light grey flannels playing against a young and deliciously pretty girl in a white dress. Will recognized the players. The man, whom his family called Boots, was Sammy's eldest brother. The girl, Rosie, was Boots's daughter. Will had come to know them when Susie took him to meet the Adams family.

They were playing a typical father-and-daughter game, Boots teasing Rosie by making her chase from side to side, using his racquet in a lazy-looking way but making the ball fly over the net. Rosie, utterly involved, ran and scampered, the skirt of her short dress flying, her legs in white socks. She did more than chase after the ball, she yelled.

'Daddy, you stinker!'

But she was heart and soul into the fun of it, as she always was when any kind of game was just between her and Boots and she had him all to herself. All her affinity with him surfaced then.

Will thought the watching man and woman were very taken with her. Well, she wasn't bad at tennis. She had energy, enthusiasm and a good eye for a ball. Her enthusiasm was infectious. She screamed when Boots put a short one over, but she flew to get at it and just managed to plop it back. It left Boots stranded. She jumped up and down in her joy.

'Isn't she a young sport?' said Annie. 'I wish I could play tennis, it looks fun.'

'If I could play meself,' said Will, 'I'd teach you. Mind you, Annie, I've played football for the battalion. Like me to teach you that?'

'It's always been me dearest wish to play football, I don't think,' said Annie, sitting close to him because she liked being close, and Will began trying to puzzle out why the natural pleasure of the contact set off the little stirring sensations that threatened to sensitize his bronchial tubes, as they had the other evening.

Rosie yelled again.

'Daddy, I'll stick pins in you!'

'Play up, Rosie.'

'Will, what a lovely girl,' said Annie.

'She's Rosie Adams,' said Will, 'and that's her dad, Sammy's eldest brother.'

'Crikey, d'you know them?' asked Annie.

'Yes, I met all the Adams fam'ly, through Susie,' said Will.

''Ave they all turned posh, then, the Adams?'

'Not posh, no,' said Will. 'They used to live in the house we live in now. They bettered themselves when they left.'

'I don't blame them,' said Annie. 'I wish me dad had a chance to better 'imself, I bet he'd take it with both 'ands. Still, he's not down in the dumps about it, nor me. Nor you, are you, Will? I mean, well, I think we're betterin' ourselves just sittin' in the park and watchin' the tennis, don't you?'

'Are we?' asked Will, trying to ignore vibrations.

'Well, if we were sittin' on a doorstep in the Old Kent Road, we'd be more lower than better, wouldn't we?'

'More lower than better, yes, see what you mean,' said Will, who thought the strong-looking man on the other bench was concentrating a very fixed pair of mince pies on the scampering Rosie.

'It's nice we agree,' said Annie. 'I thought, when I first met you, I thought what an 'orror, I bet his parents despair of 'im. I don't know how you've managed to be such an improvin' feller; it must be the improved company

242

you've been keepin'. 'Ave you been goin' out to look at cathedrals with our vicar? He's ever so improvin', and nice as well.'

Will grinned. He watched Rosie serving, he watched her dance on quick feet as she waited for the return. He thought about Sally. Sally had quick feet and enthusiasms. He could just see her dancing about on a tennis court if she'd been given the chance to learn the game.

On the other bench, Madge said, 'Don't you wish she was yours, Henry?'

'What?' said Henry Brannigan.

'I mean don't you wish she was your daughter? She's a bit young for you otherwise.'

'I'm lookin', that's all,' he said.

'You ought to 'ave 'ad kids, Henry,' she said, 'then you wouldn't be such a lonely man. Come on, let's go back to the flat and I'll do us a nice Sunday tea, which I'd like to do, seein' 'ow good you're bein' to me.'

He had increased her allowance to two pounds a week because she was giving him suppers and Sunday dinner. She didn't think he'd only want food and company for ever. Well, when he wanted what was good for any real man, she'd be very willing.

Will and Annie left a few minutes later, Will deciding not to intrude on Boots and Rosie by making his presence known to them. Annie said he was going to have Sunday tea with her and her family, wasn't he? Will, who had kept the vibrations at bay simply by listening to Annie and watching the tennis, said he'd be pleasured.

'Pleasured?' said Annie. 'I 'ope you don't have larks in mind.'

'What larks?'

'Well, I don't know exactly how improved you are,' said Annie, 'you might not be improved all that much.'

'I think I've got larks comin' on,' said Will.

Annie's laughter gurgled.

I'll have to watch he doesn't put his head under the table again, she thought.

She experienced little vibrations then, but they weren't quite as alarming to her as Will's were to him.

'Me mum says you can stay to Sunday tea, Cassie,' said Freddy, who'd managed to resist her demands to be taken up the park again with her barmy cat. He'd persuaded her to ride around all the back streets instead, although she'd made his ears ache with her complaints that they wouldn't get to see the Prince of Wales or soldiers on horseback or the lady of a hundred and one nights. Freddy had had to ask the lady of what? Cassie, who naturally did a lot of reading, said there was a book about her and that she told stories to a sheikh on a white horse every night. Freddy said if he spent every night sitting on a white horse, he was as crackers as she was. Cassie complained he wasn't listening properly. Freddy said he was, that was why his ears were aching, and that anyone who told stories for a hundred and one nights was going a bit short of sleep. Cassie said well, she thought it was a hundred and one, and that she told her stories while she was wearing a big red ruby in her tummy button. Blimey, said Freddy, no wonder the sheikh couldn't get off his horse, with a big red ruby staring at him. Cassie complained he wasn't paying attention, and Freddy said he couldn't pay attention and ride his bike as well. Anyway, when they finally got home, Mrs Brown said Cassie could have Sunday tea with them, if she liked.

'Please, what yer got for tea?' asked Cassie.

'Boiled eggs, bread an' butter, salmon and shrimp paste, raspb'ry jam and cake,' smiled Mrs Brown.

'Crumbs, I'd like that,' said Cassie, 'but I'd best go 'ome first an' tell me dad I'm 'aving tea here.'

'I'll ride yer there,' said Freddy. A mate was a mate, even if she was scatty.

'No, I'll do a bit of walkin',' said Cassie, 'I don't think me bottom wants to sit on yer bike any more today.'

'Freddy, didn't you give her a cushion to sit on?' asked Mrs Brown.

'Course I did,' said Freddy, 'she gives me a rollickin' if I don't.'

'Yes, but I've gone all numb,' said Cassie.

'Cor,' said Freddy in glee, 'Cassie's got a numb bum.'

'Now, Freddy, you didn't ought to say that in front of Cassie,' said Mrs Brown.

'Oh, the Little Princess 'ad one of them,' said Cassie, 'when she sat on six velvet cushions that 'ad an 'ard pea under them. Well, I won't be long, I'll just go an' tell me dad.' Off she went, leaving Freddy grinning and Mrs Brown smiling. Will, Susie and Sally were all out, and Mr Brown was in the parlour, his feet up.

Along the pavement twinkled Mr Ponsonby, beaming at the sight of Cassie turning into Caulfield Place, her cat in her arms.

'Well, well, what a day, what a peaceful day,' he said, stopping.

'Yes, it's Sunday,' said Cassie.

'Sunday? Dear me, are you Cassie?'

'Yes, I'm goin' to 'ave tea with Freddy Brown,' said Cassie. She thought. 'I'm 'is mate. This is Tabby, me cat.'

'Charming, what a delightful picture,' said Mr Ponsonby happily. 'Have you had your photograph taken?'

'No,' said Cassie. 'Could yer take one, please, of me an' Tabby?'

'What a charming idea,' said Mr Ponsonby. 'I must find my camera. Dear me, where did I put it? Never mind, we must meet again, Sally—'

'I'm Cassie.'

'Why, yes, how pretty. Have a peppermint, Cassie.' Out came the paper bag. Cassie took one of the sweets. Tabby shifted about.

'Thanks ever so, I'll save it till after tea,' she said. 'Oh, could I 'ave one for Freddy?'

'Of course, of course, everyone must have a peppermint,' said Mr Ponsonby, and Cassie took one for her mate. Mr Ponsonby went pigeon-toed on his way, talking happily to himself. There were prospects, prospects.

Cassie arrived at the Browns' house with her cat. Freddy groaned.

'But 'e wanted to come,' said Cassie, ''e told me so. Well, 'e likes salmon an' shrimp paste.'

'An' boiled eggs?' said Freddy.

'No, just salmon an' shrimp paste,' said Cassie, 'as long as it's Kennedy's.'

In the parlour, Mr Brown shuffled his Sunday paper, turning again to a report on the Bermondsey murder. There was a reproduction of a Brownie snapshot of the unfortunate girl, and an artist's impression of the two missing girls. The Bermondsey scrap yard was mentioned more than once, and Collier and Son also featured. But not Adams Enterprises. All the same, Mr Brown neatly ripped out the relevant page, folded it and put it into his pocket.

Mr Brown was an old-fashioned guardian of his family's peace of mind. Susie, of course, knew the yard was the one he'd been promoted to manage, but none of the others did. More peaceful to keep it like that.

On the other hand, if the police caught the bloke, he

might have to appear at the trial as a witness to the discovery of the body. Then all the neighbours would be coming round to ask questions of his dear old Dutch and to say fancy your Jim finding that poor girl under his shed at work. Oh, well, thought Susie's cheerful dad, I'll look after that worry when it arrives, like old Noah said about the flood.

When Will finally said good night to Annie at her front door, he was in two minds about kissing her. Blimey, he thought, what a load of old turnips that was, any bloke being in two minds about kissing a girl like Annie. All the same.

'Well, Annie, it's been—'

'Lovely,' said Annie, and he wasn't given a chance then to do more shilly-shallying, because Annie wasn't in two minds herself. She kissed him. Well, of course, that did it for Will and he kissed her back, doing what came naturally instead of mucking about like a bloke who didn't know his knee from his elbow. Annie went wobbly with bliss and wondered what was happening to her legs. It felt as if they were going for a walk without her, leaving her with no support. So she hung on to Will. Ruddy marvels, thought Will, kissing her again, we're bosom to bosom and I like hers better than mine. Vibrations chased about, but nothing happened to his minor bronchial tubes. He felt A1 and in good order, and he also felt Annie was definitely just what the doctor ordered for Easter. So he kissed her some more. 'Help,' she said, coming out of a final kiss.

'Yes, I feel like a lie-down meself,' said Will. 'I'll go and collapse on me charpoy.'

'Your what?' said Annie faintly.

'Me Hindustani bed,' said Will. 'Good night, Annie, see you sometime durin' the week.'

'Good night, Will.' She closed the door when he'd gone. She felt breathless from being well and truly kissed. Oh, lor', me legs, they've run off somewhere.

It caught Will forty minutes later, the sensitization of his tubes. The time was twenty to eleven and he was just about to undress for bed in the room he shared with Freddy. Freddy was sound asleep and everyone else had retired. Knowing his coughing and wheezing would wake his young brother, Will just had time to get down to the kitchen before he began to fight for breath. He swallowed a tablet with difficulty, and then his coughing was racking him. He hoped his noisiness wouldn't disturb his parents, who occupied the downstairs bedroom between the kitchen and the parlour.

Mrs Brown lay awake listening to him and sighing for him. It was cruel, what life had done to her son, a young man only twenty. Poor Will. She wanted to get up to see if there was anything she could do for him, but she knew there wasn't, and she knew too that Will would rather be left alone.

It went on for what seemed like ages. It was for ten minutes, actually, but it left Will drained. You're bloody hopeless, mate, he told himself. It was a while before he took himself upstairs again.

Mrs Brown heard him go up.

CHAPTER EIGHTEEN

Susie had spent Sunday with her three closest girl friends, Evie Kent, Cora Bargett and Marjorie Willet, because it was her last Sunday as a single young lady. Accordingly, her friends weren't really sure if it was a Sunday of lamentation or celebration. They didn't put it quite like that, of course. If they had, they'd have thought they'd swallowed a dictionary. They'd never found the need to, not as Sammy had when establishing himself as a businessman who wasn't going to be out-talked.

As far as Evie was concerned it was more like poor old Susie, you're done for now. Cora suggested Susie could still be saved if someone came up with a just cause. Evie wanted to know what kind of just cause. Cora said some knowing bloke might be able to stand up in the church and yell bigamy on account of the bridegroom already having six wives. Evie said crikey, yes, that could save Susie. Marj said Susie might not want to be saved, that she didn't look as if she did. Susie said don't mind me, just keep talking. Evie asked her if she wanted to be saved. Only from you lot, said Susie.

Cora said Susie was bound to have worries. Have you got worries, Susie? Marj asked the question. Course she has, said Cora, she's got the terrible worry of being jumped on on her wedding night. Evie said you ain't half getting common, Cora. Come on, girls, let's clap hands and sing 'Here Comes The Bride', said Marj. Evie said what, on Clapham Common? You bet, said Cora, and let's do a knees-up as well. All right, said Marj, but let's all have a drop more port first.

Susie put a stop to that idea. A girls' picnic with port wine and lemon on Clapham Common was all right, but not a knees-up. Still, they all had a riotous hen party and tea out as well.

Susie went into Sammy's office first thing on Monday morning, presented herself to him as a very personable private secretary, said she was pleased to see him and gave him a kiss.

'I liked that, Miss Brown, and I won't say I didn't, but what was it for?'

'You,' said Susie.

'I naturally hope so, Miss Brown,' said Sammy, 'I'm against it bein' for anyone else.'

'It's for that great box of daffodils, Sammy darling.'

'A small token of me feelings, Susie, on account of you bein' invaluable in the office and highly desirable on your mum's parlour sofa. That's when your mum's not actu'lly there, of course.'

'Lucky for you she's not,' said Susie, 'she'd be shocked at the way you interfere with my bosom. Still, I love you for the daffodils, the house is full of them, except that Cassie's cat ate one at teatime yesterday, I'm told.'

'Who's Cassie?' asked Sammy.

'Freddy's young lady mate,' said Susie.

'Good on Freddy,' said Sammy. 'Did you enjoy a lively hen party?'

'Well, we had a port wine picnic and a knees-up,' said Susie.

'Where?'

'On Clapham Common.'

'Here, hold me up, I'm fallin' over,' said Sammy. 'A

250

knees-up on Clapham Common and you nearly me better half?'

'Oh, the knees-up was only nearly too,' smiled Susie. 'By the way, Boots says there's a mountain of post.'

'Right, see what our share is all about, Miss Brown, and let's get down to some work.'

'Yes, very good, Mister Sammy.'

Sammy popped into Boots's office later and asked him how Emily was. Boots said she was in her office. Sammy said he knew that. The point was, why was she getting so thin? Anaemia, said Boots briefly. You can be fat and still have anaemia, said Sammy. I know, said Boots, and you can be thin too. She needs lots of liver and exercise, said Sammy. I know, said Boots. I don't like to see her looking skinny, said Sammy. Nor do I, said Boots. Thought I'd ask about her, said Sammy. Yes, thanks, said Boots.

Just after twelve, Mrs Rachel Goodman knocked on Susie's outer door and entered.

'Good morning, Susie,' she said.

'Oh, good mornin', Mrs Goodman,' said Susie. If there was one woman she'd really been jealous of, it was Rachel Goodman, a dark and lustrous beauty who, in Sammy's younger days, had been his one and only girlfriend. According to Boots, she paid Sammy a penny to kiss her, and Sammy had acquired a small fortune in pennies from her. During his growing years, Sammy refused to kiss or be kissed unless he was given a penny. Susie suspected Rachel still had a soft spot for Sammy. Further, she really was a beautiful woman, a cockney Jewess whose father had given her an excellent education and helped her acquire a flair for always looking superbly dressed. Today she was wearing a light spring coat over a silk dress of lilac blue, and a dark blue cloche hat.

251

For her part, Rachel was careful not to go straight to Sammy's office. She had always done so before Susie became engaged to him. Nowadays she announced herself to Susie first, much though it went against the grain. As a girl she had adored Sammy, her gentile boy friend who not only took her roller-skating but also to his home to enjoy a Christian Sunday tea with his family. As a woman she still hankered after being close to him. Her husband, Benjamin Goodman, was a course bookie and coming up in the world. Horse-racing did not interest her in the least. Clothes did, and so did the rag trade. She was a shareholder in Adams Fashions Ltd and on the board of directors with Sammy, Boots, Tommy and their sister Lizzy. It was her way of being part of Sammy's life.

'Is Sammy in?' she asked.

'Is he expecting you?' asked Susie, and the fair and lovely clashed with the dark and lustrous. The dark and lustrous smiled.

'My life, Susie, must he be expecting me?'

'Oh, it's a sort of informal call?' said Sammy's extremely personable private secretary.

'Yes and no,' said Rachel, who liked Susie, as everyone did. She would simply have preferred Sammy to remain a bachelor. 'He's aware there might be a strike in the rag trade?'

'He's growlin' about it, but keepin' his end up,' said Susie.

'I've something to discuss with him.'

'I'll tell him you're here, Mrs Goodman,' said Susie. She got up, opened the door to Sammy's office and said, 'Mrs Goodman's here and would like to see you.'

'Well, I never,' said Sammy, 'ask her to step in.'

'There, you can go in, Mrs Goodman,' said Susie.

'Thank you, Susie,' said Rachel, her smile winning. She

was not a mean-minded woman, she was generous and warm-hearted. 'Good luck on Saturday, have a wonderful wedding. Sammy's a lucky man.'

'How kind,' said Susie, 'thank you.'

Rachel went in and Susie closed the door, although she would have liked to leave it open.

Sammy came to his feet. Rachel flowed towards him with soft little rustles of silk.

'Bless me soul, Rachel,' he said, 'ain't you a sight for me sore eyes?'

'Well, bless you, Sammy love, for saying so.'

'I'm up to me ears, but sit down. To what do I owe the pleasure of havin' you decorate my office?'

'You're my business interests, sweetie,' said Rachel. She parted her coat, delicately hitched her dress and sat down. Long legs gleamed in fine silk stockings.

Predictably, of course, Sammy said, 'Pardon me, but ain't that slightly out of order for a married female person?'

'Slightly,' agreed Rachel, 'but no more than you deserve, Sammy, having always been complimentary about my remarkable female legs. I'm coming to your wedding, of course, but I'll be a little mournful. You understand?'

'It won't make any difference to me respectable affections for you,' said Sammy. 'You bein' a well-behaved married woman and me bein' the reverent son of Chinese Lady, me affections have always been respectable, which if they weren't would make Susie hit me with her dad's chopper. I think she keeps it in her handbag. Choppers are injurious, Rachel.'

'Same old Sammy,' murmured Rachel. 'I should want a different one? Never. Now, what's going to happen to Adams Fashions if there's a strike that'll be injurious to our new contract with Coates?'

'I'm in touch with the mills and I've taken certain steps

concernin' buildin' up stocks,' said Sammy and put her fully in the picture. He included details of how he was going to keep the factory working.

'Ain't you a clever boy, Sammy, ain't you a love?' said Rachel, reverting to her Jewish cockney style. 'My life, what a bright boy. Oh, and my daddy says that to help you get married with two smiles on your face, he's arranged with the third party for you to sign the lease on the Oxford Street shop on Friday, the day before you go to the altar.'

'I'm touched, Rachel. Ain't you and Isaac me lifelong friends?'

'And ain't it mutual, Sammy love? Take me to lunch now, will you, while you're still a bachelor?'

'Did I catch that?' asked Sammy.

'Just a drink and a kosher sandwich, Sammy, for old times sake,' murmured Rachel, voice and eyes velvety. 'Last lunch, lovey, last time. I promise. Unless we accidentally run into each other in town.'

'I'll have to consult with me personal assistant who, bein' me personal fiancée as well, might say no and also beat me brains out.' Sammy found Susie up to her elbows in correspondence. 'Ah, Miss Brown, would you kindly note I'm about to depart on a business lunch? I'll be out for forty minutes or so.'

'Who with, if I might ask?' said Susie. 'I don't happen to have recorded any business lunch in your diary.'

'Just an oversight, I forgive yer,' said Sammy.

'Might I ask if it's with a certain married woman?'

'A member of the board of Adams Fashions,' said Sammy. Susie gave him a look. Sammy fell into her blue eyes. He coughed to clear his throat. 'Well, now I remember, she does happen to be related in marriage to her better half.'

Susie laughed. Sammy wriggling was so funny.

'It's the last time, Sammy, you hear?' she said.

'Which I've agreed on with the selfsame board member.'

'Your old flame,' said Susie.

'In a way, Susie, in a way.'

'Tell her her light's gone out,' said Susie.

'No worries, Susie.'

'I know.' Susie smiled. 'Run along, Sammy.'

'Do what? I'm hearin' things again,' said Sammy, departing.

'Well, lovey?' said Rachel.

'That Susie, what a performance,' said Sammy. 'I sometimes wonder who invented female women. Well, let's pop across to the pub, Mrs Goodman.'

'Lovely,' said Rachel, 'I want to talk to you about your old friend Eli Greenberg.'

Over lunch and sitting close to Sammy in the well-appointed saloon bar, Rachel dwelt on the present misfortunes of Mr Greenberg. He was, she said, a harassed gent. A certain lady had him in her liquid sights. Sammy asked if that meant her mince pies were floating in gin. Rachel said the lady was a respectable widow with three growing sons and had never touched a drop in her life. Mrs Hannah Borovich, that was her name.

'Russian, like Eli?' said Sammy.

'You've got it, Sammy,' said Rachel, a laugh in her eyes. The lady, she said, had made up her mind she needed a new father for her sons and had decided Mr Greenberg would fit the bill and also make her a fine husband. What, Eli Greenberg? Quite so, Sammy, said Rachel, and pointed out that Mr Greenberg, when dressed up on the Jewish Sabbath, was a handsome man. Sammy said he had to admit that when the well-known rag-and-bone man attended Chinese Lady's wedding to her second husband,

255

he looked highly presentable. Mrs Borovich, said Rachel, was prepared to devote herself to making him look presentable every day of the week. Dear Mr Greenberg was now beginning to panic, and was looking for hiding-places.

'He needs your help, Sammy.'

'What, to get out of the country?'

'No, to be saved from becoming a husband and father in one go.'

'Can't he just say no?'

'Mrs Borovich is deaf to negatives.'

'Well, poor old Eli and hard luck as well,' said Sammy.

'What help are you offering?'

'Who can help any bloke who's up against a deaf woman?'

'He's not up against her, Sammy love, she won't allow that until they're married. Mr Greenberg needs your brains. Think of something.'

'Any use offering him the loan of Susie's chopper? Well, her dad's chopper.'

'There'll be blood, Sammy. No blood, if you don't mind.'

'I'm beat,' said Sammy, but took time off to do some thinking. Rachel watched him with a little sigh in her eyes. Sammy, perking up, said, 'This deaf Mrs Boggervich—'

'Borovich, Sammy.'

'Just as you like, Rachel me affectionate friend. Point is, just how respectable is she?'

'Highly,' smiled Rachel.

'Good on yer,' said Sammy, and suggested that the only way to put off a female woman who was rigid with respectability and deaf to negatives was to personally assault her and interfere with her bosom as well.

Rachel almost choked on a mouthful of kosher beef sandwich with mustard.

'Sammy, Sammy, I'm to tell dear Mr Greenberg that?' she said, laughter choking her as well.

'With the compliments of me brains,' said Sammy.

'Never, Sammy, never. Mr Greenberg will collapse at the idea.'

'Not if he's desperate. He'll give it desperate thought. It could be all over in a couple of ticks. Chuck her on to his sofa, grab all he can of her, undo her buttons—'

'Sammy, you're killing me.'

'Hope not, Rachel, I've got fond memories of you as a roller-skater. Now, as soon as Mrs Boggervich realizes Eli is treadin' all over her widow's respectability, she'll jump out of his window and run a mile.'

'Oh, my God,' breathed Rachel, 'you're my one and only Punch and Judy, and with knobs on. Chuck the lady on to his sofa, grab her all over, undo her buttons—'

'That's just a few loose details, Rachel. Eli's got sense enough to tighten them up and to make the lady feel he's a ruddy wolf, never mind how respectable he looks on his Sabbath.'

'Sammy, I'm going to miss you as a bachelor,' said Rachel, and put her hand on his knee and squeezed it.

'Is that a personal assault?' said Sammy.

'Why couldn't you have assaulted me a bit when I was your girl?'

'What, at my age?' said Sammy.

The schools having broken up for the Easter holidays, there were kids everywhere, swarms of them. Henry Brannigan, a ganger working for contractors that specialized in demolishing buildings and clearing sites, reckoned there wasn't a pavement in London free of kids. Some of them were here, watching him and his mates clearing the site of what was left of a demolished builders' yard and sheds in Peckham. To one side was a huge fire they were feeding with wrecked timber.

''Ere, mister, can we 'ave some of that wood?' asked a boy.

'No, yer can't, so shove off, all of yer,' he growled.

'Go on, mister, be a sport.'

''Oppit, yer standin' in people's way,' he said. They were doing just that, the whole lot of them, filling the pavement just outside the barrier of ropes. Passing people had to push a way through the kids or step into the road. You could never tell about people. Some could be the kind that didn't like going under ladders or stepping on lines. These loitering kids could make life difficult for all kinds. Henry Brannigan had sympathy for kindred spirits, and life had done him a good turn for once by having him meet Madge. A bloke could talk to a woman like that, knowing she understood. She didn't mind kids herself, she didn't even mind them getting in her way.

'Mister, there's some nice bits of wood over there.' The voice was persistent.

'If you lot don't push off—' Henry Brannigan growled himself to a stop. 'Bloody 'ell, all right.' Madge wouldn't like him handing out clouts and thick ears instead of timber that was only going to finish up on the fire. ''Ere y'ar, then.' His workmates looked on in surprise as he got rid of a whole heap of timber by distributing it among the eager kids. Boys and girls all scrambled for it. Sacks materialized. Gawd blimey, he thought, look at that, the young bleeders have brought sacks. He chucked wood over the ropes at them. They scattered in retreat from a deluge of timber. Back they came when he'd finished showering the pavement. They loaded their sacks. Shafts of wood protruded.

'Ta, mister, yer a real sport.'

'Me mum'll like this lot.'

'Can we come back for some more, mister?'

'Well, all right. Now 'oppit.'

They hopped it. Away they went, dragging the heavily laden sacks along behind them. He stared at them. Look at what they were doing now, turning themselves into a sack-pulling procession, crowding the pavement with their feet as well as their sacks, and getting in everybody's way. There ought to be a law against awkward kids.

He spoke to Madge about it when they were walking that evening. Madge just said she thought he'd been kind.

'You like kids really, yer know,' she said, 'or you wouldn't 'ave 'anded out all that wood.'

'I don't like 'em gettin' in me way.'

'But they don't mean no 'arm,' said Madge. 'Well, they don't know about our superstitions.'

'Granted, Madge, but it don't do to treat fate light, I can tell yer,' he said, and they adjusted their walk as they entered the light of a street lamp. A running boy nearly cost Henry Brannigan dear. He almost stepped on a line that was plainly visible. The boy dashed by. A girl appeared. She was running too, and shouting as well.

'You Billy, come back 'ere! I'll wallop yer if you don't!' Up she came and ran straight between the man and the woman, who stopped. Henry Brannigan checked and drew a breath of relief.

'Nigh on done it in, both of us,' he said. 'Kids. Didn't I tell yer?'

'Wasn't the girl a goer, though?' said Madge, as they walked on and left the light behind them. 'Wish I 'ad one like 'er. Henry, can we go in a pub?'

'Well, you like a pub, Madge, even if you ain't much of a drinker.'

'Well, I ain't ever taken to mother's ruin,' said Madge, 'and I ain't likely to, but yes, I do like a pub and can make a glass last me a long time.'

He took her to one in the New Kent Road, where no-one recognized her or made her an offer. She wanted to stand treat, although she said it would be out of his money. He said it was always a gent's privilege to pay. He bought her the drink she liked, port and lemon, and himself an ale, and in the smoky, cosy atmosphere of the pub she told him she'd been to an orphanage near Norwood today, with the woman from next door. She'd already made friends with her, and she went with her to do a bit of voluntary work, because the place was crowded out with orphans and they were short of staff. There was a girl, nine years old.

'A girl, eh?' said Henry Brannigan brusquely.

'She's dyin' for a proper 'ome,' said Madge. 'I expect they all are, poor kids, but this one, well, she touched me 'eart. Would yer mind if I asked if I could 'ave her? I'd like to look after her, I could put another bed in the bedroom. I mean, now I'm livin' a decent life—'

'They'd ask yer for references, they'd ask if you was married.'

'Oh, gawd,' said Madge.

'No girls, anyway,' said Henry Brannigan.

'Don't yer like girls?'

'I'd be glad if yer'd drop the notion.'

'Well, all right, I will for a bit,' said Madge, 'but I know you've got a soft 'eart, and I'll ask yer again later on. You might be able to 'elp me get over any problems about references or not bein' married. You 'ave got a soft 'eart or you wouldn't be doin' for me what you are doin', settin' me up in that nice flat, givin' me an allowance an' not askin' for nothing. Yes, I'll ask yer again, Henry.'

'I 'ope you won't,' he said.

Scotland Yard had been busy. They'd established from available evidence and new enquiries that the murdered girl and the two missing girls had all disappeared during daylight hours on separate Saturday afternoons. They'd further established that not one person had seen any of them in company with a man. Enquiries concerning the possibility that someone might have witnessed an act of abduction came to nothing. But there was the reasonable assumption that Saturday afternoons suggested a pattern of acts by one man, a man whose job kept him off the streets during the day until his working week finished at Saturday midday.

The girls had disappeared in circumstances that had attracted no notice. Abduction would surely have been noticed in one case out of three.

Scotland Yard decided all three girls had known the man.

'Ton of Brooke Bond tea,' said a well-known voice on Tuesday morning, and Annie looked up from the till. Will had done it on her again, hiding himself behind a customer and then popping up.

'I think you're familiar to me,' she said.

'Hope not,' said Will, 'me mum and the Army both brought me up not to be familiar to young ladies.'

Annie glanced around. Mr Urcott and Miss Banks both had customers.

'It didn't feel like that at me front door on Sunday night,' she whispered.

'Didn't feel like what?'

'As if you didn't go in for bein' familiar.'

'Must have forgotten me manners,' said Will. 'What about the Brooke Bond?'

'How much did you ask for?'

'Quarter-pound packet,' said Will, 'plus a pound of dried apricots, a tin of mustard powder and a pound packet of salt.'

'Yes, sir, thank you, sir,' said Annie, liking the look of him very much. She served him. 'Anything else, sir?'

'Well,' said Will, who felt he ought to step aside in favour of some bloke who could offer Annie health and virility instead of a wheezing chest, 'I've decided I'd better stay in the Army. There's too much unemployment knockin' around in Southwark and Lambeth.'

'Oh,' said Annie wishing he hadn't chosen to tell her here in the shop. At home she could have talked to him about it.

Will, knowing the Army was more likely to discharge him than to let him stay on, could have told Annie so and given her the reason. But he preferred not to present himself as a semi-invalid. It was a case of a young man trying to step aside in what he thought was the way a decent bloke should.

'I'll probably be rejoinin' my battalion in India when my leave's up,' he said. The battalion, actually, was due to be posted home in a few months, when its spell of duty in India would be at an end.

Annie felt a painful blow had been struck.

'Rotten old Army,' she said bravely. Two new customers came in. 'Look,' she said, 'I'll speak to my dad. He might know if you could get a job on the railways.'

'Well, thanks, Annie,' said Will. 'How much for the groceries?'

Annie told him, he paid up, put the items into his

carrier bag, said he'd see her at the wedding dance on Saturday, gave her a smile and left. Annie felt then that some old dark blind had been drawn over her sunshine.

'Lookin' forward to dancing at the weddin', Annie?' said the Gaffer over a supper of fried mackerel that evening.

'If I get there,' said Annie, and the Gaffer glanced at her. She wasn't too lively this evening.

'But it's only down Larcom Street,' said Nellie.

'I ain't keen on dancin' meself,' said Charlie.

'Lucky you ain't been invited, then,' said Nellie.

'Nor me,' said Cassie, 'I ain't been invited, either.'

'Well, you'd only want to take the cat wiv yer,' said Charlie.

'Yes, 'e likes weddings,' said Cassie, ''e'd like to go to Lord Percy's weddin'.'

'Cassie, who's this Lord Percy you keep talkin' about lately?' asked Nellie.

'I read about 'im,' said Cassie, ''e lives in a castle with four 'undred servants.'

''Ow many?' asked the Gaffer.

'Yes, and 'e's got ten motorcars and an 'undred black 'orses an' carriages. 'E's goin' to marry a princess.'

'What princess?' asked Nellie.

'I didn't read which one it was,' said Cassie. 'Here, Tabby.' She fed a piece of mackerel to the cat, a large piece.

'Cassie, you just fed 'alf yer supper to Tabby,' said the Gaffer.

'Well, 'e likes fish,' said Cassie, 'an' besides, 'e's courtin'.'

''E's what?' said Nellie.

'It's Mrs Boddy's lady cat,' said Cassie, ''e's been out nearly all day with 'er, and it's made 'im 'ungry.'

'Why?' asked Charlie.

''Ow do I know?' said Cassie. 'I know some things, I don't know ev'rything. Annie, does courtin' make ladies blush?'

'Don't ask me, I'm not bein' courted,' said Annie.

'Oh, ain't Will courtin' yer?' asked Nellie.

'He's married to the Army,' said Annie. No, blow that, she thought, putting aside depression, I'm not going to let him get away with it. Just wait till Saturday and I see him in the Institute. I'm going to stand up for my rights. I've got rights after being kissed till I couldn't hardly stand up. 'Cassie, I suppose you read it somewhere, did you, that courtin' makes ladies blush?'

'Yes, it was in a story, it said that when the 'andsome explorer kissed Lady Penelope on 'er marble staircase, it made 'er blush all over.'

'Well, I'm blowed,' said the Gaffer, 'a kiss on 'er marble staircase, was it? I don't ever remember I kissed any lady meself except on 'er dewy lips.'

'Dewy lips?' Nellie giggled. 'Where'd you get that from, Dad?'

'Well, I do a bit of readin' meself,' said the Gaffer.

'Cassie, 'ow'd yer know Lady Whatsername blushed all over?' asked Nellie.

'Wasn't she wearin' nothink?' asked Charlie.

'Course she was,' said Cassie, 'she was wearin' a ruby velvet gown.'

'So 'ow'd yer know she blushed all over?' asked Charlie.

'It said so. It said – oh, 'elp,' sighed Cassie, looking down at the cat.

'What's up?' asked the Gaffer.

'I think Tabby's just done a wee-wee on the kitchen floor,' said Cassie.

CHAPTER NINETEEN

The horse and cart crossed the junction at Camberwell Green, entered Denmark Hill and pulled up outside the public house that was opposite the shop and offices of Adams Enterprises. Mr Greenberg climbed down, put a nosebag on his horse and crossed the road like a man so careless of his life and limb that a tram driver gave him a full clang of his bell. It was doubtful if Mr Greenberg heard it.

He arrived in Sammy's office with his hat off, his red handkerchief mopping his distracted brow.

'Hello, Eli, what's brought you?' asked Sammy.

'Sammy, Sammy, you have ruined me.'

'First I've heard of it,' said Sammy. 'Are you speakin' of bankruptcy?'

'Vorse, Sammy, vorse, ain't it?'

'Is it?'

'Vasn't it only yesterday I vas hale and hearty and a free man? A poor man, Sammy, but a free one. Today I am ill and in chains.'

'Well, I'm up to me ears in work meself, Eli, but sit down and get it all off your chest. I've got a feelin' you're referring to a highly personal matter concernin' your private life.'

Mr Greenberg, sighing, sat down and began to recount the sad story of his highly personal and private downfall. In the belief that Sammy's advice, passed to him by Rachel Goodman, would relieve him of the pressing attentions of the widow, Mrs Hannah Borovich, he received her into his house last night in his shirt, braces and trousers, which itself startled the lady, she being a woman of propriety. Forthwith, as advised, Mr Greenberg laid hands on her like a man of no propriety at all and bore her to the sofa. There, he did what he could to assault her respectable bosom in a way that would convince her to regard him as the daughters of Abraham regarded Lucifer. Calamity occurred. Mrs Borovich flung her arms around him, kissed him and declared herself his willing woman. She further declared that afterwards she would go with him at once to Rabbi Goldstein for the marriage contract to be arranged. Mr Greenberg, aghast, began to struggle. Alas, Mrs Borovich declared herself already fully compromised, for her blouse and corset were gaping, which Mr Greenberg swore to Sammy wasn't his doing.

Sammy roared with laughter. Mr Greenberg eyed him in sorrow.

'Ve are not amused, Sammy.'

'She cooked your goose for you, Eli.'

'Vhat a schemin' voman, ain't it?' groaned Mr Greenberg.

'Do you good, old cock,' said Sammy, 'seein' Rachel informed me she's a handsome lady. You saw the rabbi?'

'Vhat else could I do, Sammy? Vhat else vould she let me do? Didn't she herself take me there vithout vunce lettin' go of me, and didn't Rabbi Goldstein greet me vith a hundred smiles and shake my hand?'

Sammy said it was a lesson to both of them, that it didn't matter what kind of a straightforward plan a man thought up, any female woman could put her foot through it and set about turning him upside-down. He himself had been stood on his head by a certain young woman on frequent occasions, despite him being a self-made man of considerable brains. Which proved one thing for certain.

'Vhat thing?' asked Mr Greenberg.

'Blokes never learn, Eli, not even you and me,' said Sammy. 'I ought to have remembered that when I put my wheeze to Rachel to pass to you. Now I know why she laughed. She knew what was goin' to happen, that Mrs Boggervich was goin' to turn you upside-down. Well, I'll resign meself to your weddin', Eli, and hope you'll invite me and Susie.'

'Ah, the veddin',' said Mr Greenberg, and groaned again. 'A vife and three growing sons to be my responsibility? The expense, Sammy, the expense.'

'I feel for you, don't think I don't,' said Sammy. 'Ruination has already hit all me own pockets. Still, a handsome woman, think of the compensations. And she can cook, I suppose?'

'Sammy, I should think of food vhen my stomach don't have any heart left?'

'Look on the bright side,' said Sammy.

'But a vife and three sons, Sammy.'

'Congratulations,' said Sammy. 'There's a bottle in me sideboard there. Kindly take a nip with me on account of the blessings.'

'Vell, Sammy, a nip at a sad time like this is a velcome sign of friendship, ain't it?'

'Cassie, you ain't bringing that cat,' said Freddy. His mum had made some sandwiches for him and Cassie, and supplied an apple each as well. They were going to eat them in Kennington Park.

''E's got to come,' said Cassie, ''e keeps goin' off with Mrs Boddy's lady cat. 'E'll go off with 'er for good one day. She wants 'im to marry 'er.'

'Oh, he's said so, 'as 'e?' said Freddy.

'Yes, 'e tells me ev'rything,' said Cassie.

'Well, ask 'im to tell yer if 'e minds stayin' behind,' said Freddy. 'They won't let 'im in the park.'

'I'll look after him, love,' said Mrs Brown.

'Oh, all right,' said Cassie.

'I went up the park earlier,' said Freddy. 'They said they'd mind me bike when we get there, Cassie, but they said they didn't want yer cat around, that they'd got orders to chop its 'ead off if yer bring it. So yer'd better let me mum mind it.'

'Yes, I said all right. 'E likes fish best, Mrs Brown.'

'I'll find him something,' said Mrs Brown.

Off the boy and girl went, Cassie riding astride a cushion and swinging her legs. Going along Manor Place, she said, 'Me sister Annie's been invited to the weddin'.'

'Yes, but me bruvver Will says she can't get there till about five,' said Freddy.

'I ain't been invited,' said Cassie.

'Well, you can come with 'er, if you like,' said Freddy. 'I expect me mum'll let yer.' Up Doddington Grove they went, Freddy ringing his bell at kids. 'Do yer do dancin'?'

'Course I do,' said Cassie, dreaming of kings in scarlet and queens in diamonds. 'Is there goin' to be photographs?'

'Susie won't 'alf get vexed if there ain't.'

'I'm 'aving me photo took,' said Cassie.

'Who by?' asked Freddy, totally resigned to having a scatty mate.

'Mr Po's'by,' said Cassie.

'Is 'e goin' to charge yer?' asked Freddy, skirting a slow-moving corporation water-cart.

'Course not,' said Cassie. ''E likes me, 'e gives me peppermints.'

'Fancy that,' said Freddy. ''Ere, if you come with yer sister on Saturday, don't expect me to dance with yer.'

'I'll kick yer if you don't,' said Cassie.

When they reached the park, a keeper obligingly took care of the bike, and Cassie took care of Freddy. That is, she made him go where she went and she made him carry the shopping bag in which were the wrapped sandwiches and the apples. She also told him to get her a bunch of daffodils. There were beds of them. Freddy said not on your life, his mum didn't allow him to nick daffodils and his dad would give him a talking-to. Cassie said he didn't have to nick them, just help himself when the park-keepers weren't looking. The Queen helped herself to lots of daffodils at Windsor Castle, and the King never told her it was nicking. Freddy said as he didn't happen to be the Queen, he wasn't going to help himself. Cassie said he couldn't be the Queen, anyway, he wasn't a lady.

'Thank gawd for that,' said Freddy. Still, even if she was scatty, she wasn't such a bad mate, because when it came to eating the sandwiches she let him have two and a half while she only had one and a half. And when he'd eaten his apple, she let him have two bites out of hers, and she also let him have the core, which he crunched to juicy destruction.

A mate like that was quite valuable to a bloke.

'Here's all the letters, Boots,' said Emily that afternoon, and placed the tray on his desk. 'I'm off now to buy the fam'ly's Easter eggs.'

He looked up at her, into her green eyes. She was all green eyes and thin face.

'Good for you, Em. Sure you're not overdoing things?'

'I'm fine. And you know me, if I've got nothing to do except sit and twiddle me thumbs, I'm not fit to live with. Behave yourself now, see you at home later.' Emily kissed him, warmly and affectionately. It left him in a reflective mood, signing the letters without taking too much notice of their contents.

'I did yer room out today, 'Enry,' said Mrs Queenie Watts, intercepting her brother as he entered the house in the evening.

'What for?' asked Henry Brannigan.

'Well, you've been in a nice and 'elpful mood lately,' she said, 'and yer lookin' lots better.'

'You don't need to do me room out, Queenie,' he said, sure she hadn't done very much to any of the others. His own room was private to him, anyway.

'I'd of done yer cupboard out, given it a bit of a tidyin',' she said, 'only yer keep it locked, I notice.'

'I've got personal things in it, mementoes, like.'

'Oh, about yer poor Matty, of course. Still, I thought I'd give yer room a nice clean-up, and I put a bit of polish on the furniture.' Actually, she'd just given everything a flick with her feather duster while nosing around to see if there was anything that would point to him having found a woman.

'Good of yer, Queenie, but I can manage.'

'Well, it's pleasin' yer not so sorrerful about things,' said Queenie. 'You sure you ain't found someone that's givin' you a bit of a lift?'

'I've made a few friends lately.'

'Well, I'm glad to 'ear it,' she said, and let him go up to his room. She wondered if there was any money in that cupboard. He got a decent wage and he'd collected from an insurance company when his wife fell out of that train and went to her death, poor woman. Queenie felt she wouldn't mind a bit of a loan that would pay for her and Stan to have a week in Margate.

★　　★　　★

Scotland Yard men were in dogged pursuance of the conviction that the man they were after had been known to the murdered girl and the two still missing. For the two still missing, they had the gravest concern, and at the moment were conducting exhaustive enquiries in and around the respective areas in which the three girls had lived.

Good Friday being a holiday, Susie had a word with Sammy at four o'clock on Thursday afternoon. First, might she leave now to go to certain shops before they closed?

'You might, Miss Brown, except—'

'Thank you, Sammy.' Second, might she point out that when they next met it would be at the altar?'

'What altar?'

'Yes, I hope I remember which one too. Sammy, I just want to say thanks for everything, for givin' me a chance and believin' in me when I had my first job on your market stall, and for – oh, you know.'

'What, Susie?'

'For lovin' me and askin' me. I like it, don't you, Sammy?'

'Marryin' each other?' said Sammy.

'Yes, it's such a nice idea,' smiled Susie, 'and don't forget to promise to love, honour and obey.'

'Me? Me do what?'

'Yes, it'll be best that way,' said Susie. 'I'll speak to the vicar.'

'You Susie—'

'There's a good boy. See you Saturday, love.' Susie kissed him and departed, leaving Sammy floored. She looked in on Boots.

'Going?' said Boots, seeing she had her hat on.

'Yes, to do some quick shoppin',' said Susie. 'Boots, thanks ever so.'

'What for?'

'For bein' on my side all the time.'

'Orders from above,' said Boots. 'Years ago.'

'Your mum?'

'Yes. Make sure, she said, that your disreputable brother Sammy puts a ring on Susie's finger now she's growing ladylike.'

'I bet you said that, not your mum.'

'Same thing. Good luck, Susie.'

'Em'ly's all right?'

'Fine.'

'It's rotten about her anaemia. Oh, I've got to fly. 'Bye, Boots.'

Not until ten past five did Sammy remember something he'd forgotten. He wasn't surprised his brains were failing him. The wedding was only two fateful days away. He opened the top drawer of his desk. It contained four small packages wrapped in white decorative paper. One bore Susie's name, and the others were for the three brides-maids, Sally, Rosie and Annabelle. He took out the packets for Susie and Sally, and called Ronnie in. Ronnie arrived briskly at his desk.

'Got your bike, Ronnie?'

'You bet, sir.'

'Good,' said Sammy. Ronnie could deliver to Susie and Sally, and Boots would take care of the packets for Rosie and Annabelle. He himself would be working late. Well, it was Good Friday tomorrow, the wedding on Saturday and then the honeymoon. 'I recollect, Ronnie, that you did me a favour last week. You can do me another. Same house. Kindly hand in these packets, and make sure you don't lose either of 'em. You've heard about bein' buried alive, have you?'

'That I have, Mister Sammy, and I don't fancy havin' it 'appen to me,' said Ronnie.

'Well, it will if these don't get safely delivered. Buzz off in immediate fashion and then go home.'

'Right, sir,' said Ronnie. He looked at the names on the packets, and a little grin showed. Off he went, riding his bike at speed along the Walworth Road.

It was Freddy who came to the door this time.

'Hello,' said Ronnie, 'how's your father?'

'I'd ask 'im,' said Freddy, 'only 'e ain't 'ome from work yet.'

'Might I see Miss Sally Brown?'

Freddy turned and shouted.

'Sally, there's a bloke wants to see yer!'

Sally came to the door and Freddy left them to it.

'I know you,' she said.

'Am I addressin' Miss Sally Brown?' asked Ronnie.

'Don't start that again,' said Sally, 'or I'll call me mum to 'elp you put a sock in it.'

'Would you like me to come in an' meet her?' asked Ronnie.

'You can meet 'er at the weddin', if you're really comin',' said Sally, 'and you can 'ave a dance with 'er.' She saw the two small packets in his hand. Presents had been arriving at intervals. 'You sure you should've asked for me? I mean, are those for Susie? She's not in yet.'

'It says Miss Sally Brown on this packet, and I'm deliverin' it with the compliments of Mr Sammy Adams.'

'Honest? It's for me?'

'He asked me to safeguard it with me life or I'd get buried alive.'

'Well, I believe that,' said Sally. She took the packet

273

and saw her name on it. 'You sure 'e hasn't made a mistake?'

'Workin' as I do with Mr Sammy Adams, I can tell you he doesn't go in for makin' mistakes,' said Ronnie.

'Well, thanks for bringing this,' said Sally. He gave her the packet for Susie. 'An' for this one as well.'

'Don't mention it,' said Ronnie, 'a pleasure, yer know.'

'I don't want to keep you,' said Sally.

'All right, I'll buzz off now, shall I?'

'Yes, we're sort of busy,' said Sally, wondering what Sammy had sent her, but willing to wait a bit before opening it.

'Yes, you've got the weddin',' said Ronnie, 'so I won't come in.'

'No, all right,' said Sally.

'So long, then.'

'So long,' said Sally.

'See you at the weddin',' said Ronnie.

'You'll see my dad as well, so don't try to get off with me.'

'Why not?'

''E'll bash your face in,' said Sally.

'I still like you,' grinned Ronnie, and went off whistling again.

Sally opened her packet and disclosed her bridesmaid's present, a lovely chased silver bracelet. With it was a note from Sammy.

'*To Sally, my new sister. Lots of love, Sally love. Sammy.*'

Susie's bridal present was a gold bracelet, suitably engraved. Susie, on receipt of it, wondered if she could ask the lovely man to give Sally a job in one of the firm's shops.

Annie was preparing for battle. Not of a noisy kind or of

the kind where blood would flow. Nor of the kind that would spoil the wedding celebrations. The battlefield would be a quiet corner in the Institute. Will wouldn't finish up actually wounded, but he might have a headache as well as an earache. She'd let him know she wasn't going to be kissed like he'd kissed her and then be expected to listen to him more or less saying that the most she could look forward to was a picture postcard from somewhere in India. Just you wait, Will Brown.

Will was preparing to enjoy the wedding as much as he could, without having any idea of what was going to hit him. Aside from that, Dr McManus had asked him this morning if Annie used scent. Scent? Yes, you could be allergic to scent. That could have brought on your attack after you left her on Sunday night. I don't think Annie uses scent, said Will, but Susie does. Not every scent need affect you, said Dr McManus. I'm a case for the dustbin if any scent at all affects me, said Will.

The evening being sunny, Boots and Emily took a walk. Tim and Rosie went with them, except that Rosie took Tim by the hand and made him walk with her in advance of their parents.

'What you doing this for?' asked Tim.

'So that Mum and Dad can have lovey-dovey Easter talk,' said Rosie.

'What, about choc'late Easter eggs?' asked Tim hopefully.

'Crikey, what a clever boy,' said Rosie, 'fancy guessing right.' She was sure, however, that Boots was going to talk to Emily about her being too thin.

Emily was saying, 'Boots, I'm goin' to see Dr McManus. Dr Thompson said I could if I want, he said a second opinion might help.'

'Good idea,' said Boots.

'I don't want to end up as a collection of walkin' bones,' said Emily.

'You'd rattle,' said Boots lightly. It was one way of bringing a smile to her face, making little jokes. She didn't like anyone being a wet blanket about her condition. Wet blankets had never been a great favourite with Emily.

She was smiling as she said, 'Stop tryin' to make me laugh, I might come apart.'

'Not you, Em, you'll always soldier on.'

'Bless yer,' said Emily. 'Look at our Rosie, she's always so nice with Tim. Aren't we lucky, all of us havin' each other? Is Polly Simms goin' to write to you?'

'Hello, where did that question come from?' asked Boots.

'From all me suspicions that she's only gone to darkest Africa so's she can play hard to get,' said Emily.

'Silly girl,' said Boots.

'Who, me?'

'Yes, you,' said Boots, and put an arm around her waist. Rosie, glancing back, smiled.

'There, I told you,' she said to Tim, who was trying out a hop, skip and jump way of getting along. 'They're having lovey-dovey.'

'I like choc'late Easter eggs better,' said four-year-old Tim.

CHAPTER TWENTY

There was no day off on Good Friday for some workers, including Henry Brannigan. And of all the cursed luck, he trod on a line on his way to work. Coming out of a baker's shop, where he'd bought a couple of hot cross buns to eat with his can of mid-morning tea, he stepped aside for two women. If things hadn't changed a bit for him, he'd have stood his ground or barged his way between them. But his companionship with Madge had been making him act like a gent. He'd been stepping aside, although always with an eye for the lines. This time he did it without taking heed. He actually had a careless moment. Immediately, he knew a line was under the sole of his boot. He knew it. He looked down. Curse it, there it was, his right boot on a line. He had to start watching out for bad luck from then on.

The works manager arrived on the site at twenty to twelve. He spent ten minutes inspecting progress, then demoted the foreman on the spot. He cast his eyes around, then spoke.

'Brannigan, come here.'

This is it, thought Henry Brannigan, the bleeding bad luck's caught up with me already, and I'm going to lose a well-paid job. And that means giving Madge the push from the flat.

'What's the trouble, guv?' he asked.

'The gang's not pulling its weight, that's the trouble, Brannigan,' said the works manager. 'Your bloody foreman's useless.'

'Maybe he is,' said Henry Brannigan, 'but I ain't.'

'I grant that. How'd you get on with the rest of the men?'

'I don't spend time socializin' with any of 'em, I've got me work to do.'

'Right. You're the foreman at ten more bob a week. But you'll be out on your neck if you don't get the right amount of work out of them. That clear?'

'That's clear, guv.' Henry Brannigan gave no indication of how astounded he was.

'Right. Inform your gang and get 'em working. That includes Duffy, who's just lost the foreman's job.'

Henry Brannigan got the men working and the ex-foreman too, the while wondering if fateful bad luck was going to come chasing after good luck. Bad luck could arrive in the form of a pickaxe being accidentally dropped on his head by one of the men.

Madge spent the day helping at the orphanage with her friend, taking with her six pounds of bull's-eyes, which she had made up into little packets of five sweets each. She was allowed to give them out to the girls and boys, and was able to talk to the nine-year-old girl, Lucy Peters, who had taken her fancy. Lucy was pathetically eager to have a family adopt her. It did happen from time to time, one child or another being given a home, and they were nearly always the younger children.

'Where's that scatty girl got to?' grumbled Freddy, and went out to the gate to have another look for her. Will had taken Sally and Susie for a tram ride all the way to Purley, to help calm the nerves of tomorrow's bride and brides-maid. But we've got things to do, Susie had said. No, you haven't, said Will, everything's organized, and the pair of you are only trying to find something that isn't. So at two o'clock, the three of them left, by which time young Cassie was late. She'd said she'd come round at a quarter to two and go to Ruskin Park again on his bike. She'd bring Tabby, she said. You won't, said Freddy. Cassie said perhaps his mum would mind him again then. Mum and Dad's going for a walk, said Freddy. Oh, I'll bring his piece of string, said Cassie, and they can take him with them. Freddy ordered her to leave the daft cat at home. Oh, all right, I'll see, said Cassie.

It was now a quarter to three, and Freddy was by himself, his mum and dad out on their walk. So he rode round to Cassie's house in Blackwood Street, although he knew he might miss her if she was on her way, because she could wander dreamily in all directions before arriving in Caulfield Place.

There was no answer. Mr Ford had taken Annie, Nellie and Charlie for a bus ride to Hyde Park, the day being warm and fine, the April breeze quite balmy. Freddy started to ride around the back streets in a search for his wandering mate. He rode everywhere he could think of, stopping once or twice to ask kids if they'd seen Cassie Ford. Who's she? He described her. No, we ain't seen her. He kept going back home during his tour of the streets, but there was no Cassie, and his parents were still out. They were actually in the house of neighbours in Browning Street, having been invited in for a cup of tea and a bit of a chat.

By half-past four, Freddy was frankly a worried lad. Cassie wasn't so daft as to lose herself. He rode again to Blackwood Street, but she wasn't at home, nor was anyone else. He asked a girl if she'd seen Cassie Ford.

'Yes, I seen 'er come out of 'er house ages ago,' said the girl.

279

'D'yer know what time it was?' asked Freddy.

'Well, I might if I 'ad a watch, but I ain't. It was just ages ago.'

That really worried Freddy. Again he searched around, and again he went back home. Nobody was there. So he rode to Rodney Road police station and told the desk sergeant all about Cassie and how she was missing.

'If you're havin' us on, me lad, you're for it,' said the desk sergeant.

'Course I ain't 'aving you on,' said Freddy. 'She was comin' round to our 'ouse at quarter to two, an' look at yer clock, it's gone five.'

'Where's her fam'ly?'

'I dunno,' said Freddy, 'except they ain't in.'

'Well, she's probably with them.'

'No, she ain't,' said Freddy, 'if she'd gone with them she'd 'ave come an' told me first. She's me mate.'

'What's her name again?'

'Cassie Ford.'

'And her fam'ly live where?'

'Ten Blackwood Street,' said Freddy. He described Cassie and gave her age.

The police sergeant alerted himself then. Missing girls. Scotland Yard.

'Right, Freddy Brown, you're a bright lad, after all. We'll get someone round to her house immediate.'

'But there's no-one there.'

'There might be now, Freddy, and we'd like to talk to her fam'ly. They might know where she went if she didn't go with them.'

'But she was comin' to see me, I told yer,' said Freddy.

'She might have changed her mind. Now don't you worry, we'll see to it. You keep searchin', like you have been and come and tell us if you find her. Will you do that?'

'All right,' said Freddy.

'Good lad.'

Freddy rode back home. A taxi passed him as he turned into Caulfield Place. He was in hope that Cassie would be at his gate. She wasn't, but the taxi pulled up outside it. Freddy rode up. Out stepped a man he knew, a man he liked. It was Sammy's eldest brother, Boots. His daughter Rosie followed him out of the taxi. Father and daughter were both laden with gift parcels.

'Hello, Freddy,' said Boots, and asked the cabbie to wait.

'I got yer, guv,' said the cabbie, and kept his clock ticking.

'Hello, Freddy,' said Rosie. They'd met once. They were going to be loosely related. 'We come bearing gifts, don't we, Daddy?'

'Wedding gifts from various members of the family,' said Boots.

'Ev'ryone's out except me,' said Freddy.

'Well, we'll load them on to you,' said Boots.

Freddy led the way into the house, and Boots and Rosie placed the gifts on the parlour table. The parlour was awash with wedding presents.

'Mister Adams—' Freddy hesitated.

'What's up, Freddy?' Boots liked the boy.

'It's Cassie.'

'Who's Cassie?'

Freddy rushed into words. Boots eyed him searchingly. Rosie looked concerned.

'If you've been to the police, Freddy,' said Boots, 'how can I help?'

'I dunno, Mister Adams, honest I don't,' said Freddy,

'except I think – well, I think – Mister Adams, I dunno what I think.' What he actually thought was that Boots was the kind of bloke he needed at the moment.

'Daddy, you've got to help look,' said Rosie, 'we can't just leave Freddy here on his own. He's Susie's brother. Well, Aunt Susie's, I suppose. I mean my aunt from tomorrow. Daddy, buck up.'

'Come on, Freddy, we'll use the taxi,' said Boots, 'we'll eat up the streets with that.'

'Yes, come on, Freddy,' said Rosie, 'let's all buck up.'

Thirty minutes later, they were still riding around in the taxi. They'd been first to Cassie's house, where there was still no-one home. Boots thought that just as well in one way, for the hope was that Cassie could be found before her family were sent into a state of alarm. He had his mind on the murdered girl and the missing girls. And he didn't doubt that Cassie was somewhere in this area, whether she was lost or someone had her.

He asked the cabbie to head for the police station. Once there, he spoke to the desk sergeant, who said he had men out searching, men who were making regular calls at Blackwood Street. Boots asked to use the phone. He had a quiet authority. He phoned home. Chinese Lady answered. He explained what he was doing and that he and Rosie would be late back. Chinese Lady said she didn't mind what time he and Rosie got back, that Emily wouldn't mind either, as long as he found the girl.

'You got a tickin' meter, guv,' said the cabbie, as he re-entered the taxi.

'Never mind that,' said Boots.

'I'm with yer all the way,' said the cabbie, who knew what the search was all about now. 'Let's get goin', eh?'

They set off again, the cabbie pulling up whenever

282

required to, so that Boots or Freddy could get out and ask the relevant questions of people. They widened the search, then headed back towards Browning Street. Freddy shouted.

'It's 'er cat! Look! Mister Adams, look!'

Tabby was whisking away down the shabby street, the street in which sagging timber gates guarded the entrance to a destroyed factory.

'Pull up,' said Boots.

The taxi came to a stop outside the gates.

'Mister Adams, the cat, it came out through the gates!' shouted Freddy. 'I saw it!'

Tabby was disappearing fast. A moment later the street was deserted except for the taxi. The derelict ruin of the factory brooded in the evening light of Good Friday, a day given over to religious rites. Boots alighted, followed by Freddy and Rosie.

'Mister Adams, there's a place in there where Cassie might be, honest there is,' said Freddy, and told Boots of the time he'd been here with her, looking for her cat, and how he'd found it in what was left of the factory. He said there was a room that looked as if it was sometimes used by a night watchman. It had a bed, a table and cupboards.

'Right, Freddy, we'll go in,' said Boots.

'I'll come with yer, guv,' said the cabbie. He switched off his meter and climbed out.

'All right, troops,' said Boots, 'it's the first lead we've had, so let's see what we can make of it. Perhaps Cassie got herself locked in.'

Freddy thought what a great bloke he was, and as calm as you like. He'd been a sergeant in the war. Freddy reckoned he ought to have been a general.

Boots squeezed his way through the gap in the gates and brought Rosie through after him. Freddy and the

283

cabbie followed. Boots saw the standing section. It looked gaunt and forlorn. He led the way around the mounds of brick and rubble. Feet made crunching noises. They reached the barred and padlocked door. Boarded windows stared blankly. Freddy shouted.

'Cassie? Cassie? You there, Cassie?' He banged on the door with his fist. They listened. There was no response, not a single sound. Boots examined the padlock and the stout metal bar.

'Anything in your taxi that might help?' he asked the cabbie.

'I reckon there is,' said the cabbie, and returned to his taxi at speed.

'Daddy, could she be in there?' asked Rosie, hopeful but uncertain.

'We'll see, kitten,' said Boots, thinking that if the girl was inside or had been, then she hadn't got in by herself. The padlock was evidence of that. Apart from his set mouth, he hid his feelings, which were all to do with a murdered and buried girl, and what might have happened to Freddy's young friend, Cassie.

The cabbie returned with a wrench. Boots took it and used it to savage the bar and burst it from its timber bed. That allowed him to open the door. Silent gloom seemed to actually stare at him.

'It's upstairs, the room,' said Freddy. Boots went in. He turned.

'Rosie, stay there,' he said.

'But, Daddy—'

'Stay.'

'Yes, all right,' said Rosie. She wasn't afraid, not while he was present, but there was no way she would go against him.

'I'll stay with 'er, guv,' said the cabbie, 'you just holler if you need me.' But he knew, as Boots knew, that the only person who could possibly be inside this standing section was a girl who had been locked in. A girl who might or might not be alive.

'Come on, Freddy,' said Boots. The lad plainly was not going to stand and wait himself. Boots, however, did not let him lead the way. If there was only a body to be discovered, he was not going to let Freddy see it. He walked through the passage, stopping to open doors on either side.

'No, it's up the stairs, Mister Adams,' breathed Freddy.

'It's as well to take a look down here first,' said Boots. Reaching the wooden stairs in the gloom, he began to climb them, Freddy behind him. The stairs did not creak, but the landing did, just a little. Boots halted, the silence a lonely and discouraging one.

'It's that door,' said Freddy pointing.

'Right, Freddy, guard the other doors.'

'Guard 'em?' Freddy wanted to rush into that certain room. Boots wasn't going to let him.

'Just in case,' he said. He advanced, turned the handle of the door in question and quietly opened it. And there she was, a girl, a young girl, on a truckle bed, untidy blankets beneath her. She was seemingly asleep. Freddy deserted his post. He had to look. He appeared at the open door as Boots entered the room. He gave a yelp of joyful relief.

'That's 'er, Mister Adams, that's Cassie!'

'Stay there, Freddy.' Boots moved to the bed. The girl, was she asleep or dead? He went down on one knee and gently turned her head. He looked down into her face. Cassie sighed, but her eyes remained closed. Well, praise be to God, thought Boots, and the steel inside him became less cold and rigid. Freddy appeared beside him.

''Elp, she's asleep,' he said.

Boots caught a faint odour then. It pervaded the air around the bed.

Chloroform.

He thought then that there were other smells as well. He came to his feet.

'We won't wake her, Freddy. Let her come to by herself.'

'But we ought to wake 'er, Mister Adams, an' find out 'ow she got 'ere,' said Freddy.

'Well, I'll carry her down, Freddy. The open air will help to wake her.' Boots stooped and lifted Cassie up into his arms. 'Right, here we go.'

Freddy, following him out of the room, said, 'Mister Adams, I told yer I didn't know how you could 'elp, but I think I just knew you could.'

'No, you did it, Freddy old chap,' said Boots, carrying Cassie down the stairs. 'You spotted her cat. It meant nothing to me. It meant everything to you.'

'But I wouldn't 'ave spotted it if I 'adn't been with you,' said Freddy. 'Mister Adams, I can't think why Cassie's asleep and ain't wakin' up.'

'She'll come to in the fresh air,' said Boots, and Cassie sighed again as he brought her out into the light.

Rosie stared and the cabbie looked a happy man.

'Good on yer, guv,' he said, 'good on yer, me lad.'

'Yes, we got 'er,' said Freddy, 'but she's asleep.'

'Maybe that's just as well, poor little kid,' said the cabbie, catching Boots's eye. Boots gave a little nod.

'We still need your taxi,' he said.

'It's all yours, guv, all night, if yer want it.'

Rosie, her eyes shining, said, 'Bless you, Daddy.'

'Bless Freddy,' said Boots, holding Cassie close to his chest. He spoke to the cabbie again. 'Will you take Cassie home? Her family must be back by now, and if the police have seen them, they'll be worried sick. Freddy and Rosie will go with you. Then will you let the police know and ask them if they can get a doctor to Cassie? I think she'll need a sedative.' He hoped that was all she would need.

'Ain't you comin', guv?'

'No, I'm going to wait,' said Boots.

'But what for?' asked Freddy.

'Because whoever locked her in will be coming back,' said Boots, 'and he might arrive before the police get here. Come on.' He carried Cassie to the gates. The cabbie exerted himself and widened the gap, allowing Boots to get through with the girl. Then he took off his jacket and Boots let him place it around Cassie. Freddy and Rosie climbed into the taxi, and Boots leaned in to settle the unconscious girl between his daughter and Susie's young brother. They held her. Her head lolled and a little sighing murmur escaped her. 'Take care of her.'

'You bet,' said Freddy, 'she's me mate.'

'Daddy, you watch out,' said Rosie, not liking the thought of him coming up against some horrible man.

'I'll meet you at Cassie's home,' said Boots, and watched as the taxi moved off. Then he went back to that room. The faint smell of chloroform still lingered. On the table was an oil lamp, a box of matches and a white paper bag. He picked it up. It was empty, with a peppermint smell. He examined cupboards, of which there were two. One was empty. In the other was a large plate camera, a wooden tripod, a box of photographic plates and a T-shaped flash contraption.

He was conscious of smells. He thought again of young Ivy Connor, murdered, then buried under the floorboards of a shed. In the gloom, he inspected the bare wooden floor of this dolorous room. None of the boards seemed to have been disturbed. He went downstairs. About to examine the rooms, he checked as a sound reached his ears. It was faint but perceptible. He knew what it was. Feet moving over ground littered with chips of mortar and brick. He took himself quickly to the only entrance into the place. The door, its metal bar wrenched free, was closed. He had closed it himself. He waited behind it. The sounds of a moving man were closer. They stopped. He heard a strangely petulant exclamation. He pulled the door open.

Mr Ponsonby stared at him.

'You bugger,' said Boots.

A rolled umbrella was instantly levelled at him, and from its point a six-inch shining blade leapt and clicked into place.

'Interfering busybody!' hissed Mr Ponsonby, and made a lightning-like thrust. But he had picked the wrong man. Boots had prepared himself for a murderous reaction. If Mr Ponsonby was quick, he was quicker. He knocked the umbrella aside before the blade reached his chest, and with his left fist he hit the man savagely on his right jaw. Mr Ponsonby fell stunned. Boots reached, picked up the umbrella, and with the man flat on his back, he bent over him and slipped his left hand into the capacious inner pocket of his frock coat. He drew out a bottle with a glass stopper. He put the umbrella under his arm and pulled the stopper free. He sniffed.

Chloroform.

He replaced the stopper and stowed the bottle in his jacket pocket. The man stirred. Boot stood over him and placed the blade of the umbrella against his chest. Then he waited for the police to arrive.

CHAPTER TWENTY-ONE

Cassie came to, on her bed. Her eyes opened and she blinked. A man with a kind face smiled down at her.

'There's a good girl,' he said.

Cassie made a face.

'I feel a bit sick,' she said.

'I expect you do.' Dr Sadler had examined her. She'd suffered nothing worse than chloroform, although probably two or three applications, and some fright, no doubt. He went to the door, opened it and said, 'You can come in now, but don't smother her.' The family swarmed in. An inspector and a sergeant of the CID looked enquiringly at Dr Sadler. 'Not yet,' he said, 'give her another five minutes.'

'Right,' said Detective-Inspector Grant of Scotland Yard. They'd got the man. The cabbie had driven police from Rodney Road to the factory site, and Mr Gerald Francis Ponsonby was now under lock and key, awaiting interrogation.

'Cassie, Cassie love,' breathed Annie, appalled for her young sister.

'Safe and sound now, Cassie,' said the shaken Gaffer, sitting on the edge of the bed and taking her hand.

Cassie looked dreamy.

'I feel a bit sick,' she murmured.

''Ere, what 'appened to yer?' asked Charlie, and Cassie stared vaguely at him.

'Charlie, leave 'er be,' said Nellie, who'd shed a few tears.

'She'll tell us in a bit,' said Annie. They'd all had distracted minds from the moment the police told them Cassie had been missing for hours, and that a search was being made. Dr Sadler, having mixed a sedative, allowed Annie to give it to the girl. Cassie sat up, her dad's arm around her, and drank the sedative in the dreamy hope it would stop making her feel sick.

'That's a good girl,' said Dr Sadler again.

Cassie blinked and looked around. The Gaffer let her lie back.

''E said 'e was goin' to take a photo of me,' she murmured.

'What?' said the Gaffer, having a hard job to keep his blood off the boil.

'Who said that, Cassie?' asked Annie.

'Mister Po's'by,' said Cassie.

''Oo's 'e?' asked Charlie.

''E gives me peppermints,' said Cassie.

Annie looked at her dad, and her dad looked tight-faced and grim.

'I think the police can talk to her now,' said Dr Sadler, and called the CID officers in. Freddy had gone home to acquaint his own family of events, and Rosie had been taken by the cabbie to rejoin her father. Boots was at Rodney Road police station, making a long statement. He had phoned home again and this time had spoken to Emily.

Inspector Grant, exercising a kind paternal approach, was able to get quite a coherent story from the relaxing Cassie. On her way to Freddy's house she had met Mr Ponsonby, who had promised to take a photograph of her. He said what a busy day he was having, but if she would like to be photographed now, he could spare the time. Cassie asked him if he was going to do it in his lodgings.

He said oh, no, in his studio. Cassie, who had her cat with her, said she couldn't spare a lot of time herself, because she was going to Freddy's house. Mr Ponsonby said it would hardly take any time at all, and Cassie asked if he could take the photo with her holding Tabby. Mr Ponsonby said yes, come with me.

She went with him. It seemed a bit of a long way and she kept saying she'd be late meeting Freddy. Then they came to that place where there'd been a fire and where it was haunted, and she said she didn't want to go in there. Mr Ponsonby said no, of course not, have a peppermint. He always had peppermints. Tabby jumped out of her arms then and ran into that place through a gap in the gates, and she asked Mr Ponsonby to get him for her. He said he would, but have a peppermint first, and he offered her the bag. There was only one in it, and as she put her hand in the bag, something was pushed against her face, and she couldn't remember any more, except she did dream it happened again.

Dr Sadler thought it must have happened several times, considering how long she was in the place. The man had been playing with the girl's life, before absenting himself. And why had he absented himself? The CID officers knew he'd been caught coming back, with the bottle of chloroform still on his person, but were anxious to get the girl's story before fully interrogating the man.

'Cassie,' said Inspector Grant, 'thank you very much, you're a brave young lady.'

'I don't feel so sick now,' said Cassie. She thought. 'Fancy 'im puttin' that bit of stuff over me face, I don't like 'im any more. Does Freddy know?'

'Freddy 'elped to find you, lovey,' said the Gaffer.

'Well,' said Cassie dreamily, 'I'm 'is mate, 'e told me so.'

The CID officers left then and returned to Rodney Road police station. The cabbie was still there, so were Boots and Rosie. And so was a uniformed constable, with the news that two bodies had been discovered under the floorboards of a room below the one containing the truckle bed and a camera. Two other constables were still at the place. The bodies were of young females, but had not been touched. Inspector Grant received the news in the grimly painful fashion of a police officer who hated what it meant. However, he allowed Boots to go, thanking him for all he had done.

'I suppose you'll find all other evidence you need at his lodgings,' said Boots.

'I'm damn' sure we will, Mr Adams. Thanks again.'

Boots joined Rosie and the cabbie, and they left the station.

'Can I drive you 'ome, guv?' asked the cabbie.

'You've had a long day,' said Boots.

'So 'ave you, guv, so 'as your Rosie here. Mind, we've done some chattin', ain't we, Rosie?'

'Oh, I'm very well-versed at chatting,' said Rosie, 'I caught it ages ago from Daddy and my Uncle Sammy. But mustn't he be an awful man, the one who took Cassie?'

'Worse than that, Rosie,' said the cabbie.

'Look,' said Boots, 'I know it's asking one more favour, but could you stop at Freddy's house on the way, just for five minutes?'

'Don't mention it, guv. 'Op in, you an' Rosie.'

While Rosie talked to the rest of the Brown family in the kitchen, Boots talked with Mr Brown in the parlour. He gave him the full story. Mr Brown looked sick at the ugliness of mankind.

'So there it is, Jim,' said Boots, 'the police have nailed

the son of Satan. There's no point now in keeping it from the family. They already know what Freddy's told them. Now you can tell them the rest, to save them having to find out from the newspapers tomorrow. And at least, it's all cleared up.'

'Not the best piece of news, though, for a weddin' day,' said Mr Brown.

'It won't spoil this wedding,' said Boots, 'it's special. Sammy, the engine driver, has met his match. Get Rosie for me, would you, Jim? We need to be on our way now.'

Jim fetched the girl. Susie appeared too.

'Bless you and Freddy, Boots,' she said.

'It's been Freddy's day,' said Boots. 'It's yours tomorrow, Susie. By the way, here's something I almost forgot.' He took an item wrapped in tissue paper from the inside pocket of his jacket. 'Emily said she'd arranged to let you have something borrowed to go with something blue.'

Susie unwrapped the tissue, disclosing a pink garter.

'Lovely,' she said, 'thank Em'ly, won't you?'

'Pretty, that is,' said Mr Brown.

'Well, we'll all expect to see how it looks on Susie,' said Boots.

'Daddy, you're cheeky,' said Rosie. Boots gave her a wink and they said goodbye and left. The cabbie drove them to their home in Red Post Hill. Rosie said farewell to him, then dashed in to give Emily, Chinese Lady and Chinese Lady's husband a first-hand account of the happenings.

'What's the damage?' asked Boots of the cabbie. 'All of it.'

'Listen, guv, what kind of a bloke would I be to make a charge?'

'Fairly daft not to, I'd say. It's your living.'

'Look, I tell yer what. You place five bob in me mitt an' we'll call that fair an' square, eh?'

Boots placed five shillings in his hand, and added a pound note.

'That's the least I can do,' he said.

'Don't want it, guv. It's been—'

'There's a wedding in our family tomorrow,' said Boots, 'so have a drink on us.'

'Guv, it's been a privilege meetin' you and yer daughter. You got a sweet girl there. Any time you need a taxi from East Dulwich, I 'ope I'll be the one to oblige yer. Gus Allbury, that's me.'

'Many thanks, Gus. Couldn't have done without you today. Good night.' Boots shook hands with the cabbie, watched the taxi depart, stood for a moment thinking of young Cassie and how close she'd been to death, then turned on his heel and entered the house. There he was greeted by Emily, who wrapped her arms around him.

Charlie answered a knock on the door. Will was on the step.

'Oh, 'ello,' said Charlie.

Annie, coming down the stairs, checked for a moment.

'I thought I'd come and see how Cassie is,' said Will.

Annie came quickly down to the passage and to the door.

'Oh, it's nice you thought of us,' she said, 'and Cassie specially. Come in. She's sleepin' now. She's all right, she won't ever remember much because that evil man chloroformed her. Will, come on in, we're just makin' a pot of tea and you'll 'ave a cup, won't you?'

Will joined the family for a cup of tea around the kitchen table, and everyone talked at once. The Gaffer said next time he took his children out, he'd take them all and leave no-one behind. Only Cassie had been keen on being with Freddy. Couple of real mates, they were, he said, and while he was saying it, Annie was talking about how kind the doctor had been, Nellie was going on about the police being ever so nice, and Charlie was muttering that a certain bloke ought to have his head bashed in. The Gaffer said if it hadn't been for Freddy keeping on and on in his search for Cassie, she might not have been found. Will said Freddy was now a hero, even to his sister Sally. But he said nothing about the news that Boots had brought concerning the discovery of the bodies of two young girls. The shock of Cassie's abduction was enough for them to cope with tonight. Tomorrow would be soon enough for them to learn about all that was grisly.

Annie felt deep relief at the doctor's assurance Cassie hadn't been harmed in any way, even though she'd obviously been kept unconscious for hours. She also felt very glad that Will had called. He stayed quite a while, and helped to cheer things up no end. She decided he was really a very nice young man, not a bit loud or brash, and not at all a cocky corporal. He was a lot quieter in his manner than she imagined most soldiers were, but he had a nice sense of humour.

She saw him to the front door when he left.

'Thanks ever so much for comin',' she said.

'Well, I couldn't not pop round to see how everyone was,' said Will, and did what he'd told himself he shouldn't do. He kissed her, and at the same time tried to detect if she wore scent. He didn't think so.

'That's done it,' said Annie, when he released her lips.

'Done what?' asked Will.

'You're goin' to get talked to tomorrow,' said Annie.

'Seriously?' said Will.

'Well, it's not goin' to make you laugh, I can tell you that,' said Annie.

Under interrogation, Mr Ponsonby was querulous and petulant, but patchily informative. One of the first things Inspector Graves found out was that the reason why the man had absented himself related to his need to develop his plates. He needed to know if the photographs were satisfactory, or if he needed to take them again.

'So you kept her alive, did you, in case of that?' said the inspector.

'Of course, of course. What is the use of photographs of someone who is dead?'

He had developed the plates quickly, in his lodgings, shutting out the light by drawing the thick curtains he himself had installed. The photographs were very good. Charming, in fact, charming. Such a pretty face, and such pretty legs. Inspector Grant felt an urge to throttle him. Ponsonby, of course, had drawn back the unconscious girl's clothes. The CID officer controlled himself, and by asking questions in a sympathetic and understanding way, or so it seemed, he finally induced a full confession.

Mr Ponsonby had always thought young girls enchanting because of their purity. But it was difficult to photograph them in the way he wanted to, not without them getting upset and threatening to tell their parents. So he stole a bottle of chloroform from a hospital where he had once worked as assistant to the lady almoner. He used a chloroform pad to effect a robbery at a jeweller's shop, and to delude the hospital authorities and the police into thinking that was why he had taken the bottle. He did not like the police, he said, they were interfering busybodies, disturbing to a gentleman like him.

It was a pity, of course, but it had been necessary to let the girls ascend early to heaven after photographing them.

'How many girls?' asked the inspector in a conversational way.

'Only a few,' said Mr Ponsonby. 'Dear me, it's been terribly difficult arranging to photograph any girl. One can't be too careful, parents are unfriendly people. One simply has to win a girl's confidence before inviting her to sit for me.'

Sit for him? You nasty old sod, thought Inspector Grant.

'You gave them peppermints, Mr Ponsonby?'

'Ah, everyone had to have a peppermint.'

'From out of a bag like this?' said the inspector, producing the white bag Boots had found. It smelled of peppermint.

'Of course, yes. Dear me, dear me.' Mr Ponsonby was very petulant. 'How silly of me to leave it there.' He rubbed his bruised jaw. 'I wish to complain about the interfering busybody who struck me.'

'Complaint noted,' said the inspector. 'How many girls, how many did you say?'

'A few, just a few. Three.' Mr Ponsonby explained how he had come to know them and subsequently invited them to be photographed. The first was in Bermondsey, where he used a scrap yard's shed. No-one else seemed to be using it, and he had a key that opened the gates. He had found it one day, it had been left in the lock. The girl had been so pure, so delightful, with the prettiest legs. Unfortunately, she recovered very quickly from the second dose of chloroform and he had had to quieten her.

'Strangulation is very quietening,' said Inspector Grant.

'I trust that is not a criticism,' said Mr Ponsonby in some irritation. 'It was quick and merciful, yes, indeed.' He went on to say he had been just as quick and merciful with two other girls, after finding a most convenient place

297

in which to photograph them. After finding it, he had picked the padlock and replaced it with another. Yes, he agreed with the inspector's suggestion that he had buried the girls under floorboards. It was convenient to do so, and a kindness to the girls. One simply could not leave them lying about.

'You have the photographs in your lodgings?' said Inspector Grant.

'Of course, of course, where else? One must have the pleasure of looking at them.' He hoped he would be allowed to keep them, together with those he had taken of the charming girl Cassie. He could think of nothing more to add, and therefore would like to be allowed to go home to his lodgings.

'I note your request, Mr Ponsonby. After developing the plates at your lodgings, you returned to the factory to help the girl Cassie ascend early to heaven?'

'Much the best thing,' said Mr Ponsonby. 'Really, I can't see why you need to ask. It's late, and I must get back to my lodgings.'

'We'll see you do. We'll go with you, and perhaps you'll show us these photographs,' said the inspector.

'Oh, very well,' said Mr Ponsonby in new irritation. 'What a day, what a day.'

As the CID officers suspected, most of the photographs showed the terribly unfortunate girls unconscious and with their clothes drawn back. Much to his sense of outrage, Mr Ponsonby was arrested for murder.

Cassie slept soundly.

CHAPTER TWENTY-TWO

Annie woke up, looked sleepily at the little tin alarm clock, found it was only five past six, turned over, thought about Cassie, murmured in dreamy relief, thought about Will, wondered about him, and drifted back into sleep.

Cassie's cat woke up, sprang on to the bed she shared with Nellie, curled itself up close to the hump of her warm body and purred itself to sleep again, perhaps to dream about Mrs Boddy's lady cat.

The Gaffer woke up and got up. He was on an early shift this morning, but would finish at twelve. He looked in on Cassie. Sleeping like an angel next to Nellie. Should he stay home, just in case she woke up with upset feelings? Yes, he would. Only right. Then Annie could go off to her job without worrying. It was his place to stay home, not Annie's. Annie was looking forward to going to that wedding dance this evening. She was fond of Will, the Gaffer knew that. He'd asked her yesterday morning exactly what she thought of Will as a bloke. Well, Annie had said, he's my kind of bloke in most ways, he just wants talking to, that's all. Talking to about what? I'm giving it deep thought, said Annie.

A little later, Will woke up, thought about the fact that he hadn't had an attack after kissing Annie last night and wondered if he should take another look at himself.

Susie woke to the dawning of a sunny Easter Saturday and to the necessity of being at the hairdresser's with Sally by nine o'clock. And to saying love, honour and obey. She smiled.

Sammy woke to the dawning of married life, and to the probability that it was going to ruin his pocket. But he had a singular feeling that his pocket didn't seem to care.

Freddy woke and thought about Cassie. Crikey, it was hardly believable what had happened. He'd cycle round after breakfast to see her and to tell her she could come to the wedding breakfast. His mum had said so, and that there was a place at the tables for her because Miss Simms had dropped out. If he'd cycled round yesterday, instead of letting her walk round to him, that old geezer Mr Ponsonby wouldn't have made off with her. But she'd insisted she'd come round to him. Freddy guessed why now. She'd had her barmy cat with her, she'd have arrived at his house with it and he wouldn't have been able to do anything about it. A bloke's mate didn't ought to be a problem to him. He couldn't thump her, seeing she was a girl. Still, he could talk to her, although he had a feeling it would be like talking to the empty air. Crikey, it was Susie's wedding day today.

Mrs Brown woke to see her husband bringing a morning cup of tea to her, bless him.

Mr Greenberg, waking, thought about the privilege of carting Susie and Sammy to their Christian wedding breakfast. That reminded him his own wedding was in the offing. Should a free man take to his heels or dwell on the compensation available? The widow Hannah Borovich was splendidly handsome and also an excellent cook. But would her three growing sons eat him out of house and home? Life was a torment to a man when he had to consider taking to his heels or fulfilling the marriage contract. Ah, me, thought Mr Greenberg. He arose, washed himself, put on some old clothes, ate a simple breakfast and then went to the Old Kent Road stables to brush down his pony and polish the little cart.

Chinese Lady woke up beside her husband, Edwin Finch, recently returned from what she thought of as the Frenchified Continent, where he'd spent some months on Government business. It was nice, having him beside her again. It was what God had ordered for a woman, having a providing husband beside her. She meant ordained, of course. She smiled. It was Sammy's wedding day. That Sammy, with his sauce, it was time he found there was more to life than making money. Susie was just right for him, she'd become as ladylike as Lizzy had, and she had enough sense to see to it that Sammy turned into a responsible husband, father and provider. That was what any real man was born to be. God's orders were very strict.

Will received an official letter that morning. It informed him that as he was medically unfit for further service, he was to receive his discharge papers at the termination of his three months leave, together with back pay due to him. There was a formal acknowledgement of his past services to the Army, but no mention of a disablement pension. The family said what a rotten lot the Army high-ups were, and Sally said she hoped their roof would fall in on them and disable them all. Mrs Brown said well, let's look on the bright side, Will doesn't have to go to India any more, nor get fired at. It's dangerous, getting fired at, said Mr Brown. Yes, I just told you so, said Mrs Brown. You'll be all right, Will, she said, it's good news really, specially on Susie's wedding day. She said nothing about Mr Ponsonby, nor did any of them.

As soon as he'd had his breakfast, Freddy cycled round to Blackwood Street. There he found Cassie in the pink, the pet of her family.

''Ello, Freddy, where you been?' she asked.

'Well, I like that,' said Freddy, 'I ain't been anywhere

except in me bed an' then 'aving me breakfast.' He looked at her father. 'Is she all right, Mr Ford?'

'Right as rain,' said the Gaffer.

'She's our sunshine girl this mornin',' said Annie.

'That Mister Po's'by,' said Cassie, ''e put something over me face, Freddy, and I don't remember any more.'

Freddy could have said a lot about Mr Ponsonby. His dad had passed on the news given to him by Boots, but his mum had told him not to say anything in front of Cassie. Mr Ford and Annie weren't saying anything themselves, although Freddy knew it was all in the newspapers this morning. Well, it was in Dad's paper, and had caused his mum to say she hoped the guests wouldn't all talk about it at the wedding. It was a blessing that Mr Ponsonby's name hadn't been mentioned, she said, or the whole neighbourhood would be coming round to stare at the Mason house, where he'd been lodging. The paper just said a man was being held in custody. It was another blessing too that Cassie's name wasn't in the paper either, and that the police were working to identify the two dead girls.

The Gaffer's morning paper had sensational headlines. He'd shown the paper to Annie, and they were keeping it to themselves for the time being.

As it was, Cassie seemed herself. Her only complaint was that she'd felt sick when she woke up. She was happy to tell Freddy that her cat had come back, and that she thought Mrs Boddy's lady cat might have gone and fetched him home. Freddy said he wouldn't be surprised. He also said Cassie could come to the wedding breakfast, his mum had told him to invite her. Cassie nearly fell over in her delight. Annie, due to go to work for the day, told her dad to make sure Cassie was dressed in her Sunday best, and that Nellie could see to it that Cassie's hair looked nice, with a clean ribbon. Freddy said he'd come and fetch her, otherwise she might go wandering off and end up at Peckham Rye. Cassie said Queen Alice went to Peckham Rye once. Nellie asked who Queen Alice was. Cassie said she'd never met her, she'd just read about her, and that she went to Peckham Rye to meet a magician. She wanted him to cast a spell on a wicked witch and make her disappear, only when she got to Peckham Rye, he wasn't there. Charlie asked what had happened to him. Cassie said he'd already cast his spell, only it had gone wrong and he'd made himself disappear and no-one ever saw him again.

Cassie was back to normal.

She was so much herself that she asked Freddy if she could bring Tabby to the wedding. Annie said no, Cassie love, you just can't take a cat to a wedding.

'But 'e likes weddings,' said Cassie.

'Still, leave 'im at home, me pet,' said the Gaffer, 'and 'e might 'ave a weddin' of his own, with Mrs Boddy's lady cat.'

Cassie giggled. Annie began to get ready to go to work, and Freddy, after telling Cassie he'd come for her at a quarter to twelve, went back home to do any wedding errands that were necessary.

Just after eleven, Boots answered the phone.

'Is that Mr Adams?'

'Speaking,' said Boots.

'Inspector Grant here, Mr Adams. Sorry to interrupt, I know you've a wedding on today, but I thought I ought to speak to you.' Inspector Grant sounded as if his nerves had just taken a hammering.

'What about?' asked Boots.

'The fact is, Ponsonby's slipped us.'

'What? I'm to believe you've been as careless as that?'

'Bloody inexcusable. He got out through the lavatory window at the station an hour ago. I'm there now. If you could see the size of the window you'd wonder how anyone could have managed it. But he did, the slippery bugger. We're looking for him, of course, and not sparing the manpower, but he's a peculiar character and I don't like the thought of what he might get up to.'

'You're not asking me to join the search, are you?'

'No, no, not at all, Mr Adams. But he doesn't like you, he doesn't like the fact that you interfered, to start with.'

'He calls that interference, does he?' said Boots.

'Intolerable interference, Mr Adams, those were his words. Nor does he like you for knocking him out and handing him over to us. He's got a vindictive streak, and I've a nasty feeling it'll be aimed at you. Or your daughter. Unless we can find him first.'

'Thanks very much for that slice of cheerful news,' said Boots. 'Does he know I've got a daughter?'

'When we brought him to the station yesterday evening, Mr Adams, your daughter was waiting with the taxi driver. You were with us. Your daughter greeted you.'

'Well, damn that for what it means,' said Boots.

'Mr Adams, we'll do our very best to round the man up, and I'll let you know immediately we do. I'll have someone contact you at the wedding, if necessary. Meanwhile, can I ask you to take great care of yourself and your daughter? Ponsonby doesn't look dangerous, but you and I know he is.'

'If I were him,' said Boots, 'I'd be running for my life, not thinking about having my own back. But as I'm not him, I'll watch out. Thanks for letting me know, Inspector.'

'I'm bloody sick,' said Inspector Grant, and rang off.

Boots steeled himself to face the day.

The ceremony was for twelve o'clock. At ten minutes to, St John's Church was full to overflowing for the wedding of two people who, having been born and bred in Walworth, had risen from poverty to become, respectively, an affluent young lady and a highly reputable businessman. Susie Brown was just about the poshest young lady to be seen in Walworth, and Sammy Adams, well, what a bright spark he'd always been. But they never turned their noses up at any of their old friends and neighbours.

Mrs Brown in a spring coat and a new toque hat, sat with Will and Freddy in the front pew on the left side of the aisle. Cassie, in her best Sunday dress and a little round straw hat, sat as a special treat between Will and Freddy.

In the front pew on the right sat Sammy and Boots, the best man. Boots, with Ponsonby on his mind, had brought Rosie to the church along with himself and Sammy. He'd been able to calm Sammy's nerves by telling him to think of how to cut the overheads on the new contract with Coates. Good idea, said Sammy, your dad's quite bright sometimes, Rosie. I know, said Rosie, I live an awful trying life trying to get the better of him.

Behind Sammy and Boots sat Chinese Lady, her husband Mr Finch, Emily and Emily's four-year-old son Tim. Also present were brown-eyed, glossy-haired Lizzy, her husband Ned Somers and three of their children, Bobby, Emma and Edward. Their eldest, Annabelle, was a bridesmaid, along with Rosie and Sally. Then there were Tommy and his wife Vi. Their daughter Alice, eleven months old, was in the care of neighbours, and Vi was just over four months pregnant with her second child. Next to them were Vi's parents, known to the family as Aunt

Victoria and Uncle Tom. Aunt Victoria was inclined to find fault, though not as much as she used to, and Uncle Tom, bluff and equable, was inclined to turn a deaf ear.

Chinese Lady, Emily, Lizzy, Vi and yes, even Aunt Victoria, were all wearing new outfits purchased at Sammy's Brixton shop at such an horrendous family discount that he said he'd never lost that much profit in all his life. You're breaking my heart, said Lizzy. I feel for you, said Sammy, but that kind of thing can undermine the firm's financial foundations and ruin the whole family. Emily said there would have been no fun in the transactions if Sammy hadn't mentioned something about the discount ruining him. He thanked her for her kind words. Aunt Victoria said she wasn't sure that she couldn't have done better at *Bon Marché* of Brixton. Uncle Tom said only at twice the cost, so Aunt Victoria changed the subject. Chinese Lady told Sammy he'd got a cheek to let his shop manageress charge her at all. Me, your own mother, she said, you're heading for purgatory, my lad. I suppose I'll have to start up a new kind of business when I get there, Ma, said Sammy. Don't call me Ma, said Chinese Lady, it's common, and I didn't bring you up to be common. However, Vi was so delighted with her outfit and the huge discount that she gave Sammy tuppence, which entitled her to give him two smacking kisses. Sammy was so touched he gave her a penny back.

At five minutes to twelve, with the church waiting for the arrival of the bride, Boots got up and walked along the side aisle to the open doors. The three bridesmaids were there, with the vicar. In their cerise pink, all three girls looked enchanting. Sally, suffering a crush on Boots, blushed as he smiled at her.

'Daddy, it can't be all over,' said Rosie, 'Aunt Susie hasn't arrived yet.'

'I'll tell your Uncle Sammy that,' said Boots, and spoke a few words to the vicar while looking around. He'd noticed a policeman outside the church, a uniformed constable. He was still there. A few people were at the gates, waiting to see the bride. Boots felt the constable was a safeguard for Rosie, and rejoined Sammy.

Mrs Rachel Goodman sat in a pew with Mr Greenberg, and neither felt out of place in this Christian church simply because they did not feel out of place with a family of gentiles whom they had known for years and had come to love. Rachel wore a midnight blue costume and hat, as close to black as she could get in letting Sammy see she was in mourning for the imminent loss of his bachelor status. Mr Greenberg, in handsome grey, looked a figure of solemn and august maturity. A nephew of his had charge of the pony and cart for the duration of the service.

Rachel wondered why Polly Simms wasn't present. She knew she'd been invited. She also knew the brittle and amusing Polly was incurably attached to Boots. They'd both served in the war, and they had a shared experience of its horrors. But Polly would never get Boots. Rachel knew the family so well she was absolutely certain none of Chinese Lady's diverting sons would indulge in an affair. And Boots had fine steel beneath his easy-going exterior. Was Polly not going to attend the wedding because she could no longer stand being on the outside of the family?

The church was buzzing, not only in anticipation of the bride, but because of newspaper headlines. A man was being held in custody over the murder of a young girl in Bermondsey and two right here in Walworth. Horrible. Still, Mrs Brown didn't look too upset about it.

Susie was punctual. She had made up her mind not to be late for her wedding. At two minutes past twelve, the organist turned his head. Sammy and Boots came to their feet, and the whole church rose as the Wedding March began to peal out. The vicar, the Reverend Edwards, a rosy-faced and gentle man of God, entered in the van of the bridal procession. Susie was on her dad's arm, and her dad, gammy leg and all, looked as if the Queen of Sheba couldn't have made a better bride than his Susie. Her gown of white silk was soft, shimmering and flowing, her little circular headdress of white silk roses supporting a full veil. Slowly she floated, Sally behind her, Rosie and Annabelle following, all bridesmaids holding little bouquets, circlets of pink silk roses adorning their heads. Sammy, Boots and Ned had covered the expense of outfitting the bridesmaids.

Mr Greenberg, turning his head, beamed at Susie. Rachel emitted a little sigh. Emily, watching the advance, thought of her own wedding, a wartime one, when Boots was still blind and she had had to be his guide and his mainstay. They had had a good marriage, hadn't they? She hoped so, even if she was in doubt of herself sometimes. Needing reassurance, she received it from him, and unfailing affection too, to help her through her illness.

Mr Brown brought Susie to her bridegroom and relinquished her, not without a little throaty swallow.

Sammy whispered to the bridal veil.

'Is that you in there, Susie?'

'It's me, Sammy.'

'Bless you, then.'

'Bless you too, Sammy.'

Boots smiled. Sammy and Susie were always going to be a star turn together.

The ceremony over, the photographer posed the principals and their retinue outside the church and in the bright sunshine. Susie had her veil over her head, her eyes a bright sparkling blue, her bouquet colourful against the white of her gown. Sammy's smile was that of a businessman who had just signed the most valuable contract of his life, never mind the crippling overheads. The forecourt was crowded with people, and there were others outside the church gates.

Henry Brannigan, on his way home from his Saturday morning's work, checked his measured stride and took a look at the scene on the forecourt. He saw scores of people in their glad rags, and a shimmering bride with a lovely laughing face. A ruddy wedding. Still, they weren't in his way. He eyed the newly-weds on the church steps and listened to the shouted remarks of amateur comics. He took in the enchantment of the young bridesmaids. He gave them their due, they were sweet-looking right enough, but he'd bet they took their turns every day to get in people's way. All kids did. Still, he had to admit girl kids could look like angels as bridesmaids. They didn't always grow up like angels. One or two did. Come to think of it, Madge wasn't far short of being an angel of cheerfulness. Good company, she was, not moody, like his wife had been at times.

Look at the kids there. Little terrors they probably were, but look at them now with their clean faces. Madge was keen on kids. She hadn't given herself much of a chance to have any.

He walked away, his mood thoughtful. Ruddy hell, he was treading on lines. He adjusted his step. Too late now, though. He'd have to watch out for bad luck. Wait a tick, no bad luck had caught up with him after he'd trodden on that line outside a baker's shop the other day. Far from it. Not only had he been made foreman, but this morning the works manager had told him he'd already proved himself and the job was his for good. On top of that, when he was up a ladder an hour later to gauge the best way for the gang to tackle a dismantling piece of work, one of the sods had kicked the ladder from under him. Accidental, of course, you bet it wasn't. He might have broken his neck, but he didn't even bruise himself in the fall. If that wasn't a large slice of good luck, what was? He'd spoken to the ganger, he'd delivered himself of a few choice words, and he knew it wouldn't happen again.

Life had turned round for him. He reckoned that was all due to Madge. His lucky charm, that's what she was.

Henry Brannigan began to tread on lines with careless abandon.

The photographs had been taken, and Mr Greenberg, having received permission from the vicar, drove his sleek pony and polished cart into the forecourt. The guests made way for him and he pulled up outside the church doors. Lifting his hat, he beamed down at Susie.

'Vhy, ain't it Mrs Sammy Adams, I presume?' he said.

'Hello, Mr Greenberg,' smiled Susie.

'Might I have the pleasure of cartin' you and Sammy off to the place of reception? My vord, Susie, vat a pleasure, ain't it?'

'Oh, it's a handsome offer, Mr Greenberg,' said Susie.

Boots, his hand on Rosie's shoulder, watched as Sammy helped his bride up into the cart. Sammy looked at Emily, all huge green eyes that seemed a little moist. Leaving aside Chinese Lady, Emily was first among the wives. Boots was the first of the brothers, and Sammy and Tommy acknowledged he had always worn his seniority with distinction. That made Emily the first lady of the family, again leaving aside Chinese Lady.

'Emily, up you come too,' said Sammy, 'and Boots, and the bridesmaids.'

'In the cart?' cried Rosie. 'Oh, spiffing! Come on, Annabelle!'

Boots lifted the two girls, one after the other. Sally moved forward.

'Might I lend you a hand, Miss Sally Brown?'

Sally turned, and there was Ronnie from the Camberwell offices, all togged up in his best suit and wearing an admiring grin.

'Oh, it's you,' she said.

'What a peach,' said Ronnie, 'I can't wait to shake a leg with you later.'

'Not if I see you comin',' said Sally, and then she was up in the cart too. So was Emily, and so was Boots.

'Full cartload, Eli,' said Sammy, 'so don't gallop. There's no hurry.'

'Vhy, that there ain't, Sammy,' said Mr Greenberg, 'so I'm cartin' you all the vay round, through the Valvorth Road and down Browning Street, and so on, ain't it?'

'Blessed saints,' said Rosie, 'what a palaver, ain't it?'

They were all perched on the narrow side seats, Sammy and Susie, Boots and Emily, and the three bridesmaids, much to the uproarious delight of the guests.

'It's a lovely weddin', Jim,' said Mrs Brown to Mr Brown.

'Our Susie, eh?' said Mr Brown. 'Ain't you proud of her, Bessie?'

'That I am, Jim.'

'Sammy's got himself a lovely wife in Susie,' said Vi to Tommy.

'I've had one for a few years meself,' said Tommy.

'That's funny,' said Vi, 'I've had a nice husband a few years meself.'

'Good on yer, Vi.'

'Good on you too, Tommy.'

'Who's goin' to be on top out of those two?' asked Lizzy of husband Ned.

'Well,' said Ned, 'if Sammy does what comes naturally—'

'I didn't mean that, Ned Somers,' said Lizzy. 'Honestly, your mind, if I don't straighten it out I won't be able to take you anywhere.'

'Not even to church?' said Ned.

'You're not goin' to dodge that,' said Lizzy. 'There, they're off.'

Mr Greenberg drove the pony and cart out through the gates, turning left for the Walworth Road, and after the cart went the younger guests who, of course, began to sing.

'My old man said follow the van . . .'

Susie waved her bouquet at everyone the cart passed in Larcom Street. Emily remembered her own wedding, her own ride in the cart with Boots and others. She slipped her arm through his.

'We did this,' she said. It had been nearly ten years ago.

'So we did,' said Boots, leaving alone the fact that he'd been blind at the time. He watched the street. He wondered if Ponsonby knew of the wedding. The man knew his name. Inspector Grant had mentioned it in the man's presence. Ponsonby had lodged only a few doors away from the Browns and would have known, as everyone in the street did, that Susie was engaged to Sammy Adams. The man was clever enough to make the right assumptions and to ask questions that would turn assumptions into fact. He'd have to ask those questions of people in the neighbourhood. He was on the loose, unless the police had caught up with him again. Boots was willing to take his chances with the man, but in no way was he going to leave Rosie at risk. Tim at the moment was with his cousin Bobby, Lizzy and Ned looking after him. But Boots felt that if Inspector Grant was right, Ponsonby would be after Rosie or himself, or just Rosie. The vicious lunatic had a fixation on young girls.

'Boots, it's a lovely day,' said Emily.

'Specially arranged by Sammy, Em.'

'Well, it's gladsome, don't you think?'

'I'd say so, Em.'

Rosie, utterly delighted with everything, with her place in the cart, with waving to people in the Walworth Road and with the singing young people following the cart, whispered, 'Mummy, are you and Daddy having happy talk?'

'Well, it's a weddin' day,' said Emily. 'Oh, lor', I forgot about Tim. Who's lookin' after him?'

'Aunt Lizzy and Uncle Ned,' said Rosie.

The bridal cart nearly stopped the traffic, especially when the young people began to sing to the bride.

'*If you knew Susie like I know Susie, oh, oh, oh what a girl . . .*'

Boots noticed then that the uniformed constable was following.

Inspector Grant was obviously convinced that Ponsonby would make an attempt to strike.

CHAPTER TWENTY-THREE

St John's Church Institute was by no means unattractive, with its stage at one end and a gallery at the other. Cloakrooms were accessible on either side of the stage, as were kitchen amenities. The local Boy Scout Troop used the hall, made their Friday evening cocoa there and sang camping songs around the piano on the stage.

Today, the two families and their guests sat down to the wedding breakfast at large trestle tables covered in white cloths and placed together to form an open-ended rectangle. The top tables were occupied by the bride and groom, their families and two friends who were rather special, Rachel and Mr Greenberg. Sammy and Susie had both agreed that to have put them elsewhere would have put them among strangers for the most part. Rachel was touched, Mr Greenberg beaming. There was kosher food for them.

There were over seventy guests and the caterers served an excellent meal. Susie, looking around and taking everything in, remembered the years of desperate poverty, when the best her dad could do for his family was a cheap flat in Peabody Buildings in Brandon Street, and she never seemed to have any frock that hadn't already outlived its time. The occasional rat poked about around the dustbins of Brandon Street yards, and the numerous cats enjoyed active nights hunting mice. She would never forget the day when, in her sixteenth year, Sammy gave her a job helping to run his market stall. She'd been a shabby and hungry-eyed waif at the time. The memory made her put a hand on Sammy's knee and squeeze it.

'Hello, who's doin' that?' he asked.

'Me,' said Susie.

'I hope it's not goin' to cost me,' said Sammy.

'Say a tanner, Sammy.'

'Make it a tiddler, Susie.'

'Fourpence,' said Susie, laughing. Sammy gave her two pennies. 'That's only tuppence,' she said.

'I'll have to owe you the rest, Mrs Adams,' said Sammy, 'it's been a ruinous week.'

'Uncle Sammy, what're you doing?' asked Annabelle.

'No idea,' said Sammy, 'it's been like that for a year, Annabelle.'

'You're funny, Uncle Sammy.'

'Point is,' said Sammy, 'will I recover?'

It was like that all around the hall, and the breakfast turned into an exhilarating affair, riotous with laughter. There was beer for the rousing cockney element, such as old friends and neighbours like Mr and Mrs Blake, Mr and Mrs Higgins, and Mr and Mrs Pullen, as well as Sammy's factory friends Gertie and Bert. There were soft drinks for the children and wine for those adults who fancied it. Ned, who now had a very good job with a wine merchant of Great Tower Street, had supplied the wine.

Susie caught Will's eye. She framed words.

'All right, lovey?'

'Fine.'

Will was actually finding himself in a waiting mood. Not for an event, nor the speeches. It was Annie. Everyone seemed to have someone. Sally, unattached, seemed to have a pleasant-looking boy sending her pencilled notes by the hand of one of the caterers' waitresses, and each one had her giggling. Will kept thinking about Annie, lively, spirited and always giving as good as she got. But she wouldn't be here until about a quarter to five. He felt it was going to be a long wait. But what was the point of thinking about her? Here he was, chucked out of the Army on account of his asthma and having to look for a job that would be kind to him. He was no sort of a catch for a girl like Annie, or for any girl. Ruddy great balls of fire, he thought, I'm a mess, I'll probably have an attack as soon as she arrives. Blow that for a lark.

Boots felt Rosie was safe for the time being, except that there was something lurking in the back of his mind, something that he couldn't get hold of. What was it? The atmosphere of revelry was interfering with concentrated thought, and it prolonged the breakfast. But when it was finally over, Susie's dad was the first to make a speech. It was in honour of the guests.

On his feet, he began by saying, 'I don't want none of you to worry, because I'm not goin' to get you to listen to more than you want to 'ear.'

'Good speech, Jim!'

'Short an' sweet, old mate.'

'Give 'im a cheer.'

'No, give 'im a beer.'

Rosie made herself heard with the aplomb of a girl already self-assured.

'Don't take any notice, Mr Brown, we're all ears,' she said. 'At least, I am and so's my Uncle Sammy.'

'Thank you kindly, Rosie,' said Mr Brown. 'Anyway, I've only got a few words to mention, which is that me and my wife, Mrs Bessie Brown, who's wearin' a new titfer, wish to thank all of you for bein' here in honour of our daughter Susie and 'er new better 'alf.'

'What's she done with 'er old one, then?'

'Got 'im under the table, has she, Jim?'

'If you don't all keep quiet,' said Freddy, 'me dad won't make 'is speech.'

' 'Ooray!'

' 'Ooray twice!'

'Where was I?' asked Mr Brown.

'In honour of Susie and Sammy,' said Boots.

'Thank you kindly, Boots,' said Mr Brown. 'Yes, me an' Bessie thank you all for bein' with us today an' for all your good wishes, and we 'ope everyone 'as a fine time without falling over, which some guests did when we got married ourselves. Is that the lot, Bessie?'

'Yes, it's our pleasure, Jim,' said the smiling Mrs Brown.

'Well, then, me an' Bessie drink yer very good 'ealth,' said Mr Brown.

'Same to you, Jim!'

'Same to you, Bessie!'

Boots was on his feet a few minutes later, with Rosie looking ready to giggle, Chinese Lady looking suspicious of the lurking smile on his face, and her husband Mr Finch looking as if his eldest stepson was going to be worth listening to.

'Ladies—'

'Where? What ladies?' asked a wag.

'Ladies and gentlemen—'

'What's he talkin' about?'

'You mean who's he talkin' about.'

'They're after you, Daddy,' said Rosie.

'Let's have it, Boots,' said Ned.

'I'll fire the next clever gent out of a cannon,' said Boots.

'Now, Boots, we don't want any aggravatin' talk,' said Chinese Lady, 'not on Sammy and Susie's weddin' day.'

'Duly noted, old girl,' said Boots. 'Now, ladies and

gentlemen, family life that begins with marriage needs to be blessed with good plumbing, and the first principle of good plumbing is all to do with frost-proof pipes. Frost-proofing can be achieved in several ways, all of which are described in Stopcock and Company's plumbing manual.'

'What's that only oldest son of mine talkin' about, Edwin?' asked Chinese Lady of her husband.

'Plumbing,' said Mr Finch. 'Good plumbing is dear to the hearts of all of us.'

'Not at a weddin' it's not,' said Chinese Lady.

'I expect you all want to know how to deal with a burst pipe,' said Boots. 'You first find out where all the water's coming from.'

'Is that a fact?' asked Tommy.

'It's news to me,' said Sammy.

'It's useful information for newly-weds,' said Boots, and went on to say that his mother, bless her cotton socks, had twice been a newly-wed and twice endowed with worldly goods, including good plumbing.

'Is it me who's goin' barmy, or is it Boots?' asked Mr Higgins.

'I knew it,' said Chinese Lady, 'I knew that son of mine would go off his 'ead one day, I always said he would, but I never thought it would happen at his brother's weddin'.'

'Sounds all right to me, Mrs Finch,' said Will, 'and I know for a fact that Susie's expectin' Sammy to endow her with good plumbin'.'

'Plumbing's serious,' said Sammy.

'Especially if you can get ten per cent discount,' said Susie.

Guests rolled about, and the bridesmaids were all in fits.

318

'In addition to good plumbing,' said Boots, 'newly-weds need an efficient mangle.'

'Of vhich I have a stock at five bob each,' said Mr Greenberg, 'and no charge for delivery.'

'Good on yer, Eli!'

'Ve are all friends,' beamed Mr Greenberg.

'Efficient mangles are a must,' said Boots, 'and so are ladies' undergarments. Particularly for brides.'

'Daddy!' shrieked Rosie.

'Stop him, someone,' begged Susie.

'Hit him, you mean,' said Lizzy.

'While I can't speak as a gentleman,' said Boots, 'I can say, as a common or garden bloke, that brides not only go for good plumbing and efficient mangles, they've also got a thing about reliable elastic.'

'Sammy, stop him!' cried Susie.

'Why, what's he said?' asked Sammy.

'Keep goin', Boots,' said Will, hoping that laughing moments wouldn't affect his tubes.

Rachel thought, I should miss this? Not likely. What a family.

Boots touched on the subject of bridal trousseaux. He said he hadn't seen Susie's trousseau, but he had it on good authority from her sister Sally that it wisely contained some winter warmers.

'I can't hardly believe what I'm hearin',' said Chinese Lady.

'Nor me,' said Sally, close to hysterics.

'It's the winter weather,' said Boots. If Sammy was rarely lost for hitting English on its head, Boots was never lost for whimsical or deceptive patter. And he was talking as much to divert himself as the guests. Something was still worrying him, something he felt he'd forgotten or overlooked. He caught Rosie's eye, and Rosie waited in delight for his next piece of nonsense. 'You'll all be interested to know that Susie's bottom drawer is as good as she hopes Sammy's plumbing will be.'

'Never mind the plumbin',' said Sammy, 'just give me a list of me fancy expectations.'

'Well,' said Boots, 'how'd you like the sound of four ladies' woolly vests down to the knees, two red flannel petticoats and one plumbers' spanner for giving you a headache?'

'That's out for a start,' said Sammy. 'I don't like headaches except as a matter of business.'

'I never heard anything more deplorable in all me life,' said Chinese Lady, 'and I can't take kindly to you laughin' about it, Edwin.'

'Believe me, Maisie, I'm not laughing,' said Mr Finch, 'I'm crying.'

'So am I,' said Susie.

'Don't see why,' said Will, 'I like the sound of four woolly vests down to your knees, sis.'

'I'll kill Boots,' said Susie.

'You've done it now, Daddy,' said Rosie.

'Regarding the happy couple,' said Boots, 'I've known Sammy all his life, and it's my considered opinion that if there were two more like him, the rest of us would be walking backwards.'

'Granted,' said Sammy.

'Seconded,' said Tommy.

'Thirded,' said Lizzy.

'I've known Susie since she was sixteen,' said Boots. 'Sammy runs on electricity, Susie runs on sunshine. If you put two people like Susie and Sammy together, they'll never have a freeze-up, even if their plumbing is a major disaster.'

'Is that son of mine makin' sense?' asked Chinese Lady.

'Now and again,' said Mr Finch.

'Sammy fell on his head when he first met Susie,' said Boots, 'and he's still not right way up. Long may Susie keep him like that, it's one way of emptying his pockets. Ladies and gentlemen, I give you the bride and groom and a long-lasting marriage.'

'Well done, Boots,' said Mr Finch, and everyone came to their feet to toast the happy couple. After which, Rosie whispered to Boots that she was sure his mum was going to box his ears.

'Never a dull moment in this family, kitten,' he said.

'Mummy's still laughing,' said Rosie, 'I think she's getting better, don't you?'

'Thumbs up to that, Rosie.'

Sammy's speech was appreciated by one and all. He admitted Susie had floored him, and that she answered him back as well, but it hadn't been painful all the time, and he was hoping to make a recovery. He further admitted he had had to hand Susie all his worldly goods on account of the vicar listening, and he could only hope she'd let him have enough back to take care of his overheads. He thanked Mrs Brown for having had Susie as a result of a twinkle in Mr Brown's eye, and he thanked them both for making sure that Susie hadn't run off with a floor-walker, as that would have upset him no end. He hoped that as his wife she'd cure herself of answering him back. He thanked everyone for their presents, and he thanked his mother for bringing him up to be virtuous, charitable and a bit of all right in the business world. Modesty prevented him saying more than that. He complimented Mr Finch on becoming his stepfather, and he complimented the bridesmaids on looking highly adorable. He proposed a toast to them, and he himself toasted his bride.

'Good luck, Susie!'

'Good on yer, Sammy!'

'Bless you both,' said Mrs Brown happily.

There was an interval before the three-piece band arrived and dancing began. Ladies took themselves off to their cloakroom and Boots took himself into the street. The uniformed constable was patrolling about. Boots asked him if he was acting under instructions. The constable said yes, that his orders were to make sure that Ponsonby, the wanted man, did not enter the Institute or intrude on the wedding celebrations in any way. A colleague was just round the corner in Brandon Street to check on people entering Larcom Street. There was a third man near the vicarage and church, watching people coming up from Charleston Street or from the Walworth Road. In addition, there were scores of men combing the whole area.

'Thanks,' said Boots, 'I'll have cups of tea and some wedding cake sent out to you and your colleague in a while.'

'Kind of you, Mr Adams, we'll appreciate that. Good luck, sir.'

He and Rosie needed that, did they? If so, how much? Ponsonby, obviously, was still at large. He went back into the hall. Everyone, of course, knew about the murders and a man who'd been charged by the police. What they didn't know was that the slippery bugger had escaped custody. Well, there was no point in telling them, no point in introducing an ugly note. It was Susie's big day. Let it stay like that.

There was a queue tailing back from the ladies' cloakroom beyond the stage, and the caterers were busy setting out cups and saucers and making huge pots of tea. The cake was waiting to be cut. Susie and Sammy were circulating in dutiful and sociable fashion, talking to as many guests as possible. Boots looked instinctively for Rosie. Young Tim was his pal, Rosie his sweetheart. He sometimes had to be careful not to show more attention to the girl than the boy, and Rosie herself took care to see that Tim was never pushed into the background.

Will came up, a smile on his face. Boots liked Will, he liked the whole of the Brown family, very much a reminder of his own when they were living in Caulfield Place.

'How's it goin', Boots?' asked Will.

'It's going well for Susie,' said Boots. 'Have you seen Rosie?'

'She's over there, with Freddy, Cassie and your niece Annabelle. Sally's gone into hidin'. There's a young bloke from your offices tryin' to turn her into his girlfriend.'

Sally appeared then, a young vision in pink.

'Who's this?' asked Boots.

'Boots, it's me,' said Sally.

'Well, don't go home too early,' said Boots, 'not before I've had a dance with you.'

Sally turned a thrilled pink that almost matched her cerise dress. Boots was her hero after what he'd done for Cassie yesterday. Will recognized her then as a girl with a crush.

'Oh, I'll be ever so pleasured,' she said. 'Boots, 'as Will told you the Army's goin' to discharge 'im?'

'Is that a fact, Will?' asked Boots.

'Had an official letter this mornin',' said Will.

'With an offer of a pension?' asked Boots, glancing across the hall at Rosie.

'Not a word,' said Will.

'Well, we'll go to work on it together,' said Boots. 'I'll come and see you sometime next week.'

'Oh, ain't you nice?' said Sally.

'The Ministry of Pensions won't think so,' said Boots.

'Blow them,' said Sally.

'I won't say five bob a week wouldn't be useful,' said Will.

'We'll start by getting you to ask for two quid,' said Boots.

'Two quid?' said Sally, blinking.

'Will won't get it,' said Boots, 'but it'll send the Ministry into a panic. That'll give Will a chance to settle for twelve and six, or ten bob at the worst.'

'I'm not proud,' said Will.

'Nor am I,' said Boots, 'it alters the shape of your face.'

Sally laughed. Boots had a quiet word with a waitress about tea for the policemen.

The tables had all been folded and stowed away, except for two covered with cups and saucers. The hot tea was ready and the wedding cake was cut amid the sounds of revelry. Boots went across to Emily, who had just taken young Tim in hand and was trying to show him how to dance the Boston Two-Step. Boots collected a cup of tea on the way and gave it to Emily.

'Lovely,' she said, 'just what I need.'

'Sit down and drink it,' said Boots. The chairs now lined the walls.

'But I've already been sittin' for ages,' said Emily.

'Well, good for you,' said Boots, 'now do some more. I'll see to Tim. Come on, young 'un, let's go out to the yard and see if we can have five minutes football before the band arrives.'

'Crikey, could we, Dad?' asked Tim, plainly preferring that to the Boston Two-Step.

'Did I hear someone mention football?' asked Emily.

'Yes, Dad did,' said Tim.

'Not likely you're not,' said Emily, 'not in your suit, me lad, nor your dad in his. I don't know, goin' out to a yard to kick a ball about when there's a weddin' on. Your grandma will have a fit. So will I. That dad of yours wants talkin' to sometimes.'

'No football, then,' said Boots, 'just a look at the fresh air. It's getting a little warm in here.'

'Well, lovey, if it's fresh, bring some back 'ere,' said Emily.

'I'll find a paper bag,' said Boots, and took Tim around the stage and through the kitchen to the back door, which opened on to an alley used as a yard for dustbins. He wanted to check the door, to find out if the caterers were keeping it locked. They weren't. They were using the dustbins. But just beyond the entrance to the alley, he glimpsed a constable. So there he was, the colleague of the man on duty outside the Institute. Inspector Grant was taking seriously his feeling that before Ponsonby attempted to slip off to wider pastures he meant to revenge himself for being handed over to the police in that factory wasteland. With other police officers swarming elsewhere, Ponsonby must be feeling squeezed, wherever he was.

'Look, there's a bobby, Dad,' said Tim, 'I'll go and ask him the time.'

'What for, young feller-me-lad?'

'Dad, you always ask a bobby the time,' said four-year-old Tim.

'No, you don't,' said Boots, catching hold of his energetic young son before he had a chance to slip the parental leash. 'Up you come.' He picked the boy up and slung him over his shoulder. Tim yelled with delight as Boots carried him back into the hall. Chinese Lady intercepted father and son, a cup of tea in her hand, her hat a wedding triumph.

'So there you are,' she said.

'Hello, old lady,' said Boots, eyes picking out Rosie.

'What's that boy doin' over your shoulder, might I ask?'

'What boy?' asked Boots.

'Me!' yelled Tim.

'What's he doin' up in the air?' demanded Chinese Lady.

'Search me,' said Boots, and his mother put on her severe look.

'I don't know what I'm goin' to tell people about that speech of yours,' she said. 'It's a mystery to me where you got that tongue of yours from.'

'It's a mystery to me too,' said Boots, 'so we're both in the same boat. Well, you do the rowing, old lady, while I keep a lookout for the old man of the sea.'

'What old man of the sea?' asked Chinese Lady suspiciously.

'The one with all the answers,' said Boots.

Chinese Lady's firm mouth twitched.

'Put that boy down,' she said.

'Down you come, Tim,' said Boots, and set the lad on his feet. 'Go and get yourself a cup of tea and a slice of cake. Then I'll show you how to turn cartwheels for your grandma.'

'Crikey, yes,' said Tim, going at a run.

'Lovely wedding, old girl,' said Boots.

'It was,' said Chinese Lady, 'till you started talkin' about Susie's bottom drawer. I was never more embarrassed for any of my sons. Sammy's bad enough, but at least he 'asn't got any of those Frenchified ways you picked up in France.'

'Well, that's something to be thankful for,' said Boots. The three-piece band had arrived, a little surprised to have been closely inspected by a policeman. They were now up

326

on the stage and getting ready for their part in the proceedings. As soon as everyone had had a cup of tea and a piece of wedding cake, the caterers would finish clearing the hall.

'I can't for the life of me think why Edwin don't disapprove of that tongue of yours,' said Chinese Lady, who wouldn't have allowed him to, in any case.

'Never mind, live in hope,' said Boots. He glimpsed a movement in the gallery. 'Just a moment.' He walked to the far end, climbed the stairs and came upon Freddy and Cassie. 'Hello, what's happening up here?' he asked.

Cassie regarded him in dreamy adoration, having been told he was the man who had helped Freddy bring her home.

''Ello,' she said shyly. 'Me an' Freddy's lookin' for Queen Mary's best 'at.'

'Well, she's lookin',' said Freddy, 'I'm just bein' wore out.'

'Yes, Queen Mary come up 'ere once,' said Cassie, 'and lost 'er best 'at. I read it somewhere. It's got green feathers. Mister, 'ave you met Queen Mary and 'ad Sunday tea with 'er?'

'Not lately,' smiled Boots.

'There, I told yer, Freddy,' said Cassie. 'I told yer 'e was bound to 'ave met Queen Mary.'

'Yer'll 'ave to excuse 'er, Mister Adams,' said Freddy, 'she can't 'elp bein' scatty.'

'I ain't scatty, am I, mister?' said Cassie.

'I like scatty girls,' said Boots. 'We're all a bit that way. In fact, the whole world's barmy, Cassie.' He ruffled the girl's hair. 'Enjoy yourselves. Hope you find Queenie's hat.'

The band struck up then. The tables were all out of the way, the hall clear. The dancing began.

And Annie arrived.

CHAPTER TWENTY-FOUR

Annie entered the Institute at five minutes to five. Crikey, she thought, it must be an important wedding to have a policeman on duty outside. Actually, there'd been quite a few about. Had she bought an evening paper on her way home from work she'd have known why. They were head-lining the escape of the man held in custody. His name was revealed and his description, together with the warning that he was dangerous.

The atmosphere of revelry reached Annie at once. The guests were dancing to the music of a three-piece band, and the hall was a picture of colour and movement. Girls were all dolled up, and all the women looked wedding-worthy. Annie noticed some very smart ladies and some posh-looking men. She supposed Sammy Adams had friends all over because of his business. Young men looked frisky, and the middle-aged women looked kind of mellow, as if beer and port had been flowing. The band were playing 'Miss Annabelle Lee', and the dancers were doing a quick-step. It all looked lively and exciting, and there wasn't a gloomy face anywhere. The bride herself was dancing, her white gown swirling and floating, and she was laughing up into the face of a very interesting-looking man. Combing the vague recollections she had of seeing Sammy Adams at his market stall, Annie felt sure she was seeing him now. There were chairs along the side walls, but not many people were using them at the moment. Most were dancing. Annie looked around for a sight of Will. Not seeing him, she slipped into the cloakroom to take off her hat and her light raincoat, and to unnecessarily tidy up her face.

She emerged in her highly fashionable loose-waisted white dress, her stockinged legs gleaming. The first person she saw was Cassie, who was in argument with Freddy. Freddy was in a new grey suit with long trousers, but still looked very much a boy.

'Hello, you two,' she said, 'what's up?'

'I just don't believe it, but it 'appened,' said Freddy. 'Cassie's barmy cat 'as invited itself.'

'D'you mean it came in 'ere?' asked Annie.

'Well, Tabby likes weddings,' said Cassie. 'I keep tellin' Freddy, but 'e keeps not listenin'.'

'Crikey, Annie, don't yer look posh?' said Freddy.

'Do I, Freddy?'

'I bet Will's goin' to fall over when 'e spots yer,' said Freddy.

'Annie, Tabby's gone in the men's cloakroom,' complained Cassie, 'an' Freddy won't go an' get 'im.'

'Beats me 'ow it got here,' said Freddy, 'but I ain't fetchin' it. D'you know what she wants to do? Take it round in a dance.'

'Well, Tabby likes dancing,' said Cassie. ''E used to dance as Dick Whittington's cat in a pantomime.'

'Bloomin' Muvver O'Grady,' breathed Freddy, 'she ain't real.'

The dance came to an end. Annie watched couples leaving the floor. There was no sign of Will with a partner.

'Hello.'

Annie turned, and there he was, smiling and looking a fine young man in his new grey suit, bought for the wedding.

'Hello, Will.'

'You're lookin' highly fashionable again, Annie,' he

said, thinking her just about the nicest girl a bloke could hope to walk out with.

'I don't like the way you say highly,' said Annie, 'you're as bad as me dad.'

'Well, it's not our fault you look good enough to eat,' said Will. 'Come on, come and meet the bride and groom and lots of other people.' He took her to that part of the hall where the Brown and Adams families were sociably grouped. He introduced her first to Susie and Sammy. Susie, recognizing her and wanting her to be a bright light in Will's life, greeted her like an old friend. Sammy, who had been told about her and what had happened yesterday to her sister Cassie, shook hands warmly with her. She was immediately conscious of electric energy.

'What a pleasure,' he said. 'Are you the girl my new brother-in-law Will found in a pushcart?'

'Sammy!' Susie shook a finger at him.

'Oh, I can't believe it,' said Annie, looking at Will. 'You've done it on me again.'

'Not me,' said Will. Susie was the guilty party, actually. She thought the incident the funniest thing ever, although she was aware Annie didn't.

'I'd give five bob to see Susie in a pushcart,' said Sammy. 'Unfortunately, I can't afford it at the moment.'

'Sammy, go and stand in a corner,' said Susie.

'Who said that?' asked Sammy, and Will, grinning, introduced Annie to his mum. She'd already met his dad. Mrs Brown was that taken with the girl she almost gave her a motherly cuddle. Mr Brown said hello again, Annie, glad you could come, but watch some of the fellers here, they'll be after you. Annie met Chinese Lady, introduced to her as Mrs Finch, and her husband Mr Finch, ever such a distinguished-looking man. She also met Boots and Emily, Lizzy and Ned, Tommy and Vi. Then there was a quite beautiful woman whom Boots introduced as Rachel, a friend of the family, and a dark-bearded fatherly-looking man with whom all Walworth was acquainted, Mr Greenberg. Annie, knowing Boots was the man who had been such a great help to Freddy in finding Cassie, discovered him to be distinguished-looking himself, but with a very easy-going air. His wife Emily had marvellous auburn hair and magnificent green eyes, but was awfully thin. Then there were two people called Aunt Victoria and Uncle Tom, and several children. Lord, thought Annie, why am I meeting all these people if I'm just someone who's only going to get a picture postcard from India, and perhaps not even that?

Guests were dancing again, and most of the people she had just met melted away to take the floor. Annie waited for Will to ask her. Instead, he began chatting to Sammy's mother. Annie ground her teeth. Tommy came up.

'Now we've met and me wife Vi's havin' a sit-down,' he said, 'might I have the pleasure? I'm Tommy, in case you've already forgotten.'

'I'm Annie, if you've forgotten,' she said.

'Which I haven't,' said Tommy, and so she danced with him, but she was wild with Will.

Boots was taking Aunt Victoria round. Emily had said he ought to, for the sake of family relations. Aunt Victoria was saying that she was very complimented. Boots said well, you can still shake a fine leg for a woman of forty. Aunt Victoria, well past forty, felt so pleasured by this further compliment that she overlooked his mention of her limb. It was a lovely wedding party, she said, and she didn't want to complain, but she thought the caterers' port was a little vinegary, that it was very inconvenient that in the ladies' cloakroom one of the cubicles was out of order, that she was sure Mr Higgins was getting drunk on all the beer he was ordering free from the waitresses, and that some of the children seemed a little rowdy. Well, I'm like you, Aunt Victoria, said Boots, I don't want to complain, either, and I'm glad you agree we shouldn't. Well, I was just mentioning one or two things, that's all, she said. Boots smiled, and Aunt Victoria went girlishly giddy in his arms.

The dance over, Annie looked for Will, a fierce light in her eyes. He'd gone missing, the coward. She intercepted Susie.

'Susie, could I ask you, doesn't Will dance?'

Susie looked at her and saw vexation. She realized Will had said nothing about his condition to this very attractive girl. Susie felt she knew why. All the same, Annie should be told, it was only fair. They stood together in the middle of the hall. Waitresses appeared with trays of beer, port and soft drinks. Spirits in the church hall weren't allowed.

'Annie, Will's got asthma. That's why he's home from India, and why he's havin' to leave the Army. He received a letter today, telling him they were goin' to discharge him. He hasn't told you, obviously. He gets attacks, sometimes not for a day or so, sometimes three a day. He probably thinks he'll have an attack if he dances, and he's a bit fed-up with himself.'

'He's got asthma?' said Annie. She felt very upset. 'Oh, that's not like consumption, is it?'

'No, of course not,' said Susie, still softly brilliant in her wedding gown. She and Sammy weren't going on their honeymoon to Devon until tomorrow. They were spending their wedding night in their new home. Susie was having nervously excited moments about it, and Sammy was wondering if Susie was going to wear a black silk nightdress. 'It's just that it makes Will feel he's only half a man some days.'

'Oh, where is 'e?' said Annie. 'Fancy not tellin' me. If I

can put up with bein' dumped in a pushcart and havin' him tell everyone about it, he can put up with tellin' me about his asthma.'

'Well, good for you, Annie,' said Susie. 'Look, there he is, up in the gallery, watchin' us.'

The band struck up again as Annie made for the gallery stairs. It didn't take her long to corner Will and to speak her mind. She didn't make the mistake of being sad and pitying, although she did feel sad.

'Will, you silly, you ought to be ashamed,' she said, 'takin' me out, kissin' me till I didn't know where me legs were, and not tellin' me you've got a bit of a chest complaint. Lots of men 'ave got chest complaints, but they don't go round deceivin' girls.'

'Deceivin'?' said Will.

'Well, it is deceivin', isn't it, not confidin' in a girl who's your young lady?'

'I thought it was best if—'

'As if I care you've got a funny chest—'

'You haven't. Yours is—'

'Don't be cheeky. I want to know all about the attacks you 'ave. Will Brown, look me in the eye when I'm talkin' to you.'

'Annie, I've even been chucked out of the Army.'

'Thank goodness for that,' said Annie. 'I don't want my young man in any Army, anyway. And you're still not lookin' at me.'

'Can't,' said Will.

'Why can't you? What's wrong with me?'

'If I look at you, I'll kiss you.'

'Well, that's nice. I like you sayin' things like that. Let's sit down in the corner over there.'

'Annie, if I get an attack, you won't like what it does to me.'

'Well, come and sit and talk to me,' said Annie, 'about what makes you have attacks. We don't 'ave to dance, just sit together.'

Will gave in. Annie put her arms around him and kissed him. Nothing chronically disastrous happened, even though Annie was wearing a little scent. Well, when a girl had made up her mind to be someone's young lady, a little scent was a great help.

The band played on, and on, contributing to the revelry infectiously and exhilaratingly, especially after each member had been served with a pint glass of the free beer. Old-fashioned dances alternated with lively modern fox-trots, and young people nearly fell over themselves in their delighted dash on to the floor to perform the Charleston. Sammy's office girls rushed with young men. Into the fray went Lizzy, Vi, Emily and Susie with their husbands. In went Rosie and Annabelle to dance it with each other. In went Cassie, dragging an appalled Freddy with her.

Chinese Lady could hardly believe her eyes. Those short frocks, and Sammy's office girls all wearing pink garters, the delight of flappers. She knew where they came from. Sammy's ladies' shops. That disreputable young man was heading for purgatory all right. And look at Boots, her only oldest, he was performing with three partners now, Emily, Rosie and Annabelle. And that Tommy, going it with Vi. As for Lizzy, well, there she was with Ned, and Ned performing as if he didn't have an artificial leg. Well, thought Chinese Lady, if I don't have something to say to all of them, my name's not Mrs Maisie Finch.

'I never saw anything so shockin',' she said to her husband.

'Wait until they're performing "Mother Brown",' said

Mr Finch, well-versed in this cockney ritual, known as a knees-up.

'Oh, that's different,' said Chinese Lady.

Emily emerged exhausted at the finish of the Charleston, and Boots made her sit down. Ned came up, and advised Boots a bloke wanted to see him, he was waiting at the door.

'I'll get Emily a port, Boots, while you go and see the bloke.'

Boots found a detective-sergeant waiting for him.

'Sorry to disturb you, Mr Adams, but Inspector Grant asked me, as I was comin' this way, to drop in on you.'

'You've copped Ponsonby?' said Boots.

The CID sergeant said no, not yet. What he wanted to say was that they'd traced a call made by Ponsonby on a shop in King and Queen Street, near the market. He'd made the call not long after his escape from the Rodney Road police station. He'd bought a toy periscope.

'A what?' said Boots.

A toy periscope, said the CID man, made of cardboard with two small mirrors and sold to kids for tuppence. Boots asked where Ponsonby had got the money from. Wasn't it standard practice for the police to empty a suspect's pockets? Yes, and that had been done, said the sergeant, but in making enquiries in the market, they'd discovered Ponsonby had sold his silk-lined waistcoat to a second-hand clothes stall for threepence. Incidentally, they'd also found a stack of money in a cupboard in his lodgings, which was believed to relate to a robbery. Anyway, the point was, Inspector Grant was convinced Ponsonby was still somewhere in this area, and he wanted Mr Adams to take great care, especially when the wedding celebrations were over and he left with his family to go home. There would be police around, and if Mr Adams didn't mind, they'd like to give him an escort to his home.

Bloody hell, thought Boots, how the devil can I tell Emily and Rosie that there's a maniac after my blood, and how the devil could Ponsonby have really worked out that I'm here with them? And what the hell did he want a periscope for?

'Look, Sergeant,' he said, 'Ponsonby could have been sharp enough to find my address from the telephone directory. Can you ask Inspector Grant to check the area around our house?'

'Good idea, sir,' said the CID sergeant, 'I'll get that message to him. He's not far away. Sorry if I've worried you as well as disturbed you, but Inspector Grant doesn't like the bugger or what he's capable of gettin' up to.'

'Tell him I share his feelings,' said Boots, and the sergeant left. Boots rejoined the party. He saw Rosie and Annabelle talking to Chinese Lady. Sally, in retreat from Ronnie Jarvis, who had managed to collar her for the Charleston, begged Boots to save her from more of the office boy's larks.

'I think you're playing hard to get, Sally,' he said. A waltz had just begun. 'Is this our dance?'

'Oh, crikey, could we?' breathed Sally in hero-worship, and Boots took her into the waltz. Sally was swoony all the way, but plucked up enough courage to ask him if he thought Sammy would give her a job in one of his shops. Boots said as an apprentice shop assistant? Oh, lor', would he, d'you think? The advantage is all yours, Sally, you're one of the family now, said Boots. 'Oh, bless yer, Boots,' said Sally, and swooned on.

Will had managed a cautious dance with Annie, she bright-eyed now that she knew exactly where she stood, and that she had made him understand where he stood himself. They were walking out. Officially.

The atmosphere was rousingly festive. Cockneys didn't believe in enjoying themselves quietly. Ain't there goin' to be a knees-up? Later. What about a knees-up? Later.

Sammy, noting Will and Annie sitting together and looking as if they were already thinking of good plumbing, efficient mangles and bottom drawers, decided he couldn't let Susie's likeable brother suffer unemployment as well as asthma. He told Susie he'd find him a job that wouldn't crucify his chest. Susie hugged him and let his own chest introduce itself pleasurably to her bodice.

'Lord love yer, Mrs Adams,' he said, 'not here if you don't mind. Later.'

'Love you, Sammy.'

Rosie spoke to Emily.

'You all right, Mummy?'

'Fine, Rosie love.'

'I expect you're getting a bit tired.'

'I'm not goin' to be too tired for the knees-up,' smiled Emily.

'We're really going to have one?' said Rosie.

'There'll be a riot if we don't,' said Emily.

Boots appeared.

'Rosie,' he said, 'I don't think I've had the pleasure yet. How about it, kitten?'

'Well, I think I'm disengaged, Daddy, yes, I think I am,' said Rosie. 'You can have the pleasure.'

'Come on, then,' said Boots and they went flying into the Boston Two-Step, Rosie in sheer exhilaration. Cassie couldn't get Freddy to participate, so she made him go and look for her cat. She did some more looking herself, and tried the ladies' cloakroom. No-one was there. She looked and she called. Tabby didn't miaow or show himself, it was just ever so quiet in the cloakroom, the door of one cubicle locked and chalked 'OUT OF

ORDER'. She didn't like it being so quiet and she ran out.

It was not Cassie Mr Ponsonby was waiting for, however.

It was Rosie.

Rosie, coming off the floor with Boots, said, 'I'll tell Miss Simms that just everyone was here this evening, Daddy – oh, silly me, I can't. She's gone to darkest Africa. I'm sorry, aren't you? I think she liked you lots. Never mind, I'll tell all my school friends just everyone was here.'

'From all the noise we're making, I should think everyone knows already that just everyone's here, Rosie. We might—' Boots stopped. It hit him then, the point he'd overlooked. Everyone included Ponsonby. Boots recalled the scene in the police station, when there was the necessity of making a statement. Quite close was the handcuffed Ponsonby, who knew by then whose daughter Rosie was. Boots had said, 'Let's get it all over with now, Inspector, I'm attending a wedding here, at St John's Church tomorrow, with my family.' It was a wedding Ponsonby knew about, and he probably knew too that the reception was taking place at the Institute. And at that point he also knew the man who had knocked him out would be there with his family. He had seen Rosie, he had heard her. '*Hello, Daddy.*'

It was after nine-thirty now, and Ponsonby was somewhere close, Boots was absolutely certain of that now. He told Rosie to get hold of Tim, and for the two of them to give Emily a little company until he got back. He was just going to the cloakroom. Rosie looked at him. The hall was alive with laughter and uproarious jokes, with young people awaiting the next dance.

'Daddy, something's worrying you,' said Rosie.

'Oh, just the thought of doing the knees-up,' said Boots.

338

'Daddy, I'm not silly, you know,' said Rosie. His worries were her worries, his pains her pains.

'Nor am I, I know when I need to go to the cloakroom,' said Boots. 'Collect Tim, Rosie, and go and sit with Mummy, there's a sweet girl.'

'Yes, all right, Daddy,' said Rosie and went looking for Tim. The band struck up for the next dance. Rachel intercepted Boots as he crossed the hall.

'Boots, may I?' she said, her smile affectionate.

'In two ticks, Rachel, promise,' he said, and off he went to check the back door again. It was still not locked, the caterers were still using the dustbins. They were on duty until ten-thirty. But this time, there was a policeman on duty in the alley itself. In the darkness, Boots made him out. A street lamp beyond the alley cast a faint light over the entrance. It would pick out anyone entering.

Boots returned. Rachel was waiting. Rosie was watching, and she watched the person she loved best in all the world dance a fox-trot with the most beautiful woman in the hall. Rachel was purring.

'Lovely,' she murmured.

'I am?' said Boots.

'God, I hope not,' said Rachel. 'Not you or Sammy or Tommy. I like you all for being men, not pretty ones.'

'Bless your proud bosom, Rachel,' said Boots, thinking, thinking.

Will suddenly came to his feet.

'What's up?' asked Annie.

'Something's hittin' me tubes,' said Will. 'Give us a few minutes, Annie.'

'Yes, all right, Will,' she said, and watched as he made his way to the cloakroom, where he entered a cubicle, locked it and stood with his back against the door. He drew in breath. The danger signals fluttered and weakened. He sighed with relief, but guessed he'd have an attack by the time he got home, if not before.

Boots came off the floor with Rachel, and they both sat with Emily to let Rosie and Tim join Lizzy's children. Susie appeared in a swirl of white.

'Knees-up after the next dance,' she said, 'everyone in.'

'I should be worried?' said Rachel. 'Susie, I can't wait.'

'I've got a wooden leg,' said Boots.

'No excuses,' said Susie, and delivered the order next to Chinese Lady, Mr Finch, Mr and Mrs Brown, and Mr Greenberg.

'Well, I don't mind any company doin' a knees-up,' said Chinese Lady, 'but I'm not sure—'

'No excuses, Mum,' said Susie, now a daughter-in-law.

'Well, my goodness, Susie, at my age and all.'

'No excuses, Maisie,' said Mr Finch, who had come back from Germany with definite worries of his own, all concerning the political ambitions of a man called Adolf Hitler.

'Ve are all friends,' beamed Mr Greenberg, 'and vhat is a knees-up for if not for friends, ain't it?'

Guests swarmed again as the band struck up 'On Mother Kelly's Doorstep'.

'Come on, Boots, let's you, me, Timmy and Rosie all do this together,' said Emily.

They collected Tim, and Boots called Rosie.

'Yes, in a minute, Daddy,' said Rosie, coming up, 'but I've got to shake hands with the water board first.' That was a family thing. Spending a penny was called going to shake hands with the water board. Rosie dashed off. Boots, taking hold of Tim's hand and Emily's hand, was hit by a shaft of light.

Ponsonby. The ladies' cloakroom. Two cubicles, one out of order. The curate, knowing a large wedding party was using the Institute today, would have moved heaven and earth to ensure there was no inconvenience of that kind. Plumbing, for God's sake.

'Just a moment, Em,' he said, and was away, skirting the dancers. Then he ran to the ladies' cloakroom. He opened the door without knocking. Rosie was there, waiting. She turned, her mouth opened. Boots put a finger to his lips, then beckoned, urgently. Rosie came out into the passage.

'Daddy, what *are* you doing?' she whispered.

Boots, pulling the door to, said, 'Rosie, I think there's a man in the other cubicle.'

'Ugh,' said Rosie.

'Do you remember the man you saw at the police station last night? He escaped.'

'Oh, blessed saints,' breathed Rosie. 'He's in there?'

The door opened and Mrs Higgins emerged.

''Ello, 'ello, what's all this 'ere?' she said.

Rosie pulled the door to again.

'We're thinking up larks, Mrs Higgins, Daddy and me.'

'Oh, I'm all for larks, Rosie, specially with Boots.'

'You're wanted at the moment by Mr Higgins for "Mother Kelly's Doorstep",' said Boots.

'Oh, I ain't missin' that,' said Mrs Higgins. 'I'll 'ave me larks later, Boots.' Away she went, pink and hearty with beer.

'Rosie,' said Boots, 'we don't want any fuss, do we? We don't want the party spoiled, do we?'

'Daddy, are you sure that man's in there? Oh, is that what you've been worrying about?'

'Listen, kitten, go through the back door. You'll find

341

there's a policeman out there. Ask him to come through to this cloakroom and to bring his colleague with him.'

'Oh, Lord,' breathed Rosie. 'I do want to shake hands, though.'

'All right, kitten. Speak to your Uncle Ned. I don't think he'll be dancing this one. Ask him to take you to the men's cloakroom, and then you can speak to the policeman. Uncle Ned will want to know what it's all about. Tell him to come and see me.'

'Good idea, Daddy, ever such a good idea,' said Rosie, and dashed to find Lizzy's husband.

Boots remained where he was, outside the door of the ladies' cloakroom. While the dance was on, the ladies would stay away, he hoped. He thought about Ponsonby. It would have been the easiest thing in the world for him to have slipped into the Institute this morning, while the caterers had the place opened up. And then to print 'OUT OF ORDER' in chalk on a cubicle door before locking himself in. He'd been prepared to stay there all day, waiting and hoping. Which meant it was Rosie he was after. A young girl. But how would he have known of her entry?

The toy periscope!

Boots knew that the wall dividing the two men's cubicles did not reach the ceiling. There was a foot-high gap. Exactly how disgusting could a sadistic man get?

Ned arrived.

'What's up, Boots?'

Boots told him. Ned took the details in with a soft whistle.

'Is the cubicle the one against the outside wall?' he asked. 'If so, and if it's like the men's, there'll be a window. A small one, but probably no smaller than the one he climbed through in the police station. The moment he suspects something, he'll be after worming his way out. That'll land him in the alley. Leave the alley to me, Boots. You stay here.'

Ned met two constables on his way through to the back door. He nodded to them. Rosie was beside the first policeman, looking a little pent-up.

'No worries, Rosie, all under control,' said Ned reassuringly and carried on to the alley. Rosie led the policemen to the cloakroom, where Boots stood with his back to the door. They could hear the band and the sounds of dancers filling the hall with rousing revelry.

Boots explained briefly but concisely to the uniformed men.

'Right, got you, sir,' said one constable, 'he might be in there or he might not.'

'He's in there,' said Boots. 'I'll prove it. Rosie love, go and talk to Annabelle.'

'Must I?' said Rosie.

'Off you go, kitten.'

Rosie went, but hardly knew how she was going to keep quiet about what was happening.

Boots opened the door of the cloakroom. The cubicles were on the left, facing him, a row of clothes pegs on the right. The policemen watched from the doorway. He opened the door of the vacant cubicle in noisy fashion, then stood back a little and kept his eyes on the top of the dividing wall. The gap was wide enough for a man as slim as Ponsonby to worm through, to fall headlong on to his victim, or, if no-one else was in the cloakroom, to catch her when she left the cubicle. He heard the faintest of sounds, and the next moment the square open head of a cardboard periscope appeared. It angled, and Boots knew its mirror could pick up a vision of head and shoulders, the head and shoulders of anyone using the seat. That would be enough. Ponsonby had waited all this time, certain of course that Rosie would be in his sights eventually. The mirror picked up nothing now. It turned, stayed still for a brief second and then vanished. Boots gestured to the policemen, then turned the handle of the door marked 'OUT OF ORDER'. It was locked, of course. The two policemen were in. There was the noise of a window frame vibrating. Facing each other, shoulders pointing at the cubicle door, the policeman hit it together, and with all the force they could muster. The door crashed open at a moment when the band and the dancers reached the noisy crescendo of the finale.

Ponsonby was standing on the closed lavatory seat, his socked feet on tiptoe, his head already through the window, eyes staring down at the shadowy figure of Ned, who had a dustbin lid in his hand. Ponsonby's elastic-sided boots, tied together, were hanging around his neck. The policemen hauled him down, pinned him and handcuffed him.

'Ruffians, ruffians!' hissed Mr Ponsonby. 'What a day, what a terrible day.'

Boots saw the intended instrument of Rosie's death, a shiny new leather bootlace. It was wound around the man's left wrist, one end loose and dangling.

Dear God, his Rosie.

The policemen took the demented man out through the back door, much to the gaping astonishment of a caterers' assistant.

'Boots dear, I don't want to complain,' said Aunt Victoria ten minutes later. The wedding party was resting on its laurels, using an interval to gather itself for the last number of the evening and waitresses bringing the last orders for the free drinks. Boots, Rosie and Ned alone knew what had taken place in the out-of-sight ladies' cloakroom.

'Complain? I'm sure you don't, Aunt Victoria,' said Boots, Rosie beside him.

'Well, not at Sammy's wedding, Boots dear,' said Aunt Victoria, 'but would you believe, someone's gone and smashed in that door that was out of order.'

'Yes, I think other people are talking about it,' said Boots. 'I put it down as the act of some desperate woman. Good idea for none of us to complain, Aunt Victoria. It'll only embarrass the woman, whoever she was.'

A hand squeezed his, and he looked down into the moistly shining eyes of Rosie.

She swallowed, then said, 'I think everyone's getting ready for the knees-up, Daddy.'

'Not before time,' said Boots.

In the flat above the shop in the New Kent Road, Henry Brannigan cleared his throat.

'It's been a real 'omely evenin' with yer, Madge,' he said.

'You've been very welcome, Henry,' said Madge. 'You're 'omely yerself, and I know you've got a soft 'eart under that waistcoat of yours.'

'I've been thinkin'.' He cleared his throat again. 'Yer a warm woman, Madge, and yer fond of kids. You'd like to 'ave that orphanage girl for yer own, but you can't because you ain't married. Well, Madge, I'll marry yer if yer'll 'ave me, and give yer a real 'ome where we can bring the girl up decent an' proper.'

Madge stared at him.

'Henry, you mean that, you'll marry me? After what I've been?'

'It ain't what you've been, Madge, it's what you are. But

345

I reckon we'd better leave Walworth an' make our 'ome in Peckham, say.'

'Henry, you can put a ring on me finger any time you like,' said Madge, 'and I won't let yer down, ever. And you can stay the night, if you want.'

'Your kind offer is appreciated, Madge, but I 'ope it won't offend yer if I say no. I'm a bit of what they call conservatyve, and I like doin' things proper. I'll wait till we're married, if that's all right with you.'

'Well, I'd just like to get married quick, Henry.'

'Real quick, Madge?'

'I'm a woman, Henry, and you're a man.'

The centre of the hall was clear, the band at the ready on the stage. Pianist, accordion-player and drummer all had grins on their faces. Susie and Sammy advanced amid loud and encouraging cheers. Sammy looked electric with anticipation. Susie, still in soft shimmering white, smiled.

'Ready, Sammy?'

'Ready, Susie.'

'Here we go, then,' said Susie, and hitched her gown and underskirt. Her silvery stockings flashed.

The band launched itself into the music everyone had been waiting for, and Susie and Sammy began to set the example for all to follow. The whole company provided the vocal accompaniment.

Knees up, Mother Brown, knees up, Mother Brown,
Under the table you must go,
Ee-i-ee-i-addy-oh!
If I catch you bending, I'll saw your legs right off!
Don't get the breeze up,
Just get your knees up!
Knees up, Mother Brown!'

Up went Susie's knees, one after the other, and up went

Sammy's. Into the heart of the cockney ritual came their families, friends and neighbours. In came Will and Annie, Will willing to chance it, his young lady willing to be with him through thick and thin, to help him lay the ogre of asthma. In came Freddy and Cassie, Sally and Ronnie. In came Lizzy and Ned, Annabelle, Bobby, Emma and toddler Edward. In came Mr Finch, bringing Chinese Lady with him. In came Boots, Emily, Rosie and Tim, followed by Tommy, Vi, Aunt Victoria and Uncle Tom. In came Gertie and Bert and all the old friends and neighbours of Caulfield Place. Rachel and Mr Greenberg entered the lists, so did the office girls and, of course, Mr Brown with his beaming old Dutch, Mother Brown herself.

'*Knees up, Mother Brown, knees up, Mother Brown . . .*'

Skirts and dresses whisked and flew, the floor vibrated and frisky quips alternated with shrieks of laughter.

'Mind me eye, Susie.'

'I know where both your eyes are, Sammy Adams.'

'*Under the table you must go,*
Ee-i-ee-i-addy-oh!'

'Get 'em up, Annie.'

'What, higher, Will Brown?'

'Gawd save us, Annie, no higher, or I'll have an attack – a heart attack.'

'*If I catch you bending, I'll saw your legs right off!*'

''Ere, watch it, Cassie, yer nearly showin' yer knickers.'

'Freddy, did yer know Queen Mary wears royal blue ones? And you better find me cat after this, or me dad'll wallop yer.'

'*Don't get the breeze up, just get your knees up!*'

'My life, Rachel, vhat's all this?'

'Me remarkable legs, Eli. Get yours up, old love, it's Mother Brown's night.'

'*Knees up, Mother Brown!*'

'Get 'em up, Vi.'

'Not likely, Tommy Adams, there's two of me.'

'*Just get your knees up, knees up, Mother Brown!*'

'What's happened to your knees, Maisie? Where are they?'

'Where they should be, Edwin Finch, hidin' under me skirt.'

'*Under the table you must go, ee-i-ee-i-addy-oh!*'

'Steady as you go, Em.'

'I'll last out, Boots, you see if I don't.'

It went on and on, towards the time that heralded the finish of the celebrations, half-past ten. Faces shone and legs kicked. Susie was flushed, blue eyes entranced. Sammy was grinning all over. Boots was watching Emily, whose nervous energy showed in the sparkling glitter of her eyes. But it went from her, suddenly, just as the final notes were played, and there was a look of dismay on her face as she sagged. Boots was beside her at once, one arm around her, a strong arm. She looked up at him, her eyes dizzy.

'Thanks, lovey,' she said huskily, 'but I lasted out, didn't I? Hold me, Boots, it's been a lovely fam'ly weddin'.'

Aunt Victoria's voice was heard.

'I don't want to complain, but who let that mangy-lookin' cat in?'

A month later, Polly Simms, standing on the verandah of a rambling bungalow in Kenya, looked out over the brick-red earth and wondered why love would not go away.

THE END

SERGEANT JOE
by Mary Jane Staples

Everyone liked Sergeant Joe. From the huge jolly Beavis family with whom he had lodgings in Newington Butts, to Mr George Singleton, Charing Cross Road bookseller, who employed Joe in a little lucrative and harmless forgery, Sergeant Joe was a universal favourite. Quite a few people wondered why he didn't get married.

But it wasn't until he bumped into Dolly Smith – in a London peasouper, that he met a girl who made an impression on him. Dolly was quick, lively, and full of cockney cheek. She was also a little frightened – running from a vicious-looking thug and a sinister foreigner who seemed to think she had stolen something valuable. When Joe took Dolly under his wing he thought he was just helping her in a momentary predicament. He didn't realize his peaceful existence was going to be wrecked. For Dolly was both bewitching and beguiling – and she was also involved in something quite dangerous that was finally to give Sergeant Joe the surprise of his life.

0 552 13951 3

THE PEARLY QUEEN
by Mary Jane Staples

The Pearly Queen was really Aunt Edie. She was thirty-nine, had a good job in a factory, lived in a flat just off Camberwell Green, and had never married. Her fiancé had drowned in the Thames when she was a girl and since then she had been on her own, though not from choice. Everyone loved Aunt Edie – but especially the Andrews family.

Jack Andrews was having a tough time. He'd come back from the First World War to find his wife had 'got religion'. She'd got it so badly that she finally went off, left Jim and the three children and joined Father Peter's League of Repenters. She never really came home again. Jack and the children managed as best they could, but things were pretty tough when Aunt Edie turned up. The first thing she did was give her cousin, Maud Andrews, a piece of her mind for running off and leaving her family. But when that didn't do any good, Edie moved in and took over the Andrews family. For the time time in years life began to look good again. Aunt Edie was warm, generous, kind, and, above all, she was their very own Pearly Queen.

0 552 13856 8

THE LODGER
by Mary Jane Staples

Maggie Wilson was only thirty-three, but life in the teeming streets of Walworth was not that easy in 1908 – not if you were a widow with four young daughters. It was pretty much a hand-to-mouth existence and without the lodger Maggie really wouldn't have managed at all.

Constable Harry Bradshaw thought the Wilsons were a gutsy and brave little family – from the youngest and cheekiest, Daisy, up to the elegant Trary, thirteen-years-old and quite the young lady. But the one who won most of his admiration was Maggie herself, fighting her lonely battle against total poverty.

And his fears for her concerned more than just their lack of money. For a murderer was loose in South London – a rather sinister strangler who obviously knew the local streets and alleys very well indeed. A full scale investigation was put in hand, and Harry was told, in particular, to inquire into any new lodgers who had moved into the district. And there was something very peculiar indeed about Maggie Wilson's lodger.

0 552 13730 8

A SELECTION OF FINE TITLES
AVAILABLE FROM CORGI BOOKS

☐	13855 X	ELLAN VANNIN	*Lyn Andrews*	£3.99
☐	13718 9	LIVERPOOL LOU	*Lyn Andrews*	£3.99
☐	13600 X	THE SISTERS O'DONNELL	*Lyn Andrews*	£3.99
☐	13482 1	THE WHITE EMPRESS	*Lyn Andrews*	£3.99
☐	13289 6	MOVING AWAY	*Louise Brindley*	£2.99
☐	13499 6	THE INCONSTANT MOON	*Louise Brindley*	£3.99
☐	13829 0	THE SMOKE SCREEN	*Louise Brindley*	£3.99
☐	13260 6	AN EQUAL CHANCE	*Brenda Clarke*	£3.99
☐	13690 5	BEYOND THE WORLD	*Brenda Clarke*	£4.99
☐	13557 7	BRIEF SHINING	*Kathleen Rowntree*	£3.99
☐	12375 7	A SCATTERING OF DAISIES	*Susan Sallis*	£3.99
☐	12579 2	THE DAFFODILS OF NEWENT	*Susan Sallis*	£3.99
☐	12880 5	BLUEBELL WINDOWS	*Susan Sallis*	£4.99
☐	13756 1	AN ORDINARY WOMAN	*Susan Sallis*	£3.99
☐	13136 9	RICHMOND HERITAGE/FOUR WEEKS IN VENICE	*Susan Sallis*	£3.99
☐	13136 9	ROSEMARY FOR REMEMBRANCE	*Susan Sallis*	£3.99
☐	13346 9	SUMMER VISITORS	*Susan Sallis*	£3.99
☐	13545 3	BY SUN AND CANDLELIGHT	*Susan Sallis*	£3.99
☐	13299 3	DOWN LAMBETH WAY	*Mary Jane Staples*	£3.99
☐	13573 9	KING OF CAMBERWELL	*Mary Jane Staples*	£3.99
☐	13444 9	OUR EMILY	*Mary Jane Staples*	£3.99
☐	13856 8	THE PEARLY QUEEN	*Mary Jane Staples*	£3.99
☐	13845 2	RISING SUMMER	*Mary Jane Staples*	£3.99
☐	13635 2	TWO FOR THREE FARTHINGS	*Mary Jane Staples*	£3.99
☐	13730 8	THE LODGER	*Mary Jane Staples*	£3.99
☐	13850 9	THE BIRD OF HAPPINESS	*Sally Stewart*	£3.99
☐	13637 9	THE WOMEN OF PROVIDENCE	*Sally Stewart*	£3.99